COCKWOMBLE

HP Heritage Productions, Ltd.
Houston, Texas

Cockwomble

Paperback ISBN: 978-0-9663548-5-0
eBook ISBN: 978-0-9663548-6-7
Hardback ISBN: 978-0-9663548-8-1

Library of Congress Control Number: 2026908705

Edited by: Robin Cain & Robin Cooper

First Edition

Author contact: heritageproductionsltd@gmail.com

Published by Heritage Productions, Ltd., Houston, Texas

COCKWOMBLE

A Novel

Ben Cooper

For Jody and Robin

ONE

At 9:15 p.m. Saturday, a partially clothed woman fell from the seventh floor of the Overlook Hotel. She reached forty-five miles per hour before striking the ground face-first, dying instantly from massive blunt-force trauma. A heavy, visceral thud—followed by a wet crackle—cut through the night, then the blood-curdling screams of bystanders.

Earlier that evening, retired FBI agent Alexander Christian sat on the balcony of the Fort Lauderdale condominium he shared with his significant other, Jana Wilson. He scanned the hotels to the east as he sipped a twelve-year-old scotch. It was his evening routine. A routine Jana wasn't thrilled with, but tolerated.

Sunset in South Florida. The golden hour. A bird-watcher's dream. Even among the dense cluster of high-rise condos, hotels, restaurants, and constant traffic, vibrant wading birds, raptors, and coastal species filled the skies above Fort Lauderdale. Roseate Spoonbills, White Ibises, Great Egrets, and Black Skimmers drifted on the warm air currents.

On rare occasions, Alexander would spot an American Bushtit, a species more common in the West, or some exotic import—perhaps illegally introduced—like a Fluffy-backed Tit-babbler or a Blue-footed Booby.

Sunset also brought out what Alexander privately called the double-breasted swallow. Scantily clad young women appeared on hotel balconies—some clutching towels or robes, others already bare—stepping into the amber light. A few hesitated at the railing before turning, arching, and posing. Waiting to be photographed in front of the setting Florida sun.

Unlike Jana, who found his habit unsettling, Alexander didn't consider himself a voyeur. He preferred to think of it as appreciating composition—light, color, motion. The binoculars resting on the wrought-iron table beside his scotch weakened his argument. Still, he rarely used them, only for something truly rare.

Even with Daylight Saving Time, darkness settled in by the time Alexander started his second drink—at least as dark as Central Beach ever became. The birds disappeared. Traffic noise softened. The Atlantic, a block to the east, whispered against the shore. The cooler air made it difficult to leave his fourth-floor perch.

When he lowered the glass and glanced toward the hotel, something moved—fast—dropping from a balcony. For a fraction of a second, his mind refused to interpret it. Not a bird. Too large. Not debris. Too regular. He froze.

Was that a...person?

The lower floors of smaller buildings blocked his view of the pavement. He leaned forward, scanning upward, tracing the vertical line where the shape had fallen. Balcony after balcony. Sliding doors. Curtains. Shadows. He caught a glimpse of someone stepping inside a room, but couldn't tell from which level.

Then the screams came. Sharp. High. Multiple voices overlapping. The unmistakable sound of people reacting to a catastrophic event.

The screams confirmed it. *It was a person he'd seen fall.*

Alexander bolted from his chair, grabbed a pair of boat shoes, and hurried to the door.

Jana glanced up from her iPad. "What the...?"

"A person fell off a balcony."

"What?"

Alexander didn't hear her question. He was already out the door and waiting impatiently for the elevator. He managed to put one shoe on while he waited, the other on the ride down. When the door opened, he ran through the lobby, down the block, and arrived on the scene slightly out of breath.

A small crowd gathered around the body. Stunned silence had replaced the initial screams. Each bystander had their phone out, taking pictures of the partially clothed woman whose face was splattered on the parking lot. Alexander hoped at least one had had the decency to call 9-1-1.

"Back off," Alexander ordered the growing crowd. He knew it was useless, but he knelt next to the body and checked for a pulse. There was none. He stepped back and again told the people to back off. Reluctantly, Alexander used his phone to take pictures of the body, the gawkers, and the backside of the hotel from where the woman had fallen.

The first uniformed police officer arrived moments later. A second officer arrived soon after the first. They moved the crowd to a safe distance, then slowly approached the body. One of the officers checked for a pulse, shook his head, and looked up at the high-rise hotel. He turned his attention to the crowd. "Did anyone see her fall?"

No one answered. A few shook their heads without taking their eyes off the girl's body.

Alexander stepped forward. "I did. I saw a little of the fall."

"What do you mean by 'little'?"

"I live in the building with the orange roof." Alexander pointed to the eight-story condo unit in the distance. "I was sitting on the balcony and caught a glimpse of what I thought was a person falling. When I heard the screams, I knew I'd seen a body fall, so I came running."

"Did you see where she fell from?"

"No, unfortunately, I didn't. When she was out of sight, I looked at the balconies where she might have fallen from. I caught a glimpse of a person leaving one of the balconies, but now I'm not sure which floor that was."

The officer looked at the few people who remained at the scene, then back at Alexander. "You said you saw someone leave the balcony she fell from?"

"I saw someone leave a balcony. I'm not sure it's the one she fell from."

"How long from the time she fell until you arrived?"

"A matter of minutes."

"Did you see anyone who seemed particularly upset? Like they'd lost a friend or loved one?"

"No. It didn't seem like anyone knew who she was."

The officer made a few notes in a small notebook. "Do you mind waiting for a detective? One's on the way."

"Not at all." Alexander moved away and sat on a metal bench outside the hotel's back door. He watched as the officers cordoned off the area around the body with yellow police tape. Several more officers and an ambulance arrived. EMTs performed a quick check on the body, shook their heads, and told an officer to call the coroner's office.

Alexander pulled out his cell phone and called Jana. "Alex, what the hell happened?"

"It's a young woman. She either fell, jumped, or was pushed off the balcony."

Jana's gasp was loud and clear through the phone.

"I didn't see much, but I'm going to hang around and talk to the detective." Alexander paused and watched a middle-aged, heavyset man in a suit approach the body. "I think he's here now. I should be home shortly."

"Okay. See you soon."

Alexander put the phone back in his pocket and watched as the uniformed officer talked to the detective. The detective nodded intently and took notes. Both men alternated their gazes between the body and the building's balconies. After several minutes, they looked at Alexander, then back at the body. The detective then made his way to where Alexander was waiting.

"Sorry it took so long," the detective said. "I'm Detective Amos. I understand you saw the victim fall?"

Detective Rick Amos was in his mid-forties. He sported a bushy mustache that went out of style in the 1980s, a suit he'd purchased when he was fifteen pounds lighter, and a haircut that only accentuated his receding hairline.

"No problem. I'm Alex. I guess you could say I saw her fall. I was sitting on the balcony of my condo when I happened to look up and see what I thought was a person falling. I got over here as soon as I could."

"Why?"

"I beg your pardon?"

"I'm curious, why would you come to the scene? To gawk or did you think you could help?"

Alexander scratched the back of his head. The first question was legitimate; the second, he thought, was condescending. He didn't appreciate the comment—or the tone. "I witnessed a body falling. I thought someone might be interested."

The sarcasm in Alexander's voice didn't go unnoticed by Detective Amos. "I apologize. The victim is a young female. It appears she landed face-first. It's not a pretty sight, and all those assholes standing around taking pictures really pissed me off."

"Apology accepted. I get it. I have a confession. I took a few pictures too. A couple of the dead girl, but mostly of the crowd."

The detective looked over his shoulder at the few people still standing next to the yellow police tape. Most of the onlookers had left the scene, already busy posting images of the body on social media. Those who remained watched the coroner load the black body bag into the rear of his van.

The detective studied Alex, who stood 6 feet 4 inches tall, had broad shoulders, and looked to be in good shape. Not muscular, like a gym rat, but fit. "You a cop?"

"No. FBI. Retired."

"And you think if someone had something to do with the girl's death, they might have hung around to photograph their handiwork?"

"It's been known to happen."

"More often than we know, I'm sure. Did you see anything else?"

"As soon as the body disappeared, I scanned the balconies. I couldn't tell which floor she fell from, but it had to be near the top. I spotted her about four or five floors down. Just a glimpse—but on one of the upper floors, I'm pretty sure I saw someone duck back into a room."

"You're pretty sure?"

Alexander pinched the bridge of his nose. "Our condo is lower. It's a fairly steep angle, so all I could see was a head and shoulders. Again, it was only a glance. It could have been someone who heard a scream and ran out to see what the commotion was, and when they saw the body below, they ran back inside to call 9-1-1. They may not have even been on the same floor. As I said, I don't know which balcony she fell from."

"My partner's inside the hotel, trying to get an ID and find out which room she was in. We can't do much without an ID, and I have a feeling she's going to be hard to identify."

"Why?"

"Most likely, she's a prostitute and a junkie as well. I'd bet she was high and either fell or jumped."

"Could she have been pushed?"

"It's possible there was a fight, and she was thrown off. Not likely. Guys who take hookers to hotel rooms only want sex. The last thing they want is to get involved in a death. If it was a messed-up hooker and she jumped, whoever rented the room is long gone."

"He won't be hard to find."

Detective Amos laughed. "No. No doubt he left a credit card when he checked in. We'll give him a few days to stew. Gather more evidence and then go have a little chat with him."

"Discreetly?"

The detective laughed again, louder this time. "In case he's a family man? It all depends. I'd hate to ruin his life if he was only getting a little strange while on an out-of-town business trip or vacation."

Alexander nodded. "I like the attitude. I know a lot of cops who would go in with guns blazing."

"I'm homicide. I couldn't care less what people do—as long as they don't kill anyone. Before you say anything, I know, I'm sworn to uphold all laws. Well, we're too short-handed to care about people having sex. As long as they're adults and it's consensual."

"I understand. We could talk about ethics all night. For now, I should let you get back to work."

Amos reached into his suit jacket. "Here's my card. If you think of anything else, give me a call. Do you have any ID?"

"I don't. I left the condo in such a hurry that I forgot my wallet. I can run back and get it."

Alexander's attire—boat shoes, khaki shorts, and a Hawaiian shirt—had not gone unnoticed by Detective Amos. "No, it's fine. Give me your name, address, email, and phone number."

Amos wrote down Alexander's information. "To refresh my memory, where were you when you saw the body fall?"

"On my balcony. There." Once again, Alexander pointed to the eight-story condominium building in the distance. Its orange roof glowed brightly against the evening sky. "We're on the fourth floor."

"We?"

"I live with my girlfriend."

"Was she there when you saw the victim fall?"

"Yes, but she was inside. I ran past her on the way out."

"That's all I have. I appreciate you waiting around and talking to me. I'll be in touch if I have anything further."

"I'll be around. Would you mind keeping me updated on the case? I'm curious what happened to her."

"Not likely. You're retired, right?"

"Yes."

"Yeah, I'm not at liberty to share any details about an ongoing investigation."

"I didn't think so, but I had to ask. Thanks."

Detective Amos gave him a sly grin. "Tell you what. Send me all the pictures you took at the scene, and I'll see what I can do about giving you an update."

"Deal." Alexander glanced at his watch. "It's getting late. I'll send you the images in the morning."

The men shook hands. Alexander strolled toward the street as a uniformed officer rolled up the yellow caution tape. Firefighters washed the pavement where the girl had landed. By morning, there would be nothing to indicate that a young woman had died there. No sign of the blood, bone, or brain fragments on the concrete.

TWO

Jerry Kurtz sat on the end of his brown leather sofa with a bottle of beer in one hand and a Smith & Wesson Model 19 357 magnum in the other. He set the beer bottle on the end table, double-checked that the cylinder was empty, aimed the gun at the muted television, and squeezed the trigger.

The heavyset man, dancing like a fool on the LED screen, kept dancing. The sixty-five-inch TV was still intact. There was no ringing in Jerry's ears. But, for a split second, the feeling of euphoria reduced the anxiety that had been building since he was given the news earlier in the day.

Jerry was still pointing the revolver in the general direction of the television when he heard the knock on the front door of his condo. Before he could react, the door swung open. He instinctively pointed the gun in the direction of the door.

Sam stepped through the door, saw the gun pointed at her, and impulsively turned sideways and dropped to her knees. "What the hell, Jerry?"

After he lowered his weapon and Sam's heartbeat slowed, Jerry said, "I'm sorry. I just put a round through that big son-of-a-bitch's head."

Sam—Samantha Barnes—stood and stared at her friend. She was sure he was speaking metaphorically, but he was a trained killer. Sam's primary mission, like most CIA agents, was intelligence gathering and analysis. Jerry was Staff D. Kill Squad. Trained in lethal techniques and weaponry for covert operations.

"So, other than killing the president, how are you doing?"

"Much better, thanks."

"Maybe I should try it," Sam said.

Jerry spun the cylinder one more time to make sure it was empty, then handed her the 357. "It's empty. Go ahead."

Sam raised the gun and pointed it at the TV. The image on the TV changed to an attractive woman touting a cream that would significantly reduce itch...fast.

"You missed your opportunity," Jerry said. "You hesitated. Never hesitate."

"There'll be other chances. You mind if I grab a beer?" Sam headed to the refrigerator. If Jerry answered her, she didn't hear him. She returned a few seconds later with two beers and set one next to his near-empty bottle on the end table.

She took a swig from her bottle and sat on the couch. "What are you going to do?"

"I haven't given it much thought. I've only been unemployed for a few hours. What about you?"

Sam glanced at the TV. The local weather came on. She had missed her opportunity to take her imaginary shot at the president. "Same. I might not do anything for a few weeks and see if this gets reversed. I'll update my resume, but I doubt I'll do any serious job hunting. I'm not sure what I could do. How many job openings are there for a person with a psych degree and a tad over two years with the CIA?"

Jerry laughed. "I bet more than for a guy who's trained to kill people."

"I don't know. You might be in high demand. Seriously, you have other skills."

"I was a math major. Joined the CIA right out of college and went to the Farm after CIA 101. I'm sure I can become an analyst somewhere, but I'll be starting at the bottom."

Sam noticed the president was back on the TV. She grabbed the Smith from the couch, cocked, aimed, and squeezed the trigger. She smiled when the hammer slammed down on an empty chamber. "That does feel good." She repeated the process six or seven times until a commercial came on.

"You know, one shot would likely do the trick. A double-tap for good measure. What you did was overkill. Besides, it's a Smith & Wesson. You only get six."

"I know, but it was fun. I'm sorry, dry firing probably isn't great for the gun either."

"It's fine. Smiths can handle it, but don't make a habit out of it."

Sam put the gun on the couch. "We should get pictures of him and go to a range and actually put a few holes in his head. I haven't shot much, but I did qualify. I bet I can hit him every time from twenty feet."

"I bet you could. Unfortunately, neither the owners of the range nor the other shooters—especially the other shooters—would appreciate you putting holes in the president's head. They're liable to shoot you."

"Oh, yeah. Good point. It was a thought."

"It was. But we need to stick with pretend shooting and do it in the privacy of my living room."

"Maybe not," Sam said.

Jerry waited for her to continue the next line, but she went to the kitchen for another beer instead.

When she returned, she turned off the TV and hovered over her friend. "The CIA killed one president, why can't they...or we...kill another?"

Jerry chuckled, but then realized she was serious.

Sam sat on the couch and faced Jerry. "There's a bunch of us that lost our jobs today because of that jerk. We'd have to approach them delicately, but I'd bet several would be on board."

Jerry was trying to wrap his head around what he'd heard. "Let's back up a bit. You said the CIA killed one president. I assume you mean Kennedy."

"Yes, of course."

"There's no proof."

"No. The CIA did its job. But there are clues."

"Clues? Or conspiracy theories?"

"Facts. Facts that tell the story. You can call them what you want, but when you put it together, it's obvious Oswald didn't act alone. I'm sure he was involved, but I'm not convinced he was the shooter."

Jerry took a deep breath and slowly exhaled. "Okay, let's hear the facts."

Sam squinted at him.

Jerry recognized her disdain and could tell she thought he was patronizing her. "Please, tell me. I'm interested in your thoughts."

"Well, what jumps out at me is when Oswald was arrested, a reporter asked him if he killed the president. He said he was a patsy. Who says that? Had he killed Kennedy, he would have said, 'No,' or 'It wasn't me.' He'd deny it. If he hadn't shot Kennedy, he would have been confused and said something along the lines of, 'I have no idea what they're talking about.' But, instead, he said, 'I'm a patsy.' He knew he was being framed and, most likely, who was framing him."

Jerry crossed his arms and wrinkled his forehead. "Oswald's claim that he was a patsy is compelling. In fact, those words became fodder for conspiracy theorists. But it doesn't mean the CIA was involved."

"No, of course not. But that's only one item. There's the limo driver—"

"William Greer."

"Right. I'm surprised you knew who it was."

Jerry smirked. "I know a bit about the assassination. Most agents have done a little research into it at some point."

"So, you're aware that the first shot, the one right after the limo made the turn, most likely hit the traffic light."

"I've heard that, yes."

"There's a gunshot. Mr. Greer was with the Secret Service. He would know the sound of a gunshot. But he didn't speed up. He kept the car at the same pace. Then the second shot. He still didn't accelerate. It's only after the third shot, the kill shot, that he turns around, sees JFK with his head blown apart, and speeds up."

Jerry nodded, agreeing with Sam's assessment.

"There's more, but those two examples should prove that there was a conspiracy. Oswald was a loner with ties to Russia. Greer was with the Secret Service. Someone had to put them together, and who better to orchestrate it than the CIA?"

"My money's on the Mafia."

"The Mafia? You're kidding."

"I'm not. Sure, the CIA could arrange an assassination, but there wouldn't be a patsy. No one would ever know who did it. The Mafia, on the other hand, haphazardly recruited Oswald, Greer, and a few others to do the job. Then, they recruited Jack Ruby to kill Oswald to shut him up and to send a message to all the others involved—keep quiet or die."

"Ruby knew he'd be caught. Do you think he'd willingly shoot Oswald, knowing he'd go to prison for the rest of his life, for the Mafia?"

"If they told him it was either him or Oswald. Give him a choice—life in prison or a slow, painful death now."

Sam took a long pull from the beer bottle. "You make a valid argument for Mafia involvement. Does that mean you actually believe they were involved?"

"Not sure. Whether Oswald was the shooter or, as he claimed, a patsy, I don't know. If I'm being honest, the CIA could have been involved. The Warren Commission investigated and came up with an eight-hundred-plus page report saying Oswald acted alone. Lee Harvey Oswald didn't act alone. The only way they could have come to that conclusion is if the evidence was tampered with."

"And who better to hinder an investigation than the CIA?"

"Exactly."

Sam ran her fingers through her brown hair. "Wait. So now you're saying the CIA was involved?"

"Yeah, I guess I am...to some extent...I don't know. Having said all that, it's possible Oswald took a rifle to work, waited at the window for the motorcade, shot three times, which hit the president twice, got caught, knew they had him, and said he was a patsy to throw the detectives off."

Sam threw her hands in the air. "You've come full circle! What do you believe?"

Jerry stood and looked at the woman on his couch. "I believe we will never know. It's been over sixty years. Everyone who may have had even the least amount of involvement is dead. There's not going to be any new evidence. Unless someone wrote a true confession—a documented confession—and buried it in a time capsule, we'll never know what happened on that day in 1963. I need to water my horse. I'll be right back."

Jerry disappeared down the hall toward the bathroom, leaving Sam to think about what he'd said. She put her head in her hands, trying to make sense of what she and Jerry were contemplating.

A few minutes later, Jerry returned from the bathroom. "I can tell you're thinking about it."

Sam leaned back and rubbed her eyes. "I have. I can't believe we discussed the idea of assassinating the president."

"I had a few seconds to mull it over, too. It was an interesting topic of conversation, but I'd never do it."

"Right. No matter how much he deserves it, it's not in me." Sam paused for a moment, then cocked her head. "Having said that, the idea that the CIA was behind the Kennedy assassination intrigues me. Could they have pulled it off?"

"It would be a hell of an op if they did."

"It would. Could we do it?"

Jerry raised an eyebrow. "I thought—"

"I don't mean do it—just plan it. Work out the details. Figure out the how, the where, and the players."

"You want to plan an assassination down to the smallest details, but not go through with it?"

"Yes. Exactly."

"You realize if we get caught, no one would believe we're only planning the assassination. That's conspiracy. Conspiracy to murder. The penalties for conspiracy are damn near as harsh as for murder."

"We'll have to be extremely careful."

THREE

Alexander was breathing hard when he reached the condo door. He pressed his thumb to the sensor. A green flash—then the bolt clicked open. Jana was waiting inside the door.

"Are you okay? You're winded."

"I'm fine. Maybe a bit upset by what I saw. I took the steps instead of the elevator, trying to clear my head."

"Would a scotch help?"

"Tremendously. Do you mind making it?"

"Not at all," Jana said, heading for the kitchen.

"I'll be on the balcony."

Instead of sitting in his usual chair, Alexander leaned against the metal rail and stared at the hotel he had just come from. He held his hand in a "thumbs-up" position and eyeballed the column of rooms directly above the point where he believed the girl had landed.

"I can tell you're in deep thought. Care to share?" Jana said, handing him a scotch on the rocks in a stemless wine glass. She had a glass of white wine.

"It was a young girl. Hard to tell her age, but I'd bet she was barely eighteen." Alexander took a sip of the whiskey. "Nude, except for panties. If you call them that."

"A nude young girl. What did she look like?"

"Don't know. She landed face-first on the concrete driveway."

Jana gasped. "Do you think…it was…an accident?"

"I'd say no. I've been staring at that building, trying to reconstruct exactly what I saw. It was brief. A body falling. I don't recall any movement, except for her dropping. If she had fallen, been pushed, or thrown off, I feel she would have been kicking her legs, waving her arms, and probably screaming. She just fell. Either already dead, unconscious, or drugged."

Jana put her arm around Alexander's waist and hugged him. "I'm sorry you saw her fall. I'm sure the police will find out what happened."

"I hope so. I've been studying the building. I know where she landed, so I know about where she fell from. I don't know which floor. Best I can recall, I noticed her around the fifth or sixth floor. While I was at the scene, I counted the floors with balconies. There are ten. She had to fall from the top four or five floors. I'm sure the detective got CCTV footage from the hotel. They should know exactly which room. I'll let him know my thoughts in the morning." Alexander continued to stare at the hotel.

"Alex."

"Yeah?"

"Look at me."

Alexander slowly turned his head.

"Let the cops handle it."

"Don't worry, I will." After a few moments of silence, he sighed. "I want to share what I know with them while it's fresh. As I said, once they see the video, they'll know exactly which room she was in and who was with her. It won't be hard to track down whoever was with her—if they haven't already. Finding evidence that it was murder and not an accident will be more difficult. That's why they need to know what I saw. Of course, the tox report will tell them if she'd been drugged and, if she was, to what extent. That still doesn't prove it was murder. Whoever was with her could say she was high and fell. With no witnesses…"

Jana slapped the railing. "That sucks. Are you saying if you want to kill a person, all you have to do is take them to a high-rise building, throw them off, and claim it was an accident?"

"There's a little more to it. Computer models can simulate how a body would fall under different circumstances. The pathologists can analyze the injuries, looking for inconsistencies that might suggest foul play preceding the fall. If there are no witnesses or other conclusive evidence, it's not always possible to determine with a hundred percent certainty whether the person was pushed or fell. The fact that I saw what appeared to be a limp body falling should be enough for them to give it a thorough investigation."

Jana swirled the wine in her glass. "I'm sure the detectives know, but it seems to me, if I'm falling from a building, even if I'm committing suicide, I wouldn't go face-first. Maybe on my back, if I could. I don't know. Now that I think about it, I wouldn't go feet first. It would be quick, but shattering my legs right before I die doesn't sound like the way to go."

Alexander laughed. "You make an interesting point. I never investigated a jumper. I wonder if they consider the landing. Head first would be the way to go, but not face first. People are vain. They don't want to mess up their faces. If they were falling and couldn't roll to their back, they'd use their arms to cover their face, or at least turn their head."

Jana shivered. "Jeez, Alex. Let's change the subject. This one gives me the willies."

"The willies? I haven't heard that saying in a long time."

"I haven't had them in a long time."

"Do you know what they are?"

"Huh? The willies? Something that kinda makes your skin crawl. Or gives you goose bumps."

"Close enough." The origin of the term was, in Alexander's opinion, interesting. Still, he wasn't particularly in the mood to tell it, and he had a good idea Jana couldn't care less. He decided to save it for another time. Instead, he said, "I could use another drink. Shall we go in?"

Jana agreed, and they went inside where Jana refilled their glasses and joined Alexander on the long sofa.

Jana watched him for several seconds. "Alex, are you okay?"

"Sorry, it just dawned on me that the top four or five rooms in line with where the body fell were dark."

"They could be unoccupied. Or the blackout curtains were drawn."

"At least one room was occupied. The one the girl was in before she fell. Someone was in the room with the girl. It hasn't been that long since I left. The detective hadn't even gone inside yet. There should be a forensics team going over every inch of that room."

"Maybe the forensics hadn't arrived. Or they don't know for sure which room it is."

"Excuse me a sec." Alexander walked back onto the balcony, picked up his binoculars, and focused on the hotel's top rooms in line with where the body fell. He could see that the curtains were open and all the rooms were dark. He lowered the binoculars, let out a harrumph, and went back inside. He added ice and scotch to his glass and joined Jana on the couch.

"The rooms that she could have possibly fallen from are dark. I don't like it."

*****

Sam paced throughout her one-bedroom apartment in McLean, Virginia. She loved her apartment, which was only about fifteen minutes from Langley. The bedroom was small, but it had plenty of room for her. Because the bedroom was small, the kitchen and living room were spacious for a 750-square-foot apartment. The view was amazing.

Most mornings, Sam would either be at the office or sitting on her couch, enjoying a cup of coffee. Being unemployed, she felt she should be sitting on the porch with her coffee, enjoying the view. Instead, she paced, thinking about her conversation the night before with Jerry Kurtz.

In her heart, she knew there was no way she'd ever attempt an assassination of the president, no matter how corrupt and incompetent he was. But she couldn't help smiling when she thought about it. *But it would be fun to see if they could pull it off.*

To get her mind off murder, Sam tried to remember when her lease was up. Now unemployed, with her job prospects in McLean and DC limited, she would have to move from her three-thousand-dollar-a-month apartment. The thought depressed her.

Her phone buzzed. She opened the message.

> **Jerry: I bet I know what you're thinking.**
> **Sam: You'd probably be right.**
> **Jerry: Can I come by?**
> **Sam: Sure.**
> **Jerry: Be there in ten.**

Sam wondered if his coming by was a good idea. She glanced around the apartment. It was clean enough for Jerry. She wasn't a slob, but cleaning wasn't her forte. If she cleaned the bathroom once a month, she was happy. After paying rent, her salary as a CIA analyst didn't leave enough money for a housekeeper. At least not monthly.

Jerry arrived exactly ten minutes after his last text. Once inside, he glanced around the apartment. "Oh, man, I've always loved this place."

Sam sighed. "Me too. I'm sure I'll have to move when the lease is up."

"When's that? You might find a new job close by."

"Not likely. Even if I did, I couldn't afford this place. I'd already reached a GS-11 pay grade. I'll be starting over. Entry level."

"Maybe so, but you're still better off than me. I have no idea what I'm going to do. Luckily, I've got a decent nest egg. Because I traveled the world for my job, I didn't spend money on travel or food. I have a beater car, and I rent a small, dirt-cheap garage apartment. Cheap for McLean and DC standards anyway."

"Any idea what you'll do when you have to find a job?" Sam wasn't sure if she should ask.

"I'll probably end up with a police department as an intelligence analyst. Same as you, most likely."

Sam hadn't considered her future. Too soon. "I hope there's plenty of those jobs available. Every out-of-work agent is going to be applying."

She stared out the window and said, "I don't know. I may look for a totally different line of work. Move to Florida and become a skipper on the Jungle Cruise."

Jerry laughed. "That's funny. I can't see you spending your day telling dad jokes. Especially for fifteen bucks an hour."

"They make that much? Sign me up."

Jerry laughed again, then turned serious. "Speaking of Florida, you want to take a ride down there with me?"

"To Disney World? Are you serious?"

"More like Fort Lauderdale."

"Fort Lauderdale? Why? Oh, I know. Shit!"

"Yep. You know why. I thought we could find an extended-stay hotel and set up shop. Do a little reconnaissance while we take in the sights. Would you mind sharing a room?"

Jerry Kurtz stood five-nine, two inches taller than Sam. He was attractive with a firm jaw, brown eyes, and a full head of sandy-blonde hair. Sam considered him a good friend but was never romantically attracted to him.

"Uh, share a room? Jerry, I—"

"Sam! Have I ever been inappropriate with you?"

"No, now that you mention it, you haven't."

"Have you ever wondered why?"

Sam squirmed in her chair and didn't make eye contact with him. "No. We work together. I always thought we were friends."

"We are. But, also, you're not my cup of tea."

The comment surprised Sam. She had shoulder-length brown hair, blue eyes, and an average but well-toned body—compliments of the apartment gym where she worked out five days a week. Most men found her attractive.

Her head snapped toward Jerry. "What exactly is your type?"

Jerry stared at her, head cocked. An awkward lull ensued.

"You like bigger boobs?"

He smirked. "No. Actually, I prefer smaller. Much smaller."

Sam tilted her head.

"Samantha, seriously, you don't know? I'm gay."

FOUR

When Jana awoke the following morning, she knew something was amiss when Alexander wasn't beside her. She was the early bird, normally getting up around six. He would usually sleep until eight or eight-thirty.

There was only one thing that would get him up this hour...that girl.

She wondered if he'd slept at all or if every time he closed his eyes, he would see the image of the girl's face planted into the parking lot of the hotel.

Knowing Alexander would prefer to be alone with his thoughts, Jana lounged in bed until a full bladder and a parched mouth forced her out. After using the bathroom, she went into the kitchen. Alexander was sitting on the balcony.

Jana filled a cup with coffee and joined him. "You been up long?"

"Not too long. Awake, yes. Up, no. I didn't sleep well last night."

Jana took a sip of coffee and looked at the hotel. "I figured. So you've been sitting here staring at the hotel?"

"Basically, yes."

"Anything happening?"

"Nope. The rooms of interest are all dark."

"Rooms of interest?"

"Those are the rooms that are three windows over from the left side of the hotel. Then, from the top floor and the four below it. The more I stare at that damn building, the surer I am that I spotted the girl falling when she was even with the fifth balcony from the top. She had to come from the top five floors, three balconies from the left."

"And nothing is going on in any of those rooms?" Jana asked.

"I can't see the top floor all that well, but the four rooms below it are dark."

Jana put her hand on Alexander's shoulder. "I know it was traumatizing seeing that girl lying in the street like that. Are you going to be all right? Do you want to talk to a professional?"

"Like a shrink?"

"Yeah. It wouldn't hurt."

"I'll be fine. What I want to do is talk to that detective. I've got a few questions for him."

"What kind of questions?"

Alexander took a drink of his now lukewarm coffee. He wiped his chin on the top of his sleeve. "I want to ask if he has the girl's name and if he knows anything about her. If they figured out which room she was in, and of course, if they know what happened."

"He'll share the information with you if he has it?"

"It's an ongoing investigation, so he won't tell me much, but he should give me the basics. He seemed to be a seasoned detective. He'll be forthcoming."

Jana sat next to Alexander and put her hand on his thigh. "What do you plan to do with this information once you have it?"

"Absolutely nothing," Alexander replied. "Knowing who she was, if she had any family, and most importantly, what happened—was it an accident, murder, or suicide—will give me closure. Then I'll be able to get her out of my head."

Jana studied his cold blue eyes. She could tell he was only telling half the truth. He'd be satisfied only if the case were simple and clean. If the girl had been high and fallen, or suicidal and jumped. Even if someone had thrown her off the balcony, an arrest would at least give Alexander answers he could live with.

But any unanswered questions would eat away at him like buzzards pecking away at roadkill. Jana hoped he'd get closure quickly, but she had a feeling he wouldn't.

"I glanced at the pictures I took at the scene. No smoking gun. No one standing around stood out."

"Except you. Taking pictures."

"Everyone was taking pictures. Most so they could post on Instagram or Facebook. I took pictures as evidence. I planned to give them to the police."

"Have you?"

"Not yet. I'm going to send them to the detective this morning along with my questions. Since I'm sending the pictures, he'll be more likely to answer me."

"I hope so. I'm going in for coffee and to do Wordle. You want coffee?"

Alexander didn't answer. Jana watched him swipe through a couple of pictures on his phone, then she went inside.

The images were as clear in Alexander's mind as they were on his phone. He zoomed in on each photo and studied the faces of the people who had encircled the graphic and grotesque splattering of biological matter.

From his limited experience with physiognomy, no one stood out to him as being involved in the incident. Most of them were expressionless. A few appeared physically upset by what they were seeing, yet were unable to turn away. The images revealed nothing new.

As much as he didn't want to, Alexander zoomed in on the girl. From her back, it was impossible to tell her age. Still, he estimated she was young, between seventeen and twenty-one. Her hair was black, and her skin was light brown. She was likely Hispanic. Given that this is South Florida, Cuban would be a good guess.

Beginning at her feet, Alexander inspected the lifeless body inch by inch. He was looking for any soft-tissue damage inconsistent with a fall from a tall building. Since the girl landed face-first, any lacerations, bruises, or contusions on her back would indicate foul play.

Alexander's stomach tightened at how the young girl's limbs were unnaturally splayed. The feeling worsened as he inched upward along her torso. Her skull was split open like a coconut. The coir fibers were replaced by a matted wad of jet-black hair. Her brain matter was propelled mainly forward, forming a carpet of goo on the hotel parking lot.

Seeing corpses wasn't a new experience for Alexander, but this corpse was particularly gruesome. He put his phone down, took a deep breath, and swallowed hard. His focus turned back to the hotel where she had fallen. He shook his head to clear the images from his mind, then checked his phone. 6:47 AM.

"Way too early for alcohol," he whispered.

*****

Jerry Kurtz's revelation lingered in Sam's mind the next morning. She'd always thought he was attractive, if a little diminutive, but after two years of friendship, she'd had no idea he was gay. She found herself wondering why he'd never told her. Had he not been ready to come out? She tried not to dwell on it, but she couldn't help but feel a bit hurt that he hadn't trusted her enough to confide in her.

After finishing the last of her morning protein shake, Sam headed to the apartment gym. She wanted one final workout before she and Jerry drove south. As she warmed up on the treadmill, her thoughts drifted back to their conversation from the night before.

Then it dawned on her.

Jerry had been with the agency for ten years. As far as Sam knew, his record was impeccable. On the other hand, she had also joined the CIA immediately after college. She'd only been with them for two and a half years. It made sense that she was let go. But why Jerry?

In Sam's mind, there was only one reason. He'd been outed. The current administration was purging the government of gays. It didn't matter if they were a CIA agent or a four-star general. If they were gay, they were gone. Even being a supporter of gay rights or DEI was grounds for termination.

"Assholes!" Sam said much louder than she intended due to the music level of her earbuds. She glanced around the gym. She was alone. "Fucking assholes."

She cranked the treadmill faster to channel her anger into her workout. Her Apple Watch flashed an incoming call notification just as her leg muscles began to burn. It was Jerry. Sam slowed the machine to a walk and answered her phone.

"Did I get you at a bad time?"

"Uh, no. Why?"

"You're breathing heavily. I thought you were—"

"No, I'm in the gym. Working out." Sam could tell by Jerry's tone what he was thinking.

"That's what I was going to say," Jerry said sarcastically.

"Sure, you were. What's up?"

"Are you ready for a road trip?"

"A road trip? Seriously?"

"Yes, we talked about going to Florida."

"I know, but I didn't expect it would be so soon." Sam stopped walking.

"I talked to a friend of mine who was also fired. He wants in. He's got a condo in Fort Lauderdale. We can stay with him."

Sam wiped her face with a towel. "Jerry, are you kidding? I'm not sure you should be telling people what we're doing."

"I agree, but you are the one who said we should recruit others. His name is Willie. He's a good friend, and he's in the same boat."

Sam wanted to ask how close they were. She had never been comfortable with public displays of affection between men. Other than occasional bouts of jealousy when she saw a particularly good-looking gay man, she had no feelings one way or the other towards them. She did wonder if her discomfort was from an internalized homophobia. She decided against asking.

"So he is ex-CIA?"

"Yes. He spent a lot of time in the Caribbean. Mostly Haiti, the Dominican Republic, Martinique, and Trinidad and Tobago. That's why he lives in South Florida. It was a short hop to the islands."

"He was recently fired as well?"

"Yep. Another casualty of the current administration."

Sam felt her face flush. "I assume he's Black."

"Very. Most likely a victim of the DEI purge."

"He was a DEI hire?"

"Not hardly. Willie's got a Master's in Political Science from Tulane. Smart guy. But he's from deep Cajun country. He can dumb it down and talk coon-ass with the best of 'em. I shouldn't say this, but he looks dumber than a stump, too. You know how there are people who just look dumb?"

Sam laughed. "I do. I bet he was a good agent."

"Top notch. He's excited about our 'experiment'."

"I'm glad someone is." Sam's voice trembled.

"Are you getting cold feet? Do you want to call it off?"

"I know we aren't going through with an assassination attempt, but...I don't know...I keep thinking about what might happen if what we're doing gets out. The authorities might not believe it's an 'experiment'. We could end up in serious trouble."

Neither of them spoke for several seconds.

"I know. Other than Willie, no one will know," Jerry finally said. "We'll discuss it only in person or on the phone. No texts or emails. No trail."

"That should be safe. Perhaps we should get burner phones and use them when we're discussing. You know as well as I how easy it is to bug a cell phone."

Jerry didn't feel burner phones were necessary. Yes, what they were planning could get them in hot water. Still, nothing they were going to do should put them on the radar of any intelligence organization. He decided to appease Sam.

"Let's wait until we get a little further along. If we decide it would be better or necessary, we'll get the phones."

"I guess that makes sense." Sam took a deep breath and exhaled slowly. Her diaphragmatic breath didn't go unnoticed.

"We'll be fine," Jerry reassured. "What time can you be ready? Pack for a couple of weeks."

"Uh, I need to shower and pack. Give me a couple of hours."

"Perfect. I don't know if my old car will make it to Florida, so I'm renting one. A rep from the car rental company is picking me up in an hour. I'll come back, load my stuff, and pick you up. We're getting a late start, but I figure we can drive for five or six hours before we stop for the night."

"Sounds good," Sam said, hoping her reluctance wasn't apparent.

"Oh, Willie said we use a code name for the president. He suggested 'Cockwomble'."

<u>FIVE</u>

At 9:30, Alexander sent the photos from the scene to Detective Amos.

Ten minutes later, a reply landed in his inbox. After reading the email, Alexander reread it. "Is he kidding?"

"What?" Jana asked.

"What?" Alexander echoed. "Oh, I got an email from the detective. He said, 'Thanks for the photos. The case is closed.'"

"That was fast," Jana said.

Alexander crossed his arms and stared at the laptop on his lap. "Too fast. I doubt they even have the toxicology reports."

"Could they have had a compelling reason to close the case? Like a confession? Did he mention the outcome?"

"No. He said the case was closed. I'm going to text him with a few questions."

"Alex, why don't you forget about it. Let's go to your place in Texas. You haven't been fishing in forever. That would take your mind off that girl."

Alexander leaned back. His eyes darted around the condo. "Going fishing does sound good. But I wouldn't be able to enjoy it until I know what happened to the girl."

"I get it," Jana said. "Once a detective...you do what you have to do. An old friend is in town and asked if I wanted to meet for lunch later."

"An old friend?"

"Yeah, from way back. She's in town for a few days."

"Enjoy," Alexander said. Another time, he might have asked for details. At the moment, his mind was on the girl and Detective Amos.

Should he email or text? He chose to text. The text would be long, but he could confirm whether Amos received it. It would be harder for the detective to ignore his request.

Diana Krall crooned softly from the high-end audio system while Alexander stared at his phone. What he thought would be a simple text was anything but. He had so many questions. It was likely that the detective would only answer one or two, maybe three, but not the dozens Alexander had swirling in his head.

"Why was the case closed?" was the question Alexander most wanted to ask...and get an answer to. But he had a feeling the direct approach might not be the best. In an attempt to organize his thoughts, he leaned back in his chair and closed his eyes. He sat quietly, listening to Diana. His mind wandered to an unrelated question: What did Diana see in Elvis Costello?

A slight smile crossed Alexander's lips. Wondering why Diana Krall married Elvis Costello was the first time since he witnessed the girl fall from the building that he hadn't thought about her. After a deep breath, he went back to the text he had been trying to compose for the past twenty minutes.

"What the hell?" he said aloud. "I'm not writing a novel. Ask the damn question."

After writing, deleting, and rewriting several times, Alexander decided to keep his text to Detective Amos simple:

> **Detective, you said the case was closed. I have questions—lots of questions—for my own peace of mind. Did you identify the girl? Did you figure out what happened...why she ended up on the pavement in front of the hotel? Were any arrests made?**

If Detective Amos replied and answered any of the questions, Alexander would press for details unless it happened to be an open-and-shut case. If the girl was tossed off the balcony, and the person who threw her off was waiting in the hotel room and confessed. That would make it a closed case. Alexander didn't believe that was what happened. He pressed the blue arrow on his phone's display to send the text.

Scott Hamilton's tenor sax was streaming through Pandora. The music was so clean and pure that it gave him goose bumps. He closed his eyes and let the soft jazz carry his mind far away from the dead girl who had infiltrated his head and refused to leave.

He had just begun to relax when his phone rang.

*****

Sam was pacing in her condo when Jerry pulled up and parked a newer model Ford Edge. Before he could get out, she was halfway to the car, pushing her twenty-four-inch, aqua blue, hard-sided suitcase.

"What took you so long?" she asked when she reached Jerry, standing outside the car.

"I wanted an SUV. The rental company said they had one. Then they had to wait for one. They finally showed up with it. Late. Since it's going to be a long trip, I thought a SUV would be more comfortable than a little sedan."

"That makes sense. I thought you might have changed your mind about the trip."

"Were you hoping I had?"

"It's hard to say. I'm still not sold on the idea of plotting to assassinate the president of the United States, but I can't sit around the condo all day and mope. A road trip will be fun. I'll worry about the operation another...uh, what did you call it?"

"I didn't name the operation. We have a code name for the president: Cockwomble."

"What the hell is 'cockwomble'?"

"I'm glad you asked. I had to Google it." Jerry walked to the rear of the SUV and opened the hatch. He tossed Sam's bright blue bag next to his plain black bag. "Hop in. I'll explain on the road."

When Sam got in the passenger side, Jerry was already seated, typing on his phone. "Fort Lauderdale is roughly fifteen hours from here. One thousand miles straight down I-95."

"Oh, that sounds fun."

Jerry ignored her sarcastic tone. "Is there any place you'd like to see on the way down?"

"What's there to see between here and Florida?"

Jerry didn't need his phone to get from Sam's condo to I-95. Once they were out of her neighborhood, he said, "I'm sure there's lots to see. Beaches, theme parks, golf, and NASA. Probably a lot more."

"Disney World!"

"Yeah, there is that. When we get to Florida. Do you want to go?"

"I don't know. I was there once when I was little. It would be fun to go again. I bet it's changed a lot in the last fifteen years."

Jerry shrugged. "I've never been. I did see the Jungle Cruise movie. We should stop on the way back."

"A celebration stop. Or it would be, if what we were planning was going to happen." Sam watched as Jerry made his way to the freeway. "Jerry, I've got two questions. Why didn't we fly to Florida, and when are you going to tell me what a cockwomble is?"

*****

"This is Alex."

"Alex, this is Detective Amos. I got your text. I thought I'd give you a call."

"Thanks, I appreciate it. What can you tell me?"

There was a hesitation before the reply. "Nothing."

"Nothing? You—"

"Not over the phone. You said you lived near the hotel, right?"

"Yes, about a block west."

There was another hesitation from Amos, much longer than the first. "There's a Starbucks on Beach Road, close to where you were last night."

"I know it."

"Can you meet me there in half an hour?"

Alexander knew the place well. It was a four-minute walk from his condo. "I can. It's close. I can be there anytime."

"Thirty minutes." Detective Amos hung up.

*****

Jerry followed Dolly Maddison Boulevard to the Capital Beltway Outer Loop. Traffic wasn't overly heavy, so he stayed in the main lanes instead of jumping into the express lane. He drove at the posted speed limit, even as cars flew past him.

Fifteen minutes later, he took the exit toward Richmond and merged onto Interstate 95. It hadn't been a difficult drive, but Sam noticed Jerry's intense focus, punctuated by his deathlike grip on the steering wheel.

Once on I-95, Jerry seemed to relax. His breathing had steadied. Sam was now more interested in the answer to her first question.

"Jerry, why didn't we fly to Florida?"

"I don't drive a lot—"

"No shit."

Jerry gave her a sideways glance. "I grew up in New York City. We didn't own a car. I was in college before I learned to drive. In DC, I usually take public transportation or Uber. I have my old junker, but I only drive it short distances or when I'm going to the store and will have groceries. For work, I was usually in a foreign country where I didn't drive. To answer your question, since I'll be getting a new job, I felt I needed to get more comfortable driving. What better way than a thousand-mile road trip?"

Sam had already kicked off her sneakers. She stretched her legs out as far as they would go. "I guess I'll get comfortable. You'll be doing all the driving. I don't suppose you'd like any driving tips?"

"I'd prefer not."

After thirty minutes of silence, Jerry asked, "What kind of tips?"

"For one, if you go the speed limit, we'll never get to Florida. If you're worried about a ticket, go ten over the limit. Cops rarely stop you for ten over. If you aren't worried, go twenty over."

Jerry kept his eyes on the road, occasionally glancing at the speedometer. The section of I-95 they were on had a speed limit of fifty-five miles per hour. Jerry slowly accelerated to sixty-five. "Better?"

"A little. I have a feeling that by the time we get to North Carolina, you'll be doing fine."

Sam watched Jerry as he drove. He seemed to relax more and more with each mile. She had to wonder how a man who was a trained killer could be terrified of driving a car. "They didn't give you pursuit driving classes at spy school?"

"No, they didn't. They also didn't give me an Aston Martin DB5 with a machine gun, flame thrower, or ejection seat."

"Probably because they knew you didn't know how to drive."

Jerry gave Sam another side-eye. "How long have we known each other?"

"Uh? Oh. I guess about two years. Why?"

"In all that time, we never talked about much other than the case we were on. Even if we weren't on a case, we talked about a case...or cases. We never got too personal in our conversations."

"That's true. Like you never told me you were gay."

"No, I didn't. But it wasn't you. I pretty much stayed in the closet. Not many people knew."

She sat quietly, hoping Jerry would divulge more "tea."

"We're about thirty minutes into a fifteen-hour road trip," Jerry said. "I'm already seeing a side of you I didn't know. I hope we're still friends by the time we get to Florida."

"Me too, considering your profession. I mean, ex-profession," Sam said with a smirk. Jerry gave her a glance but said nothing. She wondered if she had crossed the line.

"Obviously, I've never driven this direction. I checked the map. There are lots of places to hide a body between Richmond and Jacksonville."

Sam leaned forward and glared at Jerry.

He burst out laughing. "Hey, you said it, not me."

"But you sounded serious. Too serious."

"Spy school."

"Touché," Sam said, leaning back in the seat. "You're right. We're going to know each other a lot better at the end of this trip. I still have another question."

"Yes."

"The code name your friend wanted to use for the president? Uh…"

"Cockwomble."

"Yeah, that's it. It's not an easy word to remember. Sounds dirty, too. What's it mean?"

"It's a British term. It's a person who makes foolish and outrageous statements or exhibits inappropriate behavior, often while holding an inflated sense of their own importance or wisdom. It's used as an insult to describe someone who is particularly foolish, arrogant, and irritating."

"How fucking appropriate."

<u>SIX</u>

Alexander arrived at the Starbucks exactly thirty minutes after his call with Amos, but he didn't see the detective. A young woman sat alone at a round table, drinking a Frappuccino and working on a laptop. Another couple sat facing each other against the back wall.

After ordering a Starbucks Dark Roast, black, and waiting too long for it to be poured, Alexander chose a table in the corner. He took a sip of coffee, pulled out his phone, and checked for messages. He had none.

"Mr. Christian."

Alexander flinched. He looked up to find Amos standing next to him.

"I'm sorry, did I startle you?"

"A little. I didn't hear you walk up. And, it's Alex."

"It's the shoes. Clove Classic. They claim to be the quietest shoes on the market, and they're incredibly comfortable. Healthcare workers wear them. They're on their feet all day, and they need to be quiet. They're also fluid-repellent. I'm guessing that's another reason healthcare workers wear them. I like that feature as well."

The shoe story was nice, but that wasn't why Alexander was meeting Amos. Still, he felt he needed to complement his shoes. "They're nice.

I'll check 'em out." Alexander said, despite thinking the shoes were butt-ugly.

"I'll send you a link. Let me grab a coffee." Detective Amos went to order.

Alexander noted that the detective's coffee didn't take nearly as long as his. It was probably because of the way Amos stood, hands on his hip, pushing his sports coat back enough for the young barista to see the badge and Glock attached to his belt.

Amos returned to the table and sat down. He glanced around and leaned forward. "I bet you're wondering why I asked to meet you here."

"To be honest, I am."

Amos took another glance around the room. The young woman was busy typing on her computer. The couple against the wall seemed to be having a healthy discussion. The barista had her back turned, working on a coffee machine.

"I told you the case is closed."

"You did."

"It came from the top. Close the case. Don't ask questions."

"Isn't that a bit unusual?"

Amos rocked his head back and forth slightly. "Yes, and no. It's not the first time, but it doesn't happen often."

"Let me guess. The last time it happened, a young girl was involved."

The detective's eyes widened. "As a matter of fact, I think so. I wasn't the detective on that case, but it seems like it was a young girl, and her death was suspicious. Maybe a drug overdose. They called it an accidental drug overdose and closed the case. Again, I don't remember the details."

"Was it recent?"

"About four or five months ago."

"You don't happen to know where?"

"No. I think it was in one of the nicer hotels."

Alexander took a sip of coffee to allow what he'd heard a chance to sink in. He wanted to give the detective a little time to think about what he'd said. It didn't take long.

"Well, fuck me. I guess I couldn't see the forest for the trees. Here in Fort Lauderdale, we have twenty-five to thirty homicides a year. It doesn't sound like much, but it keeps us busy. A lead detective is assigned to the case, and the other detectives provide assistance. Who assists depends on the location of the crime. We all usually hear about the case, but if we don't work on it, we don't get all the details." Amos leaned back in the chair and rubbed the day-old stubble on his chin. "As I said, I don't remember much about the young girl from a few months ago. But now that you mentioned it, damn, it sure is similar."

"Can you get the details of that case? I also have lots of questions about what happened last night."

Amos averted his eyes. "No."

Alexander's jaw dropped. He knew there were extenuating circumstances, but he expected a little cooperation from Amos.

"I'm sorry. I can't. Word came from high up. Last night was a suicide. Case closed. If the previous case was closed as quickly, I'm sure the orders had come from high up as well."

Alexander scratched the back of his neck. "But aren't you curious? This has to be—"

"A cover-up. Yes, I'm sure it is. Am I curious? Hell yes. Am I pissed about it? You bet. Am I going to act on it? Nope."

Alexander's deep blue eyes narrowed.

Amos saw the look and continued. "I joined FLPD after two years of junior college. I worked my ass off from patrol cop to detective. I've got twenty-five years in. I could retire, but I couldn't live on the pension. I need another ten years. If word comes down from the top to close a case, I close it."

"I get it," Alexander said. "I suppose I'd do the same in your Core Classics."

Amos laughed, impressed that Alexander remembered the name of his shoes. "You're a detective, right?"

"I have a private investigator license in Texas. Not sure you'd call me a detective."

"But you were, at one time."

"Yes, I was an FBI agent for twenty years."

"So you have skills. As I said, I'm not happy about this, but I can't risk my job."

Alexander could see where the detective was heading. "But I can do a little investigating since I don't have a job to risk?"

"Yep."

"Will I get any cooperation from the police department?"

"Not a bit."

"None? Not even running a background check?"

"I can do that. Discreetly."

Alexander nodded. "Of course. If I need to get in touch, can I text you at the number on your card?"

"Yes, it's a BYOD phone."

"BYOD?"

"Bring Your Own Device. The department doesn't issue phones."

"I've never heard the term. The FBI issued phones. Not good ones, but phones. At least they did later in my career."

"You think I'm paranoid. Maybe I am. But I was told to forget this case so fast it frightened me a bit. Now that you've reminded me of a similar case, I don't want to take any chances. Call me, don't text. Texts stay in the network and can be downloaded with a warrant for probable cause."

"Would investigating a crime give them probable cause to search your cell records?"

"This has to be a high-level cover-up. I wouldn't put it past them."

"What about WhatsApp? It's end-to-end encrypted. The data isn't stored on their servers. If you delete the messages from the app, they can't be retrieved."

"I've used WhatsApp, but not a lot. It should be okay. I'll delete any texts as soon as I read them."

Amos checked his phone to make sure WhatsApp was still active. It was.

"I want to help," he told Alexander. "What happened last night is bullshit. All the detectives know it, and I'm sure the others would like to help. But none of us can afford to get crosswise with City Hall. Or the feds. Whoever it is pulling the strings."

"I understand. The death of a young girl isn't worth getting fired or losing your pension over." Alexander watched Amos for a reaction. There was none because Amos was fully aware that he valued his pension more than the girl.

It made Alexander wonder about the detective. Although Amos seemed to be on the up and up, it could have been a ploy. There was a chance Amos didn't want to share information or assist because he didn't want to, not because he was worried about the consequences. Alexander decided he would be careful what he shared with the detective, at least for a while.

"Amos, I know you don't want to, but I may need some inside info. Nothing that would get you fired. What I need should be easy for you to get. For instance, did you identify the girl from yesterday before you got called off?"

"I didn't. If the medical examiner identified her, I didn't get the report. It's early, though. It's possible she hadn't ID'd her. I've got a feeling I'll never see the ME's report."

"That's sad. She could have family out there wondering what happened to her. Has there been a missing person's report filed for anyone matching her description?"

"Not that I know of. I'll check the computer. I'll ask around. I have to be careful."

"Would your computer have all of Broward County, or only Fort Lauderdale reports?"

"We get the missing persons reports for all of South Florida. I'll check it, but a young, thin Hispanic female with long black hair will be there. There will likely be ten or twenty of them."

"Pretty common, huh?"

"Very."

"Do you know the ME? Is he or she approachable?"

"Fort Lauderdale doesn't have a medical examiner. All our cases are handled by Broward County. The Chief ME is a woman. I don't know much about her. She joined recently. I believe they also have an intern on staff."

"That's the only way we're going to identify the girl. Without knowing who she was, there isn't much to go on. I'll see what I can find out from the ME. Speaking of Broward County, I suppose they handle all of the homicides outside Fort Lauderdale's city limits."

"They do." Amos nodded a few times. "You want to know if there have been homicides in the county that were covered up."

"It would be worth taking a look at. Any idea how to get that info?"

"Without getting myself fired?"

"That would be preferred."

Amos rubbed his forehead. "I'll have to think about it. I know several of the detectives at the Sheriff's Office. Like me, they'll be reluctant to talk. I don't know them well enough to know if I can trust them. I'll talk to a couple and feel them out. If I decide I can trust any of them, I'll see what I can find out and get back to you."

"I appreciate it." Alexander pushed himself away from the table and started to stand.

"Wait," Amos said. He stared out the window for a few seconds. "That previous case I mentioned, I think that may have been in the county, outside the Fort Lauderdale city limits. The Broward Sheriff's handled the case. They read us in, and then, like the next day, said the case was closed. That was unusual, but it wasn't our case, so we didn't think anything about it."

"It didn't strike you as odd?"

"Maybe. I don't remember. I'm sure I was busy with my own case."

Alexander nodded. "I suppose that's not something you would care to look into."

Amos sighed. "No, it's not. I'm sorry."

"No worries. I appreciate what you've shared. I should go now."

"If you don't mind, let me go first," Amos said. "Wait a few minutes before you leave."

Alexander thought Amos was being a bit clandestine, but agreed. The two men shook hands while sitting. Amos stood and scampered out the door. His Core Classics didn't make so much as a squeak.

*****

I-95 south of Lorton, Virginia, the eighteen-foot-high wall that protected neighborhoods from the sounds of the freeway gave way to rows of small native deciduous trees, including oaks, maples, and the occasional poplar. A bit further south, the rows of trees turned into gentle, rolling hills.

For most of the drive, Sam had remained quiet. She was content to play DJ on Sirius while Jerry concentrated on driving. He seemed content with the arrangement, complaining only when Sam chose an AC/DC tune—any song by AC/DC.

"Please change it," he would say. "I can't stand that band. The guitar riffs are great, but the singer's voice is like fingernails on a chalkboard to me."

Sam would oblige and select a different station.

"Hey, a sign back there said there's a McDonald's at the next exit. I need to pee." Sam read the next sign. "We're in Emporia."

"Sounds like a booming metropolis."

"Don't be snide."

Jerry took the exit off of I-95, followed the loop around, and a half mile later found the McDonald's. "Not exactly an easy on, easy off location. That was exit 11-A. We're eleven miles from North Carolina. Check the gas app and see if gas is cheaper in Virginia or North Carolina."

Sam brought up the app on her phone. "There's not much of a difference. Do you need gas?"

"We have over half a tank. We'll keep going."

"We're here, and there are several gas stations. Go ahead and fill up. You never know when you might hit a stretch without services."

"In North Carolina? I doubt I could spit without hitting a gas station. It's not like we're in Wyoming or some other godforsaken place. But yeah, we're here, I'll top off."

Sam wondered if Jerry had ever been to Wyoming. She hadn't, but from what she read, it wasn't a godforsaken place—except in the winter.

Jerry pulled into the Shell station and stopped before he reached the pumps.

"What's wrong?" Sam asked.

"I don't know which side of the car the gas cap is on."

"Seriously? Look at the fuel gauge on the dashboard."

"Okay."

"See the little arrow next to the picture of a pump?"

Jerry nodded.

"Which way is the arrow pointing?

"To the left."

"That's where the gas cap is."

"What the hell? I never noticed."

"Your car doesn't have a little arrow?"

"I don't know. I know on my car, the filler cap is on the right side." Jerry eased the left side of the Edge next to a pump. He swiped his credit card, selected regular grade unleaded, put the nozzle in the filler hole, and locked the nozzle's handle into position. He took the squeegee from the plastic water trough and cleaned the front windshield.

He finished the last swipe just as the pump clicked off. After squeezing a few more drops into the tank, he put the nozzle back in the electronic head. When the display asked whether he wanted a receipt, he pressed YES and waited for it to eject. He began to wonder if he should have used his credit card for the gas purchase.

"I was thinking," Jerry said when he was seated back inside the SUV. "We aren't committing any crimes, per se, but should I be leaving a paper trail? I paid for the gas with my credit card."

"Is your cell phone on?"

"Of course."

"Our movements are being logged. If an agency wanted to, they could subpoena our phone records and track every move we make. I wouldn't worry about credit card transactions. As you said, we aren't doing anything illegal. We're heading to Florida for a little R and R."

"I guess I'm a little freaked."

"Ya think? Let's roll. I need to pee. I hate gas station bathrooms."

Jerry pulled around the corner to the McDonald's. "You pee. I'll order. What do you want?"

Sam glanced at her phone for the time. "This is lunch. Get me a double cheeseburger, fries, and a large Dr. Pepper."

"Healthy."

"I'm on vacation."

Unhealthy or not, Jerry thought Sam's order sounded good, and ordered the same. Back on I-95 Southbound, they ate in relative silence. Sam rotated the Sirius dial searching for a tune she liked. Her tastes ranged from classic rock to current pop to country. She found a Sabrina Carpenter song and clicked on it.

When they finished eating, Sam gathered the trash and used napkins and stuffed them into the McDonald's bag. After a few more miles of silence, Sam turned the radio volume down and said, "How many people have you killed?"

SEVEN

Alexander waited a few minutes after Detective Amos left. He thought the detective was being a bit overcautious, but he understood and played along. Losing his job at his age would be disastrous. He'd still have his pension, but, as Amos had told him, it wouldn't be enough to live on. It could affect his current and retirement insurance.

Alexander stood, glanced at the barista busy making coffee, and left. Outside, he turned left and strolled up the sidewalk along Jimmy Buffett Memorial Highway. It was a cool day in Fort Lauderdale for late March. Low-seventies. The onslaught of summer was still several weeks away.

As he walked north along the coast, Alexander could see the hotel from which the girl had fallen. The image of her falling and lying dead on the ground still haunted him. The fact that the Fort Lauderdale Police had closed the case pissed him off. Had the case remained open for a few days and been closed after a thorough investigation, he could have accepted it.

As it was, there had to have been a cover-up. Someone powerful was in that room with the girl, and when they were finished with her, they tossed her off the balcony like a cigarette butt. Less than twelve hours later, she, like a smoked cigarette, was nothing but ash. Forgotten. As though she never existed. But she had existed. She had family. A family who would never know what happened to their girl.

Alexander was seething by the time he reached the hotel. He turned the corner to go to his condo, which led him directly past the spot where the girl died. He looked up at the balcony, then down at the ground. The only sign a young woman had died there the previous evening was a piece of yellow police tape tied to a small palm tree. The tape, with the letters "CRIME SCENE DO" flapped in the light breeze. The remainder of the warning had been ripped away.

"I will find out who you were, and I will bring those who did this to justice," Alexander whispered. He noticed CCTV cameras mounted on the rear of the hotel were pointed in his direction.

There's a chance.

He walked through the hotel's back entrance, still searching for cameras. When he approached the counter, a smartly dressed middle-aged woman with short black hair streaked with what could be premature grey, large seventies-style Elton John glasses, and a nametag that read 'Janice' greeted him.

"Can I help you?"

"I hope so...Janice," Alexander said. "I was here last night, and I parked my car in your rear lot. There's a huge dent in the door. It must have gotten backed in to."

The woman cleared her throat. "I'm sorry, but we aren't responsible for vehicles parked in the lot."

"Yeah, I get that. I spoke with my insurance company, and they asked if I could obtain the hotel's video footage of the lot to see if I could get the tag number of the car that hit me."

"Oh, no, I'm sorry, we don't release surveillance video. Only to the police and only with a warrant."

Alexander's eyebrows rose. "Seriously? If the cops requested the video, you wouldn't give it to them?"

"Not without a warrant."

"I bet that makes you popular with local police."

"Never had a problem with them."

Alexander detected some snarkiness. "Hmm. What about last night? When I was leaving, I saw several cop cars here."

The woman shuffled behind the counter. "Uh, I was off last night. I wouldn't know about that."

"There were lots of cops. No one mentioned it this morning?"

"No." The woman's eyes didn't stray from her computer screen. She started to type. "I'm busy. Is there anything else I can help you with?"

Alexander couldn't resist one last dig. "There is. In the past, oh, six months, how many young women have died in your hotel?"

Janice's eyes grew large. Her breathing labored. "I...I wouldn't know about anyone dying in our hotel."

"Right," Alexander said with a wink. He turned and walked out of the building.

Janice's facial expression answered his question. Last night's death wasn't the first in the hotel. The question was, how many more were there? Detective Amos mentioned there was at least one other mysterious death where the investigation was closed without due process. But that was in the county, not within Fort Lauderdale's city limits.

When Alexander left the building, he took another look at the four balconies from which he believed the girl had fallen. Then, at the spot where she landed. He shook his head as he walked past and pulled out his phone.

*****

"What?" Jerry said, not taking his eyes off the interstate.

"You heard me. How many people have you killed?"

Jerry stayed silent. He only removed his hand to rub the side of his nose.

"You aren't going to tell me?"

"I'm considering it."

"So many that you need to think about it? Jesus."

Jerry let out a soft laugh. "How long have we known each other?"

"A couple of years. What does that have to do with it?"

"And in those years, we did quite a few ops together. All intelligence gathering, right?"

"Yeah."

"Did you ever see me pull my gun?"

Sam thought about the question. "No. As a matter of fact, I didn't. We were never in a situation where you were required to."

"Exactly. That was the case in most of my assignments."

"Wait. So you're saying you never killed anyone."

"Never."

"But I thought you were..."

"A trained killer. I was trained to kill, but never did. I could have, if ordered to. But, unlike the movies, the CIA doesn't put out hits on every enemy of the state. Assassinating a foreign leader can get kinda messy. If it's someone like Osama Bin Laden, Qasem Soleimani, an Ayatollah, or Ayman al-Zawahiri. In those cases, they're taken out by the military in a raid or a drone strike."

"Interesting. I thought a lot of the work we were doing was research, so you could kill a terrorist."

"When I joined, I thought that too. I thought I'd be traveling the world, taking out foreign presidents and dictators who were anti-US. In the sixties and seventies, the CIA was heavily involved in targeted killings and assassination attempts of foreign leaders. Times change. I won't go so far as to say it no longer happens."

"You trained so long. Are you sorry you didn't, uh, I hate to say it, but you didn't kill anyone?"

"Not at all." Jerry twisted in his seat and stretched his back. "Why'd you ask?"

"Our mission. Yes, it's hypothetical, but if you were going to attempt to assassinate the president, how would you do it?"

"You mean if I was going to do it personally? Not plot out an elaborate scheme with a team and blame it on a patsy?"

"Sure, let's go with that scenario for now. How would you do it...personally?"

Jerry adjusted his Ray-Bans and ran his hand through his hair. "The main objective after the kill is not getting caught. If I could get close enough to the target's car, I'd put a bomb under it with a cellphone trigger. But I'd never get close enough to the president's car. Getting decent explosives isn't easy either. I doubt I'd be able to poison him. Although if I had enough time, I could analyze his movements and get into the kitchen of a restaurant he was eating at and spike his water. But more than likely, the Secret Service would be all over the kitchen, and you might accidentally get the wrong person."

Jerry took a long drink of the McDonald's Dr. Pepper. "Realistically, the best way...if you want to use the term 'best'...is with a sniper rifle."

"That makes sense," Sam said. "Most of the publicized assassinations are done with rifles. Kennedy, King, the attempted assassination of Trump, and Charlie Kirk. But none of them got away with it. So why is using a rifle best?"

"There are also many assassinations where a pistol was used. Bobby Kennedy, Lincoln, and John Lennon. The attempts on Ford and Reagan were both with a pistol."

Sam cocked her head. "And none of them got away with it either. So, again, why use a rifle?"

"None of them got away with it because they didn't plan well. They plan the assassination, but they never plan the escape. They were amateurs. John Hinckley Jr., who wounded Reagan, did it to try to impress Jodie Foster. Most would-be assassins are nut jobs."

"Okay, so how should one assassinate a person? I don't mean some Joe off the street, I'm talking about a public figure who would have decent security."

"With a sniper rifle. Like the Snipex Alligator."

"What the fuck is that?"

"I'm glad you asked." Jerry chuckled softly. "The Alligator is a large-caliber, anti-material rifle developed in the Ukraine. It was designed to engage targets like vehicles and communications systems at long range. It's heavier than hell, over fifty pounds, but the weight gives the gun stability and accuracy. It can penetrate over half an inch of armor. You can imagine what it would do to a human."

"Good Lord," Sam said, trying not to picture what a bullet capable of penetrating armor would do to a person.

"The record kill, which is documented, is almost two and a half miles. It happened in Ukraine, so the distance was measured in meters. Four thousand meters is what they said."

Sam looked ahead, trying to gauge how far two and a half miles were. "Over two miles. Damn. So why isn't it the weapon of choice for all shooters?"

"They aren't easy to come by. If you can find one, it will cost around twenty thousand bucks. It shoots a fourteen-point-five-millimeter round. If you can find those, they'll cost anywhere from fifty to seventy-five bucks a round. The weapon is heavy and takes practice to become proficient. You don't pop into your local gun range with one of those bad-boys and start shooting. To become decent with it, you'd have to fire at least a hundred rounds. That's five grand in ammo."

"I see your point. It's not a gun that a person runs down to the local gun store and buys off the shelf."

"Nope. And if you did, shooting from two miles away, you'd have to account for bullet drop and windage. And the kicker is that at that distance, the bullet takes four or five seconds to reach the target. If your target is human, it has to remain still. You need them sitting or standing stationary."

Sam wrinkled her nose. "So why even mention it? It's nearly impossible to get the gun and ammo, and it's unlikely anyone but a highly trained shooter could make the shot."

"All true. But that's how you get away with it. If you have the gun, the ammo, and the training, once you pull the trigger, you're gone before the bullet reaches the target. Not like anyone would be looking for you when you're over two miles away."

"Realistically, how would a trained assassin go about shooting a high-level target if they hoped to get away with it?"

"A skilled shooter with a good rifle can accurately hit a target close to a mile away. Realistically, a thousand yards. Depending on the conditions, a little further."

Sam did a quick calculation in her head. "That's over half a mile. How long would it take a bullet to go that far?"

"About a second."

"Hmmm...So the target would have to be somewhat stationary."

"It would make it easier. A good shooter could hit a moving target. One walking or riding in a car, as long as they were moving at a steady pace."

An overhead sign approached, indicating the next exit was half a mile away. Sam squinted to see the exit. "Geez, I can hardly see that far."

"The rifle would have a scope. It's not that hard."

"Is a half a mile far enough to get away?"

Jerry thought about it. "It depends on the location. The guy who shot Kirk was about a hundred and fifty yards away. He was on the roof of a building. He would have gotten away, but he couldn't help talking about it. His father turned him in. If it's a suburban area with lots of buildings, one-fifty to two-hundred yards is good. At four or five hundred yards, you can shoot, slip away, and never be caught. You need to be mindful of cameras. Cameras are everywhere. Wear generic clothing, a hat, a fake beard, and dark glasses so you won't be recognized. And keep your mouth shut. You could get away with it pretty easily."

"A gun like that, is it pretty easy to get?"

"In most states, yeah. You can buy a hunting rifle in most sporting goods stores."

"Damn. No wonder we have so many shootings in the US."

"Truth be told, that's not the gun of choice in most of the mass shootings..."

Sam waited a few seconds before saying, "So, what is?"

"How should I put this? What do you know about guns?"

Sam shrugged. "Not a lot. I've got a Glock. A Glock 26."

"You're petite, I thought you'd shoot a 43. It's a tad smaller and lighter."

"That's the one I wanted. My instructor suggested the 26. He said it was a little bigger, but it held ten rounds, with an option for more, as compared to the 43, which only holds six rounds."

Jerry laughed. "So you weren't a very good shot."

"I qualified. At seven yards, I'd hit a person every time. Anyway, you were saying..."

"Oh, yeah. The weapon of choice for most mass shooters is an 'AR' style rifle. I was reluctant to say 'AR' because it confuses people. They think it stands for assault rifle, but it doesn't. It stands for 'ArmaLite Rifle.' ArmaLite was the company that made the first AR-15. Which is an assault rifle. The original patent expired, so dozens of other companies now make similar rifles. All are semi-automatics, and most come standard with a thirty-round magazine. They shoot either a 5.56x45mm NATO or a 223 Remington round. Either round is deadly."

Sam's face flushed, and her nostrils flared. "Why are AR-style guns legal?"

"Simple. The NRA—the National Rifle Association—has to keep its base riled to keep donations coming in. They tell these idiots that it's their right, per the Second Amendment, to own a gun. If you let the government take away your AR, then they'll come after your handgun. The NRA lobbies to keep the thirty-round magazines, too."

"Idiots. I'm not a great shot, but if I can't take out a threat with ten rounds, I shouldn't be carrying a gun."

"A hundred years ago, machine guns—Tommy guns—were legal. Gangsters used them. The NRA helped outlaw them. The NRA was useful back in the day. Now, they're more interested in keeping members and keeping them agitated. They can't give an inch, or they lose members, which means they lose revenue."

"That sucks."

"It does. Especially for all those people killed by an AR with a thirty-round mag." Jerry stared at the road ahead. "I've shot an AR. I don't have much use for them. I prefer a sniper rifle. I've got mine in the back, if you want to shoot it when we get to Florida. I'm sure we can find a range."

"You ARE kidding? What is it?" Sam squinted at Jerry.

"Accuracy International AXSR. I wouldn't be without it."

"But—"

"I know, it's not an everyday carry gun. I'm not going to carry it around for defensive purposes. I like having it close. Don't worry, I'm not going to climb on a perch and open fire on a bunch of civilians or open fire on a gay bar."

Sam couldn't stifle her laugh. "I'm sorry. That's not funny, but it's what I expected you to say."

"It was meant to be ironic. Our conversation was getting a little deep. Depressing. My thought is, guns are like cars. Any idiot can buy a car. When they do, they drive too fast and lose control, or fall asleep at the wheel, or get drunk and drive, and they end up killing themselves and often others. Did you know nearly fifty thousand people die in auto-related accidents each year? And cars have all the safety gear—airbags, seat belts, and advanced warning systems."

"How does that compare to gun-related deaths?"

"Oddly, close. The difference is that a large number of gun-related deaths are suicides. I don't remember the exact number, but there are about twenty-five to thirty thousand suicides by gun each year. I imagine if the person didn't have a gun and wanted to kill themselves, there are ways. But with a gun, you get the urge, you put it to your head, and bang—you're dead."

"We could discuss this all the way to Florida," Sam said, "but I'm getting tired. Are you okay? Do you mind if I take a nap?"

"Not at all. I'm fine. I'm getting a little pissed at all these assholes going ninety miles an hour. I had tactical driving training years ago at The Farm. I didn't drive much, so I never got the chance to use those skills. I'm tempted to chase those bastards and do a pit maneuver on them. At ninety miles an hour, I bet they'd flip and roll forever."

Sam stared at Jerry wide-eyed but said nothing. She reclined the seat, pulled the seatbelt tight, leaned against the door window, and closed her eyes. She hoped he was joking.

EIGHT

The caller ID on Bat's phone surprised him. It had been a while since he'd heard from his friend. "Alex, how the heck are you?"

"I'm good. How are you?"

Bat, Bartholomew Epaphroditus Farnsworth the Third, was Alexander's best friend, computer expert, and neighbor when Alexander lived in Bolivar, Texas.

"Can't complain. No one would listen if I did." Bat took a breath, "Why do I feel this isn't a social call?"

"Is it ever?"

"Come to think of it, no, it never is. What's up?"

On his walk from the hotel where the girl died to his condo, Alexander told Bat about the girl's fall, the case being quickly closed, the detective's reluctance to investigate, and being rebuffed by the hotel when he asked about CCTV footage.

"What are the chances you can hack into the hotel's computer system and download the videos from last night?"

Without hesitation, Bat said, "Should be a piece of cake. Most hotels have horrible security. Many have open Wi-Fi, and once you're on their network, it's easy-peasy to hack their entire system."

By the time Alexander gave Bat the hotel details, he had reached the door to his condo. "If you need anything else, let me know."

Bat said he would and disconnected. Alexander pressed his thumb against the sensor on his door. The lock buzzed open.

"Hey," Jana said, "how'd it go?" She was sitting on a long white sofa, wearing pink pajama sleep shorts with an elastic waistband and drawstring, and a white tank top with a scoop neck. She had her laptop open on her lap.

"Not good," Alexander replied, flopping on the couch next to her. "Amos said they've closed the case. It came from the top. He didn't have much to say, but said he would try to help me. He's worried he'll get fired if he's caught giving me info."

"Fired? Case closed? What's it mean?"

"It means someone with a lot of power wants this swept under the rug. I asked Amos if there had been any other cases closed similarly to this one. One rang a bell. It was in the county. A young girl died, and the case was closed without much of an investigation. He didn't know the details, but he said he would try to get me what he could."

Jana slowly closed her laptop. "Alex, you're going to investigate this, aren't you?"

"I have to," he replied.

"I wish you wouldn't. If someone can toss a young girl off a balcony and have the power to cover it up, and then they find you poking your nose into it..."

"I'll be careful. I won't do too deep a dive. If I dig up anything useful, I'll send it to the FBI and let them handle it."

"You can't call them now and tell them what you told me? That should be enough for them to investigate."

"I could, but I'd be willing to bet there's already a full-blown cover-up. There are probably fake Medical Examiner reports stating it was a suicide, or that there were enormous amounts of drugs in the girl's system. It wouldn't surprise me if there's a witness statement saying she jumped."

"Damn," Jana said. "Who would...could pull it off?"

"That's what I intend to find out."

"Oh, Alex, I wish you—"

Alexander's cell phone rang. He answered immediately. "Bat, that was quick."

"Too quick. The hotel is like a fortress. It features advanced encryption, unlike anything I've seen before—and I've seen most of them. Hell, I invented many of the encryption algorithms."

"So you can't get in?"

"I'm not saying that, but it will take a while. How soon do you need the video?"

"The sooner the better. I've got nothing to go on now. I'm going to get on the computer and research Jane Does to see if there are any other similar cases, but to move forward with this one, I need to see what was going on inside the hotel. What floor was she on? Who was she with? Who left the room after she went over the rail?"

Bat was quiet. Alex knew he was thinking.

"If I could get into the hotel and get their Wi-Fi password, it should be a lot easier," Bat finally said. "Their external firewall is doing the heavy lifting."

"Not a problem. How long will it take you to get to Hobby Airport? There are several flights from Houston to Fort Lauderdale International every evening."

Bat checked his watch. "It's ten after eleven here. Give me an hour to pack and an hour and a half to get to Hobby, add an hour of wait time, and any flight after three will be fine."

"Start packing. I'll compare the flights and book the best one. Hey, I appreciate this."

"My pleasure. Mayte's in Florida visiting her sister. She's been there a week. I'll spend some time with her while I'm there. Oh, don't forget to book a room in that hotel."

Alexander rang off and went for his laptop.

"I'm way ahead of you," Jana said. "There are only two non-stops from Hobby to FLL. One at 7:05 this morning, the other at 7:05 this evening, Houston time. It arrives at 10:25 our time."

"Damn," Alexander said. "We're losing a lot of time between three and seven. It can't be helped. Book it."

"What's his full name?"

"Uh, Bartholomew Epaphroditus Farnsworth…the third."

Jana looked up from her laptop and frowned. "Spell it."

Alexander spelled out the letters F U C K   T H A T.

Jana laughed. "You don't have a clue, do you?"

"None at all. That's why he goes by 'Bat'." Alexander texted Bat, asking him to send his full name to Jana. She received the text a few seconds later.

"'Fuck that,' was right." She entered Bat's name into the Southwest Airlines ticketing system. "Done. One way. We'll book the return flight later. I'll send him the itinerary as soon as I get it."

Alexander didn't acknowledge her or take his eyes off his laptop.

"Alex?" Jana said.

"Uh, sorry. I'm looking at the hotel. There aren't any rooms available for tonight. I don't see any for at least a week."

"Not a problem. Bat can stay in our guest room."

Alexander shook his head. "That's not the point. He needs to stay at the hotel to access their Wi-Fi. Let me call him."

Alexander had a brief conversation with Bat, then turned to Jana. "He said it's not ideal, but if we could get him a room close, like in the hotel next door, he might be able to get their Wi-Fi. He said he could hack a guest's phone and then load a virus on it. I don't know why. He lost me."

Jana was hastily typing. "The hotel across the street is available. Should I book a week?"

"It shouldn't take him a couple of hours. One night. Two at the most."

"Bat said Mayte was in town. I booked a week. Give them a little vacation." Jana flashed a cheesy grin at Alexander, then typed more on her laptop. "I sent the details to Bat. I told him to Uber to the hotel. We'll reimburse him. I know you wanted to pick him up and talk shop on the way back to the hotel, but it will be almost eleven by the time he gets his luggage. You can meet him at the hotel or wait until morning to talk to him."

"Good call. I'll talk to him in the morning. He may have the video for me by then."

*****

Sam woke and gazed out the window. The scenery hadn't changed much since she'd fallen asleep. She was happy the car was still on the road and moving, and that Jerry had not been consumed by road rage and attempted a pit maneuver on an unsuspecting speeder.

"Have a nice nap?" Jerry asked.

Sam adjusted her seat upright, stretched, and yawned. "I did. I was hoping you wouldn't hit a car and make it a permanent nap."

Jerry's head snapped toward Sam. "What, you don't think I could pit a car without crashing this one?"

"At a hundred miles per hour? No. I mean, yeah, you'd hit the car, but you'd kill them and us. The death toll from auto-related incidents you mentioned would have climbed."

Jerry tilted his head and shrugged.

"Plus, you're afraid to drive. What the hell? A few hours behind the wheel and you're ready to run people off the road? How well did you score on your tactical driving training?"

"About as well as you did on your pistol qualifying."

"Okay. No more talk about fucking with the other drivers. Let 'em go."

"While you were asleep, I decided I shouldn't try to hit them with the car. I should shoot out a tire as they fly by. That, I could do."

Sam laughed, but hesitantly. Again, she wasn't sure if he was joking. People change when they get behind the wheel of a car. Calm people get aggressive. Sam wondered if Jerry was one of those people.

"Where are we?" she asked.

"We crossed into South Carolina. I saw a sign that said Florence is thirty-seven miles ahead. I'm a little tired and hungry. See if there's a Holiday Inn Express or a similar option in Florence. We'll stop, get a bite to eat, and spend the night."

Sam worked on her phone for several minutes. "There is a Holiday Inn in Florence. It's on Highway 327. Exit 170. I booked a room. Two queens."

"That's appropriate," Jerry said with a snicker.

"Uh?"

"Two queens."

"Whatever," Sam said, still looking at her phone. "Florence is a decent-sized town. About forty thousand people. I'm sure we can find a nice restaurant. Do you want a chain or a local eatery?"

Jerry scratched his cheek. "We'll be in the car all day tomorrow. Let's stick to a chain. Less chance of getting poorly prepared food that won't agree with us."

Sam scrolled through her phone. "As soon as we exit, there's a Buc-ee's. Do we need gas?"

"What's a Buc-ee's?"

"Oh, my God. You've never been to a Buc-ee's?"

Jerry frowned. "What's the big deal?"

"I can't explain it. You've got to see it for yourself. They sell food too. But there is no place to sit and eat. They want you to buy the food and eat it in your car."

"Sounds like a nice place. Here's exit 170. How do I get to the hotel?"

Sam brought up Google Maps. "After you exit, turn left on 327. The hotel is less than a quarter mile on the left."

As they exited I-95, Jerry saw the Buc-ee's on the right. "Damn, it's huge. We'll stop by tomorrow and get gas."

"We might want to go by this evening, after we eat."

"Why?"

"Trust me."

Jerry pulled the SUV into the Holiday Inn Express parking lot and parked under the large porte-cochere. "I'll check us in, you wait here. I'll come out with a cart when I'm done."

"Cool. I put the reservation in your name. I didn't give them a credit card."

Sam scrolled through the Sirius radio channels while waiting for Jerry to return. She checked her email. Nothing important. A far cry from only a few days ago, when she'd have dozens of emails, many of which were a matter of national security.

"Checked in." Sam jumped at the sound of Jerry's voice.

"Sorry, didn't mean to scare you."

"All good. Funny, I don't have a single email of any importance."

"Welcome to the world of unemployment."

The two loaded the hotel's luggage cart with two suitcases, two large tote bags, an overnight bag, and an Igloo Latitude 30-quart cooler.

"We're in room 315. Third floor. Can you take the cart up? I'll park the car and meet you in the room?"

Sam walked off, pushing the cart full of luggage. Jerry parked the Ford in the nearest spot. He caught up with Sam as she was pressing the key card against the door lock.

"Hold the door," he said when it opened. "I'll push the cart in."

"Can you unload the cart?" Sam asked. "Drop my stuff anywhere. I need to pee." She didn't wait for a reply before disappearing into the bathroom.

Jerry summed up the room. When Sam returned, he asked her if she had a bed preference."

"No."

"Great. I'll take the bed near the AC. I like it cool at night."

"Works for me. What about food? I'm starving." Sam pulled out her phone and searched for nearby restaurants. "All the usual fast-food places are nearby. We are...um...about five or six miles from town. The next exit. That's where the more traditional restaurants are."

Jerry sat on the bed and exhaled deeply. "I'm tired. I'd rather not do much more driving. What's closest?"

"Uh, there's a McDonald's across the street."

"Had that earlier. What else?"

"Wendy's, Waffle House, Subway, a place called Zaxby's Chicken Fingers & Buffalo Wings. Do you wanna be adventurous? It's across the street. We can walk."

"Is it local? Can we trust it?" Jerry asked.

Sam brought up their website. "Nine hundred and seventy locations. Primarily in the South."

"Localized, in the south, but not local. Good enough for me. Let me hit the head, and we'll go."

It took three minutes to get from their hotel room to Zaxby's. They ordered at the counter: Jerry, three chicken tacos, and Sam, an avocado ranch BLT chicken taco with fried white Cheddar Bytes. Both ordered the frozen strawberry lemonade. With their order placed, they picked a booth by the window to wait for their order number to be called.

Instead of calling their number, a young, lanky Black girl wearing a black apron over a red polo shirt and blue jeans brought their order to them.

"That was sweet," Sam said when the girl left.

"We're the only people in here. Or she was bored."

Sam gently shook her head to show her frustration with the fact that Jerry couldn't accept that the girl was being nice. The subtle gesture was lost on Jerry, who was digging into a taco. She let it drop.

"This is kind of a dumb time to ask, considering we're halfway to Florida, but why are we going to Fort Lauderdale? I wanted to ask you last night and again this morning before we left, but it was like, 'Pack, I'll be there in an hour,' so I packed, and here we are. The president is in DC most of the time."

Jerry swallowed a bit of taco and took a drink. "Have you heard the phrase, 'You don't shit where you eat'?"

"Sure. Many times."

"Well, there it is. We don't want to even pretend to be committing a crime in our own backyard."

"But we know our backyard. In Florida, we're clueless."

"True. But it doesn't take long to get acclimated. I've been dropped in places I didn't know existed and, in a few days, I knew all I needed to know to get the job done."

Sam wanted to ask what the job was, but had a feeling she wouldn't get an answer.

Jerry continued. "Plus, security is much tighter in DC. The president travels with a smaller entourage in Florida and has a more established routine. In DC, he could be anywhere on any given night."

"True." Sam ate a piece of a Cheddar Byte. "Wow, these are good. Would you like one?"

"No thanks." Jerry wiped his mouth with a paper napkin. "Where was I? Oh, yeah, think about it. In the last hundred years, all the assassinations and attempted assassinations of presidents have been outside DC. It's easier to get access to them."

Sam began to feel a little queasy. It wasn't from the taco or the cheese. She kept her head down and quietly ate until she saw Jerry finish his third taco. After popping the last Cheddar Byte, she said, "Why don't we get the car and run to Buc-ee's for gas?"

"You seem obsessed with that place. Can't we wait until we head out in the morning?"

"I'd rather go tonight. Then we can go back to the room, shower, and go to bed. I checked, and we have about eight or nine hours on the road tomorrow. I want to get a good night's sleep tonight."

"And you can't unless we go get gas?"

"That's right."

"Okay then. We'll go."

Sam placed a dollar on the table for the girl who brought them their order. They walked across the street to the Holiday Inn. The sun had set, and the air cooled.

"Do you need a jacket?" Jerry asked.

"No, I'll be fine. We aren't going far."

It wasn't far. Buc-ee's was less than half a mile up 327 on the west side of I-95.

"Jeez, this place is huge," Jerry said when he turned into the parking lot. "I've never seen so many gas pumps. Crikey!"

"Wait till you see the inside."

Jerry filled the Ford Edge with gas and moved to a parking spot closer to the doors. Forty-five minutes later, he and Sam came out of the building. Jerry was carrying three plastic bags full of stuff: kolaches for dessert later, various flavors of jerky, Smokin' Nacho Cheese Puffs, Buc-ee's BBQ chips, Buc-ee's Cinnamon Sugar Pretzels, a T-shirt with Buc-ee the Beaver on it, and a large bag of Beaver Nuggets. The snacks were for the road, he claimed.

Back at the hotel, Sam showered while Jerry broke into the kolaches. When Sam came out of the bathroom wearing a sexy V-neck cami top and ruffled shorts, Jerry's eyes twinkled with delight. Sam's instinct was to cover her breasts, knowing the cool air of the room had caused her nipples to poke through the thin satin material. She didn't want to seem obvious, now questioning Jerry's claimed sexual preference. She pulled the bedspread back and slid under the covers, pulling the sheet around her neck.

"Wow!" Jerry said, staring at Sam. "These kolaches are amazing." His eyes got wider as he took another bite. "I know we get breakfast here in the morning, but we gotta stop and get more of these."

He wasn't the slightest bit interested in her breasts. Sam wasn't sure if she was happy or hurt. She turned out the light next to her bed. "What time do we want to get up in the morning?"

"How's seven sound?" Jerry mumbled with a mouthful of his new-found delight.

"Good. I'm usually up by seven. If not, wake me. Good night."

Jerry waved, but didn't speak. He stuffed the last of the kolache into his mouth.

Sam closed her eyes for a moment, then opened them. "Jerry," she said softly, waiting for him to make eye contact. "Are you considering...you know. Assassinating..."

<u>NINE</u>

Bat's plane from Houston to Fort Lauderdale was on time. He took an Uber to his hotel, the Grand Paradise Fort Lauderdale, checked into his room, and was logged onto the hotel's Wi-Fi by midnight. The Wi-Fi was decent. He used a VPN to access his home computer. Though his laptop was state-of-the-art, his home system was exponentially more powerful and provided access to hacking utilities.

After verifying a stable connection to his home computer, Bat viewed the list of available networks. He noticed several networks that likely originated from The Overlook Hotel across the street. The signals were weak. The hotel was caddy-corner to his room. He stepped out onto the balcony with his laptop and sat in a metal lounge chair with thick cushions.

When Jana made the reservation, she requested a room with southern exposure, as high as possible. The room Bat was assigned faced due south and was on the seventh floor. From the balcony, he could see straight across the street to the block of rooms Alexander thought the girl fell from.

On the balcony, The Overlook Hotel's Wi-Fi signal was stronger. All of the available networks were secured and most likely encrypted.

Bat checked the time. Almost one in the morning, only midnight Houston time, but he still felt tired.

Air travel was taxing on him. For the most part, he didn't like people, and he hated crowds—unless the crowd was scantily clad women on the beach. Even that had tempered since he met and fell in love with Mayte several years earlier. Now, he just wanted to shower and get a few hours of sleep.

He texted Alexander and Jana:

> **Made it okay. Checked in. Have a view of The Overlook Hotel and a small view of the ocean. Overlook's Wi-Fi service is decent from the balcony. All networks from the hotel are secured. Will work on it in the morning.**

After sending the message, Bat showered and went to bed. He fell asleep instantly.

*****

One block west in his condo, Alexander had a restless night. When he closed his eyes, he saw the girl lying dead in the parking lot of The Overlook Hotel. When he tried to get his mind off her, he would remember what Detective Amos had told him. Alexander needed to find out how many other young women had died a violent death in the area.

Once he fell asleep, he slept hard. When he awoke, it was still dark, but he felt refreshed. Jana was still asleep beside him. He eased out of bed, slid on shorts and a Hawaiian shirt, started a pot of coffee, grabbed a glass of juice and his laptop, and went onto the porch.

He had done a hasty search the night before. It was time for a deep dive. He was digging through every article Google could regurgitate. He read every report on the death of a female, especially any Jane Does. What he found was unsettling. There were over nine hundred open cases of missing women in Florida. Missing didn't necessarily mean dead. The number of Jane Does, dead women who were never identified, was much lower.

Lower, but still an unmanageable number of unidentified women. The time period was too long. Alexander went back to searching for news articles on women who were found dead in Broward County in the past six months. Amos had mentioned a quickly covered-up death of a young girl four or five months prior.

Three reports were of interest. Alexander read the first news article:

> **Broward Sheriff's Office detectives are investigating the death of a woman whose body was found in a Walmart parking lot on Friday morning. The woman was found by a light post around 9 a.m., according to emergency radio traffic. The sheriff's office said that based on its initial investigation, detectives do not suspect foul play.**

Article number two:

> **A young woman was found dead inside a donation box in Pembroke Pines. Police believe she became trapped inside the box, and her death was a tragic accident. No name, age, or description of the woman was given.**

The third article of interest:

> **Fishermen found a young Hispanic woman, age unknown, washed up on the beach near Haulover Pass this morning.**

There was no mention of a young woman dying from an apparent drug overdose or from falling off a hotel balcony. Alexander couldn't help but wonder how many other deaths went unreported.

Three reports of dead women and two, that he knew of, were unreported. Five deaths in six months. The number seemed high for one county. High for two counties, too, since Alexander wasn't sure which of the reports were in Broward and which were in Miami-Dade.

The sliding glass door to the balcony opened. Jana stood in the doorway wearing a t-shirt featuring Mickey and Pluto, and running shorts. "Any luck?" she asked.

"Nope. A lot of people die in South Florida."

"They call it God's waiting room for a reason."

"Right. But I mean younger people. Lots of homicides. Mostly young males. I found a few articles of interest, but what's interesting is what I didn't find. I couldn't find anything on the drug overdose Amos mentioned, and nothing on the death at the hotel. I'm sure there were reporters on the scene. I don't know any of the local news people, but I know the type. There were a few there."

"You didn't see a television news crew at the scene?"

Alexander thought for a bit. "No, now that you mention it, I didn't. They're usually the first on the scene. If it bleeds, it leads."

Jana sat in a deck chair facing Alexander and placed her long, slender legs on the balcony rail. Alexander couldn't help but admire them.

"You were one of the first on the scene, like in a matter of minutes. You said the police arrived pretty quickly, followed by an ambulance, the coroner, and the fire department."

"Right. Plus, the detective showed up about the time the coroner arrived to remove the body."

"It all happened pretty quickly. It's possible the news people weren't able to get there in time. Or they were at a more important story."

"They were probably at a high school football game and couldn't leave. Nothing's more important around here than high school football."

Jana shook her head. "I was going to say you're joking, but you aren't wrong. Except it's March. Maybe they were at a high school basketball game."

Alexander shrugged.

"Any chance the press was told to stay away?"

"It's possible. But even in Florida, if the press is told to stay away, they'd be all over it. It's more likely the press never got the word. The cover-up keeps getting more and more complex."

*****

After breakfast at the Holiday Inn, Jerry couldn't wait to load the car and get to Buc-ee's. It was all he talked about while nibbling on luke-warm scrambled eggs and overcooked sausage links.

"I'll wait in the car," Sam said after Jerry parked. "Don't be long. Get your kolaches and get out."

"Yes, dear," Jerry said, closing the car door.

Jerry wasn't long, by Buc-ee's standards. He returned with a brown paper bag full of kolaches and a plastic bag containing an assortment of items.

"I told you I wouldn't be long." He had a kolache out before Sam could reply. "Would you like one?"

Sam waved him off. "Later. Thanks."

"Ha! Like there will be any left."

"We have a long drive today. You should pace yourself."

Jerry stuffed the remaining kolache in his mouth so he could use both hands to steer the Edge. Once he was able to swallow, he said, "I know, I should, but these little treats are addictive. That will be the last one for a while."

While Jerry navigated through the mass of cars that filled the Buc-ee's oversized parking lot, trying to find the exit, Sam thought about his answer when she had asked him the previous evening if he was considering killing the president.

"No. Are you crazy?" was his reply. "As much as I'd love to, nope. And if you mean me personally, taking a shot at him from half a mile away. Hell no. I'm here to see if a few CIA agents, albeit ex-agents, could plot the assassination of a sitting president."

Sam wasn't convinced. If Jerry were straight, the exercise might have been an elaborate ruse to spend a week or two with her in Florida, hoping to go from two beds in a hotel room to one. But sex wasn't the motivator. At least not sex with her. She considered that he had the hots for his friend, Willie. Perhaps he was using her, so it wouldn't seem so obvious. She'd never met Willie Bouchette. Was he gay? She remembered Jerry describing him as "looking dumber than a stump." Sam wasn't sure what that looked like, but she figured it wasn't the look Jerry would have the hots for.

The drive through South Carolina was, for the most part, straight and flat. Loblolly and longleaf pines lined both sides of the freeway most of the way. Carolina Jasmine grew alongside the highway. Sam didn't know what the vine with bright yellow flowers that grew beside the Jasmine was, but found it astonishingly beautiful.

An hour and a half in, they stopped at a rest stop. Jerry grabbed a kolache and ate it on the way to the bathroom. After using the facilities, Sam stood outside the Edge, stretching until Jerry returned.

"We haven't been on the road long, but I needed the stop," Jerry said when he approached.

"Me, too. It must have been all the coffee we drank."

They climbed back in the SUV, and Jerry crept toward the freeway onramp. Once on it, he floored the Edge, throwing Sam back in her seat. She watched as Jerry quickly got up to speed and merged onto the freeway. She could tell he was much more comfortable driving than he had been just twenty-four hours earlier.

As they drove south, Sam kept playing disc jockey with the radio while Jerry politely listened to whatever she chose. Whenever she turned the volume up too high, he'd quietly lower it using the steering wheel controls. Sam pretended not to notice, but after a while she started turning it slightly louder than she actually wanted, knowing he'd lower it to her intended volume.

The charade continued for several hours, along with chit-chat about the South Carolina countryside. When they passed a sign noting the available food at the next exit, Sam said, "There's a McDonald's at the next exit. Let's stop. I'm hungry, and I could pee."

"You should have a kolache."

"Fuck, Jerry. If I hear another word about kolaches, I swear I'll stick one up your ass."

"Ooh," Jerry said, with a grin. "They are sausage kolaches."

"Oh, God, I'm going to be sick." Sam gagged loudly to make her point.

Jerry ignored her and took the exit. "That was exit number three. We've got a bit less than half a tank of gas. Can you see if gas is cheaper here or in Florida?"

"That was quick. It seems like I just did this." Sam opened the Gas

Buddy app on her phone. "Gas is about ten cents less in Georgia. We should fill up. Let's do it before Mickey D's."

After getting gas, they drove two blocks to McDonald's. It was a repeat of the previous day's lunch. Double cheeseburger, fries, and a large Dr. Pepper.

Back on the road, they crossed over Saint Mary's River. "Welcome to Florida," Jerry said. "That wasn't bad. Check the map, how far to West Palm Beach?"

"Four hours and twenty-six minutes. With stops, at least five hours."

"How many miles?"

"Around three fifteen."

Jerry looked at the Edge's dashboard. "According to the car's computer, we have four hundred seventy-three miles of gas. We could make it nonstop."

Sam took a big swig of her Dr. Pepper. "The car might be able to, but I can't. I figure at least three stops. Two, the third will be when we get there."

"Sounds about right. Don't want to risk running low on gas either. I'll fill up again at our second stop. Get comfy. We'll be in West Palm before you know it."

*****

Bat took a power nap before trying to hack the Overlook Hotel's network. He attempted to exploit any system vulnerabilities. It was the same trick he tried from his house in Bolivar. He didn't expect a different result, but he always went for the low-hanging fruit first. Each deeper dive delivered the same result—a dead end.

The hotel's bonded leather desk chair was uncomfortable. Bat stood, stretched, and paced around the room, stopping to look out the sliding glass door at the hotel across the street. "Who set up your security, and why do you have such a sophisticated system? What are you hiding, Mr. Hotel?"

Bartholomew Epaphroditus Farnsworth the Third was a genius. His IQ hovered in the one seventy-five range. Like most geniuses, Bat was, at times, socially awkward. He had a sense of humor, but it was often inappropriate. He could make eye contact and engage in most any conversation, not only conversations that interested him.

Bat was also frumpy, standing five feet eight and weighing well over two hundred pounds. Before he met his girlfriend, Mayte, he wore his gray-streaked hair in a ponytail and sported a scraggly beard. With the combination of weight, hair, and beard, he looked like a cross between Willie Nelson and Truman Capote. Mayte convinced him to shave and get a haircut, which helped his appearance considerably.

Bat's Achilles heel was authority. He could not tolerate being told what to do, especially by someone who knew less than he, which, in truth, was most people. Despite being good with computers, he struggled to hold a job. He found his calling when he decided to become a cybersecurity expert and started a consulting business. He could work remotely from his beach house. No boss. No set hours.

Bat was Alexander Christian's neighbor on the Bolivar Peninsula. As different as day and night, the two hit it off over their mutual admiration of fine wine, old scotch, and attractive women. The latter was much more elusive to Bat than to Alexander. Bat's newfound wealth as an in-demand consultant helped close the gap.

At seven o'clock in the morning, Bat slid the glass door open, stepped onto the balcony, and took in the view of the Atlantic Ocean. Traces of light were beginning to appear on the horizon. He looked back at the hotel across the street. Again, he wondered why they had such strong network security.

Bat went back inside and sat at his laptop. He saw no evidence of hotel guests using the hotel's Wi-Fi. Had there been, he could have installed spyware on their phone or laptop and captured the ID and password they used to log in to the hotel's Wi-Fi. That would have been too easy.

After a few more failed attempts, Bat decided a RAT—a Remote Access Trojan—might be the way to go. A RAT would infect the computer, allowing Bat to gain full control of the system. The RAT he designed was highly sophisticated, and few computers would detect it. The Overlook Hotel's system's level of sophistication concerned him.

He saw two main issues. The computer might detect the malware, and a user would have to activate it for the program to install.

Getting it installed should be easy. Attach it to a legitimate-looking email and send it to a list of hotel employees. At least one would open the email and click the link. Avoiding detection was the issue. It wouldn't be a disaster if the malware were detected; the system would simply delete it. But it might put the hotel's IT staff on high alert. Any attention would make the next step even more difficult.

Bat checked the time on his phone. Eight thirty. He sent a group text to Alexander and Jana:

I'm awake. Been working on the hack with no luck. Let me know when you're up, and we'll meet and discuss.

Jana was on the balcony with Alexander when their phones beeped with the new text. They read it at the same time.

"I'll ask Bat if he wants to talk about it over breakfast. Would you want to join us?" Alexander asked.

"Breakfast sounds good. But it's not worth listening to Bat tell you whatever it is he's going to tell you. I know I won't understand a word of it."

"I won't either, but I need to hear him out. He didn't say how long he's been working on it, but I'm surprised he's not in already. I've asked him to hack into businesses before and get me video, and he's usually gotten it in minutes."

Alexander replied to Bat's text, suggesting breakfast. Twenty minutes later, they met outside the Village Café. It was a ten-minute walk from the condo, but the food was worth it. It was early. The morning air was muggy. They decided on a table inside, near a window. A server brought coffee and menus.

Bat opened the menu, scanned it quickly, then peered over his reader glasses. "What the hell kind of place is this?"

"Jana calls it bougie. She loves it."

"Two *organic eggs*. Nice. We have to have organic. I wonder what

'Tow poached eggs' are?"

"Two?"

"I don't know. The menu says, 'Our Benedict's. Tow poached eggs – hollandaise sauce – english muffin – home fries.' Maybe they poach them with a tow truck."

Alexander shook his head. "I'm pretty sure it's a typo."

"At these prices, they should fix it. They didn't capitalize English either. Should I point it out to our server?"

"I wish you wouldn't."

"They need to be told. It's so unprofessional, especially for an establishment that is trying to be so hoity-toity."

Alexander noticed the server coming toward the table. "Order. I'll point out the typos another day. We need to be incognito."

The cloak-and-dagger idiom got Bat's attention. Though his field of expertise was cybersecurity, he worked from the comfort of his home office on a beach in Texas. Being in the field, so to speak, was mysterious. Being secretive meant intrigue or espionage. He didn't crave the excitement or the danger that might accompany it, but it was a nice change of pace.

Alexander ordered the Express Breakfast with sausage and toast. Bat, the Our Benedict—what else—with ham. Alexander, with a slight grin, watched Bat place his order with the server without commenting on the typos.

When the server left, Bat coolly scoped out the room and leaned in to whisper. "After a couple of hours of sleep last night, I tried to hack the hotel's computers. They have the most sophisticated system I've seen in a while. I tried all the usual suspects. No luck. Even the largest chain hotels, with a lot to lose if they're hacked, don't have near this level of sophistication."

Alexander leaned back in his chair. "So what does it mean? Is it new software, or have they gone out of their way to protect their network?"

Bat's voice rose to a normal speaking level. "They've gone way above and beyond. This isn't just the latest and greatest. It's stuff I haven't even seen. They're not using it to keep their guests' Wi-Fi secure, I tell you."

"Can you break it?"

"If given enough time. How much time do I have?"

Alexander scratched his head. "The longer we wait, the less chance we have of finding out what happened to the girl. The cover-up started before she hit the ground. Time isn't critical, but every minute counts."

"I've got a few clients I need to work on, but I will devote as much time as possible to the hotel. If I can't get in by tomorrow evening, I'll post it on the dark web. There are a bunch of hackers online that will love this one."

"Are you sure that's a good idea? What if one of them gets careless or the hotel's IT department notices?"

"Not likely. This dark web group is extremely good. They know what they're doing, and they're discreet."

"Will they want to be paid?" Alexander asked, but didn't care. Money wasn't an issue, and he'd be happy to pay to see the hotel's video. He would like to know whether he would have to pay and, if so, what the amount would be.

"No. They love a challenge."

Alexander's eyebrows rose. "Seriously, I thought if it was on the dark web, you paid for it...and dearly."

"Everything is for sale on the dark web. This group doesn't need money."

"Are those the guys I read about who live in their parents' basement and play video games all day?"

"Not hardly," Bat said with a chuckle. "For one, they don't play video games. Well, some may, but mostly they write code and test encryption algorithms. They stay on top of the latest malware and work on ways to detect it. There are a few who are only interested in writing malware that can bypass the latest security."

"And they don't need money because they're infecting computers and charging a ransom?" Alexander was becoming less impressed with the hackers. Theft was theft, in his opinion.

Bat shuffled in his seat. "No, they aren't creating ransomware. What they do isn't legal, but they feel they aren't hurting anyone."

"I'm listening."

"Ordinarily, I wouldn't tell anyone this, but you're a good friend. I trust you'll keep this to yourself." Bat waited for confirmation before he continued. "They each have their own plays, and they share within the group. They don't want everyone going after the same target."

Alexander crossed his arms and listened intently.

"What they do is infect company servers so they can get in and poke around. Mostly, they want to read emails. They hack publicly traded corporations, the FDA, and press release distribution services."

"And trade a company's stock based on inside information."

"You got it."

"And you do this as well?"

Bat stared out the window. Finally, he said, "I have. Not much. I do pretty well with my contracts. But occasionally, when I get a tip that's too good to ignore, I may."

"Well, you're a real son-of-a-bitch."

Bat recoiled.

"How long have you been doing this?" Alexander leaned across the table. "And not including me?"

Bat sighed. "Geez, you got me. I thought you were pissed at what I was doing."

"I am. You've been making money in the markets, and I was squeezing by on dividends."

"I'm sorry, Alex. I thought you were doing okay. As I mentioned, I don't tell anyone about this. I know we've been friends for a long time, but you're retired FBI. I knew you wouldn't turn me in, but you could let the FBI know what was happening so they could try to stop it. And, because you're retired, I wasn't sure if you'd risk getting busted for insider trading."

"You're right. I wouldn't. Well, once, for the hell of it. Don't you all worry about getting busted?"

"No. The SEC is so far behind that you'd have to be pretty stupid to get caught. We don't trade in large amounts. A few hundred here, a thousand there, depending on the stock price. We never short a stock, and we don't trade puts or calls. That's how you get busted. A person who never buys a call suddenly buys a large position right before the stock goes up. Red flag. Even the SEC's basic algorithm can spot it."

Bat took a drink of his coffee. "We make the insider trades once a month, twice at the most. Meanwhile, we buy and sell other stocks. We'll make a little, we'll lose a little. To the SEC, we get lucky once or twice a month."

Alexander smiled. "And because the virus you installed on the infected computer isn't doing any damage, no one notices?"

"Correct. Occasionally, the company will upgrade its malware protection or run a scan, and we'll get detected and deleted. I see that happen on older installs. When it does, we reinfect with a new version."

"So why don't more hackers do this?"

"Instant gratification. It takes patience to pull this off. You can't have too many big wins too often. A big no-no is buying a lot of shares of a stock the day before they release a positive press release. The best source is the company's email server. You can download all their emails and use AI to find emails about buying or selling the company. Those emails start weeks, often months, before it's public knowledge. As soon as it sounds like there is going to be a deal, we start buying shares in the company that's being acquired."

"It's a nice little scam," Alexander admitted. "As long as you don't get greedy, your chances of the SEC catching you are pretty slim."

"That's the way we figure it. Bulls make money, bears make money, pigs get slaughtered."

Alexander wondered how Bat found the group, how they vetted new members, if they allowed new members, and how the insider trading scheme got started. He decided he'd wait and ask about it over an adult beverage at a later date.

The server came by, removed the empty plates, and offered more coffee. They both declined.

"When you're ready, use this to pay." She pointed to the POS terminal sitting on the edge of the table. "No hurry. Let me know if you need anything."

"We will," Alexander said.

The server walked away.

Once he and Bat were alone again, Alexander said, "How comfortable are you with hacking police stations?"

TEN

Two and a half hours from Jacksonville, Florida, and south of Cocoa, Jerry exited Interstate 95 and pulled into a Marathon gas station. It paled in comparison to Buc-ee's, but the restrooms were clean. "Are you hungry?" he asked Sam when he pulled to the pump.

"Not really," she replied. "But I could use the bathroom. How 'bout you?"

"You go. I'll go when you get back. I may get a soda. Do you want one?"

"I'm soda'd out. I'll get a water from the cooler." Sam slid out of the door. "Are you going to leave the car here or pull up after you get gas?"

Jerry scanned the other pumps. Only one other was in use. "I'll leave it here. I'll wait until you get back so you won't get locked out."

Sam smiled and walked toward the red tile-roofed building. When the tank was full, Jerry put the nozzle on the pump, cleaned the windshield, leaned on the car, and waited.

Sam returned a few minutes later. "Sorry. There is only one Ladies' toilet, and it was occupied."

"No worries." Jerry took off at a brisk pace toward the bathrooms.

Sam fished a bottle of water from the cooler located in the

floorboard behind her seat. She did a couple of stretching exercises and got in the front seat of the car. Jerry came back just as she took her first sip of water.

"You didn't take long."

"No line for the men's."

"There never is."

Jerry ignored the remark, started the car, and steered them back onto the interstate.

"We should be a bit less than two hours from West Palm." He pulled a slip of paper from his pocket and handed it to Sam. "Put this address in your phone. It's Willie's."

Sam entered the address and started laughing.

"What's so funny?" Jerry asked.

"Did you look at the address?"

"Yes, why?"

"Greenacres, Florida? Not even Green Acres, two words, Greenacres, all one word. That's so Florida."

"I noticed when I wrote it down, but it didn't register. Now I know why Willie says he lives in West Palm."

Sam studied the map on her phone. "It's close to West Palm Beach. There are so many small towns in the area. Greenacres, Palm Springs, Lake Clark Shores, and a bunch of others. Palm Beach and West Palm Beach are the biggest. I wonder what the difference is between West Palm and Palm Beach?"

"That's easy," Jerry said. "The rich people live in Palm Beach. Their workers live in West Palm."

"Makes sense," Sam said, still looking at her phone. "Wow, from what I see on Zillow, Willie's got a nice condo."

"I'm not surprised. He spent most of his time in the islands, but he wanted a nice place to come home to."

"And he was with the agency about as long as you. So you both were GS-13 or 14." Sam typed on her phone.

"Don't bother Googling it. GS-13 is around one-twenty a year."

"Damn. I was a GS-11. I made about half as much."

"You were still fairly new and probably due for a promotion. You would've made thirteen in no time."

"Would have." Sam slumped in her seat and stared out the window.

"Don't be so pessimistic. Lawyers are fighting the firings in court. We could get our jobs back any day."

"I'm not holding my breath."

"The president could die of natural causes...or get shot."

*****

After breakfast, Bat returned to his hotel. He scanned for anyone using the Overlook Hotel's Wi-Fi. There were none. Frustrated, he walked onto the balcony and stared at the hotel. "Why are there no guests using your Wi-Fi?" It didn't make any sense. The hotel was big, ten stories. At least two hundred and fifty rooms. How could no one be using the Wi-Fi?

The only explanation was that the hotel had hidden its Service Set Identifier, making the network invisible to Bat. It was an extreme security measure—and a headache for guests—but considering the hotel's elaborate security setup, it made sense.

Bat had a plan. An evil twin hotspot. He'd create a fake Wi-Fi network that would appear legitimate to Overlook Hotel guests by using a name similar to the one they're likely using. He would need a router. One with a strong enough signal to be at or near the top of the hotel guests' available network list.

When a user attempted to log in to the fake network, Bat would install a packet sniffer and then immediately turn off the router. This would allow him to "sniff" or capture unencrypted data packets as they were transmitted. The user would assume they entered the password incorrectly. When they tried to log on a second time, this time to the real network, the packets would show the login credentials they used. The packets would also show the users' online activity. Depending on the user, it could be useful.

Bat pulled his phone from his pocket and called Alexander.

"Bat. Whatcha got?"

"It's what I don't have. A strong router."

Alexander's momentary silence told Bat his friend didn't understand.

"I need a router to broadcast a spoof network that I hope a guest at the Overlook will try to log into."

"Will Best Buy have what you need?" Alexander asked.

"Probably. If not, I can set a less powerful router on the balcony. It needs to send a strong signal to the hotel across the street. Anyone in a room facing this way or anyone outside, like at the pool, should see it at the top of the list. The problem is that we have to wait for someone to attempt to log in. Most likely, it would be someone who recently checked in and is logging in to the network for the first time. It could take a while."

"See if Best Buy has what you need. Let me know. I'll pick it up. Unless you'd like to go with me."

"I have other work I need to do. If you could run and get it, I'd appreciate it."

Bat gave Alexander the name and model number of the router he needed. He asked for at least twenty feet of Cat6 Ethernet cable and a twenty-foot extension cord.

"Best Buy is about ten minutes from here. It shouldn't take an hour. I'll bring it to the hotel."

"There's no hurry. Mayte is coming by later this afternoon. I haven't seen her in ten days. When I get busy, she seldom sees me and gets bored around the beach house, so she comes to Florida to hang out with her sister. I want to get enough work done so I can spend time with her. I doubt we'd have much luck getting anyone to attempt to log into the network tonight anyway."

"I haven't seen Mayte in a while. Would y'all like to have dinner with Jana and me tonight?"

"Of course. I'm sure Mayte would love to see you."

"Cool. If you aren't going to set up your fake network today, should I wait and bring the router when we meet this evening?"

"Yes, that works. Mayte will be here at five. Would you like to come around six?"

"Will you have enough time...to get ready?"

"Plenty." Bat didn't catch Alexander's innuendo. He was close enough to the spectrum that he often missed subtle innuendos.

Bat rang off, sat at his computer, and began pounding on the keyboard. He had clients waiting, and he needed to get as much done as possible in a short period of time.

Alexander told Jana about the plans he had made for dinner and the necessary trip to Best Buy. She was excited about the dinner but passed on the Best Buy outing.

*****

Willie Bouchette lived in the densely populated suburban community of Greenacres, Florida, a verdant town in South Florida, which was awarded the Tree City USA designation by the National Arbor Day Foundation in 1992. It took ten minutes to get to Willie's from I-95.

Jerry followed Google Maps' directions past streets of well-landscaped single-family homes. After two turns, the single-family houses were replaced by townhomes. When the female voice directing them said they were at their destination, Jerry turned onto the stone paver driveway of the two-story townhouse.

A small strip of grass, not more than two feet wide, separated Willie's driveway from the driveway next door. A small hedge and a Cordyline Red Sister Hawaiian Ti plant grew from the front of the house.

"Those plants are blocking the front of the house," Sam said, staring at the front of the unit.

"That door may be the neighbor's door," Jerry said, pointing at the door on the other side of the hedge.

"So where the hell's the front door?"

"There's a walkway going to the left. Maybe the door's that way."

"Do you want to call Willie and tell him we're here?" Sam was nervous about walking around the house.

"Nah. Let's check it out. Leave the bags here. We can come back for them."

Jerry and Sam got out of the SUV and followed the stone pavers around the side of the house.

"That looks like a front door," Sam said, relieved. "They have a lake in the back. Nice."

Jerry agreed and knocked on the door.

A young Black woman opened the door. She had long, slender legs, a flat stomach, and a gorgeous, exotic face bounded by wavy, long black hair. Her bronze skin glowed in the afternoon sun's reflection. She wore a white crop top and denim shorts. The top accentuated her ample breasts. She said nothing to the two strangers standing at the front door.

"Is Willie here?" Jerry asked after a few seconds.

"Are you Jerry?" The woman asked with an accent neither Jerry nor Sam could make out.

"Yes," Jerry replied, bobbing his head in case she didn't understand.

"Please, come. Willie is stirring da roux." She stepped back and motioned for them to enter. When they were inside, she closed the door, turned away, and yelled something. A reply came from the kitchen, which neither Sam nor Jerry understood.

"Hee's in da kichen. Dis way."

When they turned the corner from the small foyer to the kitchen, Willie was standing at the stove with his back to them.

"Sorry, I couldn't come to the door," he said over his shoulder. "I didn't expect you so soon. I thought I'd whip up a pot of gumbo. I'm cooking the roux now, and I have to stir it constantly, or it will burn. Come in. I see you've met Guerline."

"Not officially," Sam said, extending her hand to Guerline. "I'm Sam." She stepped toward Willie, "We haven't met either."

Willie switched the flat-edged roux whisk to his left hand and shook Sam's hand with his right. "I'm glad to meet you, Sam."

Sam studied the man at the stove while he chatted with Jerry. He was large, over six feet, broad-shouldered, and weighed in the neighborhood of two-fifty. Jerry had mentioned he didn't look overly bright. Sam concurred. He had a prominent upper forehead, a Nubian nose, and a pronounced underbite. His mouth naturally turned down, and hung open slightly. She expected to see drool flowing any second.

"Sam. Sam," Willie said, interrupting her thoughts.

"I'm sorry, Willie, I was thinking about the gumbo," she lied.

"You like da Gumbo?" Willie asked using a heavy Cajun accent.

"Only if you have Tony's."

"Tony Chachere's? Dis girl know her gumbo. It ain't gumbo without Tony's." Willie's natural frown turned into a broad smile, exposing his bright white teeth, complete with gaps. "I believe we're gonna get along fine. Real fine. Would ya like cold beer?"

"A beer sounds good, but I'm in a wine mood. I don't suppose you have any wine?"

Willy frowned. His forehead creased. "We may not get along so well after all."

Sam scowled. Her eyes ping-ponged to Jerry, then to Guerline, then back at Willie.

Willie glanced up from stirring the roux and let out a belly laugh. "I'm kidding. Beer goes best with gumbo, but if you prefer wine, that's okay. I'm guessing a Chardonnay."

"Uh, yes, Chardonnay would be great, if you have it."

"Yeah, let me open a box for you."

Sam forced a smile. "Thanks."

While he stirred his darkening roux, Willie continued speaking with a heavy Cajun accent. Sam couldn't understand a word.

"I'm sorry?" Sam said.

"Never mind, I mumble to myself in Cajun to not get myself in trouble. I'm offended you think I would serve a guest a boxed wine."

Sam stiffened and crossed her arms in front of her chest. "Well, fuck, Willie. We just met, I'm trying to be polite here. You already dissed me for not wanting a beer. How am I supposed to know you don't serve wine from a box?"

Willie peeked at Sam. "I knew I waz gonna like you. You got spunk. I did wonder how long you'd allow me to rag on you before you put me in my place. I thought for sure it would take a couple of glasses of wine."

"Ordinarily, it might have. But you knew how to press my buttons."

"That's my job. Knowing people. I should say, it was my job."

"Oh, jeez, I'm—"

"We're all in the same boat. I'm glad y'all are here. Now, about that wine. I bet you like a California Chard. I have a 2024 Las Brisas Single Barrel. It offers concentrated fruit flavors of pineapple, pear, and crisp apple, balanced with rich shortbread aromas. The finish has length with a hint of lime zest, which complements the profile and pairs well with chicken and sausage gumbo."

With his attention on the roux, Willie didn't notice Sam's mouth drop at his switch from Cajun to the Queen's English. She quickly recovered. "Sounds nice."

Willie continued to stir his roux. "Guerline, would you grab a bottle of Mahoney Carneros Las Brisas from the wine cooler?" He turned to Sam and Jerry. "Guys, I apologize. I thought I'd be done cooking before you got here. You have luggage?"

"Yes, we wanted to make sure we had the right house. Didn't want to be standing at the front door with an armful of bags and be at the wrong door."

"Why don't y'all get your stuff. Guerline will show you to the guest rooms. The roux is about ready for the Holy Trinity. Another fifteen or twenty minutes and I'll be done."

Jerry gave a bewildered blink. "The Holy Trinity?"

"Damn. Wat da hell I got in ma kitch'n?"

Sam grabbed Jerry by the arm. "Let's get our bags. I'll explain."

"I know'd I liked you, Sam," Willie said as Jerry and Sam turned to leave. He let out a chuckle and went back to his pot.

Outside, Sam explained the Holy Trinity to Jerry. "It's a mix of onion, celery, and green peppers. It's the flavoring of the gumbo."

Jerry stopped in his tracks. "Sam, what the fuck is gumbo?"

Sam let out a loud laugh, then stifled it by covering her mouth. "You've never had gumbo?"

"I've never heard of it."

Sam grabbed Jerry and pulled him toward the car. "Pop the hatch. Gumbo is a staple in the South, but I'm pretty sure you can find it in restaurants across the country. I can't believe you've never had it...or at least heard of it."

"Sorry to disappoint you."

"Don't get pissy. Grab your stuff, we need to get back. Oh, do you like hot food?"

"Not particularly."

"Don't put too much Tony's on your gumbo."

Back inside, the aroma of the Holy Trinity sautéing in the roux filled the kitchen.

"Wow, the gumbo smells great," Jerry said.

"Oh, just wait a couple of hours. Jerry, would you like a beer?"

"At the risk of getting shot, wine sounded good."

Willie's shoulders drooped. "Guerline, get another wine glass, please. And would you bring me a beer?" Over his shoulder, he said, "Put your stuff down. She can show you your rooms later. Y'all will be more comfortable in the living room. I'll join you in a minute."

Guerline used an opener to pop the top of the craft beer bottle and handed it to Willie. "Dis way," she said, leading Jerry and Sam to the living room. "Please sit. I will git your wine." She went back to the kitchen and returned a few minutes later with three glasses of white wine. She set two glasses on the coffee table in front of her guests and sat on a loveseat next to the couch.

"It is nice to meet you," Guerline said slowly. The words were heavily accented but comprehensible. "I am sorry, I understand English well, but I have trouble pronouncing some words. I don't know, uh, wat's it called, slang? Willie is teaching me."

"You're doing fine," Sam said. "I need to use the bathroom."

"It's next to the front door. Do you want I show you?"

"I'll find it. Thank you." Sam walked through the kitchen to the bathroom.

"I'll be joining you shortly," Willie told her as she passed. "How's it going out there?"

"Fine. Guerline is sweet. Beautiful, too. I'm curious how you met her."

"Cuz she be outta my league, ya tink?"

"That's not what I meant, although she might be." Sam couldn't resist a payback dig on the big guy. "But I meant, she is young and not American. Oh, and what's with the heavy Cajun drawl one minute and

Ivy League eloquence the next?"

"Sorry. Force of habit. In my line of work, I often needed to dumb it down a bit. Regarding Guerline, yeah, it's a long story. I'll tell y'all about her later."

"I'm anxious to hear the story," Sam said with a wink. "She's trying to talk to us, but I can tell she's a little uncomfortable with her accent."

"You don't speak French, do you?"

"A little. My Spanish is better, but I can get by in French."

"Try her in French."

Sam walked back into the room. "Merci. Je dois y aller."

Guerline's eyes sparkled. "Tu parles français?"

"Un peu. A little," Sam repeated.

"I speak Haitian Creole," Guerline said. "It's like French, from long time ago. It's not same French. But I understand basic French."

"My French isn't great. We should stick with English. It isn't polite to talk in front of someone who doesn't understand us. Do you speak French, Jerry?"

"I don't. But if you guys are more comfortable speaking it, I'm okay with it."

"English is good," Guerline said. "I need to practice more."

The three attempted small talk while they waited for Willie. Jerry and Sam learned Guerline was from Port-au-Prince. She was five when the earthquake struck in 2010. Her mother was unharmed, but she was sent to an orphanage. There, she learned basic English. She didn't know her father.

At sixteen, Guerline ran away. After living on the street and struggling for several months, she wandered into the Marriott Port-au-Prince's kitchen asking for food. With basic English and exotic looks, the kitchen manager was more than happy to offer her a job. She was quickly promoted and soon became a server in the hotel bar. There, she met Willie Bouchette.

Sam and Jerry thought privately that the job and promotion were most likely based on her looks. They couldn't help but think she had other talents she hadn't mentioned.

Guerline started to tell them about meeting Willie when he walked into the room and sat on the love seat next to her.

"What'd I miss?"

"Guerline was telling us how you two met," Sam said.

"Ah. How far did she get?"

"Not far."

Willie patted Guerline on the thigh. "I'll tell them the story, if you don't mind."

"No problem. But I need wine. Anyone else?"

Jerry and Sam nodded. Guerline hopped up and ran to the kitchen for the bottle. She returned, filled the glasses, and sat next to Willie.

"I'd been in and out of Haiti since the earthquake. After the assassination of Jovenel Moïse in 2021 and the false claims that it was a CIA operation, I was permanently assigned there. I monitored the leadership and kept an ear out for other assassination attempts. The bar in the Marriott was clean, quiet, and served a cold Prestige Lager. The scenery was nice too."

The scenery comment wasn't lost on Willie's guests. While not legal in Haiti, prostitution is tolerated and common. Guerline did not react. The remark either went over her head or she chose to ignore it. The question neither Sam nor Jerry asked was whether Guerline was part of the "scenery."

"I spotted Guerline, and damn, she was finer than frog hair. I tried to make small talk with her, but she was standoffish. One day, I spoke to her in Cajun Creole. She barely understood a word and asked me what the hell kind of language I was speaking. By then, I could speak both Haitian Creole and French well. I explained what a Cajun was, and she could relate. We became friends."

Willie took a long drink of beer and slid his hand into Guerline's hand. "I'm sitting at the bar one day, having a beer, and this dude comes up to Guerline and whispers in her ear. I couldn't hear, but I could tell from her expression that it wasn't good. The man slapped her face, grabbed her by the neck, and started to drag her off. She pulled away, but he clutched a handful of her hair and pulled her toward the elevators. I recognized the man. He was the hotel's manager. I knew I shouldn't get involved, and I wasn't, even though I had a good idea what was about to happen. Then she looked at me. I could see fear in her eyes. Nope. Not on my watch. I caught up to them and politely asked him to let her go. When he didn't, I took the hand that had her hair, and I broke his thumb."

"Ouch," Sam interjected.

"That's what he said. Not exactly, but close. I know he wanted to take me on, but I was at least six inches taller and fifty pounds heavier than he was. And he had a broken thumb. He said I'd be sorry and ran off. At that point, I figured Guerline was fired—or worse—so I asked her to leave with me."

"Did she know anything about you?" Jerry asked.

"No. To her, I was just a guy who had been coming into the bar a few times a week. I thought I'd take her to my place for a few days while I helped her find a new job. I had a lot of connections. It turned out a bigwig in the Transitional Presidential Council wanted Guerline and informed the manager. Haiti has a rotating leadership, and they were the leaders at the time. They're a ruthless group. You don't fuck with them. I'm not sure the manager knew who I was, but I wasn't taking any chances. I had a contact with a boat that could get us to Puerto Rico then..." Willie paused. "Long story. Let's say I got Guerline into the States and leave it at that. That was almost two years ago."

"Let me guess," Jerry said. "She was born in Miami?"

"Yep. Little Haiti, to be exact. She's a US citizen—born and raised."

"I'd like to hear how you pulled that off, but another time. I don't know about Sam, but I'd love to unpack and take a shower."

Sam agreed.

"Guerline will show you to your rooms. I need to add the chicken and sausage to the gumbo. It'll be ready when you finish unpacking."

"Can't wait," Jerry lied.

ELEVEN

Jana and Alexander entered the lobby of the Grand Paradise Hotel at precisely six o'clock in the evening. Alexander was carrying a large Best Buy bag containing a Wi-Fi router, two white 12-foot 3-Outlet Extension cords, and 25 feet of Cat8 Ethernet cable. Bat had requested Cat6 cable, but the sales associate recommended Cat8 cable. A quick text to Bat confirmed it was the cable of choice. Jana carried a bottle of Lytton Springs Ridge Zinfandel.

"Should I have brought two bottles of wine?" Jana asked as they waited for the elevator.

They stepped inside, and Alexander pressed the button for the seventh floor. "One should be plenty. Enough for a drink before we head out to dinner."

"We haven't seen them in a while. I thought we might talk in the room for a while."

"If we need another bottle, we can order one from room service."

"True," Jana said.

The elevator door opened. "This way." Alexander pointed to the left. "Only two doors down. That's handy."

Alexander knocked on the hotel room door. It opened instantly.

Mayte leaped into his arms. He steadied himself while holding onto the Best Buy bag with one hand and Mayte with the other.

After a long hug, Mayte let go of Alexander and slid until her feet touched the floor. She stepped to Jana and gave her a big hug. "It's so great to see you. I kept saying I was going to text you and see if we could get together for lunch or happy hour, but it's been crazy at the shelter."

Mayte led them into the room's sitting area. "I see you brought wine. Should I get glasses?"

"Unless we're going to pass the bottle around," Bat said, not turning from his laptop. "I'm almost done here. Give me two minutes."

Mayte grabbed four glasses from the coffee bar. "Two minutes. About the same amount of time he gave me."

Jana and Alexander chuckled softly. Bat ignored the comment, just as Mayte had ignored his. Mayte set the glasses on the coffee table. Alexander unscrewed the bottle cap and filled each glass.

Bat joined them as Alexander was filling the fourth glass. "Red. Is it a Cab?"

"No," Jana replied. "It's a Zin from California's Dry Creek Valley."

Bat read the label. "2022. Good year. Fairly recent. Did you know a good California Zinfandel develops more complexity and elegance as it ages?" He took a sip. "This is good. It will be terrific in a couple of years. I hope you've saved a few bottles."

Jana tasted the wine. "Oh, that is good. I asked the guy at the liquor store for suggestions. He didn't say I should keep it a while before drinking. I may go back and get more."

"You should. It has a screw cap, too. Many people still think wines with corks are better. Screw caps are reliable, and they prevent cork taint. I've read that wines intended for long-term storage should still use a cork. The article didn't explain why, and I didn't pursue an answer. You can't beat a cap for ease of opening and sealing."

"Well, I like it." Alexander raised his glass. "To good friends."

"Cheers," the others echoed, lifting their glasses to meet his with a chorus of clinks.

Jana leaned back in the chair. "Mayte, you said it was crazy at the shelter. What's going on? Does the shelter need money?"

"No. My sister said your endowment is more than enough to keep them running. Other donations are icing on the cake. Money is not a problem. As you know, most of the women...girls we take in are, technically, illegal. They were trafficked from their country, raped, and sold into the sex-slave trade. They either escaped or were freed when the place they were being held was busted. Because they're illegal aliens, ICE comes in and tries to arrest them."

Alexander slammed his empty glass onto the coffee table. "Those bastards."

"That's a polite term for them," Mayte said. "As soon as we get a girl, we get all the information and file the paperwork for asylum. Being documented doesn't mean shit to those guys. They even tried to arrest Briana because she looks Hispanic."

"Damn them." Alexander leaned forward and filled his glass with wine. "And the ICE agents say they're following orders. Most of them need to be arrested."

"Many will be as soon as we elect a new president," Bat said.

"I hope so," Mayte said. "ICE is a big reason I'm here helping. The staff has people outside watching. If we see ICE coming, we let them know and make sure everyone is out of sight. They can't come in without a warrant, and they can't get a warrant."

"I hate that," Jana said. "If you need money for good lawyers, let me know. I'll be happy to fight those guys."

Mayte choked up. She cleared her throat to regain her composure. "Between you and Alex...and Rey, you've done so much for so many girls." Her eyes shimmered, and she pressed her lips together before continuing. "You saved my life, my sister's life, and the lives of countless girls who've come through the shelter."

For a moment, the room felt smaller, quieter—like the weight of what she'd said had settled over all of them at once.

Sensing the heaviness, Mayte continued. "Have you heard from Rey?"

"Not lately. He's still in Colombia. He bought a boat and runs fishing and diving charters out of Cartagena. I gave him enough money so he wouldn't have to work, but he can't sit still. He loves working and loves the chartering business."

"I bet he loves the Colombian ladies as well," Bat added.

"I don't know. When we were all down there, our driver set him up with a smokin' hot girl. I believe he's still with her."

"I remember," Mayte said. "I forgot about the driver. Alex, didn't she hook up with your ex?"

"She did. I haven't heard from Bonita in a while..."

"As much as I'm sure you two want to hear about your exes' love lives, I have something for you, Alex," Bat said.

"Great, what do you have?"

"To be honest, I've never tried hacking a police station's network. Turns out, it's pretty easy. Limited security. I'm in both the Fort Lauderdale PD and the Broward County Sheriff's Office. I didn't have time to do much digging, but I was able to see the missing persons records. The database is well organized. There were thousands, but most closed within a month or so. I searched for open cases involving a missing female aged sixteen to thirty. I started with the most current and worked backward. The pictures connected to the report were either driver's license photos or social media images. I found a disturbing pattern. Every two weeks, with a few exceptions, a missing person report was filed, and the missing person was an attractive young woman. Many were Hispanic, as expected in South Florida. There were a couple of Caucasian girls, but no African American girls. I should say, no attractive African American girls."

"You're looking for missing girls?" Mayte asked.

"Yes. Bat didn't fill you in?"

Mayte glared at Bat. "No, he didn't say why he was here. Only that you asked him to come help you with a project."

Alexander told Mayte about the girl falling from the balcony, the police cover-up, and the lack of cooperation from the hotel.

"Oh my God," Mayte said. "The girl who died, what'd she look like?"

"Medium height, slender, long black hair. Her face was unrecognizable."

"Did she have any tattoos?"

"None I could see. Why?"

"We had a girl disappear a few days ago. She had been at the shelter for a couple of weeks. Her boyfriend wanted to pimp her out, and when she refused, he beat her. Not bad, a few bruises. She took off and found us. She's young, eighteen or nineteen, and beautiful. She had long black hair. We assumed she went back to her boyfriend, or she got in touch with family. We thought it was strange she didn't say goodbye, but that happens. Especially if they go back to their boyfriend."

"Do you have her name? The boyfriend's name? An address?"

"I'm sure the shelter does, Alex. I'll ask."

"We need to follow up. See if she's alive."

"In the morning, can you hack into the Medical Examiner's office, Bat?" Alexander asked. "They may have photos of our victim on file."

"I'm sure I can. I doubt the ME's office is very secure."

"I hope they keep their records digitally, along with photos. If we can get a picture of the girl after they cleaned her up, we might be able to ID her. The ME might even have a name that they didn't release."

Mayte stared at the wall, her shoulders slumped.

Alexander noticed and said, "The odds of our girl being from the shelter are slim. I'll look into it, but I'm sure your missing girl is fine."

"I hope so."

"I'm getting hungry. Enough shop talk, let's go to dinner," Jana said.

*****

The sun set while Jerry and Sam were unpacking. Sam was happy to have a break between the glasses of wine. She hoped she hadn't kept the others waiting. She hadn't. When she reached the table, Willie and Jerry were in a deep conversation. Guerline was fluffing a pot of rice.

Willie stood and pulled out a chair for her.

"Thank you, Willie. Chivalry is not dead."

"No, ma'am. Just severely wounded."

Willie waited until Sam was seated, then filled four bowls with rice and gumbo, returning to the table to set a bowl in front of each person. "Dig in."

Jerry took his first bite of Willie's gumbo. "This is good."

"This is great gumbo," Sam said.

"Thank you. It's my mother's recipe, her mother's recipe, and her mother's before her. They all added okra, which I don't. Can't stand that shit."

"I'm not an okra fan either," Sam said. "I can eat it, but prefer not to. What about you, Jerry? Do you like okra in your gumbo?"

The question caught Jerry with his mouth full. He held up a finger to signal, "One second." He swallowed and dabbed his mouth with a napkin. "In my humble opinion, this is perfect as is. Best gumbo I've ever had."

Willie flashed a gapped-toothed smile. "I'm glad y'all like it. Let's get down to brass tacks. Oh, and we can talk in front of Guerline. She knows why you're here."

"So, you've already put a little thought into what we want to do?" Jerry asked.

"I have, and I should mention it now. I've recruited a couple of others, too."

Sam's eyes widened. The color drained from her face. "Uh, was telling others about us a good idea?"

"Absolutely. I shared it with two friends. I trust them implicitly. They're in the same boat as us."

"Fired CIA?" Sam asked.

"Yep. Terrell Carter and Jessica Chen. Jessica is Asian. Terrell is Black."

"The way the administration is purging the agency of Blacks, women, and gays, no surprise they were let go," Jerry said.

"Uh huh. Jessica was the trifecta. She's Asian. Filipino and Chinese. A woman, and a lesbian. Butch, too. She doesn't try to hide it."

Sam leaned back in the chair. "So you've read them in on what we're doing? They understand it's an exercise. We want to see if it could be done. We're not going to kill anyone."

Willie shuffled in his chair. "Yeah, we all know that."

Sam wasn't convinced. "I hate the man as much as anybody, and killing him would solve a lot of problems, but Jesus, it would open a can of worms. His base would make him a martyr, and who knows what they might do. Calling them dumber than a box of rocks would be an insult to the rocks. Most of them own guns."

"Easy, Sam. No one's going to kill the president. We're going through the motions to see if it's possible and how the CIA might go about it, if they were so inclined. And in such a way that his base of stoops wouldn't go on a rampage."

"I'm cool. I don't want anyone to get caught up in the process and start believing we could, or should, do this. Everyone involved has a reason."

"We sure do," Willie said. "But we're professionals. We know it's an exercise."

"Do the two you recruited know that?"

"Don't worry, Sam, they know."

"I'm glad to hear it. When do we meet your friends?"

"Soon. They've taken the initiative. They're in Palm Beach casing the Eagle's Nest. Looking for patterns, security deficiencies, and routes in and out. The compound itself is a fortress. The route in and out is vulnerable."

"Wait," Sam interrupted. "Did you say the 'Eagle's Nest'?"

"Yes," Willie said, stifling a laugh. "We debated between the Eagle's Nest and Neuschwanstein. The president thinks he's the king, but acts like Hitler. No one could pronounce Neuschwanstein. The Eagle's Nest was Hitler's retreat in Berchtesgaden. It was given to him as a gift for his fiftieth birthday. Probably a bribe. We thought it was the perfect code name."

"Works for me."

"Because the compound is on a barrier island with one main road onto the island that's close to it, and another road onto the island is about two miles away, the nearest road is the one most often used. That part of the island is densely populated. The streets are narrow with a thirty-mile-per-hour speed limit. Even State Road A1A, the Jimmy Buffett Memorial Highway, is thirty miles per hour. Most of the houses are large mansions with walls—the Eagle's Nest is surrounded by a wall that ranges from eight to fifteen feet high. The walls are hidden by lush tropical foliage. A sniper could hide anywhere along the route, but it wouldn't do any good. The president's cars are all bulletproof."

"You couldn't take him out, but you can watch him," Jerry said.

"Correctamundo," Willie said. "Someone who wouldn't seem out of place—a construction worker or road crew—could track movements in and out and not be noticed."

"Is that what your friends are doing now?" Jerry asked.

"No. The president is in Washington. Jessica and Terrell are in a car gathering intel. As I mentioned, Jessica is Asian, and Terrell is Black. Anyone who isn't lily-white in Palm Beach is very out of place. They have to be careful and keep moving to avoid being noticed."

"That's a bit of a problem," Sam said. "Lily-white seems to be in the minority on this operation."

"We'll work around it. There's always a way. I have complete faith in those two. You'll meet them tomorrow. I've asked them to come by at zero-nine-hundred for breakfast. We can get to know everyone and hear what they've got."

Sam glanced at her watch. "I didn't realize it was so late. Nine o'clock in the morning? I don't know about Jerry, but I'm beat. The gumbo was delish. Thank you so much."

"You're welcome. You know where your rooms are. If you need anything, ask Guerline or me."

"I will, thanks."

"Oh, by the way. I assume you brought a weapon. I never expect trouble, but I suggest you sleep with it nearby."

TWELVE

Inside Bat's hotel room, Alexander leaned against the glass balcony door and looked across the street at the Overlook Hotel's seventh-floor sliding door. The curtains inside were pulled shut. He closed his own curtain and sat down in a faded green loveseat. Bat and Mayte sat beside him on the sofa.

"It's been five days since you got here, and you got nothin'?" he asked Bat.

Bat shrugged. "I wouldn't say that. I'm in the hotel's network. I can see the live video, but there's no history. I have a feeling the video feed is monitored. If any video needs to be saved, they save it. Otherwise, it's deleted. My guess is it's on a twenty-four-hour loop."

"Are you saying if we need to preserve the video, you could save it?"

"If I got to it quickly enough. As I mentioned, I bet the feeds are being monitored. If they don't want it to ever be seen, they'll delete it immediately."

"Good to know. I have a feeling the girl falling to her death wasn't the only sketchy thing that has happened in that hotel."

"So you know, I haven't just been hanging around the hotel with Mayte on your dime," Bat said. "I can monitor the hotel's cameras, control the elevators, and unlock room doors. If you want to check out the room across the street, I can loop the CCTV feed, so if anyone is watching, they won't see you. I can also give you elevator access to the seventh floor, which normally requires a key card."

"I wouldn't mind seeing the room, but I'm sure the room has been scrubbed. I'll keep it in mind."

"I thought it would be nice to have. An all-access pass might come in handy."

"It will," Alexander said. "What about the ME's office? Any luck there?"

"Piece of cake. But they don't have much worth hiding. I had full access, and there was barely anything in the system. My guess is they do most of their reports manually and never upload or scan them into the computer."

"Of course not. That would have been too easy," Alexander said. "I need to visit the ME and have a little chat."

"I figured you would." Bat turned to his computer. "The Chief Medical Examiner for the county is Morgan Gossamer. She graduated from the University of Texas and got her MD from the University of Texas Medical Branch, John Sealy School of Medicine in Galveston— just a ferry ride from Bolivar. She did her residency in anatomic and clinical pathology at Baylor College of Medicine before moving to Florida, where she completed a one-year Forensic Pathology Fellowship at Broward County's Office of Medical Examiner and Trauma Services. She stayed in Florida, became an Associate Medical Examiner and the Director of Medical Education, then became Chief Medical Examiner a couple of years ago. There are no dates, but I'd guess she's done all this in the past ten years. Figure she graduated from UT at twenty-two, got her MD, did her residency, did the one-year fellowship, and has been there five or six years to get the ME position. That would put her in her late thirties. She's still fairly young, and from Texas, you'll be able to get whatever you need from her."

Mayte stifled a giggle. "You said she was young, kinda young. I don't know about Alex. He's getting old."

"Thanks for the vote of confidence, Mayte. I am getting old, but I'm sure I can still get what I need from her."

"Mayte may be right," Bat added. "Maybe you should send Jana to talk to her. In this day and age, she may have more luck than you anyway."

"You guys are hilarious. I'm sure I won't have any trouble getting information from her."

"Because you're such a skilled investigator?" Bat asked.

"I am. And I know medical examiners. They work on corpses all day. They tend to talk to them. When they meet someone who can reply, they open up."

Bat quickly typed on the keyboard. "I sent her name and the address of the ME's office to your WhatsApp account. Do you need anything else?"

"No, that's good. I already know too much about her. I don't want it to appear like I've been creeping on her."

Bat and Mayte wished Alexander luck and said goodbye. Alexander used the short walk from the Grand Paradise Hotel to his condo to think about how he would play it with the medical examiner. He could give her his private detective business card and tell her he was looking into a missing persons case. Another option would be to flash his FBI credentials and say he was investigating a possible homicide at the Overlook Hotel. He scratched option two because it was too risky. If Morgan Gossamer examined his credentials closely, she would see "Retired" printed on them. By the time Alexander had reached his condo, he'd made up his mind. He'd tell her the truth. More or less.

*****

Jerry sat at Willie's kitchen table, sipping a glass of Chardonnay. He wore a button-up short-sleeve shirt, dark shorts, black socks, and black sneakers. Other than the black socks, he looked like he stepped off a 1960s Beach Boys album cover.

At the table were Sam, Willie, Guerline, Jessica Chen, and Terrell Carter. It was the group's second meeting. The first meeting was a brief introduction five days earlier at Mom's Kitchen, a quaint home-style diner fifteen minutes from Willie's condo.

Jerry addressed the group. "Although we'd like to, none of us thought we would or could kill the president of the United States. What we have been doing is a thought experiment. This started when Sam and I discussed the conspiracy theory that the CIA was involved in the assassination of JFK. If the theory is true, or even partially true, those involved had much more time than we have had to plan it. They also had access to CIA records—such as they were in 1963—while we have all been locked out. Without access to the agency database, we could still find a patsy. Even in South Florida, it wouldn't be hard to find a left-wing radical who would be willing to take a shot at the president...if we decided that would be the best way to go about it."

"I'm probably the most familiar with the subject," Jessica Chen said. She was thirty-two, short, standing five feet tall barefoot. Her hair was cropped short on the sides and longer on the top. She wore knee-length cargo shorts and a grey tank top. "Oliver Stone came to UCLA for a showing and discussion of his film, *JFK*. I was hooked on the conspiracy theories from then on. A few years after I joined the CIA, I started digging into the assassination. I didn't find any information that couldn't be found on the internet today, which doesn't prove or disprove the existence of a conspiracy. When Willie called me and told me what you were planning, I had to be part of it."

"So, do you have an idea?" Jerry asked. "Not on Kennedy, but Cockwomble."

"I do. As Willie mentioned, if we had access to the CIA database to search for left-wing radicals, we could observe them, choose one to recruit, and feed him the intel to be in a position to shoot the president. But unlike Kennedy, where the CIA, Mafia, or whoever had Oswald killed, we'd put our shooter in a vulnerable situation so the Secret Service would take him out immediately after he shot."

"Wait," Sam said. "You're saying you'd put the shooter on the roof of a building, four or five hundred feet away, and after he shoots, every officer anywhere near would open up on him and kill him on the spot? Sounds familiar."

Jessica winked at Sam. "It should."

"Shit! Are you saying the CIA—"

"No. I'm saying that is how I'd take out Cockwomble...if I were planning it."

"Gotcha," Sam said, returning a wink.

Jessica shifted in her chair. "It hasn't been easy, because Terrell and I stick out. We stay on the move and have been observing the Eagle's Nest for almost a week. It's surrounded by an eight to fifteen-foot wall. There are only two ways in and out, both gated and guarded. It's almost as secure as the White House. There are no high buildings close enough to get a shot off and still be close enough for the shooter to be shot. Ever since JFK, the president's itinerary has been kept secret. When he's on the road, local law enforcement closes the streets along his route. When he goes from his car to a building, he's obviously moving, and he's sur-rounded by his security detail. Shooting him would be tough. I should say, taking a shot at him would be easy, hitting him would be difficult."

"I agree," Jerry said. "A person with extensive training could do it, but your average nut with a gun, not likely. Especially if he was using an AR-15. We've seen how that goes."

"Right. I'm sure a disgruntled CIA assassin or an ex-Marine sniper could do it, but where are we going to find one on short notice?"

Everyone at the table, except for Guerline, looked at Jerry.

"Hey, don't look at me. Did you miss the part where the shooter gets shot right after he shoots? Jessica, do you have a Plan B?"

"Well, A1A is the only road to the Eagle's Nest. To get there, you either come in from the north or the south. Because of the location, there isn't much traffic. While we were there, the president wasn't, so we don't know if they use the same route every time or vary it. I bet they change it. Go south on odd days, north on even days. Or randomly. Flip a coin to see which way to go. I'd dress as a road crew, dig a large hole in the middle of the street, and pack it with explosives. Then wait. When the president's limo comes by, blow it up. Granted, it would take a hell of a blast."

"Damn, girl, that's bad ass," Terrell said. "You'd also have collateral damage. The driver and anyone else in the car." Terrell Carter was a thirty-three-year-old Black man who had graduated from Cornell with a degree in Criminal Justice. He joined the CIA right out of college and occasionally worked with Willie in Haiti.

"True. Plus, once the device was planted, it could be days or weeks before the car was on top of it, and whoever was holding the trigger would have to be ready to hit it at the exact moment." Jessica took a sip of wine. "I didn't say it was a good plan."

"Any other ideas?" Willie asked.

"While we were watching the compound, Jessica and I kept noticing two guys who seemed out of place," Terrell said. "They didn't seem to have a job there. One was outside most of the time, smoking cigarettes. I thought they were his drivers and had little to do when Cockwomble wasn't there, but I can't imagine them getting paid to sit around. We didn't watch twenty-four-seven, but I noticed they'd disappear for long periods of time. Cars were constantly coming and going, but I never saw them get into a car and leave. It's a gut feeling, but we should keep an eye on those two."

"I agree with Terrell," Jessica said. "Those two stood out. We couldn't watch them the whole time, but when we saw them, usually through a gate or a low spot in the wall, they didn't seem to fit in with the rest of the staff."

Willie cleared his throat and leaned forward. "Any chance these two don't belong at the compound? Snuck in, or got hired for an odd job, and are hanging around? They could be casing the joint for their own heist. They don't sound like guests."

"Not at all," Jessica said. "For lack of a better description, it was like they ran the place. From what we could see, hardly anyone talked to them. In fact, I'd say most people there avoided them. They dress like mafia wannabes."

"Hired muscle to keep people in line?" Jerry asked.

Terrell shook his head. "Not likely. From what I observed, they didn't seem to give a shit about anyone. My feeling is that they work directly for the president or the compound manager. When the president isn't in town, they seem to do whatever they want. Granted, we don't have much data to go on."

"We'll find out soon enough. A little birdie told me Cockwomble will be at the Eagle's Nest this weekend."

*****

The Broward County Medical Examiner and Trauma Services building was a one-story structure that looked more like a strip center than a trauma center. Surrounded by residential neighborhoods, Alexander had the feeling it had once been a strip center. Most likely, a convenience store and a video rental shop. A Blockbuster back in the day. The vast power grid next to the building may be the reason the building was not residential.

Alexander was a big man who loved small cars. His favorite was a MINI Cooper, but when he moved in with Jana and needed a new vehicle, the BMW X1 seemed most appropriate. He turned the X1 into the small parking lot and parked in front of the main entrance. The sign hanging above the door looked familiar. He remembered seeing the sign on the news many years earlier, when the previous medical examiner held a press conference to discuss the autopsy of Anna Nicole Smith. Alexander wasn't sure whether he should be proud or worried that he remembered the event.

When he walked through the front door, he felt a chill in the air. The inside temperature couldn't have been above sixty-eight degrees. There was an odd odor as well. It wasn't an alcohol odor like in a hospital or clinic, but more of a heavy disinfectant smell. He surmised the staff must scrub the building down several times a day.

Inside, there was no reception area. No guard checking visitors. Alexander strolled down the hall, past what appeared to be a large lecture room, its double doors propped open. He walked to the next open door, which led to an office with a large mahogany desk and a high-back leather executive chair. A woman in her late thirties with shoulder-length blond hair sat in the chair. She flinched when she saw Alexander standing in the doorway.

"I'm sorry," Alexander said. "I didn't mean to frighten you."

The woman smiled. "Don't worry about it. This is a morgue. Anytime a body I don't hear approaching appears in front of me, it scares me. Can I help you?"

"I hope so. My name is Alex Christian. Are you the ME?"

"I am. Morgan Gossamer."

The woman was smiling. The slight scare had broken the ice. Alexander thought about how to proceed. He had a feeling she didn't have many living visitors, so he wanted to get her talking. But he didn't want to put her on the defensive. In a gentle voice, he asked if he could sit. Height can be intimidating, and Alexander was towering over the woman. The ME had not introduced herself as Doctor Morgan Gossamer. He felt it was a good sign. They were more likely to chat on a personal level.

"Thank you," Alexander said, taking a seat. "I'm a private investigator." He noticed her expression didn't change. "Well, a mostly retired PI. I live in Lauderdale and have a friend who runs a women's shelter in Miami. It's mainly for abused and trafficked girls, but they'll help anyone who needs it."

"Those shelters are so important. I see a lot of women, girls really, who I wish had found a safe place before they ended up in my mortuary cooler."

"That's why I'm here," Alexander said. He told Morgan the story Mayte had shared about young girls leaving the shelter, how they might go to live with family or friends, but all too often, they go back to their abusive boyfriends. The doctor was genuinely interested.

"Last week, a young Hispanic girl disappeared from the shelter. I was told that she loved the place and was doing well. She'd gotten a job as a server in a local bar and was talking about getting a place of her own one day. She left for work, and no one has heard from her since. It's been more than a week since she disappeared."

"You think she may be here?"

"I heard a young girl who fit her description fell from a balcony in Fort Lauderdale about the time the girl disappeared. I checked with the FLPD, but they weren't much help. Her friends are worried about her and want to know if she's dead. I'm trying to get a name."

Morgan shuffled uncomfortably in her chair. Her face flushed. "I remember her. She died in the evening and was brought in around midnight. I came in at six to begin the autopsy. At seven, a group of feds came in with a warrant and took the body."

"Feds?"

"Yes. Homeland Security. They told me she jumped from the balcony when they tried to arrest her. They said she was a criminal element and was going to be deported."

Alexander leaned back in the chair, took a deep breath, and exhaled slowly.

"Pisses you off, doesn't it?" Morgan said.

"Beyond words."

"I tried to stop them, but I had no reason. It was Broward County jurisdiction, but they had the warrant."

"I get it. I'm sure you were frustrated. By chance, were you able to identify her?"

"No. I had taken her fingerprints, but they took those, along with all my other notes. When they asked if I had pictures, I said I hadn't taken any yet. I lied."

Alexander's eyes lit up. "You have pictures of her?"

"I do. She fell from a great height and landed on her face. She wasn't recognizable when she was brought in. I cleaned her as best I could before I photographed her."

"Could I get copies of the pictures? Someone at the shelter can see if it's their missing girl."

Morgan leaned back and glared at Alexander. "I'm sorry, I didn't take any pictures."

"What? Why'd you say you did?"

"Why'd you say you're a PI?"

"I don't follow."

"Bullshit. The feds come in here and take a body along with all my work, and a week later, you're in here asking about her. I have no pictures."

Alexander recoiled. "I'm on your side."

Morgan crossed her arms and stared at him.

To try and gain her trust, Alexander decided to come clean. "I have not lied to you. I may have left out a few details. My name is Alexander

Christian. I am a PI, but I also retired from the FBI several years ago. I do easy PI work to stay busy. A few years ago, I did a job for a lady whose boyfriend had been shanghaied. Long story short, I found the boyfriend, but the client and I fell in love."

"Not very ethical," Morgan snorted.

"Not at all, but that's life. Her ex fell in love and is happy. I moved into the lady's condo in Lauderdale. From the balcony, I can see The Overlook Hotel and the balcony where the girl fell from. I saw her fall."

"Oh, jeez."

"I ran to the scene. I saw the girl on the pavement. I spoke with a uniformed cop and the detective assigned to the case. The next day, I met with the detective who told me the case was closed. He said the girl was high and probably jumped. The more I asked, the more evasive he became. To be fair, I got the same vibe from him that I'm getting from you. You aren't happy, but you're following orders."

"What about the shelter? Was that bullshit?"

"No. My girlfriend funded it, and a young girl I rescued from traffickers runs it." Alexander could see the skepticism on the ME's face. "It's all true. My best friend is living with the sister of the girl who runs the shelter. I recruited my friend to help me gather evidence. His girlfriend overheard me and told me about the missing girl from the shelter."

"Well, Mr. Christian, you are convincing. But talking to you could cost me my job...and possibly my life."

"I was fairly certain there was foul play. Even more certain now. I'd love to get those responsible, but at the very least, if the dead girl had family, I want to give them closure. I'd like to show the pictures to the people at the shelter, see if they recognize her. All I can promise is I'll delete them as soon as I show them and I won't give copies to anyone or tell anyone else about them."

Morgan didn't make eye contact with Alexander.

Alexander pressed. "I tell you what. Are the pictures on your phone or a digital camera?"

"They were on a camera. I've removed and hidden the memory card. Why?"

"So you do have photos."

"Well, fuck!"

Alexander scratched his head. "I had an idea, but it won't work."

"What was it?"

"My friend can hack into the most secure systems. I was going to suggest you upload the images to a computer, and he could hack in and download them. But uploading them would only prove their existence. We don't want that."

"No, we don't."

"I took pictures at the scene, but as you said, the girl was unrecognizable. Is it possible anyone other than you could have taken pictures of the corpse after you cleaned her?"

"The feds came in early. I was the only one here. If it gets out that there are pictures, they'll know they came from me."

"And you lied about them."

"Yep. You see my reluctance to give you the files."

"Oh, I get it. From what the detective said—and what you've told me—this isn't some routine cover-up. There are people with real influence involved."

"Exactly. Which is why I can't just sit this out. You said you live near the Overlook Hotel. Can you meet me near there tonight—with your hacker friend and his girlfriend, who knows the missing girl?"

THIRTEEN

A silver lining of being recently fired by the CIA is that agents still have close contacts within the agency. The photos of the two suspicious men at the Eagle's Nest that Jessica sent her friend were grainy, but good enough for face-detection software to identify them. Her friend sent what she found about the two men.

Mark Sunday. Known as "Bloody" Sunday. Jessica cringed at the moniker. Five feet ten, two hundred thirty pounds, barrel-chested, and thighs reminiscent of Earl Campbell's. A booking photo from DeKalb County, Georgia, showed a man with long, disheveled hair. Jessica couldn't help noticing Mark's eyes. They were haughty. Even in a booking photo, his eyes showed an arrogant human who likely felt superior to those around him.

"Exactly like his boss," Jessica whispered.

Sean McIntyre was taller and leaner than Mark. No nicknames. His picture, from a Miami-Dade County booking photo, showed a face with a history of bad teenage acne, a condition that most likely toughened him. His red hair and hazel eyes, which leaned toward green, confirmed his name's heritage. A red-headed Irishman. Jessica noted he likely had a temper.

Jessica shared the information with the rest of the group. After her text was sent, she added:

These guys are NOT your typical drivers, Secret Service agents, or any other resort staff.

Willie was the first to respond:

No, they aren't what I would call a normal protection detail either. Be wary of them.
Jessica: I plan to keep an eye on them. See what they're up to. We might be able to use them.
Terrell: Be careful. I'm on the northwest side of the compound monitoring traffic. Let me know if you need me.
Jessica: Will do.

Jessica looked up from her phone. Mark and Sean were no longer in sight.

"Damn." She started the car and drove slowly past the front gate. No sign of the men. A half-mile down the road, she made a U-turn and made another pass. Still no sign of the two men.

She dialed Terrell's cell. "They've disappeared again."

"Did they go inside?"

"Probably, I don't know. It's strange. Those guys are always outside smoking or sitting on the patio. When they disappear, it's for a long time."

"Did you see any cars leave the compound?"

"Negative."

"A large, black Cadillac Escalade is coming this way."

"I'm on A1A near the main gate. I didn't notice any large, black SUVs go by."

"They just drove by. The side windows were heavily tinted, but I could see them through the front windshield. It was definitely our guys."

"How in the hell did they get out? They didn't go through the front gate or the service entry. There's another way out."

Terrell turned and followed the SUV. "We've been studying the compound for over a week. If there was another way out, we'd have seen it. By the way, I'm following them. Catch up with me."

"On my way," Jessica said. She accelerated and quickly caught Terrell and the SUV. "We should have known there was a backdoor to the Eagle's Nest."

"We can't lose these guys, and we can't be spotted. We have to tail them until they return so we can see how they get in."

"If they go in the same way they came out."

"We've never seen them come in without seeing them leave. I'm sure they go in the same way they came out. I'm a little obvious in Palm Beach. I'm going to turn off and circle around behind you. Don't follow too closely." Terrell wanted to mention that she was noticeable as well. Not so much in a car, but a flaming Asian lesbian stood out.

Terrell took the first right he came to, drove a hundred feet, and made a U-turn. When he got back on A1A, he saw the SUV stopped at a light. Jessica was two cars behind. At the light, he sent a group text:

The two men from the compound are in an SUV heading south on A1A. We don't know how they left without us seeing them. Plan to follow them until they return. Need assistance.

*****

Alexander chose the Casablanca Cafe to meet the Medical Examiner. It was the first place Jana took him when she hired him to investigate the disappearance of her now ex. Being a regular and a good tipper, Jana was waved forward by the hostess.

"Good evening, Miss Jana. The usual?"

"We need a table for five tonight. Is that a problem?" Jana handed the young woman at the podium a hundred-dollar bill.

"Not at all." A wide smile spread across her face.

"The other three should be here shortly. I told them to let you know they're with me."

"I'll keep an eye out for them. Give me one minute." The hostess walked away and returned thirty seconds later with a server who led Alexander and Jana to a table near a window with a view of the Atlantic.

"My name is Anna. I'll be your server this evening. Can I start you with a drink? A cocktail, wine, beer?"

"I'll have a scotch on the rocks. A good scotch, please," Alexander said.

"I'll have wine," Jana said. "Bring a bottle of your house wine. It's good."

The server nodded at Jana's wine assessment and left.

The hostess led Bat and Mayte to the table. "I found two of your guests," she said.

The server returned with the previously ordered drinks. "What can I get you all to drink?"

"I'll have a Dos Equis," Bat said.

"Um, what was the drink you made me at your beach house, Alex? Oh, a Piña Colada. I'll have a Piña Colada. Thank you," Mayte said. "I haven't had a Piña Colada since you left Texas. I miss having you across the street."

"I miss Texas, too. But I can't complain." Alex squeezed Jana's hand.

The hostess returned to their table with a middle-aged blond woman in tow. "I believe this is your fifth," she said.

"Yes, it is," Alexander said. He stood to greet the medical examiner. "Everyone, this is Morgan Gossamer, the Broward County ME. Morgan, this is Jana, Mayte, and Bat."

"Nice to meet you all," Morgan said.

Bat held out his hand to the ME. "Bartholomew Epaphroditus Farnsworth the Third. I go by Bat. People always ask."

"I'm sure I would have," she said, shaking his hand before sitting. Alexander spotted the expression change on her face as she studied Bat and Mayte.

"I told you about Jana, my girlfriend. I also mentioned Bat briefly. He's my friend, colleague, and computer consultant. Mayte is his girlfriend."

Alexander thought about how, twice in a matter of minutes, he had referred to his and Bat's significant others as "girlfriends." The term seemed so high-schoolish. He made a mental note to discuss it with Jana and Mayte. Personally, he'd like to change his term from "girlfriend" to "wife."

"We all know why we're here," Alexander said, deflecting an impending awkward silence. "I wish it were under better circumstances, so I'd like to get our business out of the way, and then we can have dinner."

"I guess that's my cue," Morgan said. "Alex, you said everyone knows why we're here."

"They do."

"And they're aware of the need for utmost discretion?"

"Absolutely." The others at the table agreed.

"Thank you. I asked Alex to meet and bring his hacker friend. I guess that's you, Bat."

"Guilty as charged."

Morgan flashed a hint of a grin at the cliché. "I thought if I had the photos on my phone, and Bat hacked my phone, I could honestly say I didn't give anyone the pictures. But it wouldn't clear me. I told the feds I didn't have pictures. If images of the girl ever did get out, it would be obvious who took them. I can't take the chance."

"So you aren't going to show me the pictures?" Mayte asked.

"I didn't say that. I'm angry because there was an obvious cover-up. That's why I agreed to meet you all. I can't stand the thought that the girl may have been murdered—most likely was murdered—and whoever did it is getting away with it."

"So how are you going to show us the photos?" Mayte asked. Her voice was weak.

"I'm sure I know," Bat said.

"Alex said you were the genius," Morgan said. "How?"

"You have prints."

"You are good." Morgan grinned at Bat.

"And once we see them, you're going to eat them."

Morgan laughed. "I'm not that dramatic. I will destroy them, but I won't eat them." She paused. "The question is, when do you want to see them? The images are graphic. They're not easy to look at. Mayte, if the girl is your friend, um...well, it will be disturbing, to say the least."

Mayte took a long sip of her frozen drink. "I'd like to get it out of the way. My sister runs the shelter and knows her well. I only met her a few times. I'll be alright."

"If you're sure." Morgan pulled three eight-by-ten photos printed on plain white copy paper from her purse. The prints were folded in half. She handed them to Alexander. "You should look first."

Alexander glanced around to make sure the server wasn't near, and slowly unfolded them. He looked at the first picture and exhaled deeply. He took a deep breath, looked at the other two prints, folded them in half, and closed his eyes. The images were three more on top of those already etched in his brain from in front of the hotel that he could never unsee. He slid the folded photographs across the table to Mayte.

There was silence around the table as she picked up the images. Alexander wanted to comment to deflect the stares, but couldn't find the words. Bat leaned next to Mayte and watched over her shoulder as she unfolded the images.

Mayte put her hand over her mouth and slowly shook her head. "That's...not...her." She folded the pictures and handed them back to Morgan.

"I'm sorry you had to see the pictures."

Mayte took a long sip of her Piña Colada. "It's okay. I feel sorry for the girl, but I'm happy it wasn't Sophie."

"Was Sophie her real name?" Morgan asked.

"No. It was Sophia. Sophia Sanchez. She was from Venezuela."

"The name doesn't ring a bell. I'll remember the name and watch for it. I guess we're no closer to finding out who the victim is."

"I doubt she'd be in any databases," Bat said. "But did you get her DNA?"

"No. I got scrapings from under her fingernails and did a vaginal swab, in case she'd been raped or had had sex before she died. I used a solution that preserves DNA evidence to clean the dried blood off her. It was all placed in evidence bags along with her clothes. The lab would've tested for any foreign DNA. When the feds took her body, they took all the evidence I'd collected."

"Any idea where they might have taken her?" Alexander asked.

"No. There's an Office of the Armed Forces Medical Examiner that handles federal cases, but this wasn't one. I'd bet my job she was taken to a crematorium where she and all the evidence were destroyed."

"Why?" Bat asked.

Morgan stared across the restaurant, then shrugged. "It's hard to say, but it was a cover-up. No doubt. If I had to guess, I'd say she witnessed something she wasn't supposed to witness."

"Damn," Bat murmured.

"I agree," Alexander said. "If she happened to see a high government official take a bribe, cheat on his wife, commit murder, there are any number of possibilities. They would want to silence her."

"Damn," Bat repeated.

"Powerful people will go to extremes to retain their power."

Before Bat could repeat himself a third time, the server bounded to the table with a wide smile.

"Are you ready to order?"

*****

Jerry and Sam caught up with Jessica on US1 near Boca Raton. They eased in between the big Cadillac and Jessica's little Toyota.

Terrell, now two cars behind, created a voice text to the group:

> **I'm going to take the 808 over to I-95 and head south. There are no traffic lights. It'll be much quicker. I'll swing back to One around Fort Lauderdale. Let me know if they turn or stop.**
>
> **Jessica: Copy that. Let us know when you're back on US One, and we'll let you know where we are. By then, we'll need to fall back. Text Willie and have him get in front of us, too.**
>
> **Terrell: Will do.**

Jerry and Sam in the Ford Edge, and Jessica in her Toyota, continued shadowing the Cadillac. Every few blocks, one would turn, let the other pass, and pull in a few cars behind. They were sure they had not been made. Even if Sunday or McIntyre had been keeping an eye out for a tail, it would have been difficult for them to spot them.

At a light, Jessica created a conference call with Jerry, Sam, Terrell, and Willie. The lines were connected, but there was little conversation.

"They're turning," Jessica yelled at the phone.

"Where?" Willie replied.

"They're in the left lane to exit to 838 and A1A. There's a line of cars waiting to turn. We're two back. We're safe. Where are you, Willie?"

"I'm on 95. I just passed 838. I'll take the next exit, 842, and head east."

The big Cadillac took 838, known as East Sunrise Boulevard, across the bridge over the Middle River. It continued on across the drawbridge over the Intracoastal Canal. Jessica kept an eye on her rearview mirror, making sure the bridge didn't open before the others crossed.

"Sam, did you all make it?" Jessica said. "I see the lights on the bridge flashing."

"We did. We're about ten cars behind you."

"Good. I'm going to turn off at the next intersection and let Terrell move up. I'll pull in behind you, Sam. If you can, move up a few cars."

"We will," Jerry said, now comfortable merging the Edge in and out of traffic.

"Jessica, Willie here. If they crossed over the Intracoastal, they're probably heading to A1A. I'll head there and wait."

"Ten-four, Willie. We'll let you know if they divert."

Jessica breathed a sigh of relief. The two men in the Cadillac could have been going anywhere—Miami for a day at the beach, Key West to hang out for the weekend. It could have been a long surveillance. They were heading toward A1A and would likely turn south. If their destination was north, they'd have exited earlier.

"Willie," Jessica said to the group. "When you get to A1A, find a place to wait for us. Be ready to come north. I don't think these guys are going to go any further south. I have a feeling they're close to their destination."

"I'm on it. Let me know when to move."

"They've turned south on A1A. Traffic is light," Jessica said. "Terrell, turn off and come in behind us. Jerry, if you can, come up and get in behind them."

Like clockwork, Terrell turned, Jessica slowed, and Jerry pulled in behind the Cadillac.

"Heads up, everyone," Jerry said. "They turned right onto...uh...Granada Street. I'm not going to turn; they'd spot me in a heartbeat."

"Terrell, you keep going too. I'll follow," Jessica said.

"I'm on the move, heading your way," Willie said.

Jessica slowed to allow for a little extra space between the Cadillac and herself. When she turned onto Granada, there was no large, black SUV. "I don't see them!"

"What? They have to be here," Sam said. "We turned on the next street and are at Birch Road. Had they come down Birch, we'd have seen them."

Jessica drove slowly down the road. "I see a couple of service entrances and the entrance to a parking garage on the right. The Westin Resort and Convention Center is on the left. My bet is that they're in the garage."

Jerry and Sam, with Terrell behind them, met up with Jessica halfway down the one-block street.

The three cars pulled into decrepit parking spots along Granada. A sign warned it was a Tow-Away zone. Willie pulled in beside them.

Still on the conference call, Jessica said, "They have to be in that parking garage. It's possible they went in that oversized delivery garage, but I doubt it."

"I drove past the entrance," Willie said. "There's no sign. Painted above the entrance, it says, 'Contract Parking Only'. Why would they go in there?"

"Meeting someone is my guess," Jerry said. He and Sam got out of the Ford Edge and walked to Jessica's car. "It might be the parking garage for the hotel next to it. Sam and I will take a walk-through to see if we can find the SUV. We're the least suspicious of the group."

"Be careful," Willie said. "I don't like that 'Bloody' Sunday dude."

"We'll be fine. If anyone confronts us, we'll say we're looking for our car. If pressed, we'll act confused and say we must have walked into the wrong garage."

"Keep the conference call on. We'll be listening. Are you carrying?"

"Of course," Jerry and Sam said at the same time.

When they walked off, Willie decided that since there were five cars and four drivers, it might not be prudent to test the validity of the Tow-Away sign. There were legal parking spots along Granada, all within walking distance. Leaving one person to attend to the illegally parked cars, the others moved three vehicles, walked back, and relocated the remaining two.

Inside the parking garage, Jerry and Sam took the elevator to the third floor. They walked the length of the floor, took the down ramp to the next level, crossed it, and went down to the first floor. The lot was nearly empty. The Cadillac SUV would have been easy to spot. It was not in the parking garage.

"We don't see the Caddy," Jerry said to the group on the conference call. "There aren't many cars parked in here. If it were here, we'd have seen it."

"I don't get it," Jessica said. "We know they turned on this street, and we know they didn't make it to the end."

"Hang on," Sam said. "In the far corner, there's a ramp going down, but it leads to a brick wall. We need to investigate."

"Did you hear?" Jerry asked the others in the group.

"We did."

Sam was on her way to the ramp at a brisk pace. Jerry caught her as she slowed to inspect marks on the parking garage floor.

"Do those look like fresh tire tracks to you?" she asked.

Jerry bent and lightly ran his finger over the tracks. He easily smudged the imprint. He angled himself to get the best image and took several pictures of the tracks. They walked closer to the ramp, which was about half the length of the garage.

"I'm going down," Jerry said. "Stay here and yell if anyone comes."

"Are you sure you want to go down there? There's no cover."

"I'll be quick." Jerry jogged down the ramp until he was well below the first level of the garage. The ramp took a hard right, went another twenty-five feet or so, and stopped at a large, metal garage door. He examined the door. There was no visible way to open the door. No sensors. No buttons. Surprisingly, no video cameras monitoring the door. He turned and walked quickly up the ramp.

"There's a big door down there. I didn't see a way to open it from the outside. Either they have a remote control to work the door, or they call to have it opened for them."

"Where's it go?" Sam asked.

"Good question. It's hard to say. The first floor is at ground level. The ramp definitely goes into a tunnel. A tunnel could go anywhere." Jerry brought the phone closer to his mouth. "Did you all hear me? Ideas? We're heading back to the car."

Willie greeted Jerry and Sam when they returned to the car. "Good job, y'all. From your description, I'd bet there's a tunnel on the other side of the door that runs north." He held up an iPad Pro and pointed at the parking garage they were standing near on the map. "At one time, I'd bet this garage connected to another garage, but over time, and ownership changes, the connection was closed off." He estimated where the tunnel would be, then ran his finger along a line north. "I'd bet there's a tunnel from this parking garage straight into an underground lot to here, the Overlook Hotel."

FOURTEEN

As the evening progressed, and the wine, beer, and Piña Coladas flowed at the Casablanca Café, the conversation at the table where Alexander, Jana, Bat, Mayte, and Morgan sat lightened considerably.

Morgan was particularly interested in how Bat, a vertically challenged, overweight, computer geek, had hooked up with a beautiful, young, petite Cuban girl. Mayte was quick to point out that she was five-one, and, in her eyes, Bat was not short. She also pointed out that when they met, she was forty pounds heavier, and that didn't bother him. Most importantly, she thought Bat was cute. A bit odd, but cute.

When Alexander explained how he pulled Mayte from the Gulf of Mexico after she'd jumped from a human trafficker's boat—a boat owned by Jana's ex-boyfriend—Morgan threw up her hands.

"Wait," she said. "I'm confused. I've either had too much wine or not enough."

When the laughter died around the table, Alexander explained how Jana's ex, Reymundo, had been forced to traffic women from Cuba to the US, and, with Alexander's help, they busted the traffickers and rescued the girls. The story took a while.

"So you're now with Jana, Reymundo's ex?" Morgan asked.

"Yes. That's another story. Would you like to hear it?"

"Honestly, I would, but we've occupied the table for a while," she said, eyeing the line of people standing in line to get into the restaurant. "I think they'd prefer we left."

"I'm a regular," Jana said. "We could hang around all night, and they wouldn't mind. But my butt is getting a bit sore. Why don't we walk back to Bat's hotel and have a drink in the bar?"

Everyone agreed a walk would be nice. The server brought the pay-at-the-table device. Jana glanced at the amount, tapped her credit card, added a generous tip, and handed the machine back to the server. "Are you all ready?"

*****

Willie, Jerry, Sam, Terrell, and Jessica huddled at their cars. It had been over an hour since the SUV disappeared.

"How long are we going to wait for them to come out?" Terrell asked. "We aren't a hundred percent sure they're in there."

"I'm ninety-nine percent sure," Jerry said. "Tire tracks were heading down the ramp. A vehicle has driven down there recently."

"They could be spending the night in the hotel," Sam added.

"It's possible," Willie said. "It doesn't make sense. We aren't that far from the Eagle's Nest. Why would they need a room?"

"Maybe they're closet gays and come here to be together. They sure couldn't risk being outed, considering who they work for," Jerry said.

Willie rubbed his chin. "Well, Jerry, you'd know that better than me, but we followed them because they looked unsavory. They don't look like a couple to me. I'd be more inclined to say they're after a little female companionship and don't want to be too close to the compound."

"I agree," Jerry said. "But you never know."

"Looking for women makes the most sense," Terrell said. "There's a lot more going on here as compared to Palm Beach. More bars. More tourists. More strip joints. More hookers."

"Which means we may be on a wild goose chase," Willie said.

"Maybe," Jessica said. "But they don't fit in with the others at the Eagle's Nest. I don't know what they do, but I bet it's not a traditional job. Which is why I don't feel this was a waste of time. We can use those guys. I should say, if we were going to kill the president, we could use those guys. They'd make perfect patsies."

"To be honest," Terrell said. "I'm more interested in McIntyre and Sunday than trying to see if we could plot the assassination of a sitting president and blame it on a patsy, or convince a patsy to do it. I want to know what those two do. If it turns out we could use them in our plan, even better."

"I'm curious as well. I'm going to drive to the hotel down the street," Jessica said, pointing at the ten-story Overlook Hotel. "I want to make sure there's not another exit."

"Good idea," Willie said. "Should I come with you?"

"No. I may walk to the hotel and check it out. I'll be less conspicuous alone."

Willie pursed his lips. "Let us know if you spot the SUV. We'll let you know if they come out this way. If they do, you'll need to jump on US1 and head north. If they head that way, we'll follow until they catch you, then we'll peel off."

"Sounds like a plan. It's almost dark. Let's hope the SUV comes out the way they went in, and they come out soon." Jessica walked to her car, circled the block, and parked a hundred yards from the rear entrance of the Overlook Hotel. She got out of the car and walked slowly towards the hotel.

Two smaller residences that appeared to have been converted into apartments or Vacation Rentals By Owner units were on the left. A two-story hotel with a small parking lot in front was on her right. There were no parking garages, either above or below ground. On the left was a large hotel with no visible parking entrance.

Jessica reached the Overlook Hotel's driveway, stopped, and sat on a short concrete wall bordering the parking lot. The lot was small for such a large hotel, which meant there must be underground parking. She walked to the front of the hotel, turned, and walked down the sidewalk. A few yards past the main entrance was a driveway that went down, under the hotel.

Jessica sent a text to the group:

> **There's an underground parking lot at the hotel. The only entrance is in the front, off A1A. It has a solid garage door. Can't see in.**
> **Willie: Keep an eye on it. Let us know if they come out that way.**

Another concrete wall separated the drive from the hotel next door. Jessica leaned on the wall, her back to the street, pulled out her phone, and snapped several pictures of the parking garage. To the casual observer, it would look like she was taking selfies.

A door beside the garage door opened. A heavy-set man stepped out and lit a cigarette. Night had set in, but the stoop was well-lit from the lights lining the hotel's entrance. It was Mark "Bloody" Sunday. Jessica was in the shadows. If he looked in her direction, he couldn't miss her.

Jessica turned her back to the hotel, set her phone to selfie mode, and held it in front of her. She made sure Sunday was visible over her shoulder. With the phone on silent mode, she snapped several photos. In the first four, Sunday was looking toward the hotel entrance. As Jessica scrolled through the pictures, the man's head turned toward her and stayed. "Bloody" Sunday was staring at her.

"Shit." Jessica turned and slowly walked along A1A in the direction from which she had come. She took several more selfies, exaggerating her poses to mimic what a teen girl might do. She casually glanced toward the stoop. Sunday had stepped off and was walking toward her. She picked up her pace slightly, not enough to seem suspicious, opened the messaging app, and sent a text to the group:

> **I've been made.**

*****

"I love this place," Bat said to the group standing on the sidewalk in front of the Casablanca Cafe. "It's a beach like Bolivar is a beach, but it's like night and day. I can see why you stay, Alex. This is concrete, glass, ocean, white sand, and beautiful people. Our beach is dunes infested with rattlesnakes, brown sand, brown water, and wooden houses on pilings. We do have our share of beautiful people...on occasion."

"He means beautiful females," Mayte added.

"Scantily clad, too. Although I'm no longer interested in them." Bat put his arm around Mayte and hugged her.

The group began walking north on A1A. "I guess you haven't been to our nude beach," Jana said.

Bat stopped in his tracks. "Nude beach?"

"Haulover Beach. It's about thirty minutes south."

Mayte pulled Bat by the arm. "Don't even think about it. You're pervy enough without hanging out on a nude beach. Plus, if you did get naked, your ass would get so burnt you couldn't sit for a week."

"I suppose I would look out of place."

"That's exactly what Jana said when she took me there," Alexander said.

Bat looked at Jana. The women looked then at Alexander.

"No, we didn't go in. We got as far as the sign. Jana started to take off her clothes, but I stopped her."

"Why?" Bat blurted.

"We'd just met. I was working for her. It would have been inappropriate."

Bat eyed Jana. Again, he wanted to ask Alexander why he had stopped her, but this time, he thought better of it.

"Tall, handsome, and chivalrous," Morgan said. "He's quite a catch, Jana."

Jana put her arm through Alexander's. "He is—and he's caught."

"Don't worry, I can see that. Anyway, I'm not in your class."

"Don't be silly. You're gorgeous, and you're a doctor. Guys love smart, hot women."

"You're sweet, Jana. You may not have an MD, but I can tell you're smart. I get the impression you're streetwise, too. I'm not."

"Are you kidding? As an ME, I bet you've seen it all."

"I hate to interrupt this meeting of the Mutual Admiration Society," Bat said. "But did you see that, Alex?"

"I did."

"What do you think?"

"We need to hurry along."

Alexander and Bat began walking faster. The girls quickened their steps to keep up.

"What's going on?" Jana asked.

"You see the girl up there?"

"Yeah."

"A ways back, I noticed her leaning on the wall, taking selfies. When she started walking, that guy came off the porch. He may be following her."

"What the hell? Do you think he's going to attack her?" Morgan asked.

"I don't know. If that's his plan, and we get close enough, he'll likely change his mind."

"He's getting closer. Should we run?" Mayte asked.

"No. We don't want to set him off if he's planning anything."

The girl glanced over her shoulder, noticed the man, and sped up slightly.

"She saw him," Bat said.

"And she started walking a little faster," Alexander added. "She's worried."

Alexander, Bat, and the girls were walking as fast as they could without breaking into a jog. They closed the gap on the man, who was gaining on the girl.

"Sophie!" Alexander yelled in a deep, loud voice, loud enough that the girl and the man who was following her jumped slightly and looked back at the group.

Alexander stared directly at the girl and waved wildly. She instinctively waved back. A slight smile appeared.

"Hope we didn't keep you waiting. We're running a little late."

The girl gave the man who was following her a sideways glance. He veered off toward the front of the hotel.

"No, I was taking a little walk while I waited," she said, loud enough for the man to hear. She waited for the five strangers to reach her.

"Run up and give her a hug," Alexander told Mayte, who did as asked. The girl opened her arms for Mayte.

When the others joined, the girl said, "Thank you. I had a feeling he was following me."

"Do you know him?" Alexander asked.

"Um...no, I don't."

"Let's walk this way. He may be watching."

They began walking across the street toward the next hotel.

"When I yelled, you caught on quickly. By the way, I'm Alex, this is Bat, Mayte, Jana, and Morgan."

"Nice to meet you all. I'm Jessica. Your hollering scared the hell out of me. You've got a loud voice. When I saw you with the women, I figured you were okay. Why'd you yell?"

"We noticed the guy following you and didn't like it. I had nothing to lose. If you two happened to be walking in the same direction at the same time, no harm, no foul. But he took a sharp left and went toward the hotel."

"So he was following me?"

"Pretty good chance he was."

"I wonder why?"

"We could turn around and go ask him," Bat said.

"I'd rather not," Jessica said.

The group stopped in front of the Grand Paradise Hotel.

"This is us," Alexander said. "We were going to the bar for a drink. Care to join us?"

"Uh...I don't—"

"You should. He might be watching," Morgan said.

"You're right, I should."

They all walked into the hotel bar and found a table near the front window. Alexander sat so he could see the sidewalk they'd come from.

The bartender came to the table. "Sorry, y'all, we don't have a server tonight. It's been pretty slow since Spring Break ended. We still get a few of the late breakers, but most have gone home. We peaked a couple of weeks ago. April is slow. What can I getcha?"

Alexander and Bat ordered a scotch. Jana, Mayte, and Morgan asked for chardonnay. They decided a bottle would work. Jessica asked for a beer.

"What made you think the guy was following me?" Jessica asked.

"Bat and I noticed him leave the porch right after you started walking. You sped up a little, so did he. We had a feeling."

The bartender brought the drinks. Jessica picked hers up, "Here's to you guys. You may have saved my life. Thank you."

Morgan turned to Jessica. "Can I ask why you were standing out there alone? I mean, Fort Lauderdale isn't a hotbed of crime, but a single girl, at night, alone, is inviting trouble."

"I'm from West Palm. I was with friends earlier, and they left. I wanted to take selfies by the beach. I was on the beach walking for a while, until it got dark."

"Nice story," Alexander said. "What's the real story?"

"What?" Jessica snapped.

"I don't care. I'm curious why you lied. I'm pretty sure you aren't a hooker."

"Alex," Morgan said tersely. "It's none of our business."

"No, it's not. But she was up to something at the hotel. The guy scared her off."

"Why don't you believe her?" Morgan asked. She subtly brushed the top of Jessica's hand. "I apologize, Jessica, for speaking in the third person with you sitting here."

Jessica flashed Morgan a faint smile. "It's fine. Thanks." She turned to Alexander. "I'd like to know why you think I'm lying. I mean, I appreciate you helping me, but you're being a bit of an ass."

"He's being a real ass. So much for chivalry," Morgan said.

Alexander ignored Morgan. "You're very pale-skinned. I see no evidence of makeup or sunscreen. If you'd been in the sun even a little today, there would be at least a little pink on your face. You're wearing hiking boots. Stylish, but not great for walking in the sand. Had you been on the beach, there would be sand residue all over your boots. You could shake them out for a week and still find sand."

"Alex!"

"It's fine, Morgan. No, I didn't walk on the beach. I stayed on the sidewalk because I didn't want to get my boots sandy. They're new. And, by the time I got here, the buildings were shading most of the beach. I'm not sure why I'm being interrogated. If you'll excuse me, I need to use the restroom."

Jessica left the table. Once she was out of sight, both Morgan and Jana lit into Alexander. They demanded to know why he was questioning her.

Alexander tried defending himself. "She lied. I could tell. When you've spent as long as I did interviewing suspects, you learn to tell when someone isn't being straight with you. I was abrupt. I shouldn't have been. But, she still didn't tell us the truth. I'm even more curious what she is hiding."

"No, you shouldn't have been so abrupt," Morgan said. "Okay, she has a secret. She seems sweet, and if she does, it's not our concern."

"Okay, I'll apologize."

Inside the bathroom, Jessica sent a group text:

> **Sunday got a good look at me. Even though it's dark, I shouldn't follow him. I will head home.**
> **Willie: OK. Be careful. We'll hang here a little longer to see if they come out. I'll text you later and let you know what we do. Most likely meet up in the morning and discuss.**
> **Jessica: Sounds like a plan. See you tomorrow.**

Jessica returned from the bathroom and quickly finished her beer. "Thank you for intervening when the guy was following me. I do appreciate it. But I should get going." She pulled a small wallet from her pants pocket and began withdrawing cash. Jana stopped her.

"We got this. Don't worry about it."

"And I apologize," Alexander said. "I didn't mean to pry."

"We're good. I do need to leave, though."

"I Ubered here," Morgan said. "That man could be out there lurking. Let me call an Uber, and I can drop you at your car."

"I've only had the one beer. My car is close. I think it would be safe for us to walk to it. How far is your house?"

"It's kinda far. A half an hour or so. It's not on your way."

"I don't mind a little drive. I can give you a ride home, if you'd like."

"That'd be so nice. Ubers scare me. Especially this time of night. Are you sure you don't mind?"

"Not at all."

Morgan thanked Jana for the dinner and drinks and said goodbye to the others. "If I hear anything, Alex, I'll let you know."

Jessica and Morgan left.

"Should I follow them and make sure they make it to their car?" Alexander asked.

"Together, they'll be fine. Stalkers are a rarity around here. It's usually pretty safe. We aren't even sure what the man was up to. He may have seen a single woman and was going to hit on her."

Jessica and Morgan made it to Jessica's car without incident. Jessica kept a vigilant eye out, presumably for the man who had followed her. Inside the vehicle, Jessica locked the doors, started the engine, and let out a barely audible sigh.

Morgan directed Jessica toward her apartment. The two chit-chatted briefly about the weather, traffic, and the toll roads prevalent in Florida. After a moment of silence, Morgan said, "I want to apologize for Alex. I recently met him. He seems like a nice guy. He sure came after you."

"I know. I don't know why."

"He's retired FBI. When you went to the bathroom, he said he could tell when people were lying to him. He said he shouldn't have been so blunt, but it was a force of habit."

"It was nice of him to say he shouldn't have been an ass. He's a fed?"

"Retired. He does a little PI work, which is how he met Jana. How they met is an interesting story. I know pieces of it. If you ever see him again, you'll have to get the rest of the story."

Jessica gave her a grin. Until then, she wasn't too interested in Alexander and Jana's story. "Now I'm intrigued."

Morgan navigated Jessica through a roundabout. "Turn here. My spot is on the left."

Jessica pulled into a numbered parking spot. "Would you like to come in?" Morgan asked.

"You can catch me up on what you know about Alex and Jana?"

"If you'd like, but I may have a better idea." Morgan put her hand behind Jessica's head and gently pulled her closer. Jessica offered no resistance. A gentle kiss quickly deepened into passion.

FIFTEEN

illie leaned against the hood of his car, his arms folded across his chest. "I'm going to call it," he said. "It's getting late, and those two could be in for the night. We know they came out of the Eagle's Nest via a hidden drive. We should find the drive. Whatever they're doing here doesn't help us with our plan. Let's go home and meet at my house in the morning—say at ten. We can talk about what we know and where we are."

"What about Jessica?" Terrell asked.

"She said she was going home. I haven't heard from her, so I have to assume she made it. I'll text her later and let her know we're meeting in the morning."

"Sounds good," Terrell said. "I'm sure she's fine."

After Terrell, Jerry, and Sam left, Willie circled the block one last time, hoping to spot the big, black SUV. When he didn't see it, he reluctantly made his way to the freeway and headed north to West Palm Beach. Willie turned the car's stereo down to background level.

It had been two weeks since he had been invited to join the assassination experiment. At first, it was fun. Could it be done? As the days went by, the newness had worn thin. If the CIA was involved in

Kennedy's assassination, they had much more time and resources to carry it out. More importantly, it was not a drill.

Willie knew if he were given an assignment to take out the president of another country and wanted it to look like the work of a lone gunman, he could do it. Piece of cake. But to go through the motions with no real intent was now boring. Following two men because they appeared out of place was a waste of time. They were probably in a hotel room getting laid while he was driving back to West Palm alone. He did smile when he thought about Guerline there waiting for him.

Instead of plotting an assassination, he thought he should be looking for a job. But what would an unattractive Black man with a Master's in Political Science do? Teach at a community college? He wondered whether corporations still used spies and, if so, how he would apply.

"I'm not too old for law school," he said softly. Willie said, shivering at the thought of becoming a lawyer.

Willie's thoughts drifted back to the president. If a president ever needed killing, it was this one. Campaign promises broken. Constant lies. Racist remarks. Ridiculous tariffs. Horrible policies—when he had one. What scared Willie the most was how he could have been elected in the first place. Then he remembered a line from a book he'd read years ago. A quote Adolf Hitler said in 1911: "Propaganda, only propaganda is necessary. There is no end of stupid people."

*****

"You aren't going to leave it alone, are you, Alex?" Jana asked as she crawled into bed.

"I wish I could. For the life of me, I don't know what she was doing out there."

"You have no doubt she was lying?"

Alexander leaned back on a pillow, his hands behind his head, and watched the grey ceiling fan blades slowly spin for several revolutions. "She was lying. No doubt. The fact that she left abruptly confirmed it."

"She could have had someplace she needed to be."

"No. Had I not questioned her, I'm sure she would have stayed and had a few more beers."

"Until Morgan offered to give her a ride to her car."

Alexander sat up in bed. "Do you mean…"

"Yep."

"That wasn't on my bingo card."

"You were sitting next to Jessica. Morgan was next to her. You couldn't see how they were eyeing each other. I could from across the table."

"Obviously, I have a hard time noticing when women are hitting on each other. I mean, I could tell Jessica was a lesbian. She's so, uh, what do they call it?"

"Butch?"

"Right. But Morgan? I had no idea."

"Are you disappointed?"

"What? Why would I be?"

"I've noticed that you don't mind lesbians, as long as they aren't hot."

Alexander laughed. "That may have been true at one time, before I met you. Okay, I'll admit it. I hate to see an attractive woman with another woman."

"Like it was one less you had a shot at?"

"Geez, Jana, you make me sound like a man-whore."

"Well, if the boat shoe fits. I recall you had a closet full of women's clothing in the guest room of your beach house."

"I found those items on the beach. I kept them in case any unexpected overnight guests needed a change of clothes. Remember, you were an unexpected overnight guest the night we met."

"I was. And, I must admit, you were a perfect gentleman. You waited until we found my ex alive before you fucked me."

"Jana!"

Jana rolled on top of Alexander and kissed him. "Speaking of…if you can stop thinking about Jessica and Morgan…"

*****

"Wow. What an amazing night," Jessica said to Morgan when they woke up. "Even if it hadn't been a long time since I've had sex, I'd still say it was the best night."

Morgan smiled widely. "Same. It's been a long time for me, too. Still, what a night. The best night I can remember. I'm surprised the neighbors didn't call the cops."

"I guess your apartment is pretty soundproof. Shall we test again?"

"Oh, I'd love to, but duty calls. I have to go to work. Would you like to test it tonight? Or the walls at your house?"

"I'm game."

Morgan rolled to her side and playfully caressed Jessica's chest. "Me too. I was wondering if this was going to be a one-night stand. What would you say about a date? Dinner, drinks, and back here...or your place."

"That would be amazing. We can talk over dinner. We didn't talk at all last night. I want to get to know you."

Morgan blushed like a teenager. "No, we didn't talk a lot. We went from the kiss in your car straight to my bed."

Jessica stretched and put her arm around Morgan. "I've seen it in movies, but I've never done anything even close to what we did. For me anyway, it's usually a date or two, we kiss, and if all goes well, we end up on the bed and finally...well, you know."

"I do. Same with me. People think lesbians are promiscuous and hop from bed to bed. I suppose some do, but it's not my cup of tea. By the way, did we rip each other's clothes off?"

Jessica laughed. "Pretty close. I'm sure clothes are strewn from the front door to the bed."

"I need to get to work. I know we just met, but I trust you. You can stay for a while and leave when you're ready. Or you can stay, and I'll see if I can get off early. As long as no one is dying to see me, I should get out early." Morgan laughed. Jessica stared at her expressionless. "Oh. By the way, I'm the Broward County Medical Examiner.

"OH, MY GOD. Morgan, that's...actually very funny. A little sick, but funny."

"It's an old ME joke."

"Are there others? I'd love to hear them."

"Lots. You haven't lived until you've attended an ME conference." Jessica laughed.

"I'm not joking. Medical Examiner's conferences are a hoot."

Jessica wasn't sure if Morgan was serious. "So, you're a doctor? That's cool. Beautiful, fun, smart...how are you still single?"

Morgan gazed into the distance without answering.

"It was a rhetorical question. I know you have to leave. I'll leave too. I got a text last night that some friends are meeting for breakfast this morning. Tonight, I want to know all about you."

"And I want to get to know you. I don't even know your last name."

"It's Chen. My mother is Filipino. My dad is Chinese. No, I don't speak a lick of Chinese. Hand me your phone. I'll share my name and number."

Jessica used AirDrop to transfer her contact information from her phone to Morgan's. "Done," she said, handing the phone back. "Text me when you'd like to meet tonight. I can come back here. As soon as you get off, we can go out."

"I like that idea. It's Friday, so it should be quiet. I may get a client or two later this evening—after the bars close."

"Jeez, Morgan. You're amazing, but I'll have to get used to your sense of humor."

"You will. I'm late. I need to run. Let yourself out when you're ready. I'll text you the code to the front door later, so if you get here before I get home, you can let yourself in." She gave Jessica a deep kiss and forced herself off the bed. She pulled a pair of panties and a bra from a dresser drawer, grabbed scrubs from the closet, and got dressed. She slid her bare feet into a pair of Sketchers Hands Free Slip-Ins, kissed Jessica again, and left.

Jessica lay on the bed for several minutes, then, with great reluctance, she got out of bed, peed, and walked through the house, putting on articles of clothing as she found them. The smile would not leave her face.

She checked the time. Willie's meeting was at ten. She had an hour. Plenty of time to get there, but not enough time to go home, shower, and change clothes. She sent a text to Willie:

Running a bit late. Will be there around 10:30.

Jessica closed her eyes and asked herself why she was still going to Willie's. She felt she had finally met the woman of her dreams, and she didn't want to fuck it up.

*****

Terrell arrived at ten sharp and went into the kitchen. Willie, Jerry, Sam, and Guerline were having coffee at the kitchen table. His forehead creased. "Where's Jessica? She's never late for a meeting."

"She texted this morning. Said she was running late."

"Did you talk to her?"

"No. She texted."

"Did you try calling her?"

"No. Why?"

"On the way home last night, I drove by her apartment. She lives close. Her car wasn't in her spot. I should have called or texted her, but I didn't want her to know I was checking on her."

"Could Sunday have grabbed her then used her phone to send the text this morning?"

Terrell took a deep breath. "It's possible. Last night she texted us that she'd been made."

Willie thought for a moment. "It's possible, but not likely. Why would she say she would be here at ten thirty? Thirty minutes isn't going to buy Sunday much time if he has her." Willie checked the time. "Let's give her half an hour before we start the conspiracy theories."

Terrell nodded and sat at the table. "You're right. I'm being paranoid. I don't like those guys from the compound, and the fact that one spotted her worries me."

"Either of those two outweighs her by at least a hundred pounds, but Jessica is an expert in martial arts. One of the best, if not the best, females I've seen. I'd say at the very least she'd hold her own against them and most likely kick their ass. For good measure, she carries a Smith & Wesson LadySmith .38 Special in her purse. It slaps the shit out of your hand, but I've seen her put all five rounds in the black from seven yards." Willie leaned back in his chair. "I'm sure she's fine."

"She's a pistol, alright. No pun intended." Terrell checked the time. "We should know soon if she's okay. I'll admit, I'll be worried until she walks through the front door. This situation has made me rethink what we're trying to accomplish here. I mean, it's not worth getting one of us hurt, or worse, trying to see if we could pull off a Kennedy-like assassination."

"I couldn't agree more," Willie said. "In fact—"

The doorbell rang, the door opened, and a smiling Jessica came bounding in. Terrell jumped up to meet her and gave her a hug.

"I was worried," he said and led her to the kitchen table, where she sat on a high barstool.

"We were all worried, Jessica. You're never late."

"I'm sorry. I had trouble getting out of bed this morning. No need to worry."

"You texted that Sunday had made you. Then there was a semi-cryptic text that we thought might not have been sent by you. Even this morning's text saying you'd be late was a little out of character for you," Terrell said.

Jessica pulled her legs onto the barstool and rested her head on her knees. "Again, I should have called. But I met someone. We hit it off, and I spent the night with her."

An audible gasp came from around the table. "Tell us more," Jerry said.

"Not much to it." Jessica described what happened as Sunday approached. "Then, in the group of people I met up with was a woman. A beautiful woman. She didn't seem gay, but I could tell by the way we looked at each other. We knew. Turns out, she's a doctor. The Broward County Medical Examiner."

Everyone but Jessica and Guerline pulled out their cell phones and Googled the ME.

"Morgan Gossamer. She is hot," Terrell said. "From her bio, I'm guessing she's in her late thirties. Kind of young for you, isn't she, Jessica?"

"Damn, Terrell. You know me too well. Yeah, I preferred older women. They're more mature. That was when I was younger. Morgan is extremely mature."

"I'm happy for you—as we all are. I'm glad you could make it this morning."

"Morgan had to work. Otherwise, I may not have made it."

Willie decided it was time to steer the conversation away from Jessica's new love. He took a deep breath and let it out slowly. "Here's why I called this meeting." He leaned back, crossed his arms, and stared at the ceiling to gather his thoughts. "Yesterday, we spent the day following two guys from the Eagle's Nest who could have been instrumental in our plan to assassinate the president. I wouldn't say we lost them; Jessica found them, at least one, at the Overlook Hotel. We have no idea what they were doing there. Speculation is that they were leaving the compound in search of a little action. Sunday following Jessica would support the theory."

Willie paused for a drink of coffee. "I don't want to say we wasted our time, but we didn't get much accomplished. I thought about this on the way home last night and again this morning. I'll be frank. We never intended to try to kill the president. We were running an experiment to see if we could. Unless we went out and recruited a shooter—or a patsy—I don't know if we'll ever know for sure. I know a couple of us may have been involved in a presidential assassination or two in various countries during our careers, so, yeah, we know it could be done."

Sam's eyebrows raised slightly. As an analyst, she was never involved in any covert operations. She knew the CIA was likely engaged in assassinations, but this was the first time it had been confirmed.

Willie continued. "We were all fired about the same time. It's pretty obvious why we were let go. Jerry and Jessica are gay. Terrell and I are Black. Honestly, I'm not sure about you, Sam."

Sam scratched her head. "Me either. Because I was new? A deputy director hit on me a few months ago, and I filed a grievance. Maybe—"

"We have our answer," Willie said. "My point is, we were all pissed off. I believe, in the back of our heads, we wanted to kill the president."

"Still do," Jerry said. The group looked at him. His expression was stone cold. "In fact, I did bring my Accuracy International AXSR 6.5 Creedmoor rifle. I'm accurate with it to a thousand yards. Put me a half a mile away, and Cockwomble is history."

Everyone sat in stunned silence.

"Fuck, Jerry," Sam said.

"What? We're all thinking it."

"First of all, you told me you never killed anyone. Was that true?"

"I'll take this one, Jerry," Willie said. "Sam, there's an unwritten rule. CIA assassins never, ever, talk about their kills. Not to their spouse, their friends, or even coworkers, unless the coworker was there. Even then, they rarely discuss it once it's done."

Sam stared at Willie for an instant, then at the others around the table. Slowly, Sam began to comprehend what Willie had said.

"I'm sorry, Sam. I lied to you. The story I told you when we were driving was one I fabricated and tell whenever anyone asks if I have ever killed anyone. You'd be surprised how often I'm asked. With you, I should have just said that I don't like to talk about it."

"It's okay, I get it," she said. "So, are we shifting gears from planning an assassination to attempting one?"

There was silence around the table. The collective wheels were turning inside everyone's head. Everyone except Guerline, who left the table to fetch the glass coffee pot. Without asking, she hovered the pot over each cup, watching for a signal. When the cups of those who wanted coffee were filled, she put the pot back on the coffeemaker.

"If you'll 'scuze me," she said. "I want to go upstairs for sumting."

Willie patted her gently on her butt. "Sure, hun. I'll come get you in a bit."

Willie waited until Guerline was gone. "Right after we got together, I told Guerline that whenever I start talking business, she could excuse herself. I trust her, and I don't mind her hearing, but it's better if she doesn't know what I'm planning. For a shitload of reasons." He blew gently on the top of his coffee. Small ripples formed. He took a small sip to test the temperature, then took a larger gulp. "Also, for a shitload of reasons, last night on my drive home, I came to the conclusion we should call this off. It was an interesting exercise at first, but the fun, at least for me, has worn off. I called this meeting to see how everyone else felt."

"We aren't shifting gears, we're shutting down?" Sam asked.

"I didn't say that, Sam. I said we should discuss it."

"I agree with Willie," Jessica said. "It was fun at first. A way to blow off a little steam. But I'm over it."

"Me too," Terrell agreed. "I'm about ready to pack it in and start a job search."

Once again, all eyes focused on Jerry. He leaned back and shifted his weight in the chair. "If we were all still with the Agency, and we were recruited for this, I would do it. But, unemployed, with limited resources, and no timeline, I have to agree it's a waste of time. Having said that, I do believe that stupid son-of-a-bitch needs to be taken out. And quickly. Every day, when you think he can't be any more stupid, he tops himself. There's no question he has dementia, and Congress is scared of him. They won't stop him. It's like we're living in 1939 Germany."

Jerry walked to the back door and stared at the pond for a few minutes. When he returned, he leaned forward and rested his hands on the kitchen table. "If we can plan it so I'm ninety-nine percent sure I won't get caught, I'll shoot the bastard."

SIXTEEN

At six o'clock on Saturday evening, Mark "Bloody" Sunday and Sean McIntyre took the elevator to the parking lot beneath the Overlook Hotel. They climbed into a large, black SUV and drove down a semi-hidden drive in the far corner of the garage. When they reached a large metal door, they waved at the camera above it and waited. The door opened.

The two drove down a tunnel to another large steel door. McIntyre, in the passenger seat, clicked the button on the remote control, and the door opened. When they were through, McIntyre pressed the button. They waited while the door closed, then left the parking garage.

"Take a left, then a right on Seabreeze. It'll turn into SE 17th Street. Follow it to US1. Not far, three and a half miles or so. Traffic is light. If we don't get stuck at a bridge, ten minutes. Turn right on US1," McIntyre said.

"How far after that?"

"Roughly fifteen minutes."

Sunday nodded as he calculated the total time of the drive in his head. A bit less than thirty minutes. Long ago, they determined that a half hour from the compound and the same distance from the hotel was optimal for their excursions. Not too close where they might be recognized, yet not so far that they couldn't get back to the hotel quickly.

McIntyre navigated while Sunday drove the last few blocks to Lou's Sports Bar & Grill in Hollywood. The exterior was modern and chic. At the base of the large stucco building was a single door framed by two large windows. Above the door, bright letters spelling "LOU'S" glowed in the afternoon shadows.

Lou's interior was more rustic. A long, wooden bar ran the length of the interior. A lit shelf behind the bar highlighted bottles of alcohol. A line of televisions flickered above the bar. All the screens showed talking heads, presumably discussing the Final Four. The sound was muted.

"Damn," Sunday said. "Is there a basketball game tonight?"

"I don't know. You'll need to ask the bartender."

"If so, that could be good. It'll mean lots of college girls."

A door at the far end of the bar led to the patio. Booths lined the back wall, and tables with chairs filled the area between the bar and the booths. Sunday and McIntyre sat on barstools near the front door.

"Hi, guys. What can I get ya?" The bartender was an average-looking woman in her mid-thirties. She had an above-average chest, which she displayed prominently.

"What do you have on draft?" McIntyre asked.

"Damn. Lots. What do you like? IPA, lager, ale? We got several small-batch IPAs from Crooked Can delivered this morning."

"I'll give one a try," Sunday said. "Surprise me."

"Me too," McIntyre said.

The bartender left and returned with two TropIPAlooza Piña Colada IPAs.

Sunday looked at the TV. "There's a game tonight?"

"Yes. Final Four."

"I'm surprised it's not packed in here."

"It was. Florida got their butt kicked by Houston. The place cleared out pretty quickly." She scanned the bar. "There are quite a few folks on the patio. What's left is a typical Saturday night. It'll pick up later. I think Arizona and Michigan play next. I'm not sure. I'm not much of a basketball fan. I've noticed a few T-shirts."

"I noticed too," McIntyre lied. He had been checking out the women and was only interested in their bustlines, not what was on their t-shirts.

"Would you all like to start a tab?"

"No, we'll pay cash. We're going to move to a table." Sunday handed her a twenty-dollar bill. "Keep it."

"Thanks," she said and walked down the bar to help another patron.

"This is pretty nice," Sunday said. "The beer's cold. The location is perfect. There are three strip joints within a mile of here. We've got plenty of time."

"I wish there was a baseball game on one of the TVs. I don't care for basketball."

"True, but the game may bring in some good eye candy."

"Whoa. Like those two," McIntyre said, nodding toward the two young women who walked through the front door.

Sunday spun around. The first, a blonde with huge breasts, wore a white tank top, a short, white skirt with a white belt, and white knee-high boots. The other, a sandy-blonde with smaller breasts, wore a black tube top and a black skirt. Both were in their late twenties. "Damn. Them's nice."

The two women walked past them to the end of the bar and out the back door to the patio.

"Should we follow?" Sunday asked.

"Nah. If they don't come back, we'll go out and see if they're alone later. Let's get a table. I'm hungry."

They picked up their beers and walked to a table in the corner, away from the televisions.

"We're away from the crowd, and we can watch everyone in the bar from here," McIntyre said.

A server soon appeared with menus. "Hi, I'm Amanda. I'll be taking care of you tonight. I see you have beers. Can I get you anything else? Water, an appetizer?"

McIntyre and Sunday stared at the server for several seconds, stunned. She was gorgeous. Platinum blonde hair that hung halfway to her waist, bright blue eyes, and a symmetrical, balanced, slightly upturned nose that was in perfect harmony with her facial features. Full, but not overwhelming, natural breasts, and long, slender, tan legs. She wore a tank top and low-rise denim shorts. She barely looked twenty-one.

"I'm sorry," Sunday said after the awkward silence. "You have us tongue-tied."

"Excuse me?"

"Did you ever watch the old TV show, 'Cheers'?"

"Uh, no, I didn't."

"Well, there were these two guys who were always at the bar. They considered themselves cool, but when a beautiful woman walked in, they got all flustered and couldn't speak. That's what just happened to us."

The server tapped a pen against her order pad. "Oh."

"Anyway. Uh, water would be great. And bring us two of the Florida Sunshine Lagers. The TropIPAloozas were too sweet for our taste. We should be ready to order when you get back."

"Fuck'n A," Sunday said after she'd walked away. "She's stunning. What are our chances?"

"She is stunning. But she doesn't strike me as the brightest light on the Christmas tree."

"So, there's a chance?"

After a quick glance at the menu, they were ready to order when the server returned with the beers. Sunday ordered chicken-fried steak, and McIntyre ordered a rack of ribs. Their food came promptly, and they ate in silence, occasionally pointing out an attractive young woman who'd entered the bar.

When they were finished, the server came by with the check in her hand. "Are you up for a dessert this evening?" She asked before setting the check on the table.

"No dessert, but I have something to ask you," Sunday said.

The server glanced back and forth at the two men. "Um, no, I don't think so."

"You haven't heard what I was going to say."

She frowned. "I've heard it all. I can tell what you want, and the answer is no."

"You should hear us out," McIntyre said.

"Okay, I'll humor you," she said with a smirk. "Which of you wants to ask me out?"

"Neither," Sunday said. "But you're on the right track."

"Seriously?" Her voice lowered. "What, you want me to give you head in the bathroom?"

"You're getting warmer."

The server's eyes narrowed. Her face reddened.

"We don't want to make you mad or embarrass you," Sunday said. "And, um, we certainly aren't suggesting you look the type, but—"

"I'll give you credit for a new approach. I'm not sure what you want, but I'm pretty sure the answer will be the same."

"We work for a very rich man. He's older. Actually, he's very old. Even so, he still likes women. He knows he's old, so he pays well." Sunday paused to see if the server's expression softened. When it didn't, he continued. "He's also extremely private, so it's all about sex. No going out, no dinners, no walks along the beach. You meet in a hotel room, have sex, and he leaves."

"So you guys are his pimps?"

"Glorified pimps. We do other work as well."

"Sorry, guys. It sounds...well, disgusting, to be honest."

"He normally pays ten grand."

The server's head canted slightly, and her lips pursed as she stifled a grin.

"I'll be honest," Sunday added. "You're the hottest woman I've seen in a long time. We usually get girls from a strip joint. They're thrilled to make 10k for a few hours' work. You're in a whole different league. What'd you say your name was?"

She hesitated briefly, then said, "Amanda."

"Amanda, our boss would be very pleased to see you. It would be a huge feather in our cap. How 'bout twenty grand?"

"For the night?"

"For a couple of hours."

Amanda glanced around the bar. It was obvious she was calculating how many hours she'd have to work to earn twenty thousand dollars in tips. She nibbled on a manicured fingernail with her perfectly straight, white teeth. Her face turned serious. "Is this guy a creepy asshole that's into kinky shit?"

"No. He's an old white guy who likes attractive women. When you get older, your body changes, but your tastes don't. For most men—and women too, I assume—it gets to a point where anyone you'd want doesn't want you, and anyone who wants you, you don't want. If you're rich enough, you merely buy what you want. Personally, I think the creepy guys are the rich old farts who flaunt their hot young girlfriends."

"Yeah, they're creepy. But a lot of girls would rather have a sugar daddy than be a whore. If I did this, I'd be a whore. Doesn't matter if it's a hundred bucks or ten thousand, you're being paid for sex. A whore is a whore."

"An escort sounds better. Or an entertainer. You'd be providing entertainment to an old man." Sunday shrugged. "But, you have a point. That's exactly what it is. Money for sex. A lot of money."

"Can I think about it?"

"Sure. But not long. And we have a few rules. Our boss is rich. Mega-rich. Discretion is important. You can't go into the kitchen and discuss it with your friends. Whether you come or not, you can't mention this conversation. We can't stop you, but keep it to yourself. Also, if you come with us, you absolutely cannot speak to anyone about it. Not only is he rich, but he's also powerful. If word got out about what you did, and there was even a hint it was you, he could make your life miserable. Like jail-time miserable."

"Jeez. You make it sound so wonderful. Why the fuck would I do this?"

"We already gave you twenty thousand reasons."

"And if I did bounce this off my friend in the back?"

"We'd leave. Without you."

"How would you know?"

"Sooner or later, your friend would come out and look at us. Like he, or she, was checking us out. Even if you told them not to, they would. We know the look." Sunday looked at the time on his watch. "The boss will be at the hotel at eleven. You, or another girl, will be there waiting for him. Go ahead and think about it, but you have to let us know in ten minutes."

"But I'm working."

"Go into the lady's room. Splash a little water on your face, then tell your boss you got sick and need to go home. We're parked about a block up the street. A black Cadillac Escalade. We'll leave now. Wait ten or fifteen minutes, then come to the car. If you aren't there in twenty, we'll figure you aren't coming, and we'll leave."

Amanda bit her lower lip. "This is so crazy. I've never done anything like this. What exactly would I have to do?"

"Do you have a boyfriend?" McIntyre asked.

"No. We broke up a few months ago. He was too possessive."

"Did you have sex with him?"

"Of course."

"What about since?"

"Yeah, not a lot."

"Most likely, whatever you've done before, you'll do tonight."

"You ever watch porn?" Sunday asked.

"A few times."

"If you saw it in a video, be prepared to do the same."

Amanda cringed.

"Take the initiative," McIntyre said. "Ride 'em like a rented mule. Wear his ass out. If you keep him happy, he won't ask for anything else. It'll reach a point where he'll have had enough. He'll call his driver, who'll be with us, and then he'll leave. We'll pay you and call you an Uber."

Sunday glanced at the ticket on the table. He dropped two one-hundred-dollar bills for a seventy-dollar tab. "Twenty minutes. We'll be waiting. Unless you say no right now, and that's fine, we won't have to wait. In fact, there's a blonde at the bar who I bet would come without blinking."

Amanda bit her lower lip again. "Okay, I'll do it."

*****

Alexander and Bat sat on the balcony of the Grand Paradise Hotel. The early April air had cooled, and the breeze off the Atlantic carried a chill. They kept warm with a single malt.

"Any news on the dead girl?" Bat asked.

Alexander shook his head. "Not a word. I've followed up with the detective. He'd like to help, I think, but like Morgan, he's come up empty."

"The other night, you convinced Morgan to give you a copy of the picture she took of the dead girl."

"You convinced her, Bat. It was brilliant: use AI to restore her face so it could be an Instagram or Facebook photo. No one would ever know the photo was taken in the Medical Examiner's office. How's it going?"

"So-so," he said. "I gave it a few tries, but the images aren't great. I ran one through face recognition and got hundreds of possible matches. I'll keep working on it."

Alexander swirled his drink. The ice rattled against the glass. "I doubt I'll ever know who the girl was or who covered it up. I do know whoever it was had serious pull. They were able to squash the investigation, had the body and all evidence removed from the ME's office, and scared off the local police and sheriff's office."

"Obviously, someone with a lot of money or high up politically. Probably both."

"Definitely both. No doubt." Alexander's jaw tightened. "Which pisses me off even more. It would be nice to give the girl's family closure—if she had one. But I'd like to nail the son of a bitch who tossed her off the balcony." As he'd done many times, Alexander looked toward the balcony where the girl had fallen. He suddenly sat up in the lounger and leaned forward. "There's a light on in that room."

"There's light leaking out around the drapes. I've been here two weeks. Never seen even a flicker coming from that room. They could be cleaning it."

Alexander checked the time on his phone. "At 10:35 at night?"

"A guest checked in?"

"For the first time in two weeks?"

"It could have taken two weeks to sanitize the room. We don't know what happened in there."

Alexander leaned back in the lounger. "It's possible. Kinda strange though."

"Strange isn't the word. That hotel has a security system like Fort Knox. Employees are trained not to answer questions. Network security that would rival the NSA."

"Which means an extremely powerful person owns the hotel, or frequents it enough to make it worth the cost of the security."

"Exactly, my friend." Bat leaped to his feet. "I still have access. I'll check the cameras. See if I find out what's going on." He disappeared into the hotel room.

A few minutes later, Bat returned to the balcony. "Something's going on all right."

"What'd you see?"

"Zilch. One elevator is locked and set to go only to the seventh floor. Its camera, the cameras leading to the elevator, and all the cameras on the floor are turned off."

"Can you turn them on?"

"Not without tipping my hand. The IT guy would see the cameras go on, trace it back to me, and lock me out. I bet it's monitored 24/7. They'd spot it in minutes."

Alexander rubbed the back of his neck. "Damn it. Something's going on, and we're flying blind. I don't like it."

"Should I stroll over? Go inside, and tell them I have a reservation. While they're checking it, I can take a quick look around."

Alexander stared across the street at the balcony. "You won't see anything out of the ordinary. They aren't going to be that careless, and they will have seen you. Are the lobby cameras working?"

"They are."

"Then they'd have you on video. No bueno." Alexander took a sip of his scotch. "Can you monitor the cameras inside the hotel?"

"I can."

"Do it. See if any turn on. We might catch a glimpse of enough to tell us what's happening."

"What are you planning to do?"

"I'm going to sit here, enjoy my scotch, and keep an eye on that balcony."

SEVENTEEN

Amanda paced anxiously about the hotel room. When she'd climbed into the SUV, Sunday had asked her for her phone, then he shut it off. It wasn't a good start. She wished she'd told a friend—or at least texted one—what she was doing. Her hands trembled when it dawned on her: *No one knew where she was.*

Her instructions were simple. When her visitor arrived, she would do whatever he asked. "No," would not be in her vocabulary. She wiped her palms, now damp with sweat, on her shorts and walked to the door to peer through the peephole. The two men she knew only as Mark and Sean were standing outside.

Rightfully assuming the men were standing guard and wouldn't let her leave, she crossed to the balcony door, pulled the heavy curtain aside, and looked out. The glare turned the glass into a mirror—she saw only herself. She tugged at the handle, but it was locked. Before she could fumble the lock open, the electronic beep sounded from the main door.

Amanda froze. Struggling to catch her breath, she turned to face the door. A rotund man of considerable stature stepped in, wearing a zip-up hoodie. She'd been hoping the man she was there to please would be slim and at least halfway attractive—for an older guy. When he stepped toward the light, she could tell instantly he was neither. Severely overweight, bordering on obese. Her stomach knotted as she pictured this pig on top of her, humping like a rabid Chihuahua.

The man removed his hoodie and walked up to her. He now stood in the light where she could see him clearly.

"Christ! You look exactly like the president!"

"I am the president. Take your fucking clothes off."

*****

Amanda sat on the corner of the bed, sobbing. Her hair damp, her face streaked with smeared eyeliner, she wore a white hotel robe, the belt cinched tight around her waist. She bore little resemblance to the "ten" who had walked into the hotel less than two hours earlier.

McIntyre walked to the foot of the bed and looked down at Amanda. "Come on, babe, it couldn't have been that bad."

"No?" Amanda said, her chin quivering. "He came in, told me to take off my clothes. He didn't ask, he told me. While I stripped, he undressed and got into bed. He spread his legs and pointed to his dick. He just laid there and watched me."

"What was so bad?" Sunday asked. "I'm sure you've given head before."

Amanda's nostrils flared, and her face turned red. "After a while, he grabbed his iPad and said he needed to make social media posts. I'm like, what the fuck? Did I tell you he never got hard? After maybe fifteen minutes, he told me to go into the bathroom with him. He stood in front of a mirror so he could watch us, and told me to get on my knees. I did. He grabbed the back of my head and pulled me to his crotch. I figured he wanted to watch me give him a blow job, so I did. Suddenly, he started pissing in my mouth. I gagged and tried to pull away, but couldn't. He was holding my head right there. I was finally able to turn my head, and he peed on my face and hair. It must have excited him. He finally got an erection. He pushed me down to the floor, in a puddle of his pee, and started fucking me."

Amanda stopped to compose herself. McIntyre and Sunday stared at her, stone-faced. It wasn't the first time they'd heard a similar story.

Amanda blew her nose on a Kleenex she'd been clutching. "The fat slob didn't try to support himself. His full weight was on top of me. I guess fucking me didn't excite him because he went limp really fast. That was good because I was about to pass out. I literally couldn't breathe. So, then he gets off me, sits on the toilet, grabs my hair, and pulls my head into his crotch again. I could tell he couldn't see me, so I used my hand and went through the motions. He never knew. So I'm pretending to suck him, and he grabs his iPad and starts reading. A few minutes later, he starts cussing, pushes me to the floor, calls me every demeaning name in the book, grabs a towel, and walks out. I saw this robe hanging on the bathroom door. I dried off, put it on, and I waited. I wasn't going back into the room with him. Around ten minutes later, I heard the door open, and he was gone. A few minutes after that, you guys came back."

"It may not have been your typical date, but you're being well compensated," Sunday said.

"Not well enough. He was disgusting. He didn't want to have sex. He wanted to humiliate and demean me. News flash. He's the piece of shit."

McIntyre pulled a stack of cash from his jacket pocket. "I assume you won't be joining us again?"

"Not for ten times that amount."

McIntyre laughed. "Bullshit, baby. For ten times this—two-hundred grand—you'd eat peanuts from his ass."

Amanda jumped off the bed. "Give me my money."

McIntyre stepped back a couple of steps. "Not so fast. There are a couple of rules we need to discuss."

"Like me never telling anyone what happened here tonight? Don't worry. I—"

Sunday pulled a small .22 caliber semi-automatic pistol from his pocket, pressed it behind Amanda's left ear, and pulled the trigger. Her entire body shuddered before dropping back onto the bed.

"What the fuck, Sunday. Why'd you shoot her? You fuck! I had plans." McIntyre pulled a loaded syringe from his other pocket and held it in the air like a badge of honor. He quickly grabbed a pillow and put it under Amanda's head to absorb the hemorrhaging blood.

"Yeah, like you did last time with the little Cuban hottie. Until you fell asleep, and the bitch wandered out onto the balcony. Luckily, I was out there having a smoke."

"And you threw her off the balcony."

"No, I tried to grab her. Even drugged up, she fought like a wildcat. I slugged her to calm her down, but I must have hit her a little hard because she stumbled backward and over the rail."

"We both would have been fucked if the DOJ, FBI, and Homeland hadn't helped cover it up for us."

"I learned from that. But damn, Amanda was so fucking hot." McIntyre studied the lifeless woman on the bed. "Even with a head full of presidential piss, she's still hot." He walked over to her, opened the robe, and ogled her naked body. "No worries, she's still warm." He proceeded to unbuckle his pants.

"Are you kidding me? Are you going to fuck her corpse? You sick bastard." Sunday didn't wait for a reply. He opened the sliding-glass door, walked to the railing, and lit a cigarette.

*****

"Any luck?" Alexander asked when Bat returned to the balcony.

"No. The whole hotel's on lockdown."

"Look." Alexander nodded toward the hotel. The curtain was pulled back, and a face pressed against the glass. "Can you make it out?"

Bat squinted. "No. Too dark. It's definitely a person...and...they're gone."

"First sign of life in two weeks."

"Since they've turned off most of the cameras in the hotel and locked down the one elevator, I'd say whatever it is, it's happening or about to."

"But what is it that's happening?"

"That's the million-dollar question. Let me go inside and watch the video feeds. Hopefully, one will come back on."

An hour later, Bat returned to the balcony. "Any sign of life across the street?"

"Nope. Quiet. The light's still on in the room. Did you have any luck?"

"No. The cameras are still turned off. I checked the guest list. There are a few guests, all in rooms on the east side."

"The east side faces the ocean. Everyone wants a view."

"True. But there are always a few cheap asses who wouldn't pay the premium for an ocean view room. The whole back side of the hotel is empty."

Alexander thought about it. "There are two elevators. One in the front of the hotel and one in the back. With the back side empty, no one takes the back elevator, and no one accidentally gets off on the wrong floor. No witnesses."

"Or so they won't hear anything they aren't supposed to hear."

Alexander gazed up at the brightest stars that managed to pierce the Fort Lauderdale light pollution. "Maybe the Hispanic girl got off on the wrong floor, saw something she shouldn't have, and got tossed off the balcony."

"Shit," Bat said. "That could be exactly what happened."

"Yep. So why risk it in a hotel in the middle of the city? If you're engaging in acts so nefarious that you kill anyone who sees or hears you, why do it in a hotel? If they can afford to buy out half a hotel, they could charter a yacht and have all the privacy in the world. There'd be fewer people to pay off as well."

"Hiring a yacht would make a lot more sense. Find a boat with an unscrupulous captain and crew. No worries. Didn't the *Miss Jana* fit that bill at one time?"

"Not exactly. She only trafficked young girls."

Bat laughed. "Like Mayte and her sister. They both match the description of the dead girl."

"They do..." Alexander's eyes widened. "This could be a trafficking operation. They're smuggling in young girls to sell them. They house them in the hotel, show them off to bidders, and sell them. One tried to escape and got thrown off the balcony."

"Human trafficking makes a lot of sense," Bat said.

"It does, and it doesn't. Would human traffickers have enough power to cover up a murder?"

"If it involves a foreign government like Venezuela, Russia, or Cuba, it does. I've got an idea," Bat said. He went back into the hotel room.

Alexander was curious about Bat's idea. He knew he'd find out in due time. He adjusted his lounger to a more upright position to get a better view of the balcony across the street. The ice had melted in the scotch sitting on the table next to him. He'd lost interest in alcohol.

The common wind gusts throughout the afternoon had given way to a gentle breeze. Sounds from the nearby waves breaking onto the beach were barely audible. A muffled crack broke the silence.

Alexander's head shot up. He instantly looked toward the balcony across the street. There was no movement. "Bat," he said in a hushed tone. When there was no response, he repeated, slightly louder.

Bat came to the door. "Did you call me?"

"Yes. Did you hear that?"

Bat cocked his head and listened. "No. Only the sound of the surf."

"I mean, a few seconds ago. It sounded like a gunshot."

"I didn't hear any bangs. Was it loud?"

"Not particularly. It sounded muffled, as if it came from inside a closed room. It sounded like a small caliber round. A .22 or .25. Could have been a .32, but not likely. It sounded like a sharp, high-pitched crack or pop. Not the boom or a kathump from a nine or a .38."

"You think it came from the hotel?"

"Hell, it could have come from anywhere. But my money's not only on it coming from the hotel, but coming from that room. Wait...someone's coming out the door. Duck in and turn out the room light."

Bat quickly turned out the lights. Alexander slowly slid off the lounger onto the floor, rolled over to the glass door, and stood. Moving slowly with his back to the glass, he reached the wall—out of sight from the balcony across the street.

"Is there a way to turn the front screen of the phone off while I video?"

"There is, but it's complicated. If you want to start recording now, you don't have time. Hang on." Bat ducked inside and came back with a hotel brochure. "Cover the screen with this."

Alexander started video recording, set the optical zoom to 3x, and placed the brochure over the screen. He positioned himself so he could see the hotel with one eye and pointed the camera at the man standing on the balcony across the street.

"He lit a cigarette," Alexander whispered. He knew there was little chance the man on the balcony across the street could hear him, but he took no chances. "He's looking at his phone. It's bright, but his face is tilted down. We may not get a shot of his face."

"He's standing on the balcony, having a smoke, and looking at his phone. Doesn't sound like a man who recently shot someone."

Alexander held the camera steady and kept recording. He turned his head toward Bat. "Why do you always have to make sense?" With less enthusiasm, he turned his attention back to the man across the street. "Yeah, he's just standing there, casually smoking and scrolling through his phone."

"Keep recording," Bat said from the door.

An orange glow flew off the balcony as the man flicked the cigarette butt away. He walked to the door, pushed the curtain aside, stood for a second, stepped in, and closed the door and curtain behind him.

"He's gone." Alexander lowered his phone and hit Stop. "I guess you were right. He was just having a smoke. Hotels don't allow smoking in the rooms anymore. You have to go outside to smoke."

"AirDrop the video to my phone. I'll load it onto my laptop. We'll get a much better image. We could have missed something. You coming?"

"I'm going to watch the room a little longer. If he's staying in the room, one of two things will happen. He smoked his last cigarette. He'll go in, brush his teeth, pee, and go to bed. The lights will go out soon. Or, he's a night owl, and he'll be back out for another cigarette within twenty minutes. If the lights stay on, and he doesn't come back out, I'd say I did hear a shot, it did come from that room, and he needed a smoke to calm his nerves. Now that he's had a smoke, he's inside cleaning the mess."

Bat's head bobbed. "That's a lot of ifs and speculation. Hopefully, the video will give us some answers."

Once the video was transferred to Bat's phone, he downloaded the file to his laptop. He watched it in real time first. Nothing jumped out. He restarted the video and fast-forwarded to the part where the cigarette lit. When the flame illuminated the man's face, Bat paused the video and made several screenshots.

Next, he fast-forwarded to where the man used his cell phone. The lighting was better than it was with the lighter, but the man's head was down. Bad angle. More fast-forwarding. Bat stopped when the man pulled the curtain back, then went frame by frame. "Fuck me!" he said softly, then yelled, "Alex, come in here."

EIGHTEEN

Alexander stared at the laptop screen. The frame appeared to show a girl lying on the bed. She looked to be naked—and maybe dead. The lower portion of her body was too dark to make out, possibly shaded by a person standing beside her.

"Go back to the man on the balcony," Alexander said. "He's a similar size and weight to the guy who was following the girl the other night. What was her name?"

"Jessica?"

"Yeah, Jessica. If he's the guy who was tailing her, it may be good we happened along."

"That's true," Bat said, his eyes still glued to the video. "But this is now. I think we have a dead girl and possibly another person in that hotel room."

Alexander shook his head slowly. "Or a sleeping girl."

"Who doesn't stir when another person walks in the room?"

"She could be passed out."

Bat selected the clearest frame from the video and zoomed in. "There's not enough detail, but look." He pointed to discoloration on the left side of the girl's head and the bright red pillow beneath it.

"Blood?"

"Or her hair's dyed in several colors. It's common. It could be a red pillowcase."

"Her hair isn't dyed. How many hotels have red pillowcases?"

"I agree with you, but we can't do a damn thing about it."

"Call the detective...Amos," Bat said.

"And tell him there might be a dead girl in the hotel, and she may have been shot because I thought I may have heard a gunshot which may have come from a hotel room across the street? No idea which one. That's not enough to even get him interested, let alone enough probable cause for a warrant."

*****

Mark "Bloody" Sunday took a drag off his cigarette. He'd done a lot of bad things in his life, but what his partner was doing to the girl in the hotel room crossed the line. She was beautiful, but she was dead. Sunday shivered. He took another drag and tossed the glowing butt off the balcony.

Sunday checked the time. 1:15 in the morning. Almost fifteen minutes had passed since he'd shot the girl. Plenty of time for McIntyre to abuse her corpse.

Sunday walked slowly to the room's door, opened it, and pulled the curtain aside. "You done?"

A now-dressed McIntyre stood over Amanda, admiring her. He gently squeezed her breasts. "I am. Such a waste. She was perfect."

"You knew we'd kill her when we picked her up. That's what we do."

"Not this one. I would have taken her to the boat and disappeared with her, at least for a while. She wouldn't have liked it, but in the middle of the ocean, she'd either fuck or swim. She'd have come around."

"She's still going for a boat ride. She won't fuck or swim. Just sink."

McIntyre spun and stuck his finger in Sunday's chest. "Don't be crude."

"You're the one who fucked a dead body."

"She wasn't dead. Maybe brain dead. But I could still feel her heart. It took a while for her to bleed out."

Sunday slapped McIntyre's finger away. "Never point your finger at me again, or I'll break it."

McIntyre's eyes narrowed. Sunday was bigger, likely stronger, and he had a gun in his pocket.

McIntyre took several long, controlled breaths to quell his anger. "Don't shoot any more girls until I tell you to."

Sunday put his hand in his pocket and gripped his Ruger Lite Rack LCP II .22 LR semi-auto pistol. His gun of choice for close-range killing. The .22 caliber long rifle bullet has plenty of umph to penetrate a skull. After penetration, the bullet would fragment, scattering pieces of lead, assuring the cessation of all brain function. The fragmented bullet was impossible to test for ballistics. The downside was that a .22 was only guaranteed to be lethal when fired at point-blank range, directly behind the ear.

At the moment, Sunday was standing in front of his intended target, a target who was keenly aware that he might pull his gun and was ready. Now was not the time or place.

"We need to get rid of her," he said.

"I'll get a cart and let the staff know we're done. As usual, the staff will clean the room after we remove the body." McIntyre took one more admiring look at Amanda. "Such a fuck'n waste." He left the room, took the direct elevator to the lobby, and switched to the elevator that went to the second-floor laundry room. He needed the extra-large laundry hamper in the corner, where it had been every other time he went to pick it up. He pulled it from the wall and reversed his steps back to the room.

Sunday closed Amanda's robe and tied the belt. When McIntyre returned with the laundry hamper, Sunday tossed Amanda's phone and purse into it. The two men then dumped Amanda into the hamper and covered her with a comforter from the bed.

After a quick sweep of the room to make sure they had all of Amanda's belongings, Sunday and McIntyre rolled the hamper to the elevator. Just like before, they'd have to ride down to the lobby and transfer to another elevator to reach the parking garage beneath the hotel.

It was the part of the job both men hated most. Even with only a few guests in the hotel, they were too exposed.

The Cadillac SUV was parked outside the elevator door in a reserved spot. Sunday made sure no one else was in the garage, then he opened the vehicle's tailgate. After spreading the comforter on the cargo bed, the men hoisted Amanda onto it and wrapped her. Sunday pressed the button to close the tailgate while McIntyre pushed the hamper out of the way. A staff member would retrieve it later.

At two in the morning, Fort Lauderdale traffic was light. That was the good news. The bad news was that at that hour, the few people on the road were likely coming from bars. The cops know it, and are on the lookout for drunk drivers.

Sunday drove cautiously, keeping the SUV a few miles above the speed limit at most. He braked at yellow lights rather than running them and used his turn signal for every lane change and turn.

Getting stopped for a minor traffic violation would be disastrous. A driver's license check would flag them as convicted felons, likely triggering a vehicle search. Finding a body in the cargo area would require another major cover-up.

They knew they were running low on favors. They also knew men like them rarely made it to trial. They'd seen how it worked before: a dead detainee in a holding cell, a bedsheet tied to a vent, and an official ruling of suicide.

The Back Cove 372 Downeast-style cruiser was moored at a private dock off A1A between Palm Beach and Fort Lauderdale, a thousand yards north of Hillsboro Inlet. Trees blocked the view from the street. A small, gravel road snaked around the trees to the secluded concrete dock.

Sunday backed the SUV to the ramp. Both men breathed a sigh of relief once they were parked. They popped the hatch. Amanda was still flexible—full rigor wouldn't set in for hours.

Each man grabbed an end and carried Amanda to the boat. Sunday dropped her legs onto the deck. McIntyre laid her down gently.

"What? You gonna fuck her again?"

McIntyre lunged toward Sunday and threw a wild punch that was easily dodged. Sunday countered with a right fist to McIntyre's jaw. The punch dropped him.

"Don't let a dead bitch get you killed, Sean."

McIntyre couldn't help himself. Amanda was the most beautiful woman he'd ever seen. If it were possible to fall in love at first sight, he had. He had known her fate when she had agreed to come with them. But he had had a plan: Knock her out. Put her on the Back Cove 372 and head toward the Bahamas. The boat had plenty of range and was big enough to make the passage. Once in the islands, he would've anchored in secluded coves and wooed her. He would tell her how Sunday would've killed her if he hadn't kidnapped her—though he might not use the word "kidnapped." He would tell her that he took her to save her life, that they'd have to stay in the islands for a while, and that they couldn't go back because Sunday would still kill her. McIntyre knew that eventually Amanda would have come around. She'd have fallen madly in love with him, and they'd live happily ever after, just like in every Hallmark Christmas movie.

Instead, while Sunday drove the boat toward Hillsboro Inlet, McIntyre wrapped a chain around Amanda and secured it with wire. Once in the Atlantic, Sunday throttled up the single 600hp Cummins diesel engine, and the boat quickly hit its cruising speed of twenty-five knots. In an hour, they'd be over twenty miles offshore, where Amanda would find her final resting place in seven hundred and fifty feet of water.

*****

"Does the hotel have a parking garage?" Bat asked.

"Yes. We walked past the entrance the other night."

"So it's in the front. No way to see it from here. If he leaves from the garage, we'll never see him. We could walk around to the front and watch."

Alexander grimaced. "It's late. Or early, depending on your perspective. We'd stick out standing out there. He's probably already gone."

"With or without the body?"

Alexander thought it over for a minute. "It could have been a shadow from something else, but I think there were two people in that room. I'd say they killed her and have a plan to get rid of her. The staff takes care of the room, and the killer takes care of the body."

"They take her out and dump her along the side of a road or in a dumpster?"

"Not likely. This seems to be well planned, especially if the hotel staff cleans the room. They brought a girl to the hotel, used her, and killed her. They won't leave her on the side of the road to be found. Assuming someone had sex with the girl, there would be too much DNA evidence—semen, sweat, hair, skin cells—to dump the body where it would be found. They either hauled her to the Everglades and dumped her, or took her out to sea and tossed her overboard. Either way, she'll never be found."

Bat rubbed the back of his neck. "Alex. You're close. But think about it. If the guy in the video is the guy who followed Jessica, and his plan was to lure her to his room, where he was going to rape her, and maybe kill her, how could he do it? Someone with enough clout to empty a wing of the hotel isn't going after some chick walking along A1A."

"Good point. And considering that it's likely the same room a young girl recently fell to her death from, and how the subsequent investigation was squashed, we aren't talking about some random dude on vacation picking up a girl in a bar and bringing her to the hotel for sex, and it gets out of hand and she dies."

"You're the investigator," Bat said. "What's your gut say? A tourist with big money? A local?"

"Definitely not a tourist. And I'd bet the guy from the balcony killed her, but he didn't have sex with her. Maybe sloppy seconds. No, he brought her to the room for someone else's pleasure. Someone with serious money and even more connections."

"Would you like to know what bothers me?" Bat asked.

"Sure."

"If what we speculate is true, then the operation they have going on across the street is going to be a well-oiled machine. Lure a woman into a room in a hotel. A hotel that has more security than the White House. More than likely, she's molested—raped would be more accurate—killed, and disposed of—all without a trace of evidence. What happened last time? Why did the girl fall from the balcony?"

"Good questions. I have no answers. Anything else?"

"Assuming we're correct about tonight, that's two dead women in just over two weeks. How many more are there?"

Alexander's face glowed red. He rubbed the stubble on his chin. "I hate to even think about it. Ten? Twenty? Fifty? More? We've got to figure it out and stop it."

"No doubt. But, how? The local LEOs aren't inclined to help."

"Detective Amos will help. Not with what we have now. But I have a hunch, and if it pans out, he will help."

"Care to share this hunch?"

"They picked this girl up recently. Probably last night. From the video, she's blonde. Blonde with streaks of red or pink, although I'm convinced the color we saw was blood. Black-haired Hispanic girls disappear by the droves in South Florida. Not so much with blondes. If she had any family or friends, I'd expect a missing persons report to be filed within a day or two. I'll ask Amos to watch for it. If we can identify the girl and track her movements, we might find the men who took her. At the absolute minimum, we learn how these guys operate. If we can find any solid evidence of what we think has happened, we'll give it to Amos. I have a feeling he'll help."

"We could also give the girl's family closure."

Alexander grimaced. "I don't know. If we do get a missing person report for a young—I'm assuming she's young—blonde, and we're able to ID her, unless we're one hundred percent sure she's the girl we saw in the video, or we can prove she's dead, I wouldn't want to tell the family. We could be wrong."

Light began to creep in around the closed curtains at the balcony door.

"Sun's coming up." Alexander opened the curtains and stepped onto the balcony. The early morning air was cool and damp. Dew coated the lounger. The half-empty glass of watered-down scotch sat beside it.

Out of habit, Alexander looked at the balcony. It was too light outside to tell whether the room's lights were still on. Movement in the small driveway behind the Overlook Hotel caught his eye. A young woman dressed in white tossed a plastic bag into a dumpster.

"What time is it?" Alexander asked Bat, who'd followed him onto the balcony.

"Almost seven."

"A little early for maid service to be dumping trash."

"Way early. Unless they just cleaned up a murder scene."

"We need to get that bag," Alexander said. "Do they have cameras monitoring the dumpster?"

"I can check." Bat disappeared into the hotel room and returned a few minutes later. "No cameras are active."

"Stay here. Call me if anyone comes out of the hotel."

A few minutes later, Alexander crossed the street. He hugged the wall along the hotel and slipped behind the large dumpsters. Bat saw him and gave him a thumbs-up. Alexander peeked into the bin where he saw the girl toss the bag. All the plastic garbage bags, except one, were damp with morning dew. He grabbed the dry bag and darted back to the hotel.

Bat was waiting and opened the door for him. "Good job."

Alexander tossed the bag onto the floor. "Let's hope there's evidence in it. You don't have any vinyl gloves, do you?"

Bat frowned. "Not on me, no."

"I'm not opening the bag until I get gloves. I should have been wearing gloves when I grabbed the bag, but I couldn't wait."

"The medical examiner," Bat said. "She'd have gloves. In fact, she should be here, in case there is any evidence in the bag."

"Great call."

NINETEEN

Morgan was asleep when Alexander called. She had muted her phone, so the call went to voicemail. One advantage of being a medical examiner, compared to a practicing doctor, is that the patients are already dead. There are no emergencies.

Forty-five minutes after the missed call, Morgan began to stir. The soft touch against her breast slowly pulled her from a deep sleep. Realizing it was someone's hand, she jolted awake and instinctively slapped it away.

"I'm so sorry, Morgan," Jessica said. "When I woke, you were lying there, the sheet had slid off, and you looked so delightful. I stayed still as long as I could. I had to touch you. I was tempted to lean over and nibble on you, but I'm glad I didn't. You slap hard."

Morgan stretched. "I'm sorry I slapped your hand. Next time, climb on top of me and pin me down before you touch me."

Jessica laughed. "How 'bout I nudge you awake before I touch you? Or let you sleep and wake up naturally?"

"Nudging me awake sounds good. I can sleep anytime." Morgan rolled to her side and gently kissed her bedmate. The kiss lingered and deepened before Jessica finally pulled back.

"I should go to the bathroom before we get too amorous."

"Me too. You go first."

Jessica crawled out of bed and disappeared into the bathroom. Morgan reached for her phone. She scrolled through a couple of overnight text messages and noticed a missed call. At first, she dismissed it as spam—no name, not in contacts, and who still calls anymore? Against her better judgment, she hit Play.

Hi Morgan. This is Alex Christian. We met the other night. I may have information about the girl who fell from the balcony. Well, not exactly about her, but related. I need your help. Sorry about calling so early, but it's important. Can you call me as soon as possible?

Morgan sat up in bed, hit the redial button, and put the call on speaker. Jessica came out of the bathroom, noticed Morgan on the phone, and cocked her head. Morgan held up her hand. Jessica, still curious, quietly slipped back into bed and put her arm across Morgan's waist. Alexander answered on the first ring.

"Hi Alex. This is Morgan," she said. "I woke up and saw your message. What's going on?"

Alexander explained what he and Bat had witnessed overnight, beginning with what he believed was a gunshot. Jessica sat up and listened intently to the call. When he got to the part about stealing the bag of trash from the hotel's dumpster, Morgan interrupted him.

"Don't open the bag. I'll be right over." Jessica nudged Morgan in the ribs. "Um...do you mind if Jessica comes along?"

"No...it's fine. In fact, we've got grainy images of the man on the balcony. It might be the man who followed her the other night. I'd like her to look at the pictures."

"We're twenty-five minutes away. Give us forty-five."

"We're in room 715 of the Grand Paradise Hotel. It's the hotel we had drinks in the other night."

"We'll be there shortly."

"Thanks," Alexander said.

Morgan ended the call. "We need to go."

It took the two women less time than Morgan expected to dress and get out the door. Morgan tossed two large white Tyvek HAZMAT suits she kept for the rare times she was called to a crime scene and a box of six-mil heavy-duty nitrile gloves into the car. They were on the road ten minutes after the call with Alexander.

The drive to the hotel was silent. Morgan was focused on the road and what she might do if the garbage bag contained evidence of a murder. Jessica had a sinking feeling the man on the balcony would be Mark Sunday. Or, possibly, Sean McIntyre. If either showed up in the photos, should she identify them? If she did, questions would follow. Lots of questions.

Morgan parked in the visitor lot behind the hotel. She grabbed the box of gloves. Jessica carried the unopened two-pack of suits. They walked briskly into the hotel and to the elevators. Morgan pressed the button for the seventh floor. The elevator took forever. Morgan texted Alexander:

In the lobby. On our way up.

Alexander was standing in front of the elevator doors when they opened. He reached out and gave each woman a gentle hug. "Thank you for coming," he said.

"You're welcome. I hope we find something...I mean..."

"I know what you mean. I have a similar feeling. Depending on what we find, it might mean there's another dead girl out there."

Bat, waiting at the door to the room, ushered them in. The large white plastic bag sat between the bed and the door. The four of them stood staring at it.

"I brought two suits and gloves. The suits are large, but I forgot how big you were, Alex."

"That's okay. I'm going to let you go through the bag. I'll stand by in case you need me. Otherwise, we'll observe."

Morgan looked at Jessica. "Can one of you document what we're doing?”

“I can,” Jessica said, pulling out her phone.

Morgan put on the suit and gloved up. She slowly untied the band that secured the bag’s top. A powerful wave of bleach filled the room the moment it opened. Morgan jerked back and covered her mouth and nose with her forearm. The others did the same.

“I can’t believe I forgot masks,” Morgan said. “Bat, can you open the door to the balcony?”

Jessica stepped onto the bed to get a better angle on the bag and to be farther from the smell. Alexander put on a pair of gloves and stepped closer to hold the bag open.

“Bleach. Not a good sign. You don’t use that amount of bleach in the routine cleaning of a hotel room.”

“I agree,” Alexander said. “That much bleach is used to sanitize a crime scene.”

“Fuck!” Jessica blurted.

The three snapped their heads her way.

“I’m sorry.”

“Don’t be,” Alexander said. “We all feel the same.”

Morgan dug into the bag. She stopped and looked around the room. “Fuck! We don’t have another bag to put this stuff into.”

Jessica smiled at Morgan. She knew the “fuck” was for her benefit.

“I’ll see if I can find a housekeeper and get a couple of plastic bags.” Bat left the room before anyone could respond.

“Let’s step outside until he gets back. The odor of the bleach is over-whelming.”

On the balcony, each took several deep breaths.

“You said you had pictures of the person who was in the room. Could I see them?” Jessica asked.

“Bat has them on his laptop,” Alexander said. “When he gets back, I’ll have him show them to you.”

“Could it wait until we go through the bag? I’d like to get this over with.”

“Of course,” Jessica said. “I thought since we were waiting—”

“Hello,” Bat yelled when he returned and found the room empty.

Morgan hurried back in. Bat held several bags aloft, like a hunter with his trophy.

"There was a cart down the hall. I grabbed a handful of bags."

Morgan took an empty bag and spread it out on the floor. She began slowly pulling items from the garbage bag Alexander had pilfered from the dumpster. The first few bleach-soaked paper towels she removed were white. As she pulled out more, the stains darkened. With each piece Morgan removed, the color deepened to brownish-red.

"This is blood," Morgan said. "Chlorine bleach reacts with the proteins and iron in blood, causing it to darken—turn this brownish-red color." She continued to pull out paper towels. Each one was darker than the last.

"Oh, fuck," Morgan said, the words spoken in a much deeper voice. Everyone knew the word wasn't for Jessica's benefit. "This is bad." She pulled out a blood-soaked pillowcase and held it up for Jessica to document.

"Jesus," Jessica whispered. Her body shivered, but she kept her phone steady and continued to video.

"Open a new bag, please, Alex. I want to preserve this."

Alexander opened a bag, and Morgan carefully dropped the pillowcase into it.

"Damn," she said. "I forgot a Sharpie, too."

Bat pulled a black Sharpie from his satchel and handed it to Morgan, who refused to take it.

"Thank you, but give it to Alex. Alex, tie the bag and put today's date and time on it. Add, 'Evidence Bag 1'."

Morgan returned to the original bag. She pulled out a few more stained paper towels and froze. She tilted her head and squeezed her eyes shut. After several deep breaths, she sighed heavily, opened her eyes, and pulled out a pair of pink panties.

Jessica gasped. Her phone dipped slightly before she steadied it. Alexander and Bat stared at the panties, then looked away. Morgan pulled out the last few items from the original bag. More stained paper towels and a washcloth with reddish-orange stains. She put the paper towels in the bag with the others and the washcloth in a separate bag.

"I'm going to have to notify the police," Morgan said, pulling off her gloves.

Alexander tied the tops of the three bags, labeled the other two bags, and removed his gloves. "Let's not get hasty."

"About calling the police? We must. This is definitely evidence of a crime."

"Is it?"

"What the fuck, Alex. You know it is." Morgan's nostrils flared.

"I know it is. But would a cop? Especially one who doesn't want to get involved with whatever happened in that hotel, and since it's the same room a girl fell from."

"I think a couple had been going at it hot and heavy when it was interrupted by a menstrual period, or a bloody nose. The man could have had the bloody nose," Bat said. "They slid a pillow under her ass and kept going, or if you go with a bloody nose, it would be all over the pillow. Then, when they left, she forgot her panties. The housekeeping staff was so disgusted that they threw the panties and pillowcase in the trash and disinfected the room with bleach. No crime committed."

"You're pretty close," Alexander said. "If not exactly how they'd play it. Heck, if push came to shove, they'd track down the passionate couple, who'd admit they were in the room and left it a bloody mess."

"Not to mention the evidence would more than likely disappear," Bat said.

Jessica stopped recording and set her phone down. She stepped off the bed. "What are you going to do?"

The room went silent.

Morgan carefully removed her HAZMAT suit. "First, I need to wash my hands. Excuse me."

"I should do the same." Alexander looked at the three labeled garbage bags sitting in the middle of the floor. "I should take care of these first."

"Put all three, plus the original bag, in one new bag and tie it up," Morgan yelled from the bathroom.

By the time Alexander had double-bagged the bags, Morgan was out of the bathroom. He went in and scrubbed his hands. When he came out, Morgan and Jessica were huddled with Bat over his laptop. He showed them the key moments of the video and opened the screenshots.

"He looks like the guy who followed you," Morgan said to Jessica after studying the images.

"I'm sure it is," Jessica said. "His name is Mark Sunday. They call him 'Bloody' Sunday." She brought up the booking photo of Sunday on her phone.

No one looked at the picture on Jessica's phone. All eyes were on her.

"I guess I have some 'splaining to do."

*****

When they returned from dumping Amanda's body at sea, McIntyre was still not speaking to Sunday. He sat on the aft deck, staring at the water, and thinking about Amanda. He considered killing Sunday, turning the boat around, and getting lost in the Bahamas for a while. He was tempted, but it wasn't the right time. He decided he would wait. He'd do it next time, and he'd take a girl, whoever she might be. He hoped they could find another girl as pretty as Amanda and convince her to come along. It should be easy. Most of the girls had been pretty. Not perfect, like Amanda, but close. She didn't have to be blonde either. He remembered the Hispanic girl with long black hair. She was adorable. She'd do.

"Get ready to tie up," Sunday yelled. He slowed the boat and maneuvered it close to the dock. "Sean! Grab a line," he yelled again, snapping McIntyre out of his thoughts. He nudged the boat against the dock.

McIntyre tossed rubber fenders over the side, then tied the aft line to a pier and went forward to secure the bow line. "All done," he yelled back at Sunday.

Sunday cut the engine and climbed down from the bridge. "Let's wash the deck down and get the hell out of here. It's been a long night." He pulled a hose and a mop from the dock box. He gave the mop to

McIntyre. "You swab, I'll spray."

McIntyre scowled at his partner. "Why are you laughing?"

"I was picturing how the girl must have reacted. First, when she discovered she'd be fucking the president. Then, while she was giving him head, he pissed in her mouth. I bet she'd never had a golden shower." Sunday laughed harder.

McIntyre gripped the mop handle until his knuckles turned white. His face turned red. It took every bit of anger control to not stuff the mop down Sunday's throat. Instead, he kept mopping, channeling the anger into scrubbing away any trace that Amanda had been on the boat.

One day. One day soon. I'll take care of you.

The thought put McIntyre at ease. A slight smile came to his face. "Hey, Sunday, who owns this boat, anyway?"

"Don't know. A backer of the boss, I guess. I was given the keys and a credit card to buy fuel, and told I could use it any time. I'm not sure they know what we use the boat for."

"You never let anyone know before we use it? What if we show up here one day and the boat's not here?"

"It'll be here. But if, for some crazy reason, it isn't, plan B. We'd head to the Everglades. There are plenty of hungry alligators there waiting for a warm meal." Sunday chuckled. "I think it would be a little cold by the time they got it. But still, them gators would love those sweet young honeys we've been feeding to the fishes."

McIntyre snapped the mop handle over his knee and jabbed the pointed end into Sunday's chest.

Sunday saw the fire in his eyes, and backed off. "Take it easy. What the fuck's gotten into you? Oh...Amanda."

"Yeah, so? I don't like killing any of the girls. You enjoy it."

"You want to stop?"

McIntyre knew there was no stopping. He'd never walk away from the job. He wasn't sure what would happen when the president was no longer the president. He had money, and he would still want to molest young girls. They might continue for a while.

He lowered the broken mop handle, but kept an eye on Sunday. "No, I ain't gonna find a better job. I hate killing pretty girls."

"You'd be okay killing ugly girls?"

"I didn't say that. But honestly, it would be better if they were dogs."

"You can forget it. Ain't gonna happen. We present the boss with an ugly girl, and we're both fired." Sunday inspected the deck. "That should do it. We can wrap it up here. You owe the owner a new mop."

"He can deduct it from my paycheck."

Sunday coiled the hose and stowed it in the dock box. "Take the broken mop to the next dock and toss it. There's no trash bin here. I'll pick you up after I lock the boat."

McIntyre eyed the dock, and there was a bin. Was Sunday setting him up? "Okay."

He walked down the road, hugging the row of mangrove trees. If he heard Sunday racing up behind him, trying to run him down, he could jump into the trees out of harm's way.

Sunday was waiting in the SUV when McIntyre returned from the neighboring dock. Sunday wasn't going to kill him. Not today.

McIntyre used the ride to plan his escape. He would do it on the next job. One more kill. Not a girl—Sunday.

*****

Alexander, Bat, and Morgan sat on the balcony of the Grand Paradise Hotel. They listened to Jessica's explanation of how she knew Sunday and McIntyre.

"I'm sorry," she said. "You were spot on when you said I was lying, Alex."

"I knew you were. But for the life of me, I don't understand why you weren't willing to share the fact that you and your friends were plotting to assassinate the president of the United States with five people you'd just met." Alexander laughed at his comment.

The somber mood lightened a fraction.

"In retrospect, I should have." Jessica cupped her hands over her mouth to cover her dropped jaw. "Do you know what this means?"

They all knew. Bat said it aloud: "Sunday and McIntyre work for the president. That means there's a good chance the president of the

United States was in that hotel room last night. He had sex with a girl, and the girl was killed. Same thing a few weeks ago. He's corrupt enough to do it and powerful enough to cover it up. I can't think of anyone else with that much clout."

"There had to be a major fuck-up a few weeks ago when the girl fell to her death," Alexander said. "Last night was how it was supposed to go. More than likely, the way it's gone many times before. Except last night, I happened to be sitting here and heard a gunshot. I wouldn't have heard it from my condo, even if I'd been on my balcony at that time of night. I'm sure I haven't heard any gunshots before. This is Fort Lauderdale, not Overtown. Had I heard a pop, I would've assumed it was a firecracker or a car backfiring."

"What are we going to do?" Morgan asked. "Bat's right. If I tell anyone about the evidence we have, it will disappear."

Alexander walked to the railing, and—for what felt like the hundredth time—looked at the hotel across the street. The image of the girl falling motivated him. Bat, Morgan, and Jessica sat quietly and let Alexander think.

After several minutes, Alexander turned around. "This is what we should do. Morgan, can you take the evidence to the morgue and store it?"

"Yes. Absolutely. I can put it in a cold locker. That'll preserve it."

"Perfect. I'm going to text Detective Amos and ask him to look for any blonde females reported missing. If she hasn't already been reported, hopefully, she will be soon. If we can get a name, we can investigate. Bat, check for cameras from other buildings and hotels in the area. See if you can spot a vehicle big enough to haul a body."

"Alex," Jessica interrupted. "I'm sorry, I should have mentioned it. Sunday and McIntyre were in a black Cadillac SUV. We believe they entered a parking garage two blocks over. There could be a tunnel connecting the hotels."

"Don't be sorry, Jessica, that's good info. Thank you. Anything else?"

"No. We do think there is a hidden driveway out of the president's compound, which we're calling the Eagle's Nest."

"Appropriate," Morgan said.

"The code name for the president is 'Cockwomble."

"What?" Morgan said.

"Cockwomble," Bat said. "It's a foolish, obnoxious person who makes stupid comments and has an inflated sense of their own intelligence. Our current president."

Morgan threw her head back and slapped the arm of her chair. "So appropriate. Who came up with it?"

"My friend, Willie."

"I'd like to meet him," Alexander said. "We should get together with all your friends. You said they were talking about quitting the experiment?"

"We all met yesterday morning. Willie feels the excitement has worn off. I do too, but more importantly, I don't want to risk my relationship with Morgan. Jerry said he would take the president out if we had a good plan. He's a trained CIA assassin. Hard to say if he would do it. We decided to take a couple of days off to think about it. We're going to meet tonight to decide what to do."

Had he not been up all night, the revelation that a trained assassin was contemplating killing the president would have raised alarms. Alexander was too tired to care. "Any chance they could come here? Or, we could go there to meet them?"

"I'm a bit apprehensive about telling them I told you about them. I'm not sure how they'll react."

Mention that we believe the two men you identified recruit women—for lack of a better word—to have sex with the president. Afterward, the women end up dead. Tell them Bat and I are looking into it. I assume you're in, Morgan?"

"All the way."

"And we need their help to, at the very least, stop them. Busting those two, Sunday and McIntyre, and putting them behind bars for life would be even better. Hopefully, we can nail Cockwomble too. But that will be difficult. If we can't...well...we can discuss letting your friend have his shot."

TWENTY

Morgan was as surprised as Alexander and Bat when Jessica told them how she knew Sunday and McIntyre. She felt a small sting of hurt that her new lover had not confided in her. Still, she completely understood Jessica's reluctance—the details of the group's mission were explosive.

During the thirty-minute drive from the hotel to the Medical Examiner's office, Jessica explained what her group had been doing for the past two weeks. She rambled a bit, repeating some of what she'd told them earlier.

"We're meeting later to decide what to do. I was ready to quit. I've changed my mind."

"What about Jerry? Was he serious?" Morgan asked.

"I don't know how serious he was. I heard he and Sam drove to Key West. Neither had been there. I'm not sure they realized how far it was from West Palm."

"It's a lot closer than it is to DC."

"Very true."

"The Keys are a great place to unwind, chill, and forget about the troubles of the world."

"We should go there for a long weekend when this is over," Jessica said.

Morgan put her hand on Jessica's. "Key West sounds lovely. Let's do it." Morgan paused. "Can I ask you a question?"

"Do you need to ask? Is it about what we were planning?"

"No. It's personal."

Jessica shifted in her seat to face Morgan fully. "Okay."

"You're so beautiful."

Jessica blushed. "Thank you. But that's not a question."

"Ha ha. You're also feminine. You don't come across as butch at all, even though you try to. Your hair. Your clothes. It's all part of the image, but it doesn't really fit you.

"You're right. Honestly, I don't like masculine women. But before I changed my style, that's all that would hit on me. So I thought, if I'm butch, more lipstick lesbians would notice me."

"Did that work?"

"You tell me."

Morgan laughed and slapped the steering wheel. "I guess it did. But I would have anyway, as long as I was sure you were gay." She put her hand back on Jessica's. "I love you as you are, but would you consider going back to femme?"

"What did you say?"

"Would you go femme again?"

"Before that. You said you loved me. Was it a figure of speech?"

Morgan bit her lower lip. "It was not. I know, it's way too soon, but I knew right away. I hope I haven't scared you away."

Jessica pulled Morgan's hand to her mouth and kissed it. "Not too soon at all. I love you, too. Knew it after the first night. How long until we get home?"

"Not long. We've got to stop by the office to drop off the evidence bags."

"Hurry. My heart is jumping out of my chest."

At the Broward County Medical Examiner's building, Morgan used a fresh pair of vinyl gloves to carry the evidence bags inside. She placed the bags in a cold locker, closed the door, and locked it. "That should keep anyone from tampering with it," she said.

Jessica watched with her arms crossed, tight against her chest. "This place gives me the chills. How do you work here?"

"You get used to it. By the time you get out of med school, you're used to corpses. I'm still bothered when a child is brought in. Especially a victim of child abuse." Morgan shivered. "I get pissed when I think about those cases."

"I'm sure seeing dead children has to be rough." Jessica gave Morgan a long hug. "You are amazing."

The women embraced until Morgan pulled back slightly. "We should go. I desperately need a shower."

Jessica brushed her chest with her hands and frowned.

"You're fine," Morgan said. "I wore the HAZMAT suit. I mean, I feel dirty."

Jessica exhaled. "Even so, I could use a shower too." She winked at Morgan, who smiled.

The two left the ME's office. Morgan lived less than five minutes away. On the drive, Morgan asked about the group meeting scheduled for later in the evening.

"Are you going?"

"Yes. I'd like you to go with me."

"Of course, I will. But why? I have a feeling they aren't going to be thrilled you told me and the others about your plans."

"Oh, they're going to be pissed. With you there, they may not tell me how they really feel."

"Wanna bet?"

Jessica shrugged. "The real reason I want you there is to tell them about today. And what we think led to it."

"You're going to tell them there's a good chance the president had sex with a young woman last night and had her killed when he was finished with her?"

"Exactly."

"Why?"

"Because I plan to help Alex and Bat. I'm sure my friends will want to help too. Those girls need justice, and if we can't kill the president, we can try to expose him."

"I don't know, Jess. He's such a liar. He'll lie his way out of it. His dumb-ass followers will believe him."

"Oh, they will. The far-right news will spin it. We'll need to have iron-clad evidence. Pictures, DNA, and whatever else we can find. A video of the Cockwomble molesting a young girl would be disgusting, but so good."

"As long as no more girls die. That should be the top priority—preventing another girl from dying. One more kill is one too many." Morgan turned into her driveway.

Jessica grabbed her arm. "You called me 'Jess.' No one has ever called me Jess. I like it."

*****

Alexander walked the short distance from the hotel to his condo. Jana was at the kitchen table when he pressed his thumb onto the lock's sensor. She jumped to greet him at the door.

"I was worried."

"I'm sorry. It's been a long night. I know I should have called, but I figured you were asleep. This morning has been crazy."

"Did you sleep at all last night?"

"Not a wink. I'm beat, but I need a shower. Come with me. I'll tell you about it."

Jana followed him into the bathroom. She sat on the closed toilet seat while he undressed and stepped into the shower. The primary shower was a walk-in without a door. Jana had no trouble hearing his account of the evening over the spray of the showerhead. Alexander finished the story at the same time he finished his shower.

"What are you going to do?" Jana asked.

"I'm going to go to bed."

"I figured. I mean—"

"I know what you mean. At the moment, I don't know. The ex-CIA group is meeting tonight. I don't know what their plans are, but I'd like to get them to join me. Since local law enforcement is stonewalling me,

I need all the help I can get. I've only met Jessica, but I'd bet money the others are sharp as tacks. If they decide to help—even if only Jessica does—I'm sure we'll get justice for those girls."

"Should I ask what kind of justice you're talking about?"

"Better you didn't. Legal justice is preferred. But I'll take any type."

"I was afraid you'd say that. Be careful, Alex."

"I will, don't worry."

"Sleep on it. See how you feel in a couple of hours."

"I will. I won't do anything hasty. I asked Detective Amos about missing persons. My phone's on the kitchen table. If you hear it, check it for me. You know my PIN. If he replies, wake me."

"Sure," Jana told him, but she had no intention of doing so.

Alexander crawled into bed naked and pulled the sheet to his neck. Jana looked over her shoulder at him before she closed the bedroom door. He was already asleep. She went into the kitchen and checked his phone for messages. None.

Two hours later, Alexander's phone buzzed. There was one text from Amos.

One missing person report for a Caucasian female overnight. Amanda Elliott. Age 21. Works at Lou's Sports Bar in Hollywood. She left work not feeling well. No one has heard from her since. Her car is still in the parking lot. Driver's license photo to follow.

Jana scrolled to the photo and gasped. The girl was pretty. More than pretty. Gorgeous. Jana sighed. She knew she should feel bad, no matter what the girl looked like. Still, the thought of a beautiful young girl being killed in the way Alexander hypothesized felt worse than if she had been less attractive. *You are one pretentious bitch, Jana.*

Jana checked the time. Alexander had only been asleep for two hours, and he'd been up all night. Two hours wasn't enough sleep. *What would Alex do?*

Jana pushed the Forward icon next to the message from Detective Amos. She scrolled through the contact list until she found Bat. She selected the contact, added, "This is Jana. Alex is asleep. This is from the detective," and pressed Send. She did the same with the image.

Jana immediately received a reply.

> **Bat: Thanks. I'll look into it. Also sent to the ME and her girlfriend.**
> Jana: Why?
> **Bat: Thought the ME should have it in case the woman comes across her desk. Should say table.**
> Jana: OMG!
> **Bat: This missing person might not be her. Odds are against it. This one could be anywhere.**
> Jana: Thanks.
> **Bat: Have Alex call when he wakes up.**
> Jana: I will

Jana put the phone down and imagined the girl in the picture lying on a stainless-steel slab in the morgue. She rubbed her upper arms to ward off the chill that had come over her.

Jana left Alexander's phone on the table and went to the sofa in the den. She typed in the name "Amanda Elliott" into her laptop. Google returned pictures of twelve Amanda Elliotts. All were brunette.

According to IMDb.com, there were at least seven actresses named Amanda Elliott. Not likely any were the correct Amanda. Jana then searched Facebook. As she expected, there were hundreds of Amanda Elliotts. She began slowly scrolling through the list, studying the small profile picture for any blondes. To narrow the list, she added Hollywood, Florida, in the City field. Facebook didn't find any results.

"Fuck. Why don't people put their city in? Isn't the point of Facebook to find and connect with old friends?" Jana removed the City option, stared at the screen, and went back to Google. She searched for "Amanda Elliott Lou's Sports Bar".

Bingo. Pictures of the correct Amanda. Links to Facebook, Instagram, and LinkedIn. Jana clicked the link to Facebook. The most recent post was a year old. It was a picture of Amanda in a skimpy bikini on a Florida Beach.

Instagram contained more recent images and reels. Amanda was active and popular. A reel of her doing a cartwheel, again in a skimpy bikini, had over 5,000 likes. Photos of Amanda at work in the bar had considerably fewer likes.

Jana copied and pasted the links into a WhatsApp message on her laptop and sent them to Bat.

Here's Amanda's SM accounts. Thought they might help. Pretty girl.

A minute later, Bat replied with a thumbs-up emoji.

Jana closed her laptop, leaned back on the couch, and closed her eyes. She'd seen the AI-generated picture Bat created of the girl who fell. That was sad, but she didn't seem real. Amanda was real. Her social media posts showed a beautiful young woman full of life—a life cut short by two ass hats who pimped her out to a malignant narcissist. An obnoxious, bad-mannered, arrogant, duplicitous, selfish, and all-around bad person.

Jana smiled ever-so-slightly and whispered, "We'll nail his ass, Amanda. For you and all the others before you."

*****

The hazmat suit and gloves fully protected Morgan, but as soon as she and Jessica got to her place, Morgan headed straight for the shower. Jessica was tempted to join her, but without a change of clothes, she decided against it. She lay on the bed and patiently waited for Morgan.

When Morgan came out of the bathroom, she had a large towel wrapped around her body and a small towel wrapped around her wet hair. She crawled into bed next to Jessica, who immediately slid her hand under the large towel and pulled Morgan close.

"Let's stay at my place tonight," Jessica suggested. "It's closer to the meeting. We won't have to drive so far afterward. I'm sure Willie will have nice wine too. We may have to Uber home."

"I'll pack an overnight bag."

"It's time I ditched the butch attire. I might let you see me with makeup on, too. I hope you'll still love me."

"I'm sure I will," Morgan said, pushing a wayward clump of Jessica's hair away from her face. "You've been the top in our relationship. I know I'll love the Femme Jess, but will you want to switch?"

"In the few relationships I've had, I've always been the person who tends to initiate and be more active in giving. You know I love receiving, but I love giving—especially to you." Jessica climbed on top of Morgan. "I won't change."

"I hope not." Morgan's chest heaved as Jessica removed the towel and slowly slid her way between Morgan's legs to prove that their relationship wouldn't change. "Oh, wait," Morgan said, between heavy breaths.

Jessica looked up at her lover. "You want me to stop?"

"No. Never. But if you don't, we never will, and we won't make your meeting."

Jessica hovered over Morgan on her elbows and knees. "It looks like you're going to be the voice of reason in this relationship. If we're going to meet my friends, we do need to leave. I want to swing by my house and change."

Reluctantly, the women got out of bed. Morgan threw a change of clothes and a toothbrush into an overnight bag. "What do you plan to wear tonight, Jess?"

"How 'bout a cute little dress?"

Morgan grinned. She went through her closet in search of the perfect outfit to meet Jessica's friends. Not too formal. A little sexy. In her opinion, a little sexiness was about all a woman her age could muster without looking like a slut. Luckily, her natural breasts were full and firm. Her legs were long, slender, and naturally tan. She felt her abs could use a few more sit-ups. Even though the current style was to show a little midriff, Morgan decided the bare midriff ship had sailed years ago.

After she considered several dresses that were either too short or too long, she spotted a pink midi dress with spaghetti straps, a scoop neckline, and an asymmetrical hem. The dress was fully lined, so she could go braless.

Jessica would like that.

Jessica was sitting on the bed playing Connections on her phone when Morgan came out of the closet wearing the dress. "Wow! You look fabulous."

"Thank you. I was shooting for 'good.' I'll take 'fabulous' any time."

Jessica jumped off the bed and wrapped her arms around Morgan. "You nailed it. I hope you know I'm going to nail you tonight."

"Again, that's what I was shooting for."

Jessica ran her hand up the back of Morgan's leg and rubbed her butt. "Oh my God, you're wearing a string thong." Jessica stepped back and took a breath. "We'd better get out of here, or we'll never leave."

Morgan grabbed her overnight bag, turned on an interior light, and walked out with Jessica. On the drive, Jessica filled in any gaps she may have missed in her and her friends' plans.

"In the beginning," she said, "it was like we were on a mission to prove—or disprove—the theory that the CIA could orchestrate the assassination of a sitting US president. We staked out his compound, followed a few of his workers, and mapped his routes. But as the days passed, it felt like all we were doing was watching the movements of the people who worked for him. We weren't doing any planning. Jerry said it early on: Use a long rifle. Simple, easy, and with a little forethought, almost foolproof."

"'Almost' being the keyword," Morgan said.

"Yeah. 'Almost' doesn't prevent you from going to prison for life."

"So you all were ready to call it quits."

"We were."

"How 'bout now?"

"I was ready to move on. Get a job. Spend more time with you. Travel a little?"

Their phones beeped at the same time. The console in Morgan's Lexus RX displayed: **Text message from Bat.**

"I have a text from Bat too." Jessica opened the text, read it, and looked at the picture. "Oh, fuck."

Morgan shot a glance at Jessica. "What is it?"

Jessica held up the picture of Amanda so Morgan could see it. "A missing persons report was filed on this girl this morning. She could be the girl from the hotel last night."

"Fuck."

"Bat says he wanted you to have the picture in case she comes into your office." Jessica kept staring at the picture of Amanda. "Oh, Morgan. That would be awful."

"I hate to say it, but to me she'd be just another case on my table. I've seen everything—from fashion models to people off the street. It might sound cold, but it doesn't mean I don't care. And even if she did end up in the morgue, it wouldn't prove she was at the hotel. Still, I plan to help Bat and Alex go after those guys. They've killed at least two women—probably more."

"I'm in."

"I thought you might be."

"Oh, turn here." Jessica pointed at the intersection. "Sorry. At the end of the block, turn left. I'm at the end."

Morgan followed the directions and pulled into a visitor parking spot. "Uh...these are...nice."

"It's a shithole," Jessica said. "But it's all I could afford, and it's more than I can afford if I don't get a job soon."

Morgan followed Jessica and waited while she punched in the door code. Inside, Morgan gazed around the apartment. "You've fixed it up in here. It's cozy."

"Thanks. It's all I need. Would you like a drink while I get ready?"

"I'm fine. I want to read Bat's text." Morgan sat at the kitchen table and looked at what Bat had sent. She slowly took a breath and put her phone down. She took a closer look at Jessica's apartment. It was old, but clean. The Formica countertops had faded with age. Outdated tile covered the entire apartment. Stress cracks were visible in the corners of most walls. Morgan had been there once before, but she'd only seen the bedroom.

This place was a shithole, she thought to herself. Why does she live here? A CIA agent had to make enough to afford a better place than this.

She wanted to ask Jessica about it, but although they were in love, they'd only been together a few days. And when they were together, they hadn't done much talking.

Jessica came out of the bedroom wearing a floral-print mini dress with flocked trim. She was a short girl, but her legs were slender and shapely. They gave the illusion of being much longer. The mini dress left a very small amount of her leg unexposed. She'd put on makeup. Not a lot. Just the right amount of concealer and mascara to give her a polished look. She'd applied blush to the apples of her cheeks, which gave her a gentle, youthful appearance. Her hair was pulled back in a bun.

"Wow, Jess, you look amazing."

"Thank you. It feels nice to not be wearing a black tank or flannel."

"You looked great in butch, too, but I do prefer the new you. It's my turn to say we need to get the hell out of here now, or we'll never leave."

Morgan wrapped Jessica in a hug. "Before we leave, I want to say that although we haven't known each other long, I'd love it if you'd move in with me."

TWENTY-ONE

Morgan's move-in proposal got both women a little emotional. After they agreed and the sniffles passed, they took their time fixing their makeup.

At ten minutes after five—ten minutes later than they said they'd be there—Jessica knocked twice on Willie's front door and walked in. The light chatter in the kitchen stopped cold when the two women rounded the corner.

Everyone stared at Jessica, then Morgan, then back at Jessica. The expressions ranged from surprise to shock to anger. The women froze.

"This isn't good." Morgan had whispered, but everyone heard her.

"What da fuck? Jessica," Willie said. His words were heavily Cajun-accented. Had Jessica arrived alone, his comment might have been the same, minus the accent.

"Everyone, this is...my...uh, friend. Heck, I might as well call a spade a spade. This is my girlfriend, Morgan."

"Holy mackerel, Andy. Who you be call'n a spade?"

"It's nice to meet you all. I've heard a lot about you," Morgan said. "And you, Mr. Bouchette, you can drop the phony accent. I know you have a Master's from Tulane. I have a good idea that you know that the term, 'call a spade a spade' is from ancient Greek via Erasmus, who adapted Plutarch's phrase 'calling a fig a fig and a trough a trough' into Latin and then English around 1542, using 'spade', the digging tool instead of 'trough', meaning to call things by their plain names."

"Well, aren't we a fountain of knowledge, Miss..."

"Gossamer."

"Miss Gossamer. It seems you have us all at a disadvantage. We didn't know Jessica was bringing a guest. We also didn't know she'd been sharing our information with you—which she obviously has."

Morgan walked around the table and stood next to Willie. "You're right, sir. She has. There is a reason she has, if you let me explain. I apologize for being snarky. Jess didn't deserve your comment."

Willie slowly stood and held out his hand. "I apologize. I was surprised to see you. I was also a bit surprised by Jessica."

Morgan shook Willie's hand. "She looks good, doesn't she?"

Willie glanced down at Guerline. "I'm not at liberty to say."

Light laughter broke out around the table.

"You just did," Morgan said.

Another spattering of laughter.

"Everyone, as I tried to say earlier, this is my girlfriend, Morgan. I didn't bring her here because we're seeing each other. I brought her because she wants to talk to you all. She has something to ask. Please give her a chance."

Guerline gave Morgan a light hug. "It is nice to meet you. I'm Guerline. My boyfriend tinks he is funny. Please sit. What kin I git you to drink?"

"I've heard Willie serves good wines. A wine would be fine."

"White or red? Wat 'bout you, Jessica?"

Both asked for white. Morgan and Jessica squeezed in at the far end of the table from Willie. Guerline left to get two wine glasses and a new bottle of Chardonnay.

Morgan couldn't take her eyes off Guerline. She was tall. Her cheekbones were soft, but well-defined. She had a distinct jaw, thin lips, a small, straight nose, and almond-shaped eyes. She wore studded low-rise denim micro shorts and a cropped white waffle teddy top, which hung loosely off one shoulder. Her lack of a bra was obvious. She pulled the bare midriff style off beautifully.

"I guess you know all about us," Sam said.

Morgan turned her focus to Sam. "Jessica has told me what you're doing. She didn't share any details."

When Guerline returned, Morgan noticed a slight twitch in Jessica's eye.

A hint of jealousy. How sweet.

"Okay. So you know a little bit about us. We need to address the elephant in the room." Sam looked at Jessica, then back at Morgan. "We know you know what we have been doing the past few weeks. That bothers me. I'm sure it bothers everyone here. Because what we have been doing is, technically, a felony."

Morgan knew Sam's "elephant in the room" comment was a metaphor. However, she still wondered if Sam used it intentionally. Morgan was not overweight, but she was the oldest woman in the room. She kept her feelings to herself.

Jessica twisted in her seat. "Sam, everyone, I'm sorry. I should have prepared you, but I knew if I'd asked to bring Morgan, you'd have said no. She needs our help, and once you hear her out, you'll get on board."

"Jessica, you said she wanted to talk to us," Sam said. "Let's hear it."

All eyes turned to Morgan.

"If you don't mind, I talk better standing." Morgan stood, looked around the table, and took a deep breath. "I do have something to say, to ask, of you all. I didn't realize I'd be making a speech, so bear with me." She took a sip of wine while she gathered her thoughts. She grabbed her phone and found the picture of Amanda that Bat had sent her. She passed her phone around the table.

"This is Amanda Elliott. She was reported missing this morning. We're fairly certain a woman was killed last night in the Overlook Hotel. There's a pretty good chance it was Amanda."

A murmur filled the otherwise quiet room.

"Are you a cop?" Jerry asked. His tone was a bit hostile.

"I'm not. I'm the Broward County Medical Examiner. A friend sent me the picture in case she ended up in my morgue."

"That's right," Jerry said. "I forgot. Jessica mentioned that you were the ME. Why show us the picture?"

"My friends and I are pretty sure the girl is dead. We believe this man was involved." Morgan showed them the picture of Mark Sunday.

A noticeable gasp filled the room.

"He was at the scene, for sure. Jessica identified him. After she identified him, she was forced to come clean about why she was at the hotel the other night."

Before anyone could ask, Jessica said, "Be patient. Morgan will answer your questions."

Morgan flashed Jessica a faint smile. "A few weeks ago, Alex Christian, a retired FBI agent, was sitting on his balcony in Fort Lauderdale. He happened to see a girl fall from a balcony of the Overlook Hotel. He ran to the scene. It was a young Hispanic girl. Dead, of course. At the scene, Alex met the detective assigned to the case. The next morning, the detective told him the case was closed, and the girl had jumped. Alex didn't buy it. He decided to investigate it himself. His investigation led him to me. When he asked about the girl who fell from the hotel, I told him the girl's body came into my office. I'd just started my autopsy when the feds showed up. They said they were taking over the investigation. They took the body and all the forensic evidence I'd gathered."

"A cover-up?" Jerry said.

Morgan took another sip of wine. "Big-time cover-up. Last night, Alex and his friend were on a hotel balcony across the street from the Overlook. He thought he heard a gunshot, so he and his friend started watching the hotel. When a man walked onto the balcony, they started videoing. The man smoked a cigarette and went back in. When he did, he pulled back the curtains. In the video, you can see what appears to be a woman lying on the bed. Early the next morning, they saw a housekeeper drop a bag into a dumpster behind the hotel. My friend ran across and grabbed the bag. Before opening it, he called me."

Morgan took a deep breath, picked up her wine glass, and finished it. Guerline promptly refilled the glass.

"Jess was with me when Alex called. We rushed over, and I examined the bag. It was filled with paper towels that reeked of bleach and were soaked in blood. A pair of women's panties was at the bottom of the bag."

"Not a good sign," Willie said.

"Not at all. Alex showed us the video he and his friend recorded. He thought the man on the porch looked like the man who followed Jess. That's when Jess slipped and told us who he was. We encouraged her to tell us about you all, your plan, and how you'd followed him and the other guy, uh, McIntyre, to the hotel, or to the parking garage near the hotel."

"Jessica, tsk, tsk, tsk," Willie said sarcastically.

"I know. But I was shocked when I saw it was Mark Sunday."

"With this evidence, you haven't called the police?" Sam asked.

"No. I put the items from the hotel in separate bags and labeled them. The bags are in a locked cooler at my office. If we called the cops or the feds, I'm sure it would be taken and disappear like before. For now, I'm holding on to it. Alex said the video on its own is circumstantial. The detective wouldn't act on it. He did ask his cop friend to let him know about any female missing persons with blonde hair."

"Your friend didn't tell the cop why he was asking about missing girls?" Sam asked.

"No. Alex believes he's a good cop, but he's not ready to share what he knows about the second girl...yet."

"I see why. Two girls died at the same hotel in a matter of weeks, and the first death was covered up."

"Not only the same hotel—the same room. That's not a coincidence. Oh, Bat, Alex's friend, says the hotel's security rivals the NSA's. He's a cybersecurity expert."

Morgan could see the wheels turning in her audience's collective heads. She knew they'd taken the bait. She only needed to set the hook and reel them in. "You all know more about Sunday and McIntyre than I do. It doesn't take a brain surgeon to figure out these killings weren't covered up to protect those two lowlifes. So, ask yourself, who has the power to have local law enforcement drop a case and bring in the feds to confiscate my evidence?"

"Not many," Terrell said.

"I can only think of one person," added Jerry.

"The fucking president," Sam said.

"That's our guess," Morgan said, looking at Jessica. "We—Jess, and my friends Alex and Bat—want to take these guys down. The Hispanic girl and Amanda, or whoever she was, deserve justice. Most of all, we want to get the guy who's behind it. Cockwomble, as you refer to him. You all are ex-CIA. We need your help."

The room went surprisingly quiet. Morgan thought the ex-agents would all be willing to help, considering why they were gathered around the table in the first place.

Willie was the first to speak. "It's obvious Sunday and McIntyre are the fixers. We need a tail on them twenty-four-seven. We can't let them deliver another girl."

"Or, can we?" Terrell asked. "We catch him in the act."

"Too risky," Jerry said. "We'd have to catch the president with his pants down, but before they kill her."

Morgan's chin quivered, her eyes welled up. Not only were her new friends in the game, but they'd taken the ball and run with it.

"We talked about it a little," Jessica said. "We believe even if we caught Cockwomble with the girl, even had video, he'd claim it was fake. AI-generated. He wasn't there. And he'd surely have an alibi. FOX News and the others would spin it and, more likely, we'd be the ones who get fucked."

"That's so on-point," Jerry said. "The past two weeks weren't a waste of time after all. We know the main characters. We know where this is happening. Now we need to stop him."

"You're right," Jessica said. "But we need to do more than just stop him. We need to let the world know what he did, and in a way that he couldn't lie his way out of it. Simply killing him would stop him, but it would make him a martyr in the eyes of his cult. We need ideas."

"I tink dis is gonna go on a long night. Maybe I order da pizza now," Guerline said.

*****

Alexander slept hard and woke up drowsy. He sauntered into the living room.

Jana, watching a previously recorded episode of Kimmel, paused the recording. "The detective sent a missing persons report. A cute blonde. I should say, a beautiful blonde. Her name is Amanda Elliott."

"Why didn't you wake me?"

"You were up all night. You needed your sleep."

"I did. But still..."

"I forwarded the text to Bat. He suggested I send it to Morgan in case a blonde shows up on her table...as Bat put it."

"Good idea."

"I did a little research. I found Amanda's social media pages. She was popular. I should say she is popular. Bat said just because she's missing doesn't mean she's the girl from the hotel."

"He's right there. If no one is missing the girl who was in the hotel, she may not be listed as missing." Alexander checked his phone and read the messages. "She works at a sports bar in Hollywood. I need to pay them a visit."

"Do they have food?" Jana asked.

"Probably. Most do."

"Call Bat and see if he's eaten. Ask him if he wants to go with us."

Alexander texted Bat, who replied a few minutes later with a thumbs-up emoji.

"What time?"

"I need a shower to wake up and a shave. Can you be ready in thirty?"

"Is it a fancy place?"

"It's a sports bar. Shorts and a t-shirt."

"I can be ready. I need the bathroom."

Alexander texted Bat to let him know they'd pick him up outside his hotel in thirty minutes. He used the guest bath to shower and shave. He wore khaki shorts and a Hawaiian shirt with flowers and beer bottles on it. He Googled Lou's Sports Bar and saved the address to his phone.

Several minutes later, Jana came out of the bedroom wearing white micro-tailored shorts and a ribbed, bra-free tank top. Her blonde hair was in a ponytail.

Alexander saw her and blew a long, slow whistle. "Damn, you look good. I hope those guys aren't there tonight in search of hot women. They'd go for you."

"At least you'd be there to save me."

"I should carry my Glock."

"You're going to be drinking, I'm sure. Not a good idea to have a gun on you."

"I'd leave it in the car."

"Still not a great idea."

Alexander didn't plan to take his gun, but would have liked to. Anytime he knew he'd be asking questions about a possible homicide, he preferred to be armed. He knew the evening should be routine, and he would have a few drinks. That meant no gun.

"You ready?" Jana asked. "Should I drive?"

"Sure. I'll navigate."

They picked up Bat and thirty minutes later, Jana parked in a small parking lot next to Lou's Sports Bar. There weren't many cars in the lot.

"Pretty dead," Alexander said.

"It's still a little early," Jana said. "It's Sunday too. No sports on TV."

"Maybe they'll have curling on."

They went inside. A few people sat at the bar, and a few of the tables were occupied.

"Sit anywhere you'd like," the middle-aged woman tending bar yelled.

Alexander glanced around the bar. "Let's sit close to the kitchen and the bar station. I want to see everyone going in and out and serving drinks."

They chose a table that satisfied Alexander's requirements. A few minutes later, a server brought menus.

"Hi," he said. "I'm Josh. Can I start you with a cold beverage?"

Jana ordered a Chardonnay. Alexander and Bat ordered beers and queso. Josh left to put in the order. Bat surveyed the bar. Cameras were in every corner.

"They have good surveillance coverage. I hope the cameras work."

"One way to find out," Alexander said.

The server brought the drinks and set them on the table. "Your queso will be out in a couple of minutes."

"No hurry," Alexander said. "I do have a question. Were you working last night?"

"Uh, yeah. Why?"

"Were you busy?"

"On and off. We were slammed during the first basketball game. Florida was playing. When they lost, it quieted down a little. I guess we were a little busier than usual."

"Do you know Amanda Elliott?"

"Sure. She works here."

"Have you seen her today?"

"Uh, no. I don't know if she was scheduled to work today. Do you know her? Has she served you before? I get a lot of requests for her."

"I don't know her. I'll be honest. I'm a private investigator. She was reported missing this morning. Any idea who would have reported her?"

"Missing? Jeez. No. I mean, I don't know. She's good friends with another server named Becky. Becky was supposed to work tonight, but called in."

"I see you have video cameras. Do they work?"

"I think so. Not sure. You'd have to ask a manager."

"Is the manager in?"

"Kate is the MOD—manager on duty."

"Can we speak to her?"

"Uh, sure. I'll get her."

Josh disappeared into the kitchen. A few minutes later, he returned with chips and queso. "Kate said she'd be out in a minute." He set the food down and left.

"Ugh, white queso," Jana said. Her nose twisted. "Can't anyone in Florida make decent queso? It's made with yellow cheese."

"I agree with you, Jana," Bat said. "This is not Tex-Mex queso. But it's not bad."

A woman in her early thirties with dark hair and a pleasant smile approached the table. "Hi. I'm Kate. Josh told me you wanted to see me."

"Yes. I'm an investigator. Amanda Elliott was reported missing this morning."

"Yes. Josh mentioned it. I know she left early last night, said she wasn't feeling well. She's off today."

"Do your security cameras work?" Alexander asked.

"Yes, but I'm not too sure how. We rarely need to check the videos."

"Can my associate take a look? That's what he does."

"Um, I guess so." Kate's eyes danced around the bar, then at Bat before settling back on Alexander. "I'd like to clear it with my boss. Let me give him a call. I'll let you know what he says."

"It would be a big help if we could see the video. Thanks."

Kate left. Bat and Jana had finished half the queso.

"Let's order," Alexander said. "This could be a while."

The trio read the menu and decided what to order. When Josh returned, Jana ordered "Lou's French Dip," Alexander got the "Big A$$ Hamburger," and Bat ordered a grilled chicken wrap.

"Got it," Josh said.

"A chicken wrap, Bat? You're eating healthy?" Jana asked.

"Mayte got on me a little. I've gained weight. I thought I'd start eating better."

"While you wash it down with a beer?" Jana said. "I'm kidding. That's good. Alex should follow your example."

"You should talk, Jana," Alexander said. "You're wolfing down the chips like you haven't eaten in a week."

Jana ignored the comment. "Where is Mayte?"

"She got tired of sitting around the hotel watching me work. She went to stay with her sister for a few days. I thought I'd be going back to Bolivar soon. She'll be coming with me, so she wanted to spend time with Briana."

"Do you still plan on leaving soon?" Alexander asked.

"I don't want to. If you don't mind, I'd like to see this through."

"Why would we mind?"

"You're footing the bill."

Jana laughed. "Don't worry about the bills. We need your help."

Kate returned to the table. "My manager said it was okay to view the video. He said to call him if you need help with the machine."

"Thank you," Bat said. He and Alexander got up from the table and looked at Jana.

"You guys go," Jana said. "I'll stay and finish the queso."

Bat and Alexander followed Kate through the kitchen to a small office containing an old metal desk, a faux-leather executive chair, two small swivel chairs, and a large metal file cabinet. The security system was on a shelf against the back wall.

"Sweet," Bat said when he saw the security system. "It's a Lorex Elite Series 4K 16 Channel 6TB system." He pulled a swivel chair in front of the system and sat. He went to work rewinding the video.

"What time did you say Amanda left last night?"

"Around eight or eight-thirty."

Bat watched the monitors as he rewound the video. When the time stamp reached 1800, he pressed play, then 2X forward. When two men entered the bar at the 1830-mark, Bat paused the video. He gave a side glance at Alexander, who stared blankly at the monitor.

"What is it?" Kate said. "What'd you see?"

"Probably nothing," Bat said. "Those two are wearing sports coats. It's a bit odd for a Saturday evening in a sports bar."

Bat continued the video at 2X speed. He and Alexander concentrated on the two men. They sat at the bar for a short time, then moved to a table. Soon after they sat, Amanda approached them. Bat slowed the video to real time, then to slow motion.

"Do you see something?" Kate asked.

"No," Alexander said. "One of the guys Amanda is serving resembles someone who may be involved in another case. We don't know whether it involved Amanda." Alexander did not lie.

"Bullshit! Is the other case a murder? I can tell by your faces. Do you know what happened to Amanda? Is she..."

"We absolutely do not know, Kate. Please don't start spreading any rumors. You may upset her friends and family for no reason."

"I'm her friend." Kate wiped a tear from her cheek. "Promise me Amanda's not dead."

"Until they find a body, I'm assuming she is not dead."

Kate felt relieved. "Thank you."

Bat fast-forwarded the video past any time when Amanda was not present. At the 2015 mark, Sunday and McIntyre left the bar. Fifteen minutes later, Amanda left.

"Do you have a thumb drive?" Bat asked. "I'd like to make a copy of the video."

"I don't know. There may be one in the desk. If so, I guess you can have it."

Bat rooted around in the desk and found an older 4GB thumb drive. He plugged it into the NVR and transferred the footage of Amanda talking to Sunday and McIntyre, and of them leaving the bar. He ejected the drive and slipped it into his pocket. "I'll return the drive after I copy the files."

"Okay," Kate said, her hand trembling. When Bat stood, Kate grabbed his arm. Her smile was long gone. "If you get any new information on Amanda, please let me know."

Alexander spoke up. "I will. As soon as I have any news, I'll let you know. Here's my card. If you hear anything, call me." He started to walk off and stopped. "See if you can find out who reported her missing. I'd like to talk to them."

Kate slowly nodded, still fighting back tears. Alexander and Bat returned to the table. Jana was on her second glass of wine.

"How'd it go?"

Alexander rubbed his temples and pinched the bridge of his nose. "Amanda left the bar fifteen minutes after she served Sunday and McIntyre."

"Oh, shit."

"She appears to be perfectly fine in the video. The manager said she left because she felt ill. I think she was propositioned by those two and left with them."

"Why? She's so pretty. I'm sure she gets hit on many times a day, every day. Why leave with those two scumbags?"

"Money," Bat said. "I'll bet they offered her more money than she makes in a week here, maybe in a month. Easy money is hard to resist."

"She could've recently ended a relationship, too. Feeling a little down and up for an adventure. I'm sure those guys really sold it."

Josh brought the food out and set it on the table. "What else can I get for you today?"

"Could you bring a to-go box?" Jana asked. "I got full on the queso."

Alexander glanced at Bat, who gave him a subtle nod. "Would you bring us all to-go boxes? We ate too many chips."

Shortly after Josh left to get the take-out boxes, Kate returned to the table with them. "Josh told me you all requested boxes. You saw something in the video that made you lose your appetite. What was it?"

"Kate," Jana said. "They told me what they saw. It's not good news, but it doesn't mean Amanda's in trouble. It's a lead. They need to work on it."

Kate wiped her runny nose with a napkin. "Your meals on me. Promise me you'll let me know what you find."

"You and Amanda were good friends?"

"You could say so. She has a ton of close friends. She's the sweetest..." Kate's voice trailed off. She stared at Jana. "Are you related to Amanda? You remind me of her."

"That's so nice of you to say. No, we're not related. I've seen pictures of her. She's beautiful." Jana caught herself before referring to Amanda in the past tense. Jana dug into her purse and pulled out a hundred-dollar bill. She handed it to Kate. "Thanks for the meal. Give this to Josh."

"Thank you so much. He'll appreciate it." Kate stuffed the bill into a pocket and walked away. Alexander, Jana, and Bat filled their to-go boxes and left.

Outside the bar, away from the front windows, Alexander kicked the tire of a parked car and slapped a street sign.

TWENTY-TWO

There was a renewed energy among the fired CIA agents when they met the following day at Willie's house in Greenacres. What had become an exercise in futility now had purpose. Once angry at the president for being fired, they were now incensed that at least two women were dead because of him. The fired agents would have new opportunities—there would be none for Amanda or the Hispanic girl.

"The original reason for us to be here was to see if we could do what the CIA may or may not have done to Kennedy. That was Jerry's idea. I became the de facto leader when I invited Jessica and Terrell. I'll admit, the first several days were interesting and fun. Although we didn't have the time or the resources, we figured out how it could be done, but not the who. And we didn't have a patsy." Willie took a drink of beer.

"Now, after what Morgan said, and we've all signed on, we have a mission. A complicated mission. We've been bouncing ideas around the table for a couple of hours. We know we want to get Sunday and McIntyre. They're most likely the ones responsible for the deaths. We'd love to get the man who is behind them. Cockwomble. Then there are all the others involved, which is damn near everyone at the Overlook Hotel—from the owner to the housekeepers who helped cover up the killings. Then we have those responsible for covering up the Hispanic girl's death. Obviously, it started with the president, but the FBI, Homeland, the DOJ, possibly all of them, likely had a hand in the cover-up." Willie took a deep breath. "I know, that's a lot. I want to make sure we get Sunday and McIntyre. We may not get any of the others, but I want to open a big-ass can of worms. Hopefully, heads will roll."

"Can I make a suggestion?" Morgan asked.

"Of course."

"Alex, the retired FBI agent, mentioned that any evidence we collect needs to be admissible. He removed the trash bag from the dumpster on the hotel grounds, but the dumpster wasn't locked. Anyone had access. No warrant required. My point is, if we want to get these people legally, I suggest we follow the law."

"Good point," Jerry said.

"I don't know much about the CIA," Morgan said. "Don't you guys mostly work outside the US, and often outside the law?"

"Never." The sarcasm in Jerry's voice was unmistakable. Everyone at the table rolled their eyes and avoided making eye contact with Morgan.

"I know you haven't met him, but we should ask Alex to be in charge. We need direction."

"I couldn't agree more," Willie said.

Morgan and Jessica's phones pinged at the same time. They shot glances at each other, knowing who the text was from without looking at their phones. All eyes were on them.

Morgan picked up her phone. "It's from Alex." She read it to herself, then aloud. "Last night we went to Lou's Bar and checked surveillance footage. Amanda served Sunday and McIntyre. She left the bar fifteen minutes after they left." Morgan set her phone on the table and dropped her head.

The room fell quiet. The photo of Amanda with Sunday and McIntyre at Lou's Bar didn't prove the girl in the grainy image was her, but no one doubted it.

Around the table, there was a mix of clenched jaws and pursed lips.

Willie stood, leaned forward, and placed both hands flat on the table.

"We aren't investigators. We're spies. Infiltrators. Analysts. That's what we do. Morgan, see if you can get your friend on the phone."

"Alex?"

"Yes."

Morgan rang Alexander's number and put the phone on speaker. Alexander answered on the second ring.

"Alex," Morgan said. "I have you on speaker with Jess's friends. I shared your text with them."

"I'm betting they all agree. The woman in the hotel was more than likely Amanda."

"They do. We all do. It's so sad. That's why I'm calling. Willie, he's our leader, wanted to talk to you."

"Sure."

"Hi, Alex. This is Willie. You could say I was the de facto leader, the common denominator of the group. We're all in agreement. We need to get whoever was responsible for the deaths of these two women. Not only the guys who killed them, but everyone. From the president—he's the instigator—to everyone who was involved with the cover-up, including anyone at the hotel who facilitated, from the owner to the housekeeper. We're all committed."

"Glad to hear it. Bat and I feel the same. We can use the help."

"Since you're the investigator, I think you should take charge." Willie glanced around the table. No one objected. "We all feel the same. Morgan mentioned you want to run the investigation by the book. So if anyone goes to trial, the evidence will be admissible."

"Absolutely. We don't want anyone to walk on a technicality. Whoever is behind this has money. You know anyone involved who goes to trial will have top-notch lawyers on their side."

"We're good at gathering intel and infiltrating the opponent. Tell us what you need, and we can get it."

"Sounds good. I hate to use the cliché, but this is definitely not their first rodeo. Obviously, if these two cases are related, there was a glitch the night the Hispanic girl died. I got lucky and saw it. Even luckier to have videoed what happened last night. I can't even speculate on how many times this has happened, how many young women have been killed, but I guarantee it's more than two."

"No doubt," Willie said.

"Last night wasn't likely the last either. Jessica mentioned you all had followed Sunday and McIntyre. I'd say stick with them like glue. They'll strike again. That's when we nail them. From there, we figure out how to tie in the others."

There were nods of agreement from everyone at the table.

"You know your team. You coordinate the surveillance. It needs to be around the clock. Let me know if you need our help."

"We can cover it."

"Good. How far are you from us?"

"Alex, this is Morgan. We're at Willie's house in Greenacres. We're about an hour north of you."

"That's a lot of ground to cover," Alexander said.

"We're fifteen minutes from the Eagle's Nest," Willie said.

"The Eagle's Nest?"

"Our code name for the president's compound."

"Got it. So, you're either close to the compound or close to the hotel."

Sitting on the sofa across from Alexander and listening to the conversation, Jana mouthed, "Get them rooms in the Grand Paradise. I'll cover it."

"We'll get rooms at the Grand Paradise Hotel for your group. It's across the street from the Overlook. It'll give your guys a place to stay if needed."

Willie hesitated. "Having a place close to the hotel would be great, but, uh, we're all unemployed—"

"No worries. We have a financial backer."

Jana was not an investigator or a CIA agent, so she knew her involvement would be limited. She smiled, knowing she had contributed to the effort.

"My friend Bat is in the same hotel."

"I'm sorry, what kind of name is Bat?" Willie asked.

"It's a nickname. His real name is Bartholomew Epaphroditus

Farnsworth the Third."

"Weell, fuuuuuck me," Willie said. "No wonder he calls himself Bat."

"Who said that?"

"It was Willie. He often reverts back to his Cajun roots," Jessica said.

"Alrighty, then," Alexander said. "We don't need to start following Sunday and McIntyre today, but we should soon. Text me everyone's name, and I'll arrange the hotel reservations. We should all meet in person, at least once."

"Hi, Alex, this is Sam. I was an analyst with the Agency. I'll send everyone's names and phone numbers later. Can you send me your number?"

"I can give it to you all now. Everyone ready?" Alexander read off his number. "Do you think we should use burner phones?" He glanced toward Jana, who nodded, then added, "We'll supply those too."

"Not necessary," Sam said. "Although a burner is good to have, it's an extra phone to keep track of and keep charged. Get one or two in case anyone needs to use one. Activate one with a DC area code. Either 202 or 771. You can request the area code when you activate the phone. For messages, let's use WhatsApp. The messages are encrypted end-to-end. No one, not even law enforcement, can access the content of the messages."

"Thanks for the reminder, Sam. Good idea. My WhatsApp number is the same as my phone."

"Got it. I'll text you mine. Reply with Bat's number, and I will create a group chat and add him."

"Perfect. When we're ready, we'll pick a time to meet. Lots to talk about."

"Looking forward to it. Later," Willie said.

Morgan disconnected the call. "I thought that went well."

"Me too," Willie said. "It would be good if we could all meet with Alex and Bat tomorrow. As he mentioned, I don't think Sunday and McIntyre will make a move in the next few days, but we need to get eyes on them." He checked the time. "It's late. Go home. Let's meet here at ten in the morning to plan the day."

There were no objections. Morgan and Jessica were the first to leave.

*****

The phone call with Jessica's friends was encouraging. Still, it was after midnight, and Alexander was in bed, on his back, staring at the darkened ceiling. The only sound in the room was Jana's faint breathing. Waiting for Sunday and McIntyre to strike again wasn't a valid plan. The Overlook Hotel was a veritable Fort Knox. Once they had their prey inside the hotel, it would be tough for him and the ex-CIA agents to protect her.

What Alexander wanted to do was bust them for the murders of the Hispanic girl and Amanda. But how? He ran every scenario he could imagine. First, there was the Hispanic girl. He wished they'd given her a name. Jane Doe would be better than 'Hispanic girl', but both were so impersonal. Finding who she was and calling her by her given name was what he hoped for. He decided to refer to her as HG. Going by the initials seemed a little less cold. A little more personal.

HG's death had been ruled a suicide—by someone, but not Morgan Gossamer. Her body was gone, likely cremated, along with any forensic evidence.

No video. Without knowing who she was, it wasn't possible to track her whereabouts on the day she died. Sunday and McIntyre met Amanda at her workplace. They likely met HG at her workplace, wherever that was. Missing persons was a bust. Alexander squinted in the darkness. He couldn't remember, with all the excitement of the past twenty-four hours, if Bat had run the AI-generated image of HG against the social media accounts. He opened his phone and created a note to himself to check with Bat and have him send a copy of the image to Detective Amos, so he could check it against the latest missing persons reports.

After saving the note, he opened the Photos app and scrolled through the pictures he had taken of HG the night she fell from the balcony. It wasn't HG he was interested in, it was the people standing around looking at her. Using his two fingers, he zoomed in on the faces of the bystanders, studying each one.

"Damn," he whispered. Neither Sunday nor McIntyre were in any of the photos.

Alexander closed his eyes, took a deep breath through his nose, and exhaled through his mouth. Even if he could get the girl's name, it wouldn't help the case much. Linking Sunday and McIntyre to her on the day she died would be nice, but it wouldn't prove that they harmed her. If he had a name, he could notify her family. It would be a win. A small win, but a win nonetheless. There hadn't been many to this point.

Alexander thought about Amanda. She was almost certainly dead—but there was no body. Without it, there was no proof of murder. And the only link to the men who might have taken her was the video from Lou's Sports Bar, which was at best weak. Amanda had probably served hundreds of customers that day. Claiming the two who left the bar fifteen minutes before she disappeared were responsible wouldn't hold up—it would get laughed out of court.

DNA tests would prove that the blood on the paper towels and the panties recovered from the dumpster were Amanda's. It still wouldn't prove she was dead. She could have been having sex and started her period. She could have had a bloody nose. Neither would produce the amount of blood found in the bag, but it would cast doubt on whether or not she was dead.

Alexander rolled from his back to his side, to his back, to his other side, and again to his back. Jana moaned softly and changed positions. She didn't wake. He watched her for a few minutes. When her rhythmic breathing resumed, he turned his attention back to the ceiling. Faint streaks of light on the ceiling, filtering in from outside, resembled clouds against a dark sky. Dark clouds. The clouds were hanging over him. How appropriate.

The minutes ticked by slowly. Alexander went through every detail again and again, always with the same result. No body. No evidence. No witnesses. No case. Mark Sunday and Sean McIntyre got away with murder. Two murders for sure. How many others were there?

A hypnic jerk shook the bed. Alexander took another deep breath through his nose and slowly exhaled through his mouth.

Jana stirred again. She rolled to the side to face Alexander. "You're still awake?" She spoke in a hushed, groggy tone.

"Yeah. Going over what I know. Trying to figure out what I've missed."

Jana scooted closer and rested her head on his chest. "Too bad one of the guys doesn't confess." In the darkness, Jana could not see Alexander's eyes roll or his skeptical smirk.

"Yeah," he said. "Go to sleep. I love you."

Jana drifted off. Moments later, Alexander lifted his head. His smirk turned to a slow-spreading smile. His eyes widened. The dark cloud above him lifted, replaced by a sharp, focused intensity.

TWENTY-THREE

Alexander was up early with a newfound vigor, patiently waiting to meet the group of ex-CIA agents. Jana booked four rooms and a suite at the Grand Paradise Hotel. The suite, with a large sitting area, would be used as a meeting room.

Jana and Alexander arrived at 9:00 AM to check into the rooms. Bat joined them in the suite.

"Who gets this room?" he asked.

"It's a double-edged sword. It's a beautiful room with a huge bedroom, but there could be people coming and going in the adjoining section all night," Jana said. "There's a solid door, but privacy will still be lacking. I thought Willie and Guerline might like the room. Or Jessica and Morgan, since Morgan works and won't be here every night."

"When everyone is here, we'll ask who wants it. Let them decide," Alexander said. He sent the room number to everyone using the group text Sam had created. Replies came instantly. "On our way." "Be there in ten." "Almost there."

Willie and Guerline were the first to arrive. When Alexander opened the door, he was taken aback by Willie. Jessica had warned him that Willie looked 'dumb,' but he still wasn't prepared. He wasn't ready for Guerline either. Her stunning looks were amplified by the outfit she wore: shorts and a V-neck tie-back smocked halter with a plunge neckline, low back, and front keyhole. Ample skin was showing.

Alexander introduced himself and Jana. He had difficulty not looking at Guerline's cleavage. Jana would have noticed, but she was busy sizing up the two. Alexander couldn't help but be reminded of The Beauty and the Beast.

Bat introduced himself. Willie asked about his computer setup and whether he could access the Overlook Hotel's closed-circuit TV system. After a few minutes of their technical jargon, Jana, Alexander, and Guerline's eyes glazed over.

Jana realized Bat didn't look overly smart either, but he was one of the smartest people she knew. He had a hot girlfriend, too. While Alexander feigned interest in what Bat was saying, Jana took Guerline by the hand and led her to the balcony. They bonded over current fashion and *Love Island.*

The knock on the door came none too soon for Alexander. He excused himself from Bat and Willie, who didn't notice he was leaving, and answered the door.

"Come in, Jessica. Bat and Willie are talking computers. Jana and Guerline are on the balcony. I don't know what they're talking about."

"For now, I'll join them," Jessica said.

Alexander realized neither he nor Jana had ordered refreshments, and he was in dire need of coffee. He called room service and requested a large urn of coffee, ten cups, ten bottles of water, and a mixture of donuts and Danish pastries.

The others arrived shortly thereafter. Room service came fifteen minutes later. Sam had joined Bat and Willie at the computer. Terrell and Jerry were interested in talking with Alexander.

With everyone except Morgan in attendance—she being the only person in the group gainfully employed—Alexander signaled Jana to come into the room, and he cleared his throat.

"Now that I've met everyone, and you all have met my friend Bat and my significant other Jana, welcome. I'm glad you all could come."

A smattering of acknowledgment filled the room. Alexander put his hands together, fingertip to fingertip. "I thought about this a lot last night. I went over every piece of evidence we have countless times. Everything we have is circumstantial. There may have been enough evidence to convict Sunday and McIntyre of the Hispanic girl's death, but it's gone. We likely have Amanda's DNA on a bloody pillowcase, but we don't have a body. No way they would get convicted on that. Last night, when Jana was half asleep, she said, 'It's too bad they don't just confess'."

Several "Uh-huhs," "Yeps," and "Wouldn't it be greats" came from the group.

"I think we can all agree they aren't going to confess," Alexander said. "Not without a little prodding, anyway."

"Ah ha! And we be jus da ones dat do da proddin'."

"Well said, Willie. That's exactly what I was thinking. Well, not exactly."

Laughter, along with a fresh energy, filled the room.

"I'm an investigator. I investigate crimes and gather evidence to secure convictions. We interrogate suspects, but urging a confession is a different branch. I think it would be more in your realm. I have a couple of ideas I'd like to bounce off you, but I want your input." Alexander paused, then added, "While we're figuring out how to get a confession from those guys, they're likely planning another murder. We can't allow it to happen!"

"I agree," Jessica said. "We either get a confession or stop them before they kill again."

"This confession. We want it to be admissible in court and lead to a conviction?" Sam asked.

"Preferably."

"Any thoughts on how we go about it?" Terrell asked. "We can't exactly grab one of them and stick a cattle prod up his ass until he confesses."

"No, we can't. One idea I had was for a couple of us with either CIA or FBI credentials to contact them and ask about the Hispanic Girl—which I call HG—and Amanda. I'm sure they know that only a few people outside their inner circle would know about HG, like Detective

Amos and Morgan. No one outside those directly involved would know about Amanda.

"So, we have our fake agents meet with them, and, off the top of my head, say something like, 'Amanda was reported missing, and the local LEOs are asking around.' Tell them there's a PI investigating. Then we'd ask them where they disposed of the body. We'd say we wanted to make absolutely sure her corpse wouldn't turn up."

"Basically, a sting operation. Could work," Willie said. "I do see a few holes."

"Oh, no doubt any number of things could go wrong. For one, they could say they didn't know what we were talking about. Refuse to talk to us. They could tell us to talk to their boss. They might want to check our credentials."

"We'd have to be careful flashing fake credentials, too," Jerry said. "We'd be impersonating federal officers. This could backfire, and we'd end up in jail, not them."

"We definitely need a foolproof plan," Alexander said. "At least as foolproof as we can get it. You all are the spies. I thought this would be right up your alley."

"Oh, we can come up with a plan," Willie said. "We'll need to think on it."

"Figured so. Also, we should try to get someone inside the Overlook, even if it's a housekeeper position. It would be helpful to have eyes on the inside."

"Good idea. I like it," Willie said. "I have a feeling they do serious background checks on applicants. We'd need an identity that would pass inspection. Do we have the time and resources to create one?"

The room was quiet. Most everyone looked toward Bat, who shrugged.

"Ya already have dat," Guerline said. "I was da bartender in Haiti in da hotel. If dey check on me, dey don't find noth'n."

All eyes focused on Willie.

"Uh, I don't know," he said.

"You don't have no say." Guerline snapped.

"Then we need to make sure your story is air-tight," Willie told her.

"Hopefully, they'll hire you."

Guerline loosened the tie holding her top in place, revealing more skin. "Dey will hire me."

There were no arguments. Willie was not thrilled.

When Alexander appeared to be spending more time than he should be looking at Guerline, Jana said, "Shall we move on?"

"Yes, let's move on. We have a start. We need to get eyes on Sunday and McIntyre."

Jessica nodded to Terrell, who returned the gesture. "Terrell and I will take the first shift. We've been watching them on and off for two weeks. We know to focus on them now. We'll use two cars in case they split up. Any night owls in the group? Who'd like to take the night shift?"

"Sunday spotted you the other night," Alexander said. "If he sees you, he may recognize you."

"I've changed my hair a little, my clothes a lot, and I've started wearing makeup. If Sunday catches a glimpse of me, I don't think he'll recognize me."

"Good point. I almost didn't recognize you. I like the new look."

"Thanks. Morgan does too." Jessica blushed.

"Jerry and I can take the night shift. We only have one car. If they haven't left the Eagle's Nest by, say, ten or so, they aren't likely to leave. We'll get with Jessica and Terrell and set up a schedule."

"Keep us posted," Willie said. "If they seem to be heading this way, let us know. We can intercept them and help with the surveillance."

"Roger that," Terrell said.

Alexander explained the room situation. Jessica said she'd take the bedroom adjoining the suite. She didn't think Morgan would be joining her, so she wouldn't require the privacy she might have otherwise. Jana passed out electronic key cards to the other rooms and gave everyone a key card to the suite.

"That's all I have at the moment. We've still got a lot to do. Oh, remember, keep in touch," Alexander said. "Anyone else have anything they'd like to add?"

"I'd like to say something." Jana walked over to Alexander and clutched his arm. "Alex has been consumed with this since the death of the Hispanic girl. I want to personally thank you all for helping him."

The group's consensus confirmed that no thanks were needed.

"I know you're all unemployed. You could be spending your time searching for a new job or working part-time to make ends meet. But you're here helping, and I…we appreciate it. If any of you are facing financial hardship, let me know. I'll be more than happy to help you out."

"That's very generous of you, Jana, thank you. I think we're all okay," Willie said.

"Okay. But if any of you do need help, please ask. Don't lose your home or car or go into debt because you're helping Alex."

"We'll keep it in mind," Willie said.

The meeting ended. Willie and Guerline got with Bat to do a deep dive into her online history. Jerry, Terrell, Sam, and Jessica huddled to work on a schedule.

Jessica excused herself and walked over to Jana. "Can we talk on the balcony for a minute?"

"Of course." Jana followed her outside.

Jessica's head hung between her hunched shoulders. "I hate to ask, but since you mentioned it, I could use a little help."

Jana lifted Jessica's head so she could make eye contact. "It's fine. Don't be embarrassed. I'd be pissed if you were in a bind and didn't reach out."

"It's not for me. See, my dad is Chinese, and my mom is Filipino. They met in Manila when my dad worked for a shipping company. They were married, and a little later, my dad got transferred to Los Angeles, where I was born. Dad had a work visa. Mom was qualified to visit under Dad's visa. The company was sold to a Norwegian shipping company, which transferred some of the employees to Europe and laid off the rest. Dad was laid off. I was four, and my parents wanted to raise me here in the US. They didn't want to return to the PI—the Philippine Islands—or to China. So, they stayed. Illegally. Mom cleaned houses, and Dad started a lawn service." Jessica began to tear up.

"Take your time," Jana said.

"They did okay. I got a full scholarship to UCLA, which helped.

Once I started working, I sent them money every month to make their life a little better. Now they're scared. Every time they hear a car outside, they're afraid it's ICE coming for them. They're afraid they'll be separated and sent to a prison in South America. I'm not sure about that, but they could deport Dad to China and Mom to the PI. They want to return to Manila on their own. Mom has family there. But they don't have money for airfare, and they aren't sure they can get out of the country without valid passports. Theirs expired years ago."

"Do they have a way to get back?"

"I checked into it. They can contact the Philippine embassy to obtain emergency travel documents, but of course, there's a fee. And airfare's expensive. When my lease is up in two months, I'm going to move in with Morgan. When I do, and I get a job, I could send them the money. That will be a while. They could be deported any day. I'm sure Morgan would help, but I haven't been able to bring myself to ask her. Since you offered to help, I...I thought I'd ask. I'm sorry—"

"How much do you need?"

"Um...I have a little savings. With what I have, another thousand dollars should do it." Jessica wiped a tear from her eyes.

"What's your Venmo account?"

Jessica hesitated. "I'll pay you back."

"Nonsense. It's my pleasure to help your family." Jana plugged in the Venmo info Jessica gave her.

A few seconds later, Jessica's phone notified her of the transaction.

"Thank you, Jana." She sheepishly looked at the notification. "Uh, Jana...you accidentally added an extra zero."

"No, I didn't. Take care of your parents."

Jessica burst into tears and hugged her.

Alexander noticed them hugging and came out to join them. "What happened? Are you okay?"

"Better than okay," Jessica said, wiping more tears from her face. "Excuse me, I'd better join Terrell. Thank you again, Jana...I—"

"Go," Jana said.

Alexander turned to Jana after Jessica went back inside. "What was that all about?"

"Her parents are here illegally. I gave her money to get them back to the Philippines."

"Ah...I'm glad you could help her."

"It's the least I could do. I'm not adding much to the group."

"Sure you are. Not only are you footing the bill, which is a huge help, but you and I may need to help out tailing Sunday and McIntyre. To say we are short-handed would be an understatement."

"What about your old FBI buddies? They do stings all the time. Could any of them help?"

"I reached out to a couple of them I trust. They're scared. Nobody knows what any of those idiots in charge are going to do. I told them about the HG. They were going to discreetly see if they could find out if the FBI was involved. I don't expect much out of them. If the FBI was involved, it was high-level and carried out by a tight inner circle."

"So we're on our own?"

Alexander grimaced. "Afraid so."

*****

Guerline didn't have a Facebook, Snapchat, or Instagram account. Bat took a picture of her and ran it through a facial recognition program to make sure she didn't appear on anyone else's account. The search retrieved photos of several beautiful Black women. Most of the images were from Facebook pages. Bat checked their profiles. They were either Digital Creators or Influencers. Many were AI images. None of the images was of Guerline. No hits came from any other media source. It was as though she didn't exist. Not having a profile at all was both good and bad.

Bat frowned at the computer screen. "Guerline needs a social media presence. If they do a search for her and don't find anything at all, it'll be a red flag."

"If we create her an account, it will show it was created today," Willie said. "That's no bueno."

"It would be, but I happen to have a few Facebook accounts we can use. We can change the name, add new photos, and backdate them.

Facebook allows date editing. Instagram doesn't. Between the two of you, you must have pictures on your phones."

"None we can upload to Facebook," Willie said, snickering like a teenager.

"Oh? I'll hack into your cloud account later and take a look," Bat said.

Willie's snicker turned into nervous laughter. He didn't know if Bat was joking.

"Go through your phones and pick out images I can post. Preferably ones where you're alone, Guerline. We don't want any other recognizable figures in the pictures. If you have any of you working at a bar, those would be good. Obviously, any of you in a bikini or showing yourself dressed provocatively would be good too. If they look at your page, we want them to want to hire you."

"I tink I know wat you want," Guerline said, strolling through her phone.

Willie and Guerline selected a group of photos and airdropped them to Bat's phone. Bat loaded them onto his laptop with a USB connection. He scrolled through the images.

"These are good." Bat hoped Willie didn't spot his increased heart rate or the vein in his neck throbbing as he viewed the photos of Guerline. Several of the images left little to the imagination. Though his eyes were focused on his laptop, his mind was on the images on Willie's phone, which were unsuitable for Facebook. The joke about hacking into Willie's cloud account had become tempting, but Willie was not a person Bat would wish to tangle with.

"I've got plenty to create a believable Facebook page. You'll need a CV," Bat told Guerline.

"I'll help her with it," Willie said. "If we text you all the pertinent details and dates, can you format it and print it?"

"Sure, no problem. There's a printer in the business center. I'll also send a copy via WhatsApp. You may need an electronic copy." Bat went to work on Guerline's Facebook page while she and Willie worked on her CV.

Terrell and Jessica left for Palm Beach to begin the surveillance of

Sunday and McIntyre. Jerry and Sam talked with Alexander and Jana for a few minutes before going to their rooms to rest for the night shift.

"Alex," Jana said, "I forgot to tell everyone to order room service if they get hungry. Will you let them know? I should give them a credit card to add to their wallet app."

Willie overheard. "You've done too much already, Jana. We're all in this together."

"Please, I want to help. This is my contribution."

Willie gave her a "You don't need to do it, but thank you" grin and went back to Guerline's CV.

"I'm going home," Jana whispered to Alexander.

"Give me two minutes. I'll come with you."

Alexander checked with Bat and Willie. They'd done all they could for the moment. He said goodbye and left with Jana.

On their way out of the hotel, Jana said, "That went well. You're going to nail those bastards."

TWENTY-FOUR

By noon, Bat had set up a Facebook profile for Guerline, complete with pictures. He created a one-page CV and printed it for her. At one o'clock in the afternoon, Willie drove Guerline to a Starbucks a mile from the Overlook hotel and dropped her off. She took an Uber back to the hotel and had the driver drop her at the front door. She had changed into a slightly more conservative, yet still revealing, yellow sleeveless cotton mini dress with spaghetti straps.

A staunch woman with a scowl stopped Guerline as she entered the hotel. "Can I help you?"

"Yes, please. You have a bar. I want to apply for a job." Guerline spoke slowly, working hard to pronounce her words properly. Her Haitian accent was still noticeable.

"I'm sorry. We are not hiring at—"

A middle-aged man with thick black hair and a bushy mustache interrupted. "Excuse me. Did I hear you say you were looking for work in the bar?"

"Yes, I am." Guerline flashed a wide smile and held it until the man's eyes made it from her chest to her face.

"I'm the bar manager. My name is Abdul Aziz. We happen to have an opening for a bartender."

"I'm sure you do," the woman with the scowl said before storming off.

"That's the hotel manager, Olga Sokolov. She can be a real bitch, but she lets me run the bar how I want to. Do you have any experience?"

"I do. I'm Guerline." She handed him her CV. "I worked as a bartender and a waitress in a hotel bar in Haiti. I immigrated a few years ago. I'm a US citizen."

Abdul couldn't have cared less about her experience or her citizenship. He was only going through the motions. He led Guerline into the bar and sat with her at a table in the back. He asked the basic questions. Her Haitian Creole accent came through on occasion when she answered. It didn't matter.

"We pay $10.98 an hour. That's the minimum wage for tipped employees in Florida. Are you okay with the pay?"

Guerline hesitated long enough for Abdul to think she might not take the job.

"You keep one hundred percent of your tips."

"Oh. Dat sounds good."

"When can you start?"

"Tomorrow?"

"Have you taken the Florida Alcohol Certification portion of the Florida Responsible Vendor Program?"

Guerline shook her head.

"No problem. It's an online course. It takes about two hours. Give me your phone number, and I'll text you a link. Take the course tonight and bring the certificate in tomorrow. We'll fill out the paperwork and get you started."

"Thank you, Mr. Aziz—"

"Call me Abdul."

"Thank you, Abdul. What time should I come in?"

"I'll have the night shift train you. I'm sure you'll catch on quickly. Come in at five. The bar closes at midnight on weekdays. You will close and clean up. You should be out by one."

"Do you have uniforms? What should I wear?"

"We don't have an official uniform. Most bartenders wear black slacks and a white top. You're working for tips, so feel free to wear a sexy outfit, but nothing slutty."

"I will see what I have. Thank you again, Abdul. I will see you tomorrow." Guerline scheduled an Uber to pick her up. When the ride arrived, she instructed the driver to circle the block and drop her off at the hotel next door. She paid the full fare.

Guerline made her way to the room Jana had booked for her. When she opened the door, she saw Willie stretched out on the bed. He jumped off the bed and gave her a hug.

"How'd it go?"

"I start tomorrow. Bartender. I need to go home and get clothes."

"I'll let everyone know, and then we'll go." Willie opened WhatsApp and brought up the group chat.

Guerline is in. She starts tomorrow. Bartender.

After she received congratulatory messages from the group, Guerline texted Bat and asked where he was. He replied that he was in his room. In a rather long, convoluted text, she told him Abdul asked for the Florida Alcohol Certification and asked if he could help her.

By the time Willie and Guerline reached Bat's room, he had the course up, paid for, and was several questions in. Bat had propped the door open so they could come in. "Hey," he said over his shoulder. "Sit. I found the course online. It says it will take two to three hours to complete."

Willie checked the time. "We need to run home and get your clothes. Should I go without you?"

"The course won't take three hours. Not even two," Bat said. "It's a slide show presentation and an exam. I'm a fast reader. I'll read it and give you the highlights. When I've read it, I'll take the test. We should be done in an hour. Then you can go get your clothes."

"I thought I'd keep you all company, but I'll go back to the room and see if the Rays are playing. Let me know when you're finished, and we can head out." Without waiting for a reply, Willie left the room.

Most of the course focused on legal responsibilities, ID checking, and spotting intoxicated patrons. Bat resisted the temptation to make light of the course. Guerline was taking it seriously, in case she was questioned about it when she showed up at the bar. Bat read the exam questions to her, and if she got the answer wrong, he told her the correct answer and explained why it was correct. They finished in less than an hour.

"I'll use the printer in the office center to print your certificate. I'll have it for you tomorrow."

Guerline was happy that it was Bat helping her. He didn't patronize her like Willie sometimes did...jokingly, he would say.

She thanked Bat, started to leave, then stopped. "Oh, da hotel manager's name is Olga. Olga Sokolov."

*****

On Tuesday, what they were now calling the War Room was abuzz. Guerline had infiltrated the Overlook Hotel. Getting eyes and ears on the inside was exciting. The group decided to spend the day kicking around ideas for the sting.

At 4:30 in the afternoon, Alexander walked to the Grand Paradise Hotel to meet with Willie, Guerline, Jerry, Sam, and Bat. Willie was more nervous about Guerline's first day as a bartender at the hotel than she was. Guerline saying, "I got dis," did not calm his fears.

Rather than hiring an Uber to take Guerline across the street, it was decided she'd walk. If anyone noticed, she'd tell them the driver dropped her at the rear of the hotel. Bat watched the Overlook's CCTV cameras. None pointed past the large concrete wall bordering the hotel. Guerline would say the Uber driver dropped her behind the wall if asked.

Willie went to the balcony and watched Guerline walk across the street. He came back inside the room once she entered the hotel. "I'm still not sure I like this," he said.

"As far as anyone over there knows, she's a bartender," Sam said. "Yeah, I know she was hired because of her appearance, but that happens everywhere. She'll be fine. As she said, 'She got dis'."

"But it's not a normal bar. It's inside a hotel that, in my opinion, is there for the sole purpose of accommodating deviant sexual behavior, murder, and the cover-up of young women. I doubt it's on Rick Steves' recommended list."

"It's another reason we're here, Willie," Alexander said. "Close the hotel down and put those running it in prison."

"Then let's get to it. I've been distracted with Guerline, but I've put some thought into the sting."

"I've thought about it too," Alexander said. "As I mentioned yesterday, another department handled the sting operations, so I'm far from an expert. I do know, whatever we decide to do, we need to plan it to a T. We won't be able to think of every single scenario, but we need to try. I don't want anyone getting hurt."

"Agreed," Sam said. "I've thought about it too. I had a few ideas, none of which I considered great."

"We're all new at this," Willie said. "But it can't be too hard. The FBI does it all the time." He let out a loud belly laugh.

Alexander ignored Willie's comment. "Let's focus on what we hope to accomplish. Obviously, the holy grail would be a complete confession with dates and names implicating everyone at the hotel who was involved, who is the mastermind—my guess is someone at the Eagle's Nest—who killed the women, how many women have been killed, and, of course, who was all of this for? I think we know the answer to the last question. I'd also like to get the names of the women who were killed. Undoubtedly, most are still listed as missing."

"What's a reasonable expectation?" Sam asked.

"The number of victims and their names."

"Is that all?" Sam asked. "What the fuck? All this effort for a few names?"

Alexander shrugged. "I wouldn't say letting the families of the victims know what happened is unimportant, but if that is 'all' we accomplish, I'd consider it a success—especially when you consider the scope of the cover-up used to make the death of HG go away. Even if we get a videotaped confession with the names of all the players, what would we do with it? At this point, I don't even trust the FBI. Cock-womble has them all in his back pocket."

"You're saying Sunday and McIntyre will walk?"

"They may not go to prison, but I'll guarantee they don't walk," Jerry said.

*****

Abdul intercepted Guerline in the middle of the hotel lobby. She wore black stretch pants, a white blouse, and red suspenders. Willie said the suspenders would lead the eye to her breasts, as though the eye needed any leading.

"Good afternoon. You're early. That's on time in my book. You look nice. Did you bring your Florida Alcohol Certification course certificate?"

Guerline started to open her purse to retrieve the certificate Bat had printed for her, but Abdul stopped her.

"I will take you to our HR department. You will give her the certificate. There is other paperwork too." He led Guerline behind the front desk into a cramped office containing three small desks. Two of the desks were occupied by attractive women in their mid-thirties. "This is our accounting and HR office. When you're finished here, come to the bar. I will meet you there."

The room was small and overloaded with computers, a copier, printers, and files. The space and the two women made Guerline nervous. She'd never filled out employment paperwork. Employment records weren't kept in Haiti, and she hadn't worked since coming to the US.

The women turned out to be friendly. They asked Guerline questions about Haiti and how she liked the US while they processed her paperwork. The woman who must have been the entire HR department photocopied Guerline's passport. The other gave her a W4 form to complete. Guerline had to pull her Social Security card from her wallet to enter the nine-digit number.

"We've got what we need. I'll let Abdul know you're on your way to the bar," the HR woman said. She handed Guerline her passport and grabbed her hand. "Watch out for Abdul. He's a leech."

"I will. Tank you very much."

Guerline left the small office and walked to the bar. Abdul came in right behind her.

"I guess it went well?" he asked.

"Yes. All set."

Abdul handed Guerline a two-way radio, an earpiece, and a charger. "Keep this on you and turned on at all times. Everyone has one, but we only call when we need you. For you, that usually means a high-profile client wants a drink.

"If you're called, it's your top priority—stop what you're doing and respond. We'll say your first name twice to get your attention. You answer with 'this is' or 'go for,' followed by your name. After you get your instructions, reply with 'got it,' '10-4,' or 'Roger.' Understood?"

"10-4."

Abdul chuckled. "Take the charger home with you. Charge the radio every night. This is your responsibility."

"Roger."

Abdul appreciated Guerline's "Roger," even if it sounded more like "Rojure." He signaled the bartender, an attractive young Hispanic woman in her early twenties. Guerline was beginning to see a pattern. All the employees were attractive women—except Janice at the front desk. She didn't fit the mold.

"This is Sally Sánchez. She'll train you. When she says you're ready to solo, she'll let me know. It shouldn't be more than a couple of days."

Sally took Guerline behind the bar. She showed her how to operate the two-way radio and reminded her to always have it with her and on.

"I'm surprised dey let you take da radio home. Dey should have a place to charge dem here."

"They tried to keep chargers in the office so we could leave them here. The radios kept disappearing. Now we're assigned one, and we're responsible for it."

"Dey are serious 'bout dem radios."

"They are. Funny, I've only been called on it a few times since I've been working here. I've been here almost a year. But they sure want you to keep it on you."

"It seems like a nice hotel. Quiet doh. Dat's not good when we work for tips."

"It is slow. But we get a lot of big tippers. It seems like most of the people, guys, who come in here have money."

"Dat's good to know."

Sally showed Guerline the ropes. She explained how the Wi-Fi password changed daily at 6:00 AM and that she'd receive an email with the new password.

The bar wasn't too different from the bars Guerline worked at in Haiti. There was a much larger selection of alcohol. The evening went by fast. At midnight, Sally explained the closing procedure.

By 12:30, Guerline texted Willie that she was on her way back to the hotel. He asked her to come to the suite. She walked out the back door, through the parking lot, across the street, and into the Grand Paradise Hotel. Willie, Alexander, and Bat were waiting for her.

After a big hug, Willie asked how it went. Guerline dropped on the couch and put her feet on the coffee table. She told them about HR, Sally, and how she'd been warned about Abdul. She told them about the password and the radio.

"That's a game changer," Bat said. "You must have the employee's password. The guest password doesn't change. Can I see the radio?"

Guerline handed the radio to Bat. He examined it as if George Floyd had handed him a twenty-dollar bill. "This is a Cobra PX655 Pro Business radio. Even in the city, it has a long range. Did anyone mention what frequency you're on?"

"No. Dey jus said make sure I got it on me all da time."

"We need to get a couple of these."

*****

The following morning, Willie was grumpy. After the brief meeting with Bat, he and Guerline went to their room, showered, and went to bed. Willie was hoping for a celebratory roll in the sack, but Guerline said she was too tired. She wanted to sleep. Already, Willie didn't like her working in the bar. Now he was angry about it. Instead of having sex with his bronze goddess, he lay in bed thinking about the sting. The sooner they busted Sunday and McIntyre, the sooner he would be back in his own bed with an unemployed Guerline.

Before he went to bed, Alexander texted the group saying he'd be in the War Room at 9:00 AM. He had a few ideas about the sting. Anyone who wasn't busy was encouraged to attend. He assumed Jerry and Sam, who spent the evening watching the Eagle's Nest, would be sleeping. Same with Guerline.

At nine the next morning, Alexander joined Willie, Bat, and Terrell in the War Room. Jessica was in the bedroom on the phone, updating Morgan. Alexander ordered coffee and donuts from room service.

"Bat," Alexander said. "Jana ordered six of the radios as you requested. She thought we could use them to communicate and to listen in on the hotel. She used Amazon Prime. They'll be here tomorrow."

"Perfect. Those radios have 22 channels and 121 privacy codes. That's…over 900 combinations. I'm sure there are different codes for different people, or at least departments. I can look at Guerline's radio and get her code. To make it easy to switch, I'd bet they use, say, privacy code seventeen on channel ten, then they likely use seventeen for all the channels. To talk to someone else, they only have to switch the channel. With six radios, we can sit on the balcony and monitor the channels. I doubt they change the codes too often."

"Being able to listen to them may come in handy."

"As I said last night, it could be a game-changer."

"You said you had an idea for the sting," Willie said.

"I do," Alexander said. "I've given it quite a bit of thought. It could work, but if it doesn't, and we don't get what we want, we haven't lost much. There's only one risk, other than Sunday and McIntyre shooting us. Well, shooting you. Sunday has seen me. I'm not sure we can risk him recognizing me."

"Us getting shot is the minor risk? One you're willing to take? What's the other risk?"

"You'll need fake IDs. I'm not sure which would be the best to use. FBI. CIA. DOJ. If you're caught with them, you'd be charged with impersonating a federal officer."

"And that's much worse than getting shot? Impersonating a fed is a high-level misdemeanor. With a good lawyer, explaining to a judge why we were impersonating an officer, we might get off with no charges."

"Or, if the judge is in a politician's pocket, you could be sent away for life."

"Shit. Hadn't thought about that. Got any other plans?"

Bat had been enjoying the banter between Willie and Alexander, but decided to add his two cents. "We need to hear the plan. Whatever it is. Then we can brainstorm and improve it. Once we settle on a sting, we can tweak it until we can all but guarantee no one will get shot or go to prison."

Willie frowned—more like pouted—and shook his head. "I don't knows dere boss. Sounds like I'z da one dat's gonna be do'n dis. How you gonna garaantee Willie don't get his ol' coon-ass ass shot da fuck off?"

Bat laughed. "Are you sure you're from Louisiana? Your accent has to be the worst Cajun accent I've heard."

"It's been a while. I guess I'm losing the touch." Willie turned to Alexander. "The CIA wouldn't be involved in a cover-up, but they could be gathering information for another agency. I never turned in my credentials. I'm not sure about the others."

"Sam and I turned ours in," Jerry said. "We were called in, given our walking papers, and they took our IDs and badges."

"I can use Willie's to make new IDs," Bat said. "Badges can be bought online. Etsy or eBay. They may take a few days to get here. How many do you need?"

"I'd say two. Willie has one, hopefully someone else has theirs too."

"We can't use our real badges," Willie said. "The CIA wouldn't be involved. We'll need new ones. You said two?"

"Yes. My idea is for two of you to meet with Sunday and McIntyre and say you're agents working with whatever agency we decide on, and you want to know about the fuck up they had with HG. Tell them that so-and-so—the head of whatever agency we choose—wants to make sure it will never happen again. Mention that you've seen a video of them at Lou's Sports Bar with a girl named Amanda Elliott. She's missing. Ask if she will ever be found."

"Damn. That's good," Willie said. "And if we meet them in a public place, the odds of getting shot go way down. We flash our credentials quick enough, they won't study them too closely."

"We also know their backgrounds," Bat added. "Bring up their records. DOJ, or whoever, isn't happy. If they don't want to end up back in prison, they'll answer your questions."

Willie nodded repeatedly. "I like it. And, they're not likely to shoot us in public. You did good...for a G-man.

TWENTY-FIVE

After much discussion, it was decided that the principals of the sting operation should be members of the Department of Justice. The Federal Bureau of Investigation was a close second. The Central Intelligence Agency was quickly eliminated.

The DOJ oversees the major law enforcement agencies, including the FBI, DEA, and U.S. Marshals. Having power over those agencies, the DOJ would have the power and resources to spearhead a cover-up of this magnitude. The Attorney General is the head of the DOJ, so it's less likely that anyone from the FBI or the other offices would question their authority.

It took some research, but Bat found a souvenir website that sold full-size replica Department of Justice Special Agent badges. He ordered two. On another site, he found high-quality leather credential cases with a round metal DOJ medallion on the front. He ordered two of those. Finding an image of a DOJ identification was more difficult than Bat anticipated. It was unlikely that either Sunday or McIntyre knew what a DOJ ID looked like. It was doubtful they'd study the IDs presented to them closely enough to spot a fake, but Bat didn't want to take any chances. The IDs needed to be good enough to pass more than a cursory inspection, and laminating the cards would be an issue. Most office supply stores had self-service laminating machines, but an employee might offer to assist. Laminating a Federal Agent ID might be a red flag to even the least discriminating retail employee.

The local Staples carried a nine-inch thermal laminator. It was only thirty-five bucks. Laminating pouches with a glossy finish were another twenty. A good paper cutter would have been nice, but the cards would be inside a badge holder. The edges would not be seen. Carefully cut with good scissors, the cards would pass muster.

Bat realized they'd need a printer and paper to print the ID cards. He added glossy photo paper and a decent printer to the list and texted it to Jana. She replied that she and Alexander would pick up the items later in the day and drop them off at the hotel. A few minutes later, she sent another text.

> **Jana: The radios arrived. We're leaving now. Would you like us to drop them off?**
> **Bat: Yes, please. The batteries need to be charged.**
> **Jana: Meet us outside in five.**

Bat walked out of the hotel as Jana was pulling into the front drive. Alexander handed Bat the box containing the radios. "I'll bring the printer and laminator by as soon as we get back."

"No hurry. The fake badges will take a few days. I paid for express delivery, but this isn't Amazon."

Bat returned to the war room. He unpacked and inspected each radio. "Damn," he said. He sent another group text to Jana and Alexander.

> **Bat: Pick up a surge protector with as many outlets as possible. Generic brand is fine.**
> **Alexander: Added to the list.**

Although no assignments had been doled out, Bat took it upon himself to make sure whoever was meeting Sunday and McIntyre for the sting would be properly documented. If the plan failed, it wouldn't be for lack of credentials. He leaned back in the bonded leather desk chair and thought about what he'd missed.

Suits. They should be wearing suits in their ID pictures. Handcuffs. Bat didn't know if Federal Agents carried handcuffs. Even if they didn't, it would be a nice touch. Guns. Agents definitely carry guns. He had not asked, but had a feeling they still did.

Bat closed his eyes and rested his head in his hands. One part of the operation bothered him. It wasn't his responsibility, and one of the others might have had an answer. He made a note to himself to ask when everyone was together.

*****

Jana mapped the closest Staples store. It was a half-hour away. She then searched for the closest OfficeMax. Eight minutes away. She checked the website, and OfficeMax had what Bat requested. She was sure he didn't care where she bought the items.

On the way back to the hotel, Alexander texted Bat with an ETA. When they arrived, Bat was waiting. He and Bat carried the equipment and supplies into the hotel. Jana took the car and went home.

In the War Room, Bat pointed out where to put each item.

"We may need a bigger room," Alexander said.

"I hope not. Let's wrap this up soon."

"With a little luck, we will."

"It was mentioned that Willie and Jerry would be the ones who meet with Sunday and McIntyre. It's going to be them for sure?"

"Yes, they're the operatives."

"I'll need to get them in here for ID pictures. They should wear a suit jacket and a tie. Isn't that how most fed IDs are taken?"

"They were in my day. I doubt it's changed. It won't hurt, so let's plan on it. They may have to run home and get a suit."

"Would they wear a suit on the sting?"

"They should. It looks professional. The jacket will conceal their service weapon and provide a pocket for their badge holder. I'll tell them to get a suit. Once you get the IDs made and the badges arrive, we'll be ready." Alexander stared out the glass door for a moment. "Wait, no, we won't."

"What'd we forget?"

"A recording device...or devices. Willie and Jerry should be wired."

"I thought they'd use their phones."

"Phones work well, but they need to be out, on the table. Or at least out of their pocket enough so the microphone isn't shielded. Men don't carry their phones around in their hands. It would look suspicious if either one pulled their phone out and set it on the table."

"What about a Bluetooth mike for the phone?" Bat asked.

"It would have to be small."

"I'll see what I can find. The CIA guys should know all about listening devices. I'll ask them for their opinion."

"I need to start a list," Alexander said. He checked the desk for a pad of paper and a pen. He didn't find one. "What kind of hotel is this? No pen?"

Bat shook his head, opened his laptop satchel, and pulled out a pen. It took a while, but he found a clean sheet of paper. "Write small, it might be a long list."

Alexander took the pen and paper and jotted down a few notes before realizing the room was empty. "Where is everyone?"

"Jessica and Terrell are watching the Eagle's Nest. Sam and Jerry are probably still asleep. They have the night shift. I haven't seen Willie and Guerline. She got in late, but they should be awake."

"Other than keeping an eye on Sunday and McIntyre, and what you're doing, there's not a lot more to be done...right now." Alexander patted his stomach. "I'm hungry. Why don't we call Jana and go for lunch?"

"I'd love to, but I want to begin working on the IDs," Bat said. "They need to be flawless. I also have work to do for a client. I'm a little behind."

"I keep forgetting you have a day job. I'll message everyone to meet here at five after Guerline goes to work...unless you'd like to talk to her before she leaves."

"I'm good. Five is fine."

Alexander was puzzled. He stared blankly at Bat for a few seconds. "I'm working on another idea, and I could use the local LEOs' assistance. I want to talk to Detective Amos, but I'm worried he could be part of the cover-up. I didn't get that impression, but it's hard to know who to trust."

"From what you've told me about him, he seemed genuine—if you're asking for my opinion. I'd say go with your gut. You spent twenty years with the FBI. You should have good instincts."

"My gut says to trust him."

"Then do it. If you end up dead in a few days, you were wrong."

*****

Alexander went with his gut and reached out to Detective Amos, who agreed to meet him for lunch at the Village Café. It was a ten-minute walk from the Overlook Hotel. Amos said he could be there in thirty.

Since he had time to spare, Alexander strolled along the beach. The fresh air and sound of the surf cleared his mind. He wasn't one hundred percent sure he trusted the detective, so he decided he'd only share enough information to pique his interest. As he walked along the surf line, he found a pristine sand dollar. He picked it up and put it in his pocket.

A good omen.

Despite his stroll, Alexander still arrived at the restaurant early. He requested a table in the corner away from the windows. The detective arrived ten minutes later. The men shook hands and exchanged pleasantries.

The server brought glasses, water, and menus. Amos's eyes bugged out when he saw the prices on the menu. "Jesus."

"Don't worry about it. Lunch is on me."

"Thank you, but at these prices, lunch would damn near fall into the bribe category."

Alexander thought it was a good sign that the detective was

concerned about a bribe. Then again, he could have been joking. "As long as it is only damn near, and not a bribe, we're good."

Amos laughed. "Even if you were trying to bribe me for information, you're going to be disappointed. I assume this is about the girl."

"It is. What have you learned since we last met?"

"I hate to say it, but I don't have anything new. In fact, it's worse."

"How could it be worse?"

Amos leaned in and lowered his voice. "I did a little discreet digging. As you know, we, the FLPD, were called off and told to close the case."

"Yes…"

"Quite frankly, none of the detectives were happy about it. Even the chief seemed pissed. He didn't say anything, but we could tell. I called the Medical Examiner's office—"

The server approached the table and asked if they were ready to order.

"We'll both have the Cheese Steak," Alexander said. When the server left, he turned to Amos. "Trust me on this. You'll like it."

Amos shrugged, thinking it was a little odd that Alexander ordered for him, but didn't comment on it. "The ME said the feds took the body and all the evidence. I tried to get the video from the hotel. They refused. Said they didn't have any video. I did get video from other buildings. I spent a lot of time looking for a girl with long black hair, and about the size of the one who died, entering the Overlook. Drew a blank there, too."

"Obviously, there was a cover-up." Alexander didn't want to seem too surprised that the detective came up empty.

"A cover-up of enormous proportions. We've been stonewalled."

After listening to what Amos had said, Alexander was convinced he wasn't part of the cover-up. He could be trusted. Even so, he wasn't going to show him all his cards. Not yet.

"I've been doing a little digging as well."

"I had a feeling you had."

"Can we keep what I'm about to tell you between us…at least for a while?"

"It depends."

"It's juicy."

"Are you buying dessert?"

Alexander leaned back in his chair and laughed. "I would, but we'd be getting into bribe territory. I'm not bribing you, I'm asking as a favor. Keep this quiet for a few days...or weeks. There will be a time when you can share with your team. In fact, I'll want you to—when the time is right. And...I'm going to need your assistance."

Amos turned serious. "You aren't kidding."

"No, I'm not. Do you remember the missing person you sent me?"

"The attractive blonde? Amanda..."

"Elliott. Amanda Elliott. Yes, her. I'm ninety-nine percent sure she's dead."

"Only ninety-nine? Why not one hundred?"

"Without a body, I can't be certain."

"I'm sorry, how can you be ninety-nine percent if you don't have a body? What do you have?"

"It's not what I have, it's what I may have seen." Alexander sensed Amos was growing impatient. He told the detective about the possible gunshot he'd heard from the same room the Hispanic girl likely fell from, about the man on the balcony, and how he and Bat video-recorded the man.

"In the video, we could make out a blonde lying on the bed. Early the next morning, we saw the housekeeper drop a bag into the dumpster. It was too early for normal maid service. I ran down and grabbed the bag. Inside it was a bloody pillowcase and lots of blood and beach-soaked paper towels."

Amos listened and nodded. "Sounds like you stumbled onto a murder, all right. And you think it was my missing person...based on a fuzzy video? Pretty thin if you ask me."

"There's more."

"I thought there might be."

The server brought the food and set it on the table. "Can I get you anything else?"

"We're good, thanks," Alexander said.

When she left, Alexander continued. "From the video, I thought I recognized a man I'd seen a few days earlier outside the hotel smoking. I'm sure it was the same guy who was on the balcony smoking in the video. I went to Lou's Bar, where Amanda worked, and convinced them to show me the video from the night she disappeared. Amanda served a table of two men; one was heavy-set. I recognized him as the man from the hotel balcony."

"Son of a bitch!"

"My thoughts exactly."

"You said you had evidence from the room. A bloody pillowcase. What'd you do with it? We need to test it for DNA. DNA would confirm if it was the missing girl."

"The evidence is preserved. I'm not ready to give it up. I don't want it to disappear."

Amos couldn't argue the point. "You said it's preserved. How?"

"Trust me. It is. I'll turn it over to you at some point."

"I get what you're doing, but withholding evidence is a crime."

"Only if a crime has been committed. As I said earlier, I thought I heard a shot. I think I saw a woman on the bed. She could have been having wild sex or gotten a bloody nose."

"Right. Stick with that."

"For now, I am. It's the same defense the lawyers would use if we brought in the man in the video."

"And there isn't a body. Son of a bitch."

"I told you I need your help. I've got an idea."

*****

Willie arrived at the War Room at 4:30 and went straight out onto the balcony to watch Guerline walk to the Grand Paradise Hotel. Once she arrived at the hotel, he joined the others inside. "I'm still not happy with her being over there," he mumbled to himself.

Bat was busy working on the two-way radios. Before she left, Guerline showed him her radio from the hotel. It was set to channel five, code twelve. He picked up one of the radios Jana had purchased, set it to channel one, code one, listened for a minute, and pressed the

PTT—Press To Talk—button. "Birdie num num." He released the mike and listened. No response.

Bat continued through the codes: Listening, pressing the PTT button, saying, "Birdie num num," releasing the button, and listening. Willie and Alexander watched with amusement. When Bat tried the routine on channel three, code twelve, he got a response.

"Who's playing on the radio?"

Bat switched to channel four code twelve. No response. He tried channel six, skipping channel five, the channel Guerline's radio was set to. No response. Channel seven.

"Who is this. Stop playing on the radio."

With a good idea of the sequence, Bat switched to channel nine, code twelve. "Birdie num num."

"Last warning. Stop playing on the radio. Next time, I will find you and fire you."

Bat put the radio back in its charger. "I've got the pattern," he said to Willie and Alexander. "Every other channel, code twelve on all. If he changes it, we'll get the new code from Guerline."

"Good work," Alexander said. "For now, let's set each radio on a different channel so we can monitor them. What about the ones you didn't try?"

"We have six radios. Channel one didn't seem to be in use. We can monitor three, five, seven, nine, and eleven."

"Can I see the radio?" Willie asked.

"Sure." Bat handed him a charged radio.

Willie examined it for a while and pressed several buttons. "Privacy codes act as filters, not security. If we set the radio to 'Code Off', it will open the squelch for any signal. We'll be able to hear conversations on any channel. We can also scan all the frequencies. The person on the other end was scanning. That's how he responded to Bat's transmissions."

"Good to know. It would have saved me a little time."

Willie handed the radio back to Bat. "We could have been scanning all day and not figured out the sequence. You figured the code out. Now we can program the radios to scan only the selected channels. The scan will be much faster. Scans can miss short bursts. We're less likely to miss one knowing which channels to scan."

"Because the person didn't respond to Bat when he spoke on the other channels, can we assume he's only scanning certain channels?" Alexander said.

"Correct. Which means we can pick a channel and use it." Willie said. "I suggest we test it daily to make sure it's not being monitored."

"How do we do that?" Alexander asked.

Willie set the radio to channel four and keyed the mike. "I need help." There was no response. "Anybody there?" Still no response.

"We're good. If anyone at the hotel had been listening to that channel, they would have thought a staff member needed help but had accidentally changed the frequency. I'm sure they'd have at least asked what the problem was."

"We won't need the radios much for our use," Alexander said. "But it's good we have them and know which channel we can use. We'll use channel four."

At 5:00, Jerry and Sam came into the War Room. Alexander updated them on the radios, badges, and IDs.

"I'll grab a suit in the morning when I go back to the house," Willie said.

"I didn't bring a suit," Jerry said. He eyeballed Alexander and Willie. "I won't be borrowing one from either of you."

"You're about Terrell's size. He may have one you could borrow," Sam said.

"I wouldn't worry about it. If we have to, we can buy a cheap suit," Bat said. "We have a much bigger issue."

TWENTY-SIX

With everyone gathered in the War Room, Bat asked the question that had been plaguing him. "You all may have already thought of this, but how are we going to get Sunday and McIntyre alone to pull off the sting?"

"First off, we don't need them alone," Willie said. "Or even together. We're watching them 24/7. Sooner or later, they're going to go to a restaurant or a bar. When they do, we'll scramble. Unless they venture north, away from us, they should be less than an hour from here. We should have plenty of time to meet them."

"Let me play the Devil's advocate. What if the next time they leave the Eagle's Nest, it's to grab another victim?"

"If we think they're going for a girl," Alexander said. "We call off the sting. We let them pick up a girl."

Willie's brow furrowed. "Are you kidding?"

"Not at all. We all want to nail Sunday and McIntyre. But I want to get them all. From the president on down. Everyone who's involved."

"You're pretty ambitious, Alex," Willie said.

"I know. And I have a plan. Well, to coin a phrase, a concept of a plan. For now, let's focus on the sting. If we can pull it off, the information we get will help me with my plan. I will share enough so that if we don't have a chance to pull the sting, we'll still be able to save the girl. Saving the girl is priority one."

"I thought we were going for a confession," Terrell said. "What other info are you after?"

Alexander took a long drink from a water bottle. "I don't believe for a minute that when Cockwomble wants to get laid, he rings Sunday or McIntyre and gives them his schedule. There's a middleman. Maybe at the Eagle's Nest, more likely in DC. That person calls Eagle's Nest and gives Sunday and McIntyre the date and time. He—I doubt it's a she—also gives Olga, the hotel manager, a heads-up. There are at least three, four, including the president. They're the big fish. I want them. Sunday and McIntyre will know who they are. I want to get those names."

"No doubt they know the contact at the Eagle's Nest," Willie said. "They can confirm if Olga is the contact at the hotel. That leaves one. The president's right-hand man. What are the chances Olga knows who it is?"

"I doubt it. I'd bet she only knows her contact. She may not even know a name. I think Olga gets a call with a day and time. She clears the west side of the hotel and orders the cameras off."

"And collects a nice pay day," Bat added.

"Exactly. That's why I want to get all of 'em."

Sam had been quietly listening to the conversation. "I get it. We're no longer going through the exercise of plotting an assassination. You want to bring down a sitting president. So do I. He's a sleazeball. At least two girls have died because of his deviant behavior. But look at the scope of the cover-up. I hate to say this, but no matter what we do, it might not be enough. In fact, they could end up coming after us."

Sam's statement had a sobering effect on the room. It was an outcome they'd considered privately but had not mentioned aloud. All of them wanted justice for Amanda and HG, but they would only take the risk if they had an airtight plan. Airtight on paper, anyway.

Alexander could see the mood swing. "I'm sure I know how you all feel. We'd all like to get justice for those girls, but it won't bring them back. Getting a confession from Sunday and McIntyre will at least give their families closure. I'm not willing to tell any of the families their loved ones are dead until I hear it from Sunday or McIntyre. I want them to confess and confirm they killed Amanda. I want to get HG's name. Any other names we get from them are a bonus. Once we get as many names as possible, the next goal is to stop them."

Willie looked around at his friends, slowly nodding. "I believe we all feel the same. If we don't nip it in the bud, the raping and killing might continue with two new recruiters, a different hotel, or even a different state. Let's get a confession and go from there, but keep the goal of exposing everyone in sight."

"I agree," Jerry said. "Getting the names of the girls is important, but I want the ring leaders. If we get those names, we can work on a way to bring them down. Worst case, we leak to the press that Sunday and McIntyre confessed and named names. Publish those names along with the details. It should be enough to cause an investigation, especially with the evidence from the hotel. Once it's out there, it would be difficult to cover it up. Sunday and McIntyre will be the patsies. They'll never make it to trial."

*****

Sean McIntyre still pined for Amanda. The chances of stumbling on another girl as beautiful as she was were slim. He decided to take luck out of the equation. He opened his laptop and searched for bars and restaurants between Palm Beach and Fort Lauderdale that were at least twenty miles from the compound. They had two rules: Don't hunt close to home. You might be recognized. Never return to the place where you picked up a girl.

McIntyre removed a small, folded piece of paper from a hidden pocket inside his wallet. When he unfolded it, he realized he'd not added Amanda to the list. He didn't need to, he'd remember her, but he wanted the list complete. He might forget where he met her.

In all caps, as small as he could print, he wrote "AMANDA. LOU'S SPORTS BAR." He drew a small heart at the end. "You'll be the last to die, Amanda. The next one comes away with me." He read the locations where they'd picked up the girls, folded the paper, and stuffed it back into his wallet.

There was no shortage of bars between Palm Beach and Fort Lauderdale. McIntyre focused on Delray Beach. According to Yelp, there were over a hundred and fifty bars in the area. Most were along Atlantic Avenue near the beach.

McIntyre grabbed his set of keys to the Cadillac, texted Sunday that he was going out, and left before he got a reply. He pulled out through the compound's hidden rear entrance and turned right onto US1. Delray Beach was eighteen miles south, not quite halfway to Fort Lauderdale. It was a thirty-minute drive.

Jessica pulled in behind him when he turned onto A1A. Her text to the group was simple:

The Caddy is on the move.

She followed up with:

Heading south. Looks like one occupant.

Terrell called her. "Can you tell who's driving?"

"No. It's dark, and the windows are tinted."

"Are you sure there's only one person in the car?"

"Yes. I'm behind him. I can only see one head."

"Should I join you or stay and keep watch?"

Jessica eased off the gas to keep a safe distance behind the SUV. "I'm good. Stay there. If I need you, I'll call. If we get close to Lauderdale, I'll see if Sam or Jerry can meet me...if I need help."

"Sounds good. Be careful."

Jessica texted an update to the group. She asked if anyone could stand by in case they were needed. Whenever she passed a landmark, she'd update the group on her location.

McIntyre turned right on Atlantic Avenue.

Atlantic Avenue narrowed to a two-lane road, lined with bars. Both sides of the street had on-street parking. The SUV's blinker came on, and the SUV pulled into a parking spot.

Jessica stopped to watch the big SUV squeeze into the space. The driver wasn't good at parallel parking. With no one behind her, she sat, waiting for the driver to get out. He didn't. Feeling she'd waited too long and was beginning to look suspicious, she eased past the Cadillac. She glanced over as she passed, but couldn't see the driver.

Being a Wednesday evening, the area was active, but not hopping. Jessica passed a couple of parking spots she thought were too close to the SUV and settled on one fifty yards down the street. It didn't take long for her to realize why the driver had not gotten out of the Cadillac. The sign read, in big, bold letters, "METER. FEES REQUIRED Sunday thru Thursday. 12PM to 9PM. Pay by App." She figured whoever was in the SUV was trying to use the app to pay for the parking. Jessica did the same.

She paid for parking and got out of the car. The driver was still in the SUV. She ducked behind a wall leading into a shop where she could see the SUV, but the occupant would have a hard time seeing her.

She texted the group:

> **The SUV parked on AA in front of a line of bars.**
> **I've parked and will follow. I still can't see who it is.**
> **Terrell: Be careful. If it's Sunday, don't let him**
> **see you. He might recognize you.**

"Fat chance," Jessica said to herself. "Sunday saw me in my dike stage. This is femme me. Totally different chick."

When the driver finally got out of the SUV, Jessica recognized him immediately. He walked to the sidewalk and looked up and down the street as though he was trying to decide which way to go. He turned to the right, away from Jessica. He walked half a block and went inside a bar. Jessica walked slowly in his direction.

A few minutes later, McIntyre came out of the bar, walked down the sidewalk, and entered the next bar. Jessica popped her head into the first bar and looked around. There were a couple of men sitting at the bar and a couple of tourists at a table.

Jessica came out in time to see McIntyre leave the second bar, walk a half a block, and go into another bar.

What the hell?

She peeked inside the bar. Again, it was empty except for a few patrons. The bartender was a middle-aged woman with tattoos.

When McIntyre didn't immediately come out of the third bar, Jessica walked slowly past the entrance. She could see him at the bar, a beer bottle in his hand. She kept walking past the building, stopped, and pulled out her phone.

> **It's McIntyre. He went to a bar. Stayed a minute. Went in another. Stayed a minute. He's in a third. Has a beer. I'm watching him.**

The text went to the group. Sam was the first to reply:

> **He's scoping out the bars. My guess is he's looking for another victim.**

Jessica made another pass in front of the bar. McIntyre was in a conversation with the bartender, an attractive girl in her early twenties. With McIntyre preoccupied with the bartender, Jessica took the time to peek in and look around.

Several couples were seated at tables. One couple sat at the opposite end of the bar. Several attractive college-aged girls were at the bar between them and McIntyre. When he wasn't talking to the bartender, he was checking them out.

The bartender was of medium height, about five feet six, with shapely legs. She wore a short denim skirt and a sleeveless, button-down denim vest with a V-neckline. Her tanned waist glowed from the gap between the vest and the skirt.

McIntyre didn't think the bartender was as beautiful as Amanda, but she was a close second. "How long have you worked here?" he asked when she came by to check on him.

"About six months."

"You like it? It seems like a nice little bar."

"I do. Well, I did. Christmas was good. Lots of tourists. Delray Beach is a popular vacation destination. It was a little slow in February, then Spring Break hit. This place was crazy. It's pretty much died now."

"Do you like it not being so hectic?"

"I do, but I liked the money when we were slammed. The tips were great. I have to get used to not making as much." The bartender's eyes suddenly widened, and she covered her mouth with her hand. "Oh my gosh, I shouldn't have said that. It sounds like I'm asking for a big tip. I'm not."

"Don't worry about it. I promise what you said won't affect the size of my tip."

"Um, okay." She wasn't sure if that was good or bad.

"Can I ask your name?"

"Sure, It's Sandy."

"How appropriate. You live near a beach."

Sandy sighed. "My last name is Beach." She wasn't in the habit of giving customers her last name, but McIntyre seemed harmless enough.

"You're kidding."

"Nope. My parents said they debated between Sandy and Wendy. They thought Sandy was cute."

"It is."

"It wasn't in elementary and middle school."

"I guess by high school, the kids matured?"

"No. I did." Sandy pushed her breasts together with her arms to make a point. "I grew these, got my teeth straightened, and, I guess, got kinda pretty."

"You got very pretty, Miss Beach. How 'bout another beer?"

Sandy blushed slightly. "Of course. And thank you." She got a beer from the cooler, set it on the bar in front of McIntyre, and went to check on other customers.

McIntyre watched her walk. "She's the one," he muttered. "Sandy Beach and me. On a sandy beach in the Bahamas."

His selection made, McIntyre finished his beer, laid two twenties on the bar, and left. Outside, he smiled widely, got in the big Cadillac, and drove toward the compound. Jessica called Terrell.

"He left the bar. He's headed north on US1. I think he's headed back to the Eagle's Nest. I'm halfway home. I don't see the point of following him."

"Make sure he stays on US1 for a couple of miles, then turn around and go back to the hotel. I'm sure he's coming back, too. I'll keep an eye out for him."

"Thanks." Jessica hung up. She followed the SUV a few miles north, turned off, made a U-turn, and headed back to the hotel.

While he was driving, McIntyre couldn't stop thinking about Sandy. He noticed the boat key in the drink holder, and an idea took shape. He pulled into the first service station he saw and parked. It was still early. If he waited a couple of hours, went back to the bar a little before closing, and offered Sandy a few thousand dollars to go boating, she might go with him. They could be anchored off a Bahamian island by morning. He'd offer her ten thousand dollars. Amanda was the only one who had turned ten down. It took twenty thousand to convince her.

TWENTY-SEVEN

Terrell called Jessica. "Where are you?"

"Back at the hotel."

"It's been an hour since you called. McIntyre isn't back."

"Oh, shit. I wonder if he circled back and picked up the bartender?"

"Did he spot you following him?"

"No. No way. Should I go back to the bar?"

"It's too late now. If he went back, he's got her."

Jessica's hands trembled. She swallowed hard to keep from vomiting.

Terrell could hear the gasps through the phone. "Are you okay?"

"No. I may have gotten the girl killed."

"I doubt it. That's not how they operate. There's nothing we can do about it now anyway. Hang tight."

"Okay. Please let me know when he shows...if he shows."

"I will. Bye."

Jessica hung up. She covered her face with her hands, rocked back and forth, and screamed "Fuck" at the wall.

At the service station, McIntyre sat in the parking lot, gazing into the darkness. He had time to run down to Hillsboro and make sure the boat was there. The boat held three hundred gallons of diesel. If it were full, he could easily get to the Bahamas and have plenty of fuel to explore the islands. What he didn't have was money and provisions.

He had a few hundred dollars in his pocket. Nowhere near enough. It wouldn't last long. He'd have to buy food before he picked up Sandy. Once he had her, if he stopped, she'd bolt. Even in the Bahamas, she could take off. He needed enough food and water to last at least two weeks. He knew after two weeks, she'd be in love and want to stay with him.

When he and Sunday picked up a girl for the boss, they carried at least ten thousand in cash. If the girl is hesitant, seeing the money would usually change her mind. With ten grand, they could cruise the islands for months. He would still need to stock the boat with food.

McIntyre sat in the parking lot making a list on his phone of all the supplies he would need for a month at sea. He would buy a bathing suit and other clothes for Sandy. He had a good idea of her size. Satisfied he'd made a good start to the list, he went into the service station and used the bathroom.

While washing his hands, he noticed the rusted condom machine on the wall. A crudely written sign hanging from it read, "See our selection of sexual health products available for purchase behind the counter." McIntyre didn't see the need for condoms. He and Sandy would ride bareback. Even if he had wanted them, he'd rather use the machine than ask the person behind the counter.

On his way out, he picked up a bag of Funyuns Flamin' Hot Flavored Onion Rings and filled a large cup of Dr. Pepper from the fountain machine. He paid cash at the counter. Taking a quick glance at the display of condoms, he passed.

Twenty minutes later, he pulled the SUV into the hidden driveway at the Eagle's Nest. Terrell sent a message to Jessica:

Mac is back.

*****

When Sam and Jerry relieved Terrell, he drove to his house to pick up a suit. He was about the same size as Jerry. He then drove to Willie's to grab a suit for him. Both suits were dark blue. On the drive from Greenacres to Fort Lauderdale, he couldn't get the near fuck-up out of his head. What if McIntyre had turned around and gone back to pick up the bartender?

Terrell wanted to call Jessica to ask how she was doing, but he assumed Morgan would be with her. The last thing they'd want was a call from him. When he got to the hotel, he brushed his teeth, took off his clothes, and fell into bed. Sleep came easier than expected.

Sleep came easily for Jessica, too, with Morgan beside her to listen to her and console her. When she woke, she still thought about what she'd done, but didn't feel as upset about it. Leaving was a dumb mistake, but one any of them might have made.

Morgan left for the office at 8:30. Not long afterward, Jessica heard movement in the War Room. She got up, showered, dressed, and went into the adjoining room. Bat was the only person in the room.

"You're up early," Jessica said.

"I don't sleep much. I caught up on other work last night. I thought I'd come here and get a jump on the IDs. I found a couple of good templates. I hope they look legit. I have no idea what a real DOJ ID card looks like."

She watched over Bat's shoulder as he pulled up the template images on his laptop. They were all similar. Horizontal, featuring a color photograph of a random person on the right side, the Department of Justice seal displayed on the left, and "DOJ" in big letters in the middle. One template had a barcode along its bottom edge. Another had squiggly anti-counterfeit lines in the background.

"Which looks the most real to you?"

Jessica studied the images. "I've never seen a DOJ ID. My CIA ID had a barcode along the bottom and lines in the background. Can you merge those two?"

"Sure. These could be old templates. They may even be templates made by someone who's never seen a real ID. You can't trust the shit you find on the internet these days."

"If I haven't seen a DOJ ID card, I doubt Sunday or McIntyre have. They've probably seen a lot of Secret Service IDs. I wonder if they're similar."

Bat Googled images for an SS ID. The search returned a plethora of pictures. All different. "That didn't help. Do any of you know anyone in the DOJ or SS?"

"I don't know anybody well enough to ask for a copy of their ID. The others might. But, unless they're close friends, they won't send copies of their IDs."

Bat frowned. "It was worth a shot. We'll do the best we can. Willie and Jerry will need to remember to flash the badge and ID quickly so the guys can't get a good look at it."

"I can't think of a single time I showed my credentials outside the office. Then again, we don't interrogate or arrest people. In the field, most agents don't carry their IDs, for obvious reasons. You should ask Alex how closely most people look at his badge when he flashes it."

"I will. By the way, how'd last night go?"

Jessica flinched. "Fine. McIntyre drove to Delray Beach and went to a couple of bars. He was in and out of the first two, but stayed in the third for about half an hour."

"Did you get the name of the bar? The one he stayed in for a while."

"Yes, it was the Bearded Clam."

"Sounds appetizing."

"It seemed okay from the outside. It's on the main street that runs through Delray."

Jessica watched Bat work on the IDs for a few minutes and got bored. "Unless you need me, I'm going back to my room to lie down for a while."

"I'm good."

"Cool." Jessica went into her room and closed the door. Alone, she began to imagine what McIntyre might have done after she stopped following him. She closed her eyes and tried to force it out of her mind.

Not long after Jessica left the War Room, Willie entered. He was carrying the suit Terrell had picked up for him. "I see I'm the first one here this morning. Other than you, I mean."

"Jessica came out for a few minutes. She's back in her room. I'm working on the fake IDs. I see you have a suit. Great. Once I have the picture, I can see what these are going to look like."

Willie put on the white shirt, tied the tie around his neck, and slipped the jacket on. "Where we gonna do this?"

Bat glanced around the room. The curtains were open, allowing the space to fill with natural light. He pointed to a landscape print hanging on the wall. "If we remove that picture, we'll have a blank wall and the lighting will be perfect."

The picture was securely attached to the wall with tamper-proof, theft-resistant hardware.

"What's plan B?" Willie asked.

"I don't know." Bat studied the room. "That wall is clean, but the light will be coming in from the side. Even if I use the flash, the lighting won't be good."

They decided to try it. Bat took several photos with the camera flash off and several with it on. He viewed the images on his phone.

"These aren't bad. I can adjust them a little in Photoshop. This'll work. We'll need to take Jerry's photo in the same spot. We want the images to be similar."

"I can tell ya, muh picture is gonna be way different than Jerry's. In every ID I've had, my picture is a big black blob on a white screen. Don't spend too much time on the photo. If it's too good, it'll be a red flag."

"Good to know. I'll make sure it's good enough so anyone who looks closely at it will be able to tell it's you."

"When we got our IDs made at the agency, an HR person snapped a picture. One picture. Like it or not. That's your ID photo for life." Willie removed the tie, shirt, and jacket and hung them on the door.

Bat tried to imagine how female employees felt about the one-photo policy. He laughed. "I'll work on your ID now. What name do you want to use?"

"For me, use Willie Brown. Use Jerry Jackson for Jerry." Willie thought for a minute. "Use Jeremiah Jackson for Jerry. It sounds more realistic."

"Will do. I'll let you know when it's ready for inspection."

"Okay, thanks. I'll go back to my room and hang out. I think we're going to be doing a lot of hanging out before anything happens."

"As long as nothing happens before we're ready, I'm okay with hanging out."

Willie said goodbye and left. Bat continued to work on the IDs.

*****

It became a waiting game. After being on surveillance all night, Jerry slept in. He came by the War Room when he woke up and had his picture taken. While he was there, Willie joined him. They discussed what they wanted to learn from Sunday and McIntyre. Bat joined in, throwing curve balls, hoping to knock them off their game. Neither Jerry nor Willie flinched or broke character.

"You guys are good," Bat said when he'd stopped trying to trick them.

"It's good to know all the CIA training wasn't wasted," Jerry said.

Bat smiled. It dawned on him that he was trying to trip up professionals. "Oh, jeez, I just remembered, we don't have listening devices. I started to look for Bluetooth mics yesterday and forgot all about it."

"I don't think you're going to find a Bluetooth mic small enough. Try small recording devices. They come in pens, key chains, and watches. I've seen some in the shape of car key fobs. I don't know how well they work. A pen would be good. The camera is at the top. If it's in a shirt pocket, only the lens sticks out."

"Any of them could work," Willie said. "Maybe a pen each, a key fob, and a watch. Between the four recorders, we should get every word they say recorded."

"Including video," Jerry said. "Video is always nice."

"I'll look at those and have Jana order them," Bat said.

"I hope you don't mind me asking," Willie said. "But what's her deal? She seems to be footing the bill for the hotel. Whatever we need, she pays for it. She even offered to help us out if we were hurting for money."

"Her ex was a big-time lawyer. Not a trial lawyer. Mergers and acquisitions. He was loaded. They were getting a divorce, but he died before he signed the papers. She walked away with a hefty inheritance."

"Daaaamn. That good looking and a shitload of money. You said her ex died before he could sign the papers?"

"Yep."

"Did the big guy have a hand in his dying?"

 "As a matter of fact, no. He met her much later."

"Man, some guys have all the luck. Good for him."

"I'm glad she's here and helping. I'm doing okay, but if we were paying for the printers, radios, spy cameras, and all the other stuff, I'm not sure I could afford it."

"We'd manage," Willie said. "But I sure like having those radios. I like being able to keep tabs on Guerline when she's at the hotel."

"I keep a radio on and scanning. It's been extremely quiet," Bat said.

Willie took a deep breath and exhaled. "The calm before the storm?"

*****

McIntyre spent the day on his laptop. He confirmed the range of a Back Cove 372 Yacht was roughly three hundred miles at a cruising speed of twenty-five knots. At a slower speed of seven to eight knots, the range increased to almost a thousand miles. With more time than money, he'd cruise at seven knots.

Provisions would be the trick. There needed to be enough food on board to feed two people for at least two weeks. A month would be better. As soon as Sandy figured out she'd been kidnapped, she wouldn't be happy. Explaining to her that after she had sex with their boss, Sunday planned to shoot her in the back of the head wasn't likely to calm her.

McIntyre rubbed his chin for a few minutes. He had already formulated a plan to get Sunday out of the Cadillac once they had Sandy. Originally, after Sunday was out of the car, he would knock Sandy out with a shot of Propofol, which he'd have ready in his pocket. He'd drive her to the boat, get her onboard, and take off. He'd be miles offshore before Sunday knew he'd taken the boat.

His new idea was to fake a call after Sunday was out of the car. He'd tell Sandy there was a change of plan. She'd still be paid, but they were going to take a yacht to meet his boss. It would be an overnight trip. She'd be paid double.

Instead of going out the Pompano Beach Passage, he'd follow the Intracoastal Canal to the Stranahan River and take the Jetty Buoy Passage to the Atlantic. Ironically, the canal passed within a thousand yards of the Overlook Hotel, where Sunday and the president would still be waiting for them.

Once he was in the Atlantic, Bimini was sixty nautical miles east. He'd dock at a marina on the back side of the island and tell Sandy there was another minor change of plans. They needed to get fuel and provisions, and they'd rendezvous with the boss's yacht the next morning. She'd be so impressed with the boat and the water, she'd believe whatever he said. If necessary, he'd tell her she'd be paid another ten grand. Ten thousand a day.

After he stocked up on food, water, and fuel, he'd motor to the leeward side of a secluded island and drop anchor. That is where he would break the news to Sandy that they'd be together. McIntyre closed his eyes and pictured Sandy in a skimpy bikini. Red. No, blue. Aqua blue. She'd look amazing.

"Hey!"

The loud voice snapped McIntyre out of his daydream. "What?"

"The Chief called." Chief was short for Chief of Staff. "The boss is coming in this weekend. He has golf on Saturday. They won't know if he's coming to the hotel until he's finished playing golf. We should be on stand-by at the hotel on Saturday morning. If he's coming, we won't get the word until late. We'll have to grab a crack whore from a titty bar. He won't care."

"Damn. It's only been a week. It used to be once every few months. Then, once every two weeks. Now weekly? He's pushing it." McIntyre knew he was preaching to the choir.

"I know. But what are we going to do, say no? Give all this up?"

"Don't want to do that. What time do you want to leave on Saturday?"

"We can't go hunting until we know the boss is coming. No need to get there too early. Let's leave at 11:00."

McIntyre nodded. His thoughts had already turned to Sandy.

TWENTY-EIGHT

Bat continued to work on the ID cards early Friday morning. The first few samples were good, but not great. After a little tweaking, he printed one on photo paper. The lighting seemed off. Willie had said the picture didn't need to be perfect, but a poorly lit photo might necessitate a closer look. When an ID is flashed, the picture is what people first see.

The fake DOJ badges and wallets were delivered to the condo and brought to the hotel by Alexander later that morning. Willie joined Bat and Alexander in the War Room. Each had a cup of coffee while Bat made a couple of adjustments to the image. He printed another copy, and they all thought it looked perfect. He printed Jerry's ID.

Instead of using scissors, Bat used Alexander's razor-sharp Kershaw Bel Air pocket knife and a straight edge to trim the ID cards. Inside the wallet, the cards were perfect. If, for any reason, the cards were checked outside the wallet, the photo paper would be a dead giveaway that they were fakes.

Bat put both ID cards between a sheet of laminating paper and ran them through the machine. After trimming, he held the cards up and examined them. He wasn't an expert, but he wouldn't suspect they were fake. He placed the cards inside the wallets and passed them to Alexander and Willie.

"These are good," Alexander said.

"Very impressive. Good job," Willie added.

"Thanks, guys. The recording devices are out for delivery. They'll get here today. I think we're set. All we need now is Sunday and McIntyre."

"According to Terrell, McIntyre went out last night," Willie said. "He stopped at several bars in Delray Beach, had a beer or two, then went back to the Eagle's Nest. He thinks he may have been scouting their next victim."

"Jessica mentioned it to me this morning. He went into a place called the Bearded Clam. I sent the name and address to a colleague and asked him to see if they had hackable CCTV. I told him the time McIntyre was there and gave him a description."

Alexander's brow furrowed. "You asked a colleague to hack it for you? Was that a good idea?"

"Yeah, I've got plenty on my plate. He loves hacking shit." Bat checked his laptop for new emails. "And there it is, right on cue." Bat downloaded the video and played it. Alexander, Willie, and Terrell crowded in behind him.

"Crikey. Give me a little space. Hang on." Bat turned on the TV, switched the input to HDMI, and pressed play on his laptop. The video appeared on the 55" hotel TV. The video played for a short time before it showed McIntyre entering the bar.

"There he is," Jerry said.

"The bartender's cute," Alexander said.

"She's a knockout," Bat added.

"He's got his next victim," Jerry said.

Bat paused the video and spun around in his chair to face the others. "What are we going to do about it?"

"Nothing," Alexander said.

"You're kidding. We're gonna let those two kill her?" Bat asked.

"Absolutely not. We've got them on round-the-clock surveillance. If she goes with them, which isn't guaranteed, we know where they're going. We even have a person in the hotel, and Bat has access to the video and the elevators. He hasn't used it and doesn't want to because it would give him away, but he can. There are six of us and two of them. I'm sure we can protect her."

"Why risk it?" Bat asked. "Why not notify the police and have them picked up on kidnapping charges as soon as they have the girl? It would get them off the streets."

"It wouldn't get the others. The ones who are responsible. Sunday and McIntyre are a couple of lackeys doing a job. Plus, I don't believe they kidnap the girls. They offer them so much money that they come of their own free will. Remember, Amanda left the bar about fifteen minutes after they did."

"All true," Willie said. "We need to catch 'em with their pants down."

"Exactly," Alexander said. "Catch Cockwomble with his pants down. It won't help with the other big players, like the hotel manager and whoever the big cheese is at the Eagle's Nest, but knock over the first domino, and the others will fall."

"Again, dats true. But I shoo would like to see all dim muthers go to prison," Willie said, invoking his Cajun accent for no apparent reason.

"They might. We have proof they cleaned the hotel and disposed of evidence. They also deleted the video from the night HG died. Olga will go down for that. It'll be obvious neither Sunday nor McIntyre is the mastermind. As soon as there's a new Attorney General and FBI Director, there'll be an investigation. You know all of them will want to make a deal to avoid prison. It will be interesting to see who gets Club Fed and who gets Leavenworth."

*****

McIntyre sat in the living room of the small bungalow he lived in on the grounds of the president's compound/private resort for the rich. He wanted to load up on provisions, get Sandy, get on the boat, and sail away, but needed cash. The ten thousand dollars they used to lure girls was kept in a safe, and the money wasn't given to them until they left the compound. They gave it back when they returned, minus any expenses.

The job paid well, but McIntyre's penchant for women and gambling made quick work of his bi-weekly salary. He'd tell himself to save for the future. Still, the day after payday, he'd find himself in a strip joint putting twenty-dollar bills in a girl's G-string or blowing it at an illegal craps table. He wouldn't spend all his money. He'd save enough to live on until the next payday, which would be on Saturday. One day too late. He'd stick with his plan, which was good. What McIntyre didn't like was buying provisions in the Bahamas. Selection would be limited and expensive. If tomorrow were called off, he'd come up with a plan to have the boat stocked with enough supplies to last him and Sandy at least a month. They'd eat a lot of fish, too. Stretch out the provisions.

The president's compound featured an exclusive, high-end dining room for its guests. The private club offered formal indoor dining as well as casual al fresco dining on the patio. Sunday and McIntyre were encouraged to eat on the patio. At 5:00, McIntyre strolled to the patio and sat at his usual table, which was in a corner, away from the other guests.

Sunday walked up and sat at the table.

"I'd prefer to eat alone," McIntyre said.

"Too fucking bad. Are you still pissed about the blonde?"

"I am. You shouldn't have shot her."

"You nailed her anyway. I made it easier for you."

McIntyre clenched his jaw. His eyes narrowed. "I would have been fine."

"You were going to knock her out with Propofol so she would have just laid there anyway."

"You're an asshole."

"Hey, you fucked the dead chick."

"She wasn't dead. I told you I could feel her heart beating. Your little .22 caliber bullet rattled around in her brain, messing shit up. It didn't kill her. She bled out. Probably didn't die until I'd finished."

A young female server brought two beers to the table. "The usual," she said with a heavy Hispanic accent. "The special tonight is grilled snapper."

Sunday and McIntyre nodded. Neither man smiled.

"I'll have the special," Sunday said.

"Me too."

When the server left, Sunday said, "I'd bet you she's illegal. And not a day over sixteen."

"Why doesn't the boss fuck her?"

"Too many witnesses. We couldn't kill her when he was done with her. People know she works here."

McIntyre shrugged. "He could have ICE pick her up when he was done and ship her off to a South American prison."

"He could. I'm sure they'd replace her with another cutie tomorrow. You realize that would put us out of work."

"Oh, yeah, I didn't think about that."

"I'm sorry about the blonde. You knew I was going to shoot her."

"I know," McIntyre acknowledged. "But she was so damn good-looking."

"Even covered in the president's pee?"

"Just when I was about to get over being pissed at you..."

"I make a pee joke." Sunday slapped the table and belly laughed.

*****

The pen spy cameras, watch, and key fob arrived. Bat charged them all and tested each for image and sound quality. All were surprisingly good. He put a pen in Willie's suit pocket, stood back ten feet, and spoke in a normal voice. When he played it back, the audio was loud and clear.

On the back of the pen was a tiny LED that displayed the pen's status. When powered on, the LED flashed blue. When recording, the LED was blue but hard to see. Bat went into the bathroom, closed the door, and turned off the lights. He had to tilt the pen at a forty-five-degree angle to see the blue light. There was no way anyone more than a few inches away would spot it.

The lens, embedded above the clip, was small enough that it couldn't be seen unless someone was looking for it. Bat turned the silver base to expose the ink reservoir. He scribbled a few lines on a piece of scratch paper. The pen worked. He wasn't shocked, but a little surprised.

Bat suddenly realized that agents would have a notepad. Willie and Jerry will need small, wire-bound steno pads. Bat sent a text to the group:

> **Willie and Jerry should have small steno pads. Unless Alex has any, someone should stop at a Walmart or drug store and pick up a couple.**
> **Morgan: I have a ton of those. I'll bring two to the hotel tonight.**
> **Willie: Thanks**

Not having a notepad wouldn't have been a red flag. Certainly not to Sunday or McIntyre. Having pens in their pockets with no paper, maybe. Not likely. Taking notes might make Jerry and Willie look more convincing.

Bat leaned back in his chair.

What else have I forgotten?

When the idea of sending a couple of team members to interview the two suspects was first tossed around, it seemed simple. Once it was thought out, it became much more complicated. Badges, IDs, recording devices. He was amazed that it all came together so quickly. They were ready. They had what they needed, except a way to set up a meeting.

*****

McIntyre fell asleep while planning how he would sail away with Sandy and woke up thinking about it. He wasn't prepared, but he could pull it off. He had to. He wasn't going to let Sunday shoot her.

The overnight bag he usually took to the hotel was too small for what he'd need to cruise the Caribbean for a month...or longer. He unzipped the bag a few inches, grabbed each side, and yanked. The bag split apart. "Damn, my bag broke."

The only other bag he had was a carry-on with wheels. It was small, but much larger than the overnight bag. He wouldn't need much. Underwear, five pairs, shorts, t-shirts, toiletries, and a pair of flip-flops. He'd be wearing long pants, a polo shirt, and a sports coat. If he needed anything else, he'd buy it in the Bahamas when he bought clothes for Sandy.

In his jacket pocket, he had two capped syringes loaded with propofol. If his plan didn't work, and Sandy was forced to fuck the president, he would use one on Sunday and leave with Sandy. He would tell her Sunday was going to kill her, and he still would when he got the chance. He would tell her that there was no safe place to hide. Her only option would be to head to the Caribbean with him. If she still refused, he'd use the second syringe on her. When she came around, he'd say he only did it to save her life.

He decided the new plan was better than his original idea. She couldn't go to the police. He'd tell her how the murder of the Hispanic girl was covered up. The press wouldn't believe her. *Sure, the president did what to you?*

He would tell her about the other girls, especially Amanda, and explain to her that the only way she could stay alive was to stay with him. He'd promise her they'd be able to go back in a few months after the others were sure she wouldn't tell anyone what happened. By then, Sandy would be in love with him, and she'd stay with him.

McIntyre felt this version would keep Sandy from trying to escape, and she'd have a vested interest in staying hidden. Staying hidden was the only part of the plan he hadn't worked out. Oddly, he wouldn't be hiding Sandy; he'd be hiding the boat.

The fact was, Sunday would never tell anyone what happened. He'd be pissed, for sure. But not enough to look for him. The boat owner, on the other hand, if he knew his boat was missing, would either come looking for it or report it as stolen. As far as McIntyre knew, he and Sunday were the only ones who ever used the boat. It was possible that no one would look for it, at least for a while.

The more he thought about it, the more he liked it. Don't kidnap Sandy, save her. He'd let her call her family and tell them she, on a whim, took off with a guy she met in the bar. She's fine. Don't worry. McIntyre leaned back, interlocked his fingers behind his head, and smiled. Nice plan.

McIntyre was still smiling when Sunday knocked on the door of the bungalow. He grabbed the carry-on bag and opened the door.

"You ready?" Sunday asked. "What the fuck is that?" He pointed at the carry-on. "You moving to the hotel?"

"The zipper on my other bag broke." He pointed to the bag crumpled on the floor. "This is the only other bag I have."

Sunday shrugged. "Let's go."

They walked across the compound to the maintenance garage, where the Cadillac Escalade was parked. The SUV had been washed and fueled. McIntyre popped the hatch and threw his bag into the cargo area. Sunday drove. They took the back entrance out. When they turned onto A1A, a small white Toyota followed.

Jessica rang Terrell. "They're on the move. Both of them. Heading south."

"Coming up behind you. Stay back. It's daylight, and there's not much traffic. We don't want to get spotted."

"They could be going to the store. If they get south of Delray, I'll call the others and give them a heads up."

"If they stop at the bar in Delray, let everyone know."

"Roger that." Jessica hung up. She saw Terrell behind her. They'd hang back as far as they could without risking losing the SUV. Every few miles, Jessica would turn right and let Terrell take the lead. She'd make a U-turn and come in behind him.

Jessica called Terrell again. "They just passed Atlantic Avenue, where the Bearded Clam is. They aren't going there."

"Not now, anyway."

Jessica disconnected and called Willie. She told him where they were and that they were heading south. Willie thanked her and hung up. He sent a group text:

Sunday and McIntyre are heading this way. Not sure if they're coming to the hotel. Stand by. Game on.

TWENTY-NINE

The Cadillac SUV turned into the parking garage one block from the Grand Paradise Hotel, the same garage where it disappeared three weeks earlier. Terrell parked on the side of the street, close to the garage entrance. Jessica drove to the Overlook Hotel.

As soon as the group text went out, everyone assembled in the War Room. Bat was at his laptop, monitoring the Overlook's CCTV cameras. He fed the live feed to the large-screen television in the room. "There they are, in the lobby," he said.

"Sunday is carrying a bag, and McIntyre is rolling one," Willie said. "They're staying the night."

Olga Sokolov, the hotel manager, greeted Sunday and McIntyre in the lobby. She was short, five-two, with blue eyes, fair skin, light brown hair, cut short, and an athletic build. She was attractive in a rugged, Eastern European way. A slight Russian accent could be detected in her deep voice.

They talked for a few minutes, with Olga doing most of it. She handed them their room keys. From the various cameras, the group in the War Room watched the two walk to their rooms.

"Suit up," Willie said to Terrell. "We need to go talk to those two."

"They aren't there for a holiday," Sam said. "They'll go out later to recruit a girl for tonight. Are we ready?"

"We've talked about it for days," Jerry said. "Alex put together a good plan. We've covered a lot of contingencies, but I would have liked a little more time, but if it goes down tonight, we're ready."

Bat pressed the Record button on the top of each spy pen, then handed them to Willie and Jerry. "They're recording. You don't need to touch the pens other than to write with them. Both have sixty-four gig memory cards. You can record for hours."

"Are you ready, Agent Jackson?" Willie asked.

"You betcha, Agent Brown."

The two left the hotel room and walked to the parking garage. They drove Willie's KIA Telluride. It resembled a South Florida rental. After making the block, they pulled into the Overlook Hotel's front entrance and parked. The valet attendant came around to collect the key.

"Leave it." Willie flashed the wallet containing the badge and ID. The attendant took a quick glance at Willie's ID and walked away.

Inside the lobby, the bar was to their left, the check-in counters were to the right, and an unoccupied concierge desk was at the far end. Willie and Jerry walked toward the counters. A staunch woman with a slight Russian accent intercepted them.

"May I help you?"

"Olga Sokolov?" Willie asked.

Olga's head tilted like a puppy's might when begging for a treat. "Yes."

"I'm Agent Brown, this is Agent Jackson. We're with the DOJ." Both men showed her their IDs. She took a wide-eyed glance.

"What can I do for you?"

"We'd like to talk to Mark Sunday and Sean McIntyre."

"Who?"

Willie's brow furrowed. "We flew in from Washington this morning. I'm tired and not in the mood to be fucked with." Willie made a slow pan of the lobby. "My partner and I are going to go into that bar. Go get Sunday and McIntyre and bring them down."

"I'll call them."

"No." Willie's voice got loud. "I said, go get them and bring them to the bar."

"Okay." The authority in Olga's voice had diminished, but was still present. She scurried off toward the elevators.

The fake agents went into the bar and sat at a table near the back.

"You were good," Jerry said. "If Olga had any thought about checking us out, you squashed them."

"But for how long? We need to get what we can out of those two and get out of here."

Three minutes later, Olga walked into the bar with Sunday and McIntyre in tow. Both men wore blank, confused expressions, clearly unsure why they'd been summoned.

When they reached the table, Willie and Jerry stood, showed their badges, and introduced themselves. As they slipped their IDs back into their inside pockets, they left their jackets open just long enough for the two men to notice the holstered service weapons at their sides.

"Thank you, Olga. We'll let you know if we need you," Willie said. "Have a seat, gentlemen."

"We're from the DOJ," Willie began. "Here at the request of the Attorney General. She's not happy."

"What's it got to do with us?" Sunday asked.

Willie sighed heavily. "Maybe a young girl getting tossed off the balcony a few weeks ago."

"Not sure what you're talking about."

"How 'bout the disappearance of Amanda Elliott last week? Ring any bells?" Jerry asked.

McIntyre eyed Sunday. "No, I—"

"Cut the bullshit, Mark. We aren't here for our health. Two fuck-ups in as many weeks. We were sent here to make sure there aren't any more. We've been briefed. We know exactly what's going on. We're going to ask you some questions, and we want the truth. We know the answers to most of the questions. If you lie to us, you'll be in a god-awful Venezuelan prison by midnight. The president can get his own pussy tonight."

Both Sunday and McIntyre's eyes were wide open and unblinking.

"Okay," McIntyre said. "The girl who fell, that was an accident."

"How does a dead girl fall off a balcony by accident?"

"She wasn't dead."

"No shit."

"She slipped away," Sunday said. "And I caught her on the balcony. When I hit her, she was too close to the railing and fell over."

"It's my understanding girls aren't supposed to...slip away."

"They aren't. I was a little slow. It won't happen again."

"It better not. What about the blonde, Amanda?"

Sunday looked at McIntyre. Did the agents know he fucked her? No way.

"What about her? She's dead," Sunday said.

"You picked her up at Lou's Bar in Hollywood."

"How'd you know?"

"In South Florida, young Hispanic girls disappear every day. An attractive blonde, not so much. A missing persons report was filed on Sunday morning. Our guys watched the video from the bar. Guess who she was talking to fifteen minutes before she disappeared?"

"Oh, fuck," McIntyre said.

"Oh, fuck is right," Jerry said.

"Where is she?"

"The bottom of the Atlantic. With the others." McIntyre's eyes teared up slightly.

"Good. Her body will never be found. The video has been destroyed as well. Between that and what several agencies went through to cover up the girl who fell. We want to know the name of every girl you've killed, if you have them, and where you picked them up."

"Why do you need it?" Sunday asked. His voice didn't boom with confidence.

"We need to go back and check each of them to see if you're in any video. We understand a PI viewed the video at Lou's. We don't know who he is...yet. If he keeps digging into missing persons and sees the two of you with another missing girl, and if he's good enough to find the videos, he's good enough to put two and two together. We'll send people to every place you met a girl, even if it was six months ago, to make sure there's no video."

"I'm not sure I remember many names or places," Sunday said.

"I do." McIntyre's hands shook as he reached for his wallet. He pulled out a small, folded piece of paper. "This is all of them." He slid the paper to Willie.

Willie pursed his lips to keep from smiling while he read the list. The urge quickly vanished. A knot formed in his stomach. It took all he had to keep from pulling his Glock from its holster and putting bullets in their heads. Instead, he pulled out his phone and snapped a picture of the list. "That's the first smart thing you've done. You saved us a lot of time. We may be able to catch an earlier flight back to DC." He handed the paper back to McIntyre. Willie would have liked to keep the list, but had a feeling he would be asked why. He had a reply ready, but believed a photo of the list was sufficient.

"Other than Olga, who here at the hotel knows what you do? Do the same housekeepers take care of the room every time?"

"Honestly, I'm not sure. We leave with the body and don't come back," Sunday said.

"You each have a room. You never spend the night here?" Jerry asked.

"We have rooms. It's more for convenience than sleeping. We get here early and may need to hang out for a while. The president almost always comes on a Saturday night. If he's delayed or cancels, we may stay overnight. It depends. If he's delayed and reschedules for Sunday night, we stay. He's never here on a weekday."

"Have you ever brought a girl here and had him cancel?"

Sunday's eyes narrowed. Willie wondered whether he was beginning to question the agents' validity.

"As I said earlier, we know the answer to most of our questions. We want to make sure you're telling the truth."

Sunday seemed satisfied. "Only once did we have a girl, and he canceled. Usually, by five or six in the afternoon, it's confirmed. After he's confirmed, we'll go find a girl."

"What did you do with the girl?" Jerry asked.

"We took turns with her. When we were done, Mark killed her.

She's on the list. Her name was Kayla. Or Kylie. Something like that, I don't remember."

Willie rubbed his hand on his thighs to keep from pulling his gun. "Couldn't you have let her go? You kill the girls to silence them."

"I suppose. But we would've had to pay her. We offer the girls ten grand. We're never going to pay. Patrick would be pissed."

Willie assumed Patrick was the person at the Eagle's Nest who pulled the strings. "We'll ask Olga about the hotel staff. That brings us to another question. Who at the compound, other than Patrick, knows what you do?"

"I don't think anyone does. We know a few of the staff, servers, cooks, maintenance guys, and housekeepers. Not well. We try to keep to ourselves. They think we're like a special security detail."

"What about the Secret Service? Are there any the AG should be concerned with?"

"They aren't a friendly group. The ones who accompany the president to the hotel travel with him."

"We know who they are," Jerry said. "They're hand-picked. Nothing to worry about there."

"You think there's anything to worry about?" McIntyre asked.

Jerry overexaggerated a mouth drop. "The president of the United States comes to this hotel to fuck young women, women you two supply and then kill. Do you think he should be worried about you two?"

"We've been pretty careful," McIntyre said.

"Yeah, we've seen how careful you've been. Pretty careful doesn't cut it."

"We'll be more careful from now on," Sunday said.

Willie said to Jerry. "Do you have any other questions?"

Jerry had one more question: What was Patrick's last name? He didn't know how to ask it. He pulled the spy pen from his breast pocket, dropped his hands below the table, and twisted the bottom of the pen to expose the ink tip. He pulled the steno pad from a side pocket and set it on the table. "Spell the first and last name of everyone, including Patrick, at the compound who might have even an inkling of why you two are there."

McIntyre scratched his jaw. "The head guy is Patrick Willoughby. I ain't too good at spelling. You know him, anyway."

"We do. Go on."

"Um. There's the guy who keeps the cash. When we leave, he gives us a stack of cash. We flash it at the girls. They may not be too interested until they see the big stack of hundred-dollar bills. When we get back, we give it back to him. He must know what's going on. His name is Bill. B I-L L. I don't know his last name."

"Anyone else?"

"How 'bout the guy who runs the garage. He keeps all the vehicles washed and fueled. His instructions are to clean the inside of the car with bleach whenever we return it. I'm sure he has a clue. I doubt he knows he's cleaning out the remains of a dead girl. His name's Joe." Sunday started to spell it. Willie cut him off. "We got it."

"That's it," McIntyre said. "I can't think of nobody else who might know what we do."

"When you go out to get a girl, knowing who it's for, how do you decide where to go?" Willie asked.

"We usually start in bars. If there's a hot girl in the bar or a server who's hot, we'll proposition them. We're nice about it. We tell them we understand and we don't mean to offend them. We say it's for a rich client. Not many turn us down. If we can't find a suitable girl, and it's getting crunch time, we go to a titty bar. Problem is, most of those girls are tatted up. The president don't like tats."

"So you've never failed to supply a girl?"

"Never," Sunday said. "If we did, we'd be fired."

"Or shot," McIntyre added. "I'm not sure either of us can walk away from this job."

"Why not?" Willie asked. "Who are you going to tell? You'd be hanging yourselves."

McIntyre shrugged.

"One last thing," Jerry said. "Several months back, we had to cover up the death of a young girl. It was at a different hotel. Is she on your list?"

"No," McIntyre said. "That happened at a resort hotel on

Hollywood Beach. It wasn't us. I don't know what happened or why he was there, but I heard the president was pissed. You probably know more about it than we do."

"We do. The AG wanted us to confirm that you weren't involved. That would have been strike three."

"That wasn't us, I swear."

"I didn't think so, but I had to ask." Jerry ripped a sheet out of the steno pad and wrote the number of a burner phone on it. "For obvious reasons, we don't carry business cards. This is my number. Every time you pick up a girl, text me her name and where you found her. We'll make sure there are no videos of you two."

Sunday took the piece of paper. "Oh man, that's great. Thanks."

The men stood and shook hands. Sunday and McIntyre scurried out with a fast-paced hip-swinging motion.

"Let's fuck with Olga while we're here," Willie said.

"I like it."

They walked into the lobby but didn't see her. After looking around, Willie went into the bar and asked the bartender if she would call Olga on the radio. While she was calling, Willie read her name tag. Mia. He wondered if she was the bartender who was training Guerline.

"Yes, ma'am," Mia said into the mike, then she turned to Willie. "She'll be here in a minute."

Willie thanked her and joined Jerry, who was waiting in the lobby. Olga came around from behind the counter and joined them. She, too, walked faster than she had earlier.

"You wanted to see me?"

"Yes. We have one question," Willie said. "When you clean the room the morning after, what happens to any blood evidence that might be in the room?"

"If it's bad, the housekeepers toss it. Otherwise, it goes in the laundry."

Jerry's eyes widened. "They toss it...in the trash?"

"Yes."

"You don't have an incinerator?"

"Why would we have an incinerator? This is a hotel. We've never had a problem."

"The housekeepers. Are they the same every time?"

"Yes. They've been screened and are paid very well. They're very loyal."

"Do they know who they're cleaning up after?"

"No. No one in the hotels knows. They know it's someone with money. They don't know who."

Willie gave her an exaggerated nod. "It sounds like you have your part under control anyway. The AG will be happy to let the president know that."

Olga's eyes brightened. Her face relaxed, and the stiffness melted away. "Thank you."

"Thank you for your cooperation. We have a plane to catch."

"If there's ever a problem, should I contact you?"

"We were never here."

Olga watched the two agents leave the hotel. She exhaled heavily and went into the bar. "Give me a Jack. Neat."

Willie and Jerry got in the KIA and drove south on A1A. They went three blocks and took side streets back to the Grand Paradise Hotel's parking garage. When parked, with the motor off, both took a deep breath and fist-bumped.

When they got to the War Room, everyone was waiting. They walked in and smiled.

"We got 'em," Willie said. The room erupted. There were handshakes and high-fives all around.

"Let's see what you got," Bat said, reaching for the spy pens.

"The video should be good, but check this out," Willie said. He forwarded the image of the list of names and places to the group text. Every phone in the room beeped.

"Is this what I think it is?" Alexander asked.

"It is. The name of every girl they killed and where they found her."

"Jesus," Terrell said.

"How?" Sam asked.

"I asked, and McIntyre pulled the list out of his wallet."

"This is so good. We should celebrate," Jana said.

"No time. They may be on for tonight."

"May be?" Jessica asked.

"Yeah, they said they were on stand-by. I think it means Cockwomble wants to, but he may not be able to get away."

"Regardless, we need to be ready to put Alex's plan into action," Sam said. "We need to watch the parking garage and tail them when they come out. But we're a man down."

"What do you mean?" Jessica asked.

"They know Jerry. We can't risk him being seen following them."

"I need to be here when they return. I can't leave," Jerry said.

"The three of us can handle the tail," Jessica said. "They won't be going far, and we know they'll be coming back to the hotel once they've found a girl. Terrell and I can handle it. We'll call if we run into a snag."

"The rest of us will start implementing my plan," Alexander said.

"Sunday said they usually know by five or six at the latest if they need to get a girl. If they don't leave by six, we can stand down," Willie said.

Alexander could see the excitement in everyone's faces. "If it's a no-go, it'll be a good dress rehearsal. Couldn't ask for anything better."

THIRTY

By 7:00 PM, neither Sunday nor McIntyre had left the hotel. It was a safe bet the operation was off. Jessica and Terrell were called in from watching the parking garage. If Sunday and McIntyre did leave the hotel, they wouldn't be going girl hunting.

Bat played the video on the big screen, and everyone was amazed at the quality of both the video and the audio. The recording, along with the list of victims, might be enough to convict Sunday and McIntyre. It would become fodder for late-night comedians and ignored by right-wing news. Congress would demand an investigation, but it wouldn't gain any traction.

Jana offered to take the group out to celebrate a successful sting operation. Instead of a massive celebration, they decided on a few drinks in the War Room.

Most of the conversation centered on the sting video. Willie and Jerry were the most critical of themselves, pointing out several things they thought they could—or should—have done differently. Everyone else disagreed. They thought the two had handled it perfectly.

The twenty-four-hour surveillance had taken its toll on Terrell, Jessica, Jerry, and Sam. When he wasn't on surveillance, Jerry was prepping for the sting. Whenever Guerline walked across the street to the bar, Willie worried. Worrying about her, coupled with the sting, had worn him down. Luckily, Guerline had the weekend off. She was scheduled to work the following week, Monday through Saturday. Willie was relieved she had the night off.

Not only was Bat responsible for the IDs and communications, but he also monitored the hotel's CCTV and ensured he had access to it. It could change without notice. Plus, he had to keep his clients happy.

After watching the video of Sunday and McIntyre, Alexander had become more obsessed with bringing down everyone involved, including Cockwomble.

From the recording, it was clear nothing was going to happen for a week. It wasn't late, but everyone needed to decompress. Willie and Guerline left for their room. Alexander and Jana went to their condo. Jessica and Morgan went into the bedroom adjoining the War Room. Terrell went to his room and turned on the TV. Jerry went to his room, opened the forty-two-inch gun case containing his disassembled AI AXSR rifle. Forty-five seconds later, the rifle was assembled. He took it apart and reassembled it, this time in the dark.

*****

Sunday morning arrived with mixed feelings on both sides of the street. McIntyre was disappointed he wasn't on a boat with bartender Sandy halfway to Bimini. The group in the War Room was disappointed that they hadn't executed Alexander's plan, and were on their way home. Cockwomble was on Air Force One, headed to the White House, disappointed he wasn't able to humiliate a cute teenage girl.

Alexander was the first to speak once everyone was together in the War Room. "What you all accomplished yesterday far exceeded my expectations. The video is amazing. Like you all, I thought about it last night. Not so long ago, it would have brought down the entire administration. What they had on Nixon was peanuts compared to this recording."

"Twenty-two minutes of silence on a recording took Nixon down,"

Willie said. "We have sound!"

"What we have should be more than enough, but it's a different era. What we do have are names and places. I plan to visit each of them and see if they still have video recordings. I don't have the dates, but I'm hoping, with Bat's help, we can find the dates Sunday and McIntyre stayed at the hotel. The list is chronological, with each victim added to the bottom. Amanda Elliott is at the bottom of the list. HG, whose name is Sylvia Torres, is above Amanda."

"It seems a bit morbid, but I'm glad he kept the list," Sam said.

"I'm speculating," Jerry said, "but he may have kept it so they wouldn't go back to the same place a second time."

"It makes sense," Jessica said. "They wouldn't want to go back to the same place, even a month or two later. It's unlikely, but they could be recognized as the guys who were last seen with a coworker who disappeared, especially the two of them together."

Alexander cringed. "I don't know if those two are smart enough to think that through, but whatever the reason, I'm glad he kept a list, and we have it. At the very least, as I've said before, we can give closure to families and friends who are wondering what happened to their friend or relative."

They all agreed that closure for the families would be good, but they all wanted more. "That's all I have. Does anyone have anything to add?" Alexander asked.

"I've got a question, while we're all still together," Willie said. "Should Guerline keep working at the hotel bar?"

"If she doesn't mind, I'd say yes," Bat said. "She's our eyes and ears inside the hotel, especially when they cut the video feed." He turned to Guerline. "You go back on Monday, right?"

"Right," Guerline replied.

"I wish she had gone back to work today. Last night would have been better. I'd love to know if anyone's demeanor has changed since the DOJ visited."

There was a spattering of laughter.

"I'm not watching their CCTV 24/7," Bat said. "It'd be nice to know if they had any other visitors in suits today."

"You mean like real DOJ?" Sam asked.

"Exactly what I mean. Willie and Jerry did a great job. Confident. Took no shit. Threw the weight of their position around just enough to intimidate. But Olga could be close to Willoughby, the guy McIntyre mentioned. If so, she could have called him to see if he'd been visited by two DOJ agents. Willoughby could be tight with the AG for all we know. If he is, real agents might come by with questions. They'd figure out Willie and Jerry weren't real agents."

"Bat," Willie said, "what you said makes sense, but you're giving way too many people too much credit. Even if what you said was true, and Willoughby personally called the AG and asked about agents visiting the hotel, she'd either say, 'Yes, those were her agents,' because she'd never admit that she didn't know everything happening inside her department, or she'd say she would look into it, which she never would."

"I stand corrected. Nevertheless, it would be a good idea for Guerline to stay employed for another week or so."

*****

Monday morning, McIntyre sent a text to Sunday:

> **I'm going fishing. Any reason I can't fish off the boat? It's docked close to the Hillsboro Inlet. Should be good fishing.**
> **Sunday: I don't see why not. The key is in the cupholder inside the Caddy. I wouldn't take the boat out.**
> **McIntyre: Don't plan to. Just sit and fish. Have a beer.**
> **Sunday: Want company?**
> **McIntyre: No**
> **Sunday: Fuck you.**
> **McIntyre: You already did. When you shot Amanda.**
> **Sunday: Jeez. Get over it.**

McIntyre was over Amanda, but didn't want Sunday to know it. It was part of his plan to escape with Sandy Beach. He was also over Sunday killing young girls. He enjoyed it too much, and it was such a waste.

The shack where the fishing equipment and snorkeling gear were housed wasn't far from McIntyre's bungalow. Borrowing the gear was on the honor system. Most guests who took gear returned it later the same day. McIntyre needed to keep the gear. It wouldn't be a big deal, but he'd rather not be asked about it.

Inside the shack, McIntyre selected what he thought would be the gear for fishing in the Bahamas. As stealthily as a person can carry a seven-foot fishing pole, tackle box, net, a facemask with a snorkel, a speargun, and swim fins, he walked from the shack to the garage and put the gear in the back of the Cadillac.

After confirming that his pay had been direct-deposited into his bank account, McIntyre drove to an ATM and withdrew three thousand dollars, the maximum he could withdraw per day. He could have gone inside the bank to get more cash, but three grand was plenty for what he had planned for the day.

He then stopped at a Walmart on the way to Hillsboro, where he bought three cases of bottled water, a case of French-cut green beans, a case of Chef Boyardee Spaghetti and Meatballs, a gallon of canola oil, and an assortment of women's shorts and tops he thought would look good on Sandy.

Loaded with what he thought were the essentials, he drove to the boat. He stowed the goods in inconspicuous spots inside the cabin where they wouldn't be noticed if anyone came on board during the week.

A check of the mooring lines and coiled ropes revealed they were exactly how he'd left them a week earlier. It was safe to assume no one had used the boat in the past week, and it was unlikely anyone would use it before he returned with Sandy.

McIntyre loved the little forty-two-foot motor yacht. With its thirteen-foot beam, it was plenty big enough for him and Sandy to live on for as long as he needed. The two staterooms, one forward with a queen bed and a small guest room to starboard, were nice, but he was sure he and Sandy would share the queen. There was only one head, but it had a separate shower stall. It was all they'd need.

The boat's galley included a two-zone cooktop and convection oven. The cockpit featured two captain's chairs, L-shaped seating with cushions, an aft-facing seat, and a transom door leading to a swimming platform.

McIntyre searched for information on the boat's power supply. A 9.0 kW Onan generator, which would use about a half-gallon of fuel per hour. If he only used it for cooking, with no air conditioning, it would use less than a gallon a day.

The only problem he saw with the little yacht was the lack of a tender. An inflatable with a small outboard would be nice to have, even one with only paddles. McIntyre used his phone to compare prices. A good roll-up inflatable started at a grand. A high-density polyethylene dinghy would only set him back eight hundred. He could buy a cheap inflatable raft with oars from Walmart for less than fifty bucks. It wouldn't hold up in the open ocean, but it would keep them dry when paddling from the boat to an island and back. He added it to his shopping list.

After checking the boat for other supplies and adding a few items to his list, he broke out the fishing pole. He tied on a Chartreuse Heddon Saltwater Super Spook. A large snook obliterated the lure as soon as it hit the water. The fish made an aggressive run, which included several dramatic aerial jumps.

"Yes!" McIntyre yelled after a particularly explosive jump.

It took several minutes to land the fish. He admired the long, slender, silvery fish with yellowish fins and a pronounced black lateral line running from its gills to its tail.

"The next fish I catch will be dinner for Sandy and me." He dropped the big snook back into the Intracoastal Waterway, then cut the lure from the line and stowed it along with the rod and reel. One fish was enough. He stretched out on the L-shaped seat, thought for a few minutes about what he might still need, and fell asleep.

*****

Knowing—or at least fairly certain—it would be quiet until the weekend, the group met in the War Room on Tuesday morning to go over Alexander's plan. They all felt it was a good plan, but a few had concerns.

They discussed each person's role and how to improve it. Everyone pitched in, throwing out their thoughts on what might go wrong and how to avoid it. They were all familiar with Murphy's law: What can go wrong will go wrong. They agreed that they were all professionals and could handle any scenario that might arise. There was one scenario they failed to consider.

When they felt they had beaten the dead horse as much as they possibly could, Jessica suggested they take a few days off. Recharge. Keep the plan in the back of their heads. If anyone had an epiphany, they'd organize a group video chat and discuss it. No one objected to the idea.

"Before we go," Sam said, "I have a question for Jerry. I should ask him in private, but I might not be the only one thinking it."

"Shoot," Jerry said.

"That's exactly what I wanted to ask. Shooting. We know when Cockwomble is in the room with a girl, the drapes are closed. How do you know what you're shooting at? You wouldn't want to hit the girl by mistake."

Jerry scratched the back of his head. Everyone was looking at him. They all had the same question.

"The straight answer to your question is, I won't. A thermal scope relies on infrared heat. It can't detect through glass. Glass is opaque to infrared, so a thermal scope can't see through a window. I'll have time for two shots. The first shot will obliterate the sliding glass door. With the door gone, the scope will be able to see the movements inside the room. Depending on what I see, I'll take a second shot. I'm giving myself eight seconds to assess the situation, aim, and fire. Any longer than that is too long."

"Eight seconds? Is that enough time?"

"Eight seconds will feel like an eternity. Plenty of time," Bat interjected. "Ever watch any bull riding at a rodeo? I can tell you, eight seconds is a long time."

"Wait," Jessica said. "You were a bull rider?"

"In my youth. Yes, I tried it. My entire career lasted about eight seconds."

"One ride and you quit?" Jessica asked.

"No. I attempted four bulls before calling it quits."

"Wait—"

"Yep, you did the math."

"It's a cute story, Bat. I won't ask if it's true. Anyway, back to the shot. One will do the trick. From the images Bat supplied of similar rooms, I know where the bed is and how high it is. We all know Cockwomble isn't there for conversation. He'll drop his pants and have the girl on her knees within a minute of entering the room. I'm relying on Bat to get the one camera on that shows the room door, so I know when he's entered."

"With a little luck, no one will notice one camera come on. If they do, I could be kicked off the system before I can take control of the elevators. We do have a contingency plan in case I'm booted. I hope we don't need to use it."

*****

By Thursday afternoon, McIntyre had made three additional trips to the boat. He purchased the cheap inflatable raft and stowed it, along with the oars, in a forward locker. He tested the water in the yacht's tanks, and it wasn't great. It would be fine for washing dishes and showering. They could drink the water in a pinch, but he preferred bottled water. He bought two additional cases and put them on board.

Unlike Sunday, McIntyre resisted spending his evenings at the local strip joint. He needed the cash, and soon he'd have the beautiful bartender Sandy. He still hadn't settled on which option he was going to use to abscond with her.

Ditching Sunday and taking off was the safest bet. But a lot of people would be pissed off and looking for them. Letting the president fuck Sandy first was the simplest. But he'd have to neutralize Sunday before he had a chance to shoot her. That shouldn't be a problem, but there would be a risk.

If the president did to Sandy what Amanda said he did to her, Sandy wouldn't be happy. If she didn't buy the story about Sunday planning on killing her, she could be a handful, even when they got to the Bahamas. On the other hand, if she believed him, she'd be more than happy to cruise the islands with him for a few months. If they were getting along well, he could always pretend to call in and then tell her they were still searching for her. That it wasn't safe to return.

McIntyre liked that part of the story. He decided he would use it either way. He'd tell her she knew too much. She was a loose end. The boss didn't like loose ends. He'd assure her that, in time, they would stop looking for her.

He was ready. The boat was stocked with enough provisions to last him and Sandy a month or more. He had cash. Not a lot, but when he got the ten grand, it would be plenty to keep them fed and fueled.

There was only one variable beyond McIntyre's control. Would Sandy be working at the bar on Saturday night, and if she was, would she come with them? If not, there would be nothing he could do about it. With enough time, he was sure he could find another girl as hot as Sandy. But would there be enough time? If not, they'd hit a gentleman's club and find a stripper willing to come with them. A hot stripper would be nice on the boat, but McIntyre dreamt of the beautiful girl-next-door type, one who'd be willing to fuck a random old man, sight unseen, for ten grand...or twenty. Whatever it would take.

Rumor had it that the president would be in town Saturday, had cleared his schedule, and was anxious for a Saturday night rendezvous.

THIRTY-ONE

At 7:30 on Saturday night, Sunday and McIntyre walked into the Bearded Clam and bellied up to the bar. Sandy Beach greeted them.

"Good evening. What can I get you?"

McIntyre stared at Sandy for a few seconds. He was disappointed she didn't seem to recognize him.

"I'll have Bud Light, draft, if you have it," Sunday said.

"Make it two."

Sandy walked toward the taps. "What do you think?" McIntyre asked his companion.

"She's definitely hot."

"It's not very busy tonight," McIntyre said when Sandy returned.

"No. Super slow, especially for a Saturday night. You guys want to start a tab?"

"Not tonight," Sunday said and handed her a twenty-dollar bill. "Keep it."

"Thanks." Sandy stuffed the twenty in her pocket and walked away.

"I thought she might hang out and talk with us a bit. It's not like she's busy."

The Bearded Clam wasn't a large bar. Booths lined the back wall, with eight or ten regular tables in the middle and four high-top tables closer to the bar. Two of the booths were occupied, and one of the hi-tops. Sunday and McIntyre were the only ones at the bar.

Sunday checked his watch. They had plenty of time—if Sandy agreed to come with them—otherwise, it would be cutting it close to find another girl.

"I'm a bit worried," Sunday said. "It's not crowded, but she seems to be the only bartender."

McIntyre looked around the bar. "Yeah, but if she gets sick, like Amanda did, they can't stop her from leaving."

"When she comes back, let's hit her up. If she agrees to come with us, cool. If not, we'll have one more beer and work on her."

When Sandy returned to check on the guys, they gave her the same spiel they'd given Amanda. Unlike Amanda, Sandy was interested from the get-go, albeit a bit hesitant. Not wanting to risk losing her, McIntyre quickly upped the ante to twenty thousand dollars. Sandy accepted with a wide but nervous smile. Her shift ended at nine, when her replacement arrived.

Leaving the bar after 9:00 PM would be pushing it. The president expected a girl in the room when he arrived. McIntyre convinced Sunday they should wait. Sandy was young, sexy, willing, and had no visible tattoos. It didn't take much convincing for Sunday to agree to wait for her.

Sandy's replacement arrived a few minutes after nine. It took her ten minutes to complete the handover and clock out. As they did with Amanda, the guys left the bar and waited in the Cadillac, which was parked a block up the street.

Sandy was full of excitement when she climbed into the back of the SUV. A bit of the enthusiasm waned when Sunday asked for her phone and turned it off. She accepted the reason he gave her for turning it off, but was still a bit unnerved.

McIntyre pulled the SUV into the parking garage and stopped at the metal door that led to the tunnel to the Overlook Hotel. Sandy looked at the large door, its paint faded and its hinges rusted. It resembled a prop out of a horror movie. She considered jumping from the car and running. The image of twenty thousand dollars was like a weight that kept her pinned to the back seat.

Sunday pressed the garage door opener. The large door didn't move. He pressed again. It didn't budge. He pressed harder. The door stayed closed.

"Let me see it," McIntyre said, grabbing the remote from Sunday. He pressed the button several times. Nothing. "Shit. What do we do?"

"I'll text Olga and tell them to open the door."

"That could take too long," McIntyre said.

"Then back up, drive around to the hotel," Sunday said. "I'll go in and have Olga open the door. I'm sure she can open it remotely. I'll meet you in the basement." Luckily for McIntyre, Sunday didn't check the batteries in the remote.

McIntyre backed the big Cadillac up the ramp, U-turned, and pulled out of the garage. Terrell was creeping down the street when they pulled out in front of him. He followed. McIntyre made the block and pulled next to the hotel. Sunday jumped out.

"The plans have changed," McIntyre said to Sandy once Sunday was out of the car. "Don't worry, you'll still get paid. Mark didn't know about the change in plans. Hang tight." He drove up the street and turned left on A1A. Terrell stuck with the SUV.

Jessica had parked on the side of the street between the Grand Paradise and the Overlook hotels. She was standing outside her car when the SUV and Terrell passed. "What the hell?" She called Terrell. "What's going on?"

"I don't know. I'm on McIntyre."

"Should I follow?"

"No, I got him."

"Is the girl still in the car?"

"Yes."

"What the hell is he doing?"

"No idea. I'll stay with him. We'll find out soon enough."

"I'll let the others know. This could be what they do."

"Roger. I'll send updates with the group text."

Jessica ran into the hotel and rode the elevator to the seventh floor. Everyone but Terrell and Guerline was in the War Room. "McIntyre dropped Sunday off at the hotel and took off. He turned left on A1A, away from the hotel."

"With the girl?"

"Yes. Terrell's following. He said he didn't need me."

"Do you think it's normal?" Sam asked. "Maybe they do it to make sure they aren't being followed."

"Or they knew they were being followed," Willie said. "Call Terrell and ask him if McIntyre is being evasive."

Jessica made the call and asked. When she hung up, she said, "He said no. He's driving normally. Straight up A1A."

The room was quiet for a moment as everyone considered what might be happening.

"The girl could've backed out," Bat said. "He's taking her back to the bar."

"I doubt it," Alexander said. "At this point, they'd have taken her in by force, if necessary."

"They could force her inside the room," Jessica said. "But they couldn't force her to perform. Why bother?"

"So McIntyre drops Sunday off at the hotel, then takes the girl back and tries to find a replacement? In a few hours? By himself? I'm not buying it," Alexander said.

"That would be cutting it close. I'm not sure he has enough time to find a replacement," Jessica said.

"Could they have found a different girl?" Sam asked. "Olga might have arranged for one. There could be a finder's fee, and Olga wanted in on the action."

"Willie," Alexander said. "Text Guerline and ask her what's going on."

Willie sent the text. Several long minutes later, Guerline replied that all was normal, except that Sunday was pacing the lobby, yelling into his cell phone.

"Sunday doesn't know what's happening either," Alexander said.

"What do we do?" Sam asked.

"Let's go ahead with my plan. Get in position. Then wait. If nothing happens, it's another dry run."

"And if it goes down, we're ready," Sam said.

Bat rapidly tapped on his laptop. "Jerry, room 817 is unlocked."

Jerry grabbed the black case containing his sniper rifle and left the room. After scoping out various rooms on various floors, he had determined that being one floor up would give him the best angle.

"I should get in position," Jana said.

"You sure?" Sam asked. "I can do it."

"I'm good. You need to be with Jessica. And I know the local roads better than anyone here." Jana left the room.

"You should go too," Alexander told Sam.

Sam left and met Jessica on the street. The two walked to the front of the hotel, through the front door, and into the bar. They sat on barstools at the bar.

Guerline gave them an indiscriminate nod. "Can I get you ladies any ting?"

"Rum and Coke," Sam said.

"Me too," Jessica added.

Guerline went through the motions of making two rum and Cokes, but the rum never made it into the glasses. As she placed the glasses on the bar in front of the two women, her radio squawked.

"Guerline. Guerline. Olga."

"Go for Guerline."

"Please come to the seventh floor."

Guerline wanted to ask why. She remembered what Abdul told her. If called, drop what you're doing and do what was asked. It was the first time she'd been called on the radio. "Copy. On my way."

Sam and Jessica could hear the conversation. Guerline's eyes widened, she shrugged, then left for the seventh floor.

Alexander, Bat, Morgan, and Willie heard the radio from inside the War Room.

"Ah, hell no." Willie grabbed his gun, his sports coat, and a radio before bolting from the room.

"Shit," Alexander said. "What's he going to do?"

Guerline arrived on the seventh floor and found Olga and Sunday waiting for her. "We have a special job for you," Olga said.

"Video went out on the seventh floor and the private elevator," Bat said.

"Shit."

"What special job?" Guerline asked.

"An older man will be coming soon," Olga said. "You're going to do whatever he wants."

"You mean have sex wit him?"

"That's exactly what I mean."

"Hell no. Dat's not what you hired me for."

Sunday grabbed Guerline by the arm. When she twisted away, he slapped her across the face. She winced, made a fist, and started to swing it.

Sunday pulled his gun and pressed the barrel against her lips. "You're going to go in there and do whatever he wants." He forced the gun into Guerline's mouth. "His dick or my bullet. It's your choice."

Guerline nodded. Her chin and lower lip trembled in anger, not fear. "How much you pay?"

"Twenty thousand dollars," Sunday lied. He knew the dollar amount would ensure Guerline's full cooperation.

Guerline forced a fake smile. Olga and Sunday led Guerline into the room.

"Take your bra off," Olga demanded.

"Part of the deal," Sunday said when she hesitated. He was anxious to see Guerline's breasts.

Guerline slowly unbuttoned her blouse. She knew, or hoped, that Willie, or Jessica, anyone, would bust through the door any second. No one did. She removed her blouse and unsnapped her bra, allowing it to fall to the floor.

"Nicer than I imagined," Sunday said, fondling her breasts.

Guerline stood motionless, her desire to knee him in the groin was tempered by the gun he was holding.

Olga's radio squawked. "Code red. Code red." Olga knew what it meant. The president was in the parking garage. "Put your blouse on, but don't button it. He'll be here in a few minutes. Remember, do whatever he says, or no payment."

Willie came in the back entrance of the hotel. When a staff member tried to question him, he flashed his badge and told him to get the fuck out of his way. He went straight to the bar where Sam and Jessica were sitting.

"Where's Guerline?" he asked.

"Don't know," Jessica said. "She got a call on the radio and left. What are you doing here? That's not part of the plan."

"Guerline leaving the bar wasn't part of the plan either. I heard a call on the radio telling her to go to the seventh floor."

"We heard it too. They may have needed her to make a drink."

"I don't like it. McIntyre took off with the girl. They need a replacement. Guerline gets called to the floor. You don't have to slap this coon-ass in the face with a wet mop to know that ain't right."

Willie's radio squawked. "Code red. Code red."

"What da fuck does that mean?" he asked.

"Not sure," Sam said. "But it might mean the president has arrived."

"Hang on," Jessica said. She pulled out her radio. "Bat, this is Jessica."

"Bat here, go ahead."

"Can you still control the elevators?"

"I can."

"We think Cockwomble has arrived. Willie will take the private elevator, and I'll take the regular one. Can you give us access to the seventh floor?"

"Yes. As soon as I do, they'll know their system has been hacked. I don't know how long it will take them to lock me out. Be quick."

"We will."

The president was accompanied by three Secret Service agents. They rode the private elevator that let them out across the hall from his room. Sunday opened the door. One agent stepped in, saw Guerline, then looked in the bathroom.

"Clear," he said into the microphone in his sleeve. He studied the tall, slender Black beauty on his way out and chuckled softly. After the president was inside and the door closed, the agent laughed.

"What's so funny?" Sunday asked.

"He hates Black girls. Calls 'em boogers."

"But she's hot. One of the hottest girls we've supplied."

"Doesn't matter."

Inside, the president sat on the end of the bed and stared at Guerline. She was beautiful. Her unbuttoned white blouse hung open, exposing a good portion of her breasts. Her bronze skin radiated under the fluorescent lights. She had an exotic look unlike any woman the president had ever seen.

The president stood next to the bed, staring at Guerline. He snorted, dropped his pants and underwear, and sat on the bed, spread his legs, and pointed to his penis. "Well?"

It took Jerry forty-five seconds to assemble the AI AXSR sniper rifle. Another twenty to attach the infrared scope. He had not used it often enough to attach it any faster. He pushed the curtain blocking the sliding door fully to one side and opened the door. He sat on the bed and aimed his rifle at the room across the street.

The president pushed Guerline's head down with his left hand. With his right hand, he forced his flaccid penis into her mouth. "Suck it, b—"

Jerry squeezed the trigger. The 6.5 Creedmoor round shattered the hotel room's sliding glass door with a deafening explosion. Guerline's jaw clenched. The president shrieked and bucked, throwing Guerline to the floor.

Two Secret Service agents and Sunday burst through the door. The president was writhing in pain, blood spurting from his body. Guerline crawled toward the door. Once she was out, she stood and looked around, dazed. Jessica yelled for her from down the hall. Guerline took off toward Jessica, spitting blood into her hand as she ran.

The agents radioed for an ambulance and began to render first aid to the president. Sunday stepped into the hall. The third agent was lying on the floor, bleeding. He'd been hit by the bullet after it passed through the wall. Sunday pulled his pistol and fired one round at Guerline as she dove into the elevator with Jessica.

Willie stepped out of the private elevator as Sunday fired. "What the fuck?"

Sunday whirled around. "The president's been hit," he said as Willie snatched the gun from him.

"We gotta get you outta here," Willie said. "Turn around."

"What? Why?"

"If anyone's outside watching, they'll think I've arrested you."

Sunday turned around and allowed Willie to cuff him. They stepped back onto the elevator.

Jerry disassembled his rifle, put it in the case, and was out of the room in less than a minute. He rode the elevator down, went outside, and climbed into the BMW X5 with Jana. "Go."

Inside the elevator, Guerline grabbed Jessica's radio. "Jessica's been hit."

Morgan jumped from the sofa in the War Room and headed toward the door. Alexander grabbed her.

"Guerline's got her. Sam's there. You stay here. I'll go get her. You need to glove up."

After a deep breath, a shaky Morgan agreed.

"I've got Sunday," Willie announced over the radio.

Jana glanced at Jerry. "Hell yeah," he said.

Jana turned onto A1A, went one block, and turned before the hotel. She pulled up as Willie was crossing the street with Sunday. She unlocked the doors. Willie pushed Sunday in, climbed in beside him, and closed the door. Jana drove off, much faster this time. She turned north, went several blocks, and turned back onto A1A.

Sam was at the elevator when it opened. Guerline's face was covered in blood. Jessica was bleeding from her chest.

"I'm good," Guerline said. "Help me with Jessica."

She and Sam held onto Jessica as she walked. Outside the hotel, Alexander grabbed Jessica and carried her across the street. Guerline was upright but shaky.

"Are you okay?" Alexander asked.

Guerline nodded ever so slightly.

By the time they reached the War Room, Morgan had pulled a sheet from the bed, covered the sofa, and put on nitrile gloves. All the clean towels from the bathroom were stacked on the coffee table next to the sofa.

Morgan pointed to the sofa. "Put her there. That's the best light. How do you feel, Jess?"

"I hurt."

"You'll be fine," Morgan said. "I need a knife."

Alexander handed her his pocket knife. Jessica gasped at the sight of it.

"I'm only going to cut your top off."

Morgan cut off Jessica's top and bra. She wiped the blood from her chest and examined the wound.

"Should I call an ambulance?" Bat asked, still sitting at his laptop.

Morgan pressed on Jessica's rib, under her breast. Jessica grimaced.

"No. She was hit with a small-caliber bullet. A .22 judging from the entrance wound. It went in her side at an angle, hit a rib, and ricocheted out near her back. No doubt the bullet broke a rib, but no internal damage. The bleeding has almost stopped. I should put a couple of stitches in to close the holes."

Jessica moaned.

"It won't hurt, I promise. Alex, in my car, I've got a trauma kit. It's a red box. My car's in the parking garage. Can you get it?"

"Be right back."

Bat walked out onto the balcony and looked over the edge. He came back inside. "There's an ambulance, half the police cars in the city, and what looks like every reporter in South Florida out there. I counted five news vans. All the flashing lights must have woken a lot of people. There are quite a few lookie-loos for this time of night."

Keeping pressure on Jessica's wounds, Morgan glanced at Bat. "How'd they all get there so quickly? Surely they didn't announce over the radio what had happened."

"The local LEOs and the reporters may have had an anonymous tip."

"Was that part of Alex's plan?"

"Yep." Bat checked the Overlook's CCTV. "Damn. I've been

booted out of the network. It didn't take them long."

Alexander returned with Morgan's trauma bag. She opened the bag, pulled out several sterile gauze pads, and alcohol. "This is going to sting. I'm going to need your help, Alex."

"I'm here."

"We need to roll Jess to her side and hold her steady."

"Should I wear gloves?"

"Hold out your hands." Morgan poured a generous amount of alcohol into Alexander's hands. "Don't touch the wounds."

"It's not the wounds I'm worried about touching."

Jessica laughed, then groaned in pain. "I'm sure you've touched titties before, Alex. Don't worry about it."

The best way for Alexander to hold Jessica in place was to firmly grasp her left breast. Morgan threaded a straight suture needle with Poliglecaprone 25, dabbed the front wound with alcohol, and stitched the hole. Jessica bit down and squeezed her eyes shut.

"You okay?"

"Yeah, but Alex is squeezing my tit." Jessica attempted to laugh.

Morgan sewed the exit wound, then covered both wounds with large adhesive pads. "Ease her back down, slowly."

"Now you're just feeling me up, Alex," Jessica said as Alexander slowly released her breast.

Morgan went to Guerline, who was still shaking. "I'm so sorry, Guerline. Are you hurt?"

Guerline shook her head, raised her hand, and slowly opened it. Morgan recoiled.

"FUCK! Is that what I think it is?"

Alexander jumped. Bat swung around in his chair. "What?" They both looked at Guerline's hand.

"Holy shit," Alexander said.

THIRTY-TWO

Terrell followed the black Cadillac along A1A to Hillsboro, where it turned into a small parking lot in front of a one-boat dock. He slowed, watching as long as he could, then drove to the closest place to turn around. He drove back past the SUV. McIntyre was pulling a young woman from the car. Terrell looked at the boat and instantly knew what McIntyre was planning.

A group call would have been best, but it would have taken too long to call one person, merge the call, and repeat the process until everyone was on the line. Instead, he sent a group text:

> **McIntyre is with a girl at a boat. About a half mile north of Hillsboro Draw Bridge on A1A. Standing by.**
> **Alexander: Don't let them leave**
> **Jana: We're about ten minutes from you. We have Willie and Sunday.**
> **Alexander: WTF?**
> **Jana: Will explain later.**

Mangrove trees blocked the boat's view from the street. When McIntyre and the girl were on the boat, Terrell parked behind the Cadillac. He crouched to stay hidden as he walked along the tree line. In the darkness, he watched while McIntyre unlocked the boat and turned on the cockpit lights. The girl was smiling. She didn't seem to be under duress.

Terrell crept to the dock, his weapon drawn. The girl was sitting on the L-shaped sofa, and McIntyre had disappeared below deck. Terrell sprinted the last few steps and jumped on the boat. Sandy's eyes widened.

Terrell put his finger to his lips, "Shhh."

Sandy ignored the request and let out a subdued scream. McIntyre hurried out of the cabin to see what the ruckus was. He froze when he saw Terrell's SIG SAUER stainless steel 1911 pistol.

"Get off my boat," McIntyre demanded. A brave move for a man staring down the barrel of a .45 caliber semi-automatic.

Thinking Terrell was there to steal the boat, Sandy acted like she wanted to jump him. He put out his hand, letting her know he was watching her. "What's your name?"

"Sandy."

"Sit tight. You'll be fine." He pointed at McIntyre. "Turn around, drop to your knees, and put your hands behind your back."

Sandy still had the look of a person who wanted to play the hero.

"Please, don't be stupid." Rather than trying to cuff McIntyre while Sandy had that look in her eye, Terrell stepped back and leaned against the bulkhead. He pulled out his phone and dropped a location pin to the group.

Five minutes later, Jana pulled next to Terrell's Chrysler 300. Willie got out, pulling Sunday with him. Jana and Jerry got out. Jerry led the way, gun in hand. Willie and Sunday followed. Jana waited at the car until the boat was secure.

"It's about time. Y'all walk here?" Terrell asked when he saw Jerry.

McIntyre, still on his knees, twisted to see who it was. "Agent Jackson," he said, and started to stand.

"Stay where you are," Jerry said.

"You're an agent?" Sandy asked.

"More or less. Can I get you to step out of the way?"

The sight of Jana approaching the boat calmed her. "Sure. Where to?"

"Over there, behind Terrell."

Sandy moved out of the way. Jerry handed Terrell his Glock, then slowly approached McIntyre and cuffed his hands behind his back.

"And we're secure," he said.

Willie immediately called Alexander, who put him on speaker. "How's Guerline?"

"She's shook up. Morgan's checking her as we speak."

"Can I talk to her?"

"You might want to wait until Morgan's done with her."

"Fair enough. How's Jessica? I heard she was shot."

"She was. In the side. Small caliber. Morgan patched her. She'll be fine."

"Good news. We've got Sunday and McIntyre. We're on a boat near Hillsboro. What should we do with them?"

"Ask them if they know what 'sleeping with the fishes' means," Bat said.

"Very apropos," Alexander said. "Willie, it's up to you. When Guerline is up to talking, I'll call you."

Alexander ended the call and turned his attention back to Guerline. She had calmed slightly, still holding what appeared to be a quarter of a Vienna sausage.

"I may be able to say I've seen it all now," he said.

Jessica strained to turn her head to look in Guerline's direction. "What is it?"

With a pair of thumb forceps, Morgan gently plucked the cylindrical orb from Guerline's hand. She poured a small amount of alcohol over the object to rinse off the blood and saliva, then held it up to the light and spun it 360 degrees. "I believe, my friends, this is what you would call a presidential penis. At least a piece of one." She dropped it into a hotel glass and filled it with 90% isopropyl rubbing alcohol. It resembled a small cocktail weenie that had fallen into a dry martini. She would transfer the specimen into a solution more suitable for the long-term preservation of complex tissue when she returned to the office.

THIRTY-THREE

Willie stood on the aft deck of the forty-three-foot cabin cruiser, perusing the enormity of it. "Can anyone drive this thing?"

"I can, no problem," Jana said. "I used to have a fifty-five-foot Cheoy Lee trawler. This will be a piece of cake compared to that boat. I also know these waters. We used to cruise up the canal on days when it was too rough to go outside."

"A fifty-five-footer. Wow. Did you sell it?"

"Uh, no, it sank off the coast of Colombia."

"That doesn't exactly instill a great deal of confidence in your helmsmanship."

Jana laughed. "My ex-boyfriend was driving. He scuttled her. It was sad. She was a great boat."

"Sounds like there is a hell of a story there. It'll have to wait for another day. We need to get the heck out of here. Someone could be looking for those two."

McIntyre had put the key in the boat's ignition. Jana sat on the helm seat in front of the twenty-inch wood-grain steering wheel and inventoried the console: Along with the standard throttle controls, there was a joystick for the Sleipner bow thruster, a helm position indicator, a 7-

inch Garmin display, autopilot controls, and a Cummins engine display. The stereo system and LED lighting were a nice touch.

"Put Sunday and McIntyre below. Lock them in if possible. We don't want them making a fuss on the way out," Jana said.

"I'll take care of them," Jerry said.

"Willie, can you loosen the stern line? Keep the bow line connected. I'll let you know when to cast off."

"Aye, aye, Captain."

Jana pressed the start button, and the Cummins diesel came to life. It burped a small amount of exhaust out the stern exhaust vent. She studied the controls, giving the bow thruster joystick a quick tap while she waited for the engine to warm up.

When the engine was ready, Jana eased the throttle up. The 22,000-pound boat edged forward. "Untie the boat and pull in the fenders."

Willie did as asked, then stepped back inside the cockpit and sat next to Jana. Making her way into the channel, she turned south toward the Hillsboro Inlet. She goosed the throttle, and the boat jumped. She eased it down and cruised at five knots.

Jerry came up from below. "There's a small bedroom in the front. I didn't see any weapons or tools they could use to get out of the cuffs, so I stuck them in there and closed the door. It doesn't have a lock. There's another bed on the right. It wouldn't hurt if one of us stayed on watch."

"You mean you put them in the forward berth, and there's another small berth to starboard?"

"Yeah, that's what I said."

"I'll take first watch," Willie said. "I want to check on Guerline and Jessica. I'll give them an update as well." He disappeared down the steps into the cabin.

Sandy sat on the short end of the L-shaped sofa, her brow furrowed and her head tilting slightly from side to side as her eyes moved between the others.

Jana followed the navigational channel markers through the inlet. She kept the boat at six knots. Even in light wind, the inlet could be treacherous. Shallow reefs lie on either side of the channel.

Sandy scooted along the L seat next to Jana. "Excuse me, I'm not sure I should ask, but what are you planning to do to me?"

Jana rotated the helm chair to face her. "We're going to take you for a boat ride and then take you back to the dock and make sure you get home safely."

She exhaled and blinked hard, causing a tear to run down her cheek. "Thank you." She had trouble getting the words out.

"What'd they offer you to come with them?" Jerry, who was still sitting next to Jana, asked.

Sandy turned and dropped her chin to her chest. "First, they offered ten thousand. I was tempted, but said I wasn't sure. Then they said twenty. All I had to do was fuck an older man. They said he might not even get it up. I coulda used the money. It was pretty stupid, wasn't it?"

"It was," Jana said. "But it's hard to turn down that kind of money. I get it."

Sandy looked at Jana through watery eyes.

"Would you like to know what would have happened had the one guy not taken off with you?"

"I don't know. Do I?"

"You don't," Jerry said.

"I'll tell you anyway. First off, it wasn't just a random old guy you would've fucked. He was the president of the United States."

"What the fuck? Bullshit!"

"Nope. Truth. That's what those two do. They pick up a woman for the president to abuse."

"I guess it wouldn't have been horrible. I'd have had a story to tell, even if no one would have believed me."

"First of all, from what we've heard, it would have been humiliating. He's a pig, and he loves to desecrate girls. Secondly, they couldn't have you telling anyone, so you would not have left the room alive."

Sandy's face turned pale. Then red. "What are you going to do with them?"

*****

Morgan gave Jessica a mild sedative for pain. The medicine helped, but it made her drowsy. Guerline had come to grips with what she'd done. She was on her seventh travel-sized bottle of mouthwash that Bat had removed from a service cart. She still didn't feel clean.

From the balcony of their hotel room, Alexander could see what was happening on the street below. The police had blocked off the street, keeping reporters and onlookers away from the hotel's entrances. Not long after the ambulance arrived, an air ambulance touched down on A1A in front of the hotel.

Alexander stepped back inside the room. "Life flight is here."

"The president must have lost a lot of blood if they called life flight," Morgan said.

Guerline opened another bottle of mouthwash, poured it in her mouth, swished it around, and spit it into the ice bucket she'd been holding.

Morgan was impressed that Guerline had not vomited. She had a feeling anyone who'd orally amputated a penis would have.

"Will he die?" Guerline asked after she spat another mouthful of mouthwash.

"Not likely. There's a major artery in the penis. You certainly severed it. The EMTs would have put a tourniquet on it to control the bleeding."

Guerline raised her head from the bucket of spittle. "Dey put a turnquit on his deek?"

Jessica cocked her head and peered at Guerline through vacant eyes. She blinked several times slowly before falling asleep.

Alexander was looking out the door. "The chopper took off. They must have wheeled the president out the front. I never saw him."

The television in the room was on the local CBS affiliate. Bat was monitoring CNN and FOX on his laptop. "They're all saying the president has been shot. None has updates on his condition."

"I can't wait to see how FOX spins it," Morgan said.

*****

Jana skillfully maneuvered the yacht through the inlet and into the

Atlantic. The wind was calm. Skies were clear. The ocean was glassy, with small, rolling swells. The boat glided through the water with a gentle, rhythmic movement. When the depth finder showed the water depth at thirty-five feet, she pushed the throttle up, and the boat effortlessly sped to twenty-five knots. "God, I love this boat. I forgot how much I missed the sea."

An hour later, when the GPS showed they were twenty-six miles offshore and the depth finder read 720 feet, Jana slowed the boat to a crawl.

Willie popped his head out of the cabin. "What's up?"

"I thought this would be a good place to stop and talk. If I kept going, we'd be in Bimini in an hour."

"The Bahamas? That might not be so bad."

"With two hostages and no passports? It would be bad...very bad."

"Good point." Willie climbed onto the deck, scanned the ocean, and gazed at the sky. "Wow, it's beautiful out here."

Sandy looked skyward. "It is beautiful. I've never seen so many stars."

Jana cut the engine, and the boat became dead silent. "We need to decide what we're going to do with Sunday and McIntyre."

"I texted Alex the exact question. He said it's up to us."

"I have an idea," Jerry said. "I think Jana might too. Thus, the reason we're out here in the middle of the Atlantic. I do need to get rid of my rifle. This is as good a place as any." He grabbed the rifle case from the aft deck and opened it. "This was a sweet gun."

"Isn't the barrel interchangeable?" Willie asked. "If you're worried about ballistics, toss the barrel and get a new one. You didn't leave a casing at the scene, did you?"

"Of course not. I didn't eject the spent cartridge." Jerry pulled the bolt back and ejected the spent casing. It hit the deck with a metallic clank. Terrell picked it up and handed it to Jerry. He rolled it around his fingers and tossed it into the ocean.

"While we're tossing, Jerry, it might be a good time to get rid of these." Willie pulled out his fake DOJ credentials and threw them in the ocean. Jerry did the same. The weight of the badge would ensure that it, the ID, and the wallet remained on the ocean floor.

"You're keeping the rifle?" Willie asked.

"No, it's not worth it. If investigators figure out what kind of round was fired into the hotel, which they will, I doubt there are too many rifles that fire a 6.5 Creedmoor. I wouldn't want to get stopped with one in my possession any time soon, especially one missing the barrel."

"How heavy is the gun?" Jana asked.

"With an empty magazine, about sixteen pounds. Why?"

"I dunno. I was wondering how far a person could swim tied to a sixteen-pound weight."

"Oh, my God, Jana," Sandy said. "You aren't thinking about—"

"It wouldn't be the first time."

"You've..." Sandy didn't want to say it.

"No, not in person. Several years ago, a trafficker kidnapped me. He planned to rape and kill me. His plan didn't work out. My ex's brother and his friends grabbed him, brought him out here, wrapped a chain around him, and threw him in the ocean."

Sandy sat stunned, her eyes bulging.

"They said he disappeared faster than a Twinkie at a Weight-Watcher's convention."

"Are you suggesting we do the same with Sunday and McIntyre?"

"Do you have a better idea?"

Terrell looked at Jerry, then Willie. Sandy sat on the L-seat, her mouth agape.

"We've talked about this," Willie said. "If we take them back and turn them in with the recording we made, they might go to trial. They might die in prison. One might make a deal to testify against the other. They may not be convicted. A good lawyer might have the recording ruled as inadmissible. If they do get a conviction, and Cockwomble is still the president, he could pardon them. I vote they swim with the fishes."

"You guys could kill them, just like that?" Sandy asked.

"We're ex-CIA. That's what we do," Jerry said.

"I've got an idea," Jana said. "Bring them up."

Willie went down and brought Sunday and McIntyre to the deck.

Sunday had his chin raised, wore a steely gaze, and a smirk. McIntyre was subdued. Melancholy.

"Okay, you've had your fun," Sunday said. "You can go ahead and turn the boat around and go back to the dock. We'll pretend this never happened."

"Nah, ain't gonna happen," Jerry said.

"I didn't kill any of those girls," McIntyre said.

"No, but you fucked one, after she was dead," Sunday said.

"She wasn't dead."

"No, she was still bleeding out."

"What the hell are you two talking about?" Jerry asked.

"That cute little blonde a few weeks ago. Sean got pissed 'cause I shot her before he could fuck her. He fucked her anyway."

Sandy took a few short, quick breaths. The reality of what they were saying hit her right between the eyes.

Jana patted her on the back and whispered, "You okay?"

Sandy took several deep breaths, slowly letting each out. "Yeah, I think so."

Jerry turned his attention to Sunday. He held up the small .22 semi-automatic pistol he'd taken from him. "Is this the gun you used to kill all those girls?"

"All except the one that fell off the balcony."

"I should use it to kill you."

"Bullshit. None of you look like you got it in you to shoot us in cold blood."

Jerry tossed the pistol into the water. "You're right. Turn around."

Sunday turned, facing the transom. Jerry pulled a key from his pocket and unlocked one cuff.

"Knew it. Y'all are a bunch of pansy-ass pussies."

Jerry ejected the magazine from his sniper rifle, pulled the bolt back to confirm the chamber was empty, and snapped the handcuff through the trigger guard. Using the length of the rifle, he slammed Sunday in the back, launching him and the rifle into the Atlantic. "You're right, none of us could shoot you in cold blood."

Sunday slapped at the water with his free hand. He kicked his legs as hard as he could, but the weight of the gun continued to pull him under. He'd lunge, spit a mouthful of seawater, cuss at the people on the boat, and go under. He managed to surface four or five times before disappearing for good.

"Fuck," Sandy said.

McIntyre was wide-eyed. His body shook. Dampness appeared between his legs. "I...I...I tell you, I didn't kill any of those girls."

"You may not have pulled the trigger," Willie said. "But you're just as responsible."

"I know. I didn't want to. I was quitting. My plan was to save Sandy and get out of there. That's why I brought her to the boat."

Willie laughed. "Save her? You were going to kidnap her. Hold her, and probably rape her. For how long? Until you were tired of her? Then what? Dump her body in the ocean?"

"No. Until Sandy fell in love with me. Then we'd have moved far away from here."

Sandy's stomach churned. A sudden increase in saliva filled her mouth. She leaned over the edge of the boat and spat, but didn't vomit. Her chin quivered uncontrollably.

"You hoped to gaslight her," Willie said.

"Not sure what gaslight means. I guess you're going to kill me now, too."

"Give us a reason not to," Jana said.

McIntyre shrugged lethargically.

"Tell you what. We'll give you a chance. Florida is about twenty-five miles east. Bimini is about the same distance west. We're in the Gulf Stream, and it will push you at four to six knots south. Cuba's about two hundred miles. If you can tread water, with your hands cuffed behind your back, you might make landfall in a few days."

Even in the dimly lit aft deck, it was easy to see McIntyre's face go pale.

"He could get rescued by another boat," Willie said. "Do we want to take the chance?"

"Sean, if you get picked up by a boat, head to the nearest store and buy a lottery ticket."

"I ain't gonna make it. You guys know it. Would you give a dying man a last request?"

"What is it?" Willie asked.

"Can I get a big hug from Sandy? I did plan to take care of her."

All eyes were on Sandy as she stood and walked slowly to McIntyre. When she was a foot away, she said, "That's sweet, in a sick and twisted way." She brought her knee hard into his groin.

McIntyre whelped and bent over. With both arms, Sandy shoved as hard as she could, pushing him over the transom.

"You won't be fucking any more dead girls."

McIntyre rolled to his back. He kicked his legs to keep his head above water. Each kick sent a shooting pain through his testicles.

"He's doing pretty well," Jerry said. "I didn't give him a chance in hell."

"I didn't either," Jana said.

"Should I shoot him?"

"No, I told him we'd give him a chance. I'll keep my word."

"What if he makes it?" Sam asked.

"We'll never know," Jana said.

Everyone on the boat sat quietly watching McIntyre struggle to stay afloat until he disappeared into the darkness.

"I guess we should head in," Jana said solemnly. She spun in the helm chair and pressed the start button. The diesel engine fired and purred like a kitten. "I love this boat." She headed the boat east. "Willie, let me know when we get cell reception. I want to call Alex."

"Will do. Are you going back to the same dock?"

"I don't want to. Who knows what might be there waiting for us? We should go in at the Stranahan River. It's close to my condo. We can dock at an empty slip nearby. That'll buy us time while we figure out what's going on."

Jana pushed the boat to cruising speed. "I'll see if Alex can meet us at the dock. We need to get our cars. Hopefully, no one has missed Sunday, McIntyre, or this boat, and we should be able to pick up the cars. One of us will need to take Sandy home. We shouldn't make her take an Uber." She turned to Sandy. "I trust you'll tell absolutely no one, not even your grandchildren—fifty years from now—what happened to-night."

"Don't worry. I won't tell anyone. Ever. I'm not sure I'll even believe all this is real the next time I wake up."

Jerry stepped closer to Jana and Sandy. "I took this off McIntyre—you should have it." He handed Sandy a bundle of cash wrapped in a money band with $10,000 printed on it.

"Uh, you guys should split it. I feel like such an idiot. I don't deserve any money."

"Nonsense," Jana said. "Keep it. But do good with it."

Sandy took the bundle and put it in her pocket. "Thank you. I will."

Willie came from the cabin. "I found all this in a drawer." He handed several papers to Jana. She glanced through them.

"These are the boat's papers. They're required to be on board at all times."

"Look at the owner's name."

"Fuck me."

THIRTY-FOUR

The eastern sky was beginning to lighten when Jana docked the Back Cove 372 yacht at a slip a block from her condo. Alexander and Guerline were waiting. Willie tossed the bow line to Alexander, who wrapped it around a dock cleat. They repeated the process on the stern line.

Guerline jumped on the boat and ran to Willie. After a kiss and a long embrace, Guerline said, "I sorry, Willie."

Willie shushed her. "Whatever happened in that room, it wasn't your fault. It's in the past."

A tear rolled down Guerline's cheek. She wrapped her arms around his neck and held him.

Willie leaned back slightly. "What's going on, Alex?"

"The hotel's a crime scene. When we left a half hour ago, the Overlook was still surrounded by cop cars. Bat's been monitoring the news channels, and they don't have much. They medevacked Cockwomble out in a helicopter."

"What? Medevacked? In a helicopter? Jerry didn't hit him, did he?"

Alexander glanced at Guerline. He didn't realize Willie had not heard what happened. "No, Jerry didn't hit him."

"Then why the medevac?"

"Willie," Guerline said softly, "I accidentally bit off his deek. He pushed it in my mouth. When da glass explode, it scared me. I bite. Hard. I am sorry."

Picturing the severed penis, Willie cringed. He didn't know whether to laugh or cry. He pulled Guerline to his chest and held her. "Again, it's behind us. Uh…what happened to his—"

Alexander explained. "Guerline carried it back to the hotel. Morgan put it in a glass of alcohol until she could get to the office to properly preserve it."

Jana, Jerry, Terrell, and Sandy stood on the boat, eyebrows raised and eyes wide, listening to Alexander.

"Damn," Willie said. "What about Jessica?"

"She's good. Morgan put a couple of stitches in her. She was asleep when we left. Morgan's still with her."

"We're lucky Sunday's weapon of choice was a .22. Any bigger caliber, and it might not have turned out so well."

"Very true. Jessica got lucky. We got lucky. We were thrown a couple of curves, but overall, the plan went well. I don't see Sunday or McIntyre, so I assume you figured out what to do with them."

"Yeah," Willie said. "And we have something else to show you." He led Alexander to the cockpit.

Jana gave him a hug before sitting back in the helm chair. "This is the boat's registration. Look at the owner."

"Son of a bitch. The Secretary of Defense."

"His phone number is on the registration."

Willie, Alexander, and Jana all smiled at each other.

"What are you guys thinking?" Jerry asked.

"I do love this boat," Jana said.

"Who's got a burner phone?" Willie asked.

"I left my phone in the bar," Guerline said.

Jerry handed Willie a phone. "This is the one with the DC area code."

"It can't be this easy." Willie dialed the number on the registration form. A wide-awake voice answered.

"Mr. Secretary?"

"Yes. Who is this?"

"Willie Brown, DOJ."

The line went quiet for several seconds. The secretary snorted. "Who? How'd you get this number?"

"Doesn't matter. We have your boat."

"What do you mean?" he said, his voice straining. "Where? Why?"

"I'm sure you know the answers to those questions. Where? In Florida. Why? Because it's been used to dispose of the bodies of young women."

The line went quiet again. This time for a much longer period.

Willie muted his phone. "I bet he's calling to have a trace put on the phone. It will take a while, and all he'll come up with is Florida."

The secretary finally came back on the line. "I'm sure I don't know what you're talking about."

"I'm sure you don't. So, let's cut the bullshit. I'm here to help you dispose of the boat."

"Uh, it was stolen a few weeks ago."

"Good try. I know it's early. This isn't an automobile that was involved in a hit-and-run last night. It's a yacht that's been disposing of bodies for over a year. The boys running it weren't very tidy. The boat's full of forensic evidence." Willie had a good idea the boat had been scrubbed, but figured a little white lie would help sell the story.

"Those stupid fuckers."

Willie winked at Jana. They had him.

"I'm confused. You said you were with the DOJ. Clean the boat and get rid of it. Sink it if you have to. It's insured."

"I'm part of the DOJ that isn't corrupt. Sink the boat and let you scam the insurance company? Not a chance."

"What are you suggesting? What do you want?"

"We want you to resign. It might be a good idea anyway. I'm sure you've been up all night watching the news. Your boss is going down."

"An assassin tried to kill him. His ratings are going to skyrocket."

"Not when it's leaked he was in a hotel room with a prostitute, and when he was done with her, she was going to be shot by your buddies and her body dumped at sea. Dumped off your boat."

"There won't be an investigation. Like everything he does, this will pass. I'll be fine, too."

"If you say so. Resigning is your choice. Here's what's not optional. I did a little searching and found a shelter for trafficked and abused women in the area. It's called 'Rey of Hope'. You're going to donate the boat to them."

"That's an eight-hundred-thousand-dollar boat!"

"I'm sure the organization is tax-deductible. You can write the boat off. I'll give you that. But don't brag about it. Do it silently. No one is to know."

"What if I don't?"

"Do you think the president gives a shit about you? He'll let you rot in a federal prison. In fact, anyone who's even remotely tied to his boon-doggles will likely be silenced. If I were you, I'd sign the boat over, get with the AG, and be proactive. Take HIM down."

The line was quiet again. It wasn't muted. Jana and Willie could hear strained breathing.

Thirty seconds later, "I'll donate the boat," he said. "As far as the other stuff, I don't know. You said when the info gets leaked. What did you mean?"

"You'll have to wait and see. You'll hear about it when the rest of the world does."

"Hmm. It might be time to cut and run."

"Now you're acting like a secretary, Mr. Secretary."

"Who do I sign the boat to?"

"I'll text you the information."

"I'll take care of it soon."

"I'm surprised you aren't already on a flight to Florida. I assume you will be soon. Sign the boat over. You have twenty-four hours."

"Twenty-four? I'm not sure I—"

"Don't even go there. You could have it done in ten minutes if you wanted to. Which might be a good idea." Willie disconnected the phone. "Jana, enjoy your new boat."

"Thanks, Willie. I'll wait a few months, then buy it from the shelter at the market value. They may not need it, but it never hurts to have a big chunk of cash come in. For now, we need to get our cars and get Sandy home. I'd better move the boat, too. I'm not sure whose dock this is."

"We could take the boat back to get the cars and leave it there," Willie said.

"No, I don't trust the secretary. He might send his goons to blow it up—along with us, if they get the opportunity. I kept my old boat at Bahia Mar. They have day slips. I'll keep it there until the title's transferred, and then we'll rent a slip in the shelter's name. It'll be safe then."

"My car's at the hotel," Willie said. "I can take Guerline, Sandy, Jerry, and Alex to get the cars. Guerline and I will take Sandy home. After we drop her off, we may go back to my place for a while."

"Can you deal with the boat by yourself, Jana?" Alexander asked.

"Oh, yeah. This baby handles like a dream."

"Then we should go. I've got something I need to do, too," Alexander said. "Willie, you all should clean out your room."

Jana started the big Cummins diesel. After Willie and Alexander cast off the lines, she eased the boat into the Intracoastal Canal. Once she'd cleared the dock, the others headed back to the Grand Paradise hotel.

Police barricades and news trucks still blocked the street between the Overlook and the Grand Paradise. The group walked down a block and came in on the opposite side of the hotel. Willie and Guerline went to their room to pack.

"Should I check out too?" Terrell asked.

"Can you wait a day?" Alexander said. "I don't want us all leaving this morning. It might look suspicious."

"No problem. I can hang out another day or two."

Alexander and Terrell took Sandy to the War Room. She was introduced to Bat. Morgan and Jessica were still asleep. "Any updates?" Alexander asked.

"No. Same B.S. they've been saying all night. No update on Cockwomble's condition either."

Alexander updated Bat on the boat's owner and the conversation

Willie had with the secretary.

"Pure genius," Bat said. "I'm packing and moving to my room. I should get rid of some of this stuff, too. I have a lot of equipment. It's not uncommon to have this in a hotel room, but I'd rather not be caught with it. Jerry, you should lose the ID too."

"Long gone. Willie and I tossed them in the Atlantic."

Alexander looked at the equipment in the room. "Let us know what you want to get rid of. Nobody's in the lobby. If they're awake, they're outside. We can take what you want to get rid of and dump it on the way to pick up our cars."

After careful thought, Bat decided he didn't need any of the equipment. He, with help from the others, including Sandy, carried the printer, laminator, paper, modem, router, photo paper, and a box of wires to Willie's SUV. Willie was waiting with the hatch open.

"If you see a donation box, dump all this in it. I'd hate to see it go to waste," Bat said. After they drove off, he went back to the War Room.

Inside, Morgan was up. "I heard people," she said.

Morgan listened to Bat explain what they'd done. "The place is empty," she said.

"I got rid of everything except my laptop. I'm going back to my room."

"Can you stay a little while? I need to run to the office. I should check in and make sure I'm not needed. I have a feeling it's going to be crazy there with all the buzz this morning. I'll be back as soon as I can."

"No problem. I can stay as long as you need me to," Bat said. "By the way, Terrell's coming back after he gets his car. I'm staying in my room for a few more days. You and Jessica should stay here if you can. Alex says it might look suspicious if we all left at the same time. Willie and Guerline were going to drop off Sandy and go home."

"We can stay. Jessica will be able to move around, but she'll be sore. I'm sure she won't mind staying here another night."

Bat walked out onto the balcony, leaving the door open in case Jessica cried out. Below, a crowd had gathered, many holding signs that he couldn't make out. News people were milling about. There wasn't much to report on. Bat sat in a lounge chair perusing his laptop for news updates.

*****

Motoring the Back Cove 372 down the Intracoastal Canal, Jana kept the speed under five knots. She didn't want to attract the attention of the Coast Guard or the Florida Fish and Wildlife Conservation Commission, even by accident. Explaining what she was doing in a boat registered to the Secretary of Defense was not something she wished to do.

Bahia Mar Yachting Center was less than a mile from the dock. On her way, she called to request a slip number. A dock boy was waiting when she arrived to help her tie up the boat. Once the boat was secure, she handed the dock boy a hundred-dollar bill. The tip would ensure the boat was safe and no one got close to it.

Jana Ubered back to the condo from the marina. When Alexander returned to the condo a short time later, she was asleep in bed. He tiptoed in and crawled in beside her. She smelled of a mixture of perspiration and salt air. It was a fresh, briny scent.

Jana stirred and rolled to face him. "How'd it go?"

"Perfect. I've done all I can do. I asked everyone except Willie and Guerline to come by this afternoon around five for drinks. We'll order food. We'll have a short debrief."

"Sounds too official," Jana said in a sleepy mumble. "How 'bout we'll have a bullshit session." She closed her eyes and went back to sleep. Alexander soon followed.

*****

It only took Morgan an hour to check in at the ME's office, do what she needed to do, and return to the hotel. Bat greeted her, told her that Jessica was asleep and had not woken while she was gone.

"Thank you for staying and watching her. Had she woken up while I was gone, she might have freaked out."

"My pleasure," Bat said. "Everything went according to plan with you?"

"Yes, perfectly."

"Cooley dooley. I have one more job to do—an email to send. If you'll be okay here, I'll go back to my room to write it."

"I'll be fine. I want to check on Jessica. Thanks again for waiting for me."

Bat gathered up his laptop and went back to his room. Morgan crept into the bedroom, but Jessica woke up, unsure where she was or what had happened.

Morgan sat on the edge of the bed and held Jessica's hand.

Jessica forced a smile. "It hurts to breathe. What happened?"

Morgan explained to her that she'd been shot. "I put a couple of stitches in your side and gave you a strong sedative. You'll be fine, but the bullet cracked a rib, so you're going to be sore for a few days."

"I kinda remember. It's fuzzy, but I remember some. Thank you for taking care of me."

"Of course, my love."

Jessica squeezed her eyes together and slowly opened them. "I remember...I hear it in my head, but I can't make it out."

"What does it sound like?"

"I'm not sure. Something like, 'a turnquit on a deek'. Was I dreaming?"

*****

Ten miles north on the Jimmy Buffett Memorial Highway, just past the Hillsboro Inlet, Willie and Guerline dropped Alexander and Terrell off at the dock to pick up their cars. After saying their goodbyes, they drove Sandy home.

When they arrived at Sandy's house, Willie helped her out of the back seat and gave her a hug.

"Are you okay?"

"Yeah, I'm fine. Talk about a crazy night."

"It was. Remember, you can't tell anyone what happened. I mean, no one. Don't even write it in your diary, thinking no one will ever read it."

"Don't worry. I watched one man die, perhaps two. The second one I pushed overboard. I'm not telling anyone."

"You also heard a lot today. You'll hear about it on the news, I'm sure. It's going to be hard, and you're going to want to tell people."

"I know. It's going to be hard, but I promise I will never tell anyone that I know who bit off the president's dick."

THIRTY-FIVE

Alexander and Jana woke and showered. Both felt refreshed. Bat was the first to arrive at the evening debrief—bullshit—session. Terrell, Sam, and Jerry came soon after. It didn't hurt too much to walk, and Morgan said walking would be good for Jessica, so they took a slow, leisurely walk from the hotel to the condo. They were the last to arrive.

Jana offered drinks. Alexander and Bat had scotch. Jerry and Sam requested wine. Terrell asked for a beer. Morgan showed support for Jessica and requested water for both.

"Alcohol may not mix well with the meds I gave you," she said.

Jana delivered the drinks. She poured herself a glass of wine. They all sat on the long sofas in the den. Alexander rang Willie. Everyone in the room said hello and asked if Guerline was on the call. She was and said hello to everyone.

Alexander turned the TV on, tuned to CNN, and muted it. "We're all here, more or less, for the first time since yesterday morning. What a twenty-four hours. McIntyre threw a monkey wrench into the plan when he took off with the girl, but it worked out. You all did a fantastic job. Other than a mishap with Jessica, it couldn't have gone much better."

"Mishap?" Morgan said.

A subtle laughter filled the room.

"It could have been a lot worse."

"Amen," Sam said.

"As you know, I met Morgan at her office this morning and then made a special delivery. Bat sent out an email to the local LEOs with an anonymous tip soon after. As far as I know, nothing's come of it. Bat, have you seen anything?"

"No. Last time I looked, they were still saying the president was wounded. No details. But I did see breaking news a few minutes ago: The Secretary of Defense has resigned. Effective immediately."

There was a smattering of golf applause in the room.

"I guess he saw the light," Willie said. "One down."

"Sunday and McIntyre make two...or three," Alexander said. "Bat, what about the next press release? Is it ready?"

"I wanted to run it by everyone. I didn't want to text or email it to you. There's no reason not to, I know I'm being a little paranoid." Bat retrieved the document on his tablet. "I'll read it, but it's a work-in-progress. I updated the headline this morning. Feel free to comment. The headline is: 'Assassination Attempt. President's Penis Severed.' The rest reads, 'Overnight, a bullet was fired into the president's suite at the Grand Paradise Hotel in Fort Lauderdale. The single shot was fired into the president's room around 11:00PM from an unknown location. The president was not struck. With the president was an unidentified woman, believed to be a prostitute. When the bullet exploded the glass door leading to the room's balcony, it appeared to have caused the woman to clench her teeth, severing a portion of the president's penis. The president is in stable condition at the Broward Health Medical Center. Law enforcement is searching for the woman who was with the president. A Secret Service agent posted outside the room was hit by the bullet. His condition is currently unknown.'"

"I like it," Alexander said. "I'm not an expert, but it sounds good. To the point and a little vague. It sounds official to me."

"Who's going to get the release?" Sam asked.

"I've created a document identical to a White House press release. I'll send it to Associated Press and PR Newswire with the subject, 'For Immediate Release'. Those are the top PR distribution services. I've spoofed the White House Press Office email address as the sender. With all the chaos, I'm betting they release the statement without verification. To be safe, I'm sending it directly to all the major networks. FOX won't want to read it. CBS and the others will read it as soon as they get it."

"What happens when they find out it's a fake?"

"The White House will say it's fake, but they say all bad news is fake news. They did take the president to the Broward Health Medical Center. I saw it on the news. Reporters surround the hospital. As soon as they hear the report about his penis, one of the reporters will ask a doctor to confirm that the president's penis was bitten off. He'll assume it's public knowledge and confirm it. Even FOX won't be able to put a positive spin on that."

The group took a few minutes to discuss the release. There were a few suggestions for changes, but others disagreed and thought it was good as-is.

"The only ting I don like is da part about da prostitute," Guerline said.

Willie explained why it was a good idea to leave 'prostitute' in. Guerline accepted.

"We could discuss this all night. It needs to go out, for better or for worse."

On that point, everyone agreed. Bat sent the release.

Jana refreshed everyone's drink. Jessica said she was feeling great because of the drugs and encouraged Morgan to have a glass of wine. Morgan reluctantly complied, and Jana poured her a glass of red.

The group, with Willie and Guerline on the phone, discussed the day's events. The consensus was that it went well, even better than expected, even after McIntyre took off with Sandy—the one scenario they failed to consider.

The television screen flashed "Breaking News." Bat noticed it first. "Turn up the sound."

Jana turned the volume on the TV up as the anchor read the report:

> **In breaking news, Olga Sokolov, a Russian national and manager of the Grand Paradise hotel, was arrested in connection with Saturday's attempted assassination of the president. While working on a tip, FBI agents executed a search warrant on Miss Sokolov's home. They found a box of 6.5 Creedmoor ammunition, the same type believed to have been used in the attempt. They also found a bloodied woman's top, a plastic bag containing a bloodied pillowcase, and a jar that appears to contain the tip of male genitalia.**

"They got her. And it didn't take long," Alexander said.

"You didn't have any trouble getting into Olga's house after Morgan gave you the evidence?" Jerry asked.

"No. It took a little longer than usual to pick the back door lock. I'm a bit rusty. I was in and out in two minutes. I trusted the police would get there before Olga. I left our gifts in plain sight. If she'd come home first, she would have destroyed it, but I figured she'd be tied up at the hotel. My only concern was that the anonymous tip Bat sent this morning wouldn't be enough to secure a warrant."

"By itself, it might not have been. I decided to send pieces of the recording from the bar. The tip, along with the video, was more than enough. Don't worry, guys, your faces were never seen in the video, and I used a voice modulator to disguise your voices."

"Any chance they'll lose this evidence, as they did a few weeks ago?" Sam asked.

"Not likely," Alexander said. "It's all over the news. I can't imagine how they'd do it. After what was just reported, the media will be hungry for more. They'll all run the PR Bat just sent out, no questions asked. I expect to see a breaking news report on the news within the hour."

"Look, there's more," Jana said.

The video, taped during Olga's arrest, showed the police escorting her out of the Overlook Hotel. When asked by reporters if she attempted to kill the president, she replied, "I'm a patsy."

THIRTY-SIX

It was barely nine o'clock, but everyone in the group was exhausted. Jessica had fallen asleep on the sofa. Willie and Guerline said goodbye and hung up just after the news reported on Olga's arrest. The others were hoping to see a breaking news report on the last PR Bat sent. When nothing came through within an hour, concern arose that the release had been flagged as a fake.

Morgan was the first to say she should leave. Jana offered the guest room to her and Jessica, but she declined. Instead, she asked if anyone would mind helping her take Jessica back to the hotel. Jerry and Sam both volunteered. Terrell agreed to join them.

Morgan woke Jessica and helped her off the couch. They said goodbye to Alexander and Jana, then waited for the others to do the same. When they were gone, Alexander poured himself a glass of his best scotch, and Jana filled her wine glass. They walked onto the balcony just as their friends were leaving the condo lobby. They watched them walk down the street to the hotel.

"How are you feeling?" Jana asked.

"Good. Very good. It didn't go exactly as planned, but I think we accomplished what we set out to do."

Jana laughed.

"What's so funny?"

"You set out to find out who the Hispanic girl was that fell from the balcony so you could give her family closure and, maybe, bring whoever killed her to justice."

"Yeah. I fail to see the humor."

"Jeez, Alex. Not only did you identify the girl and give her justice—I'd say tossing Sunday and McIntyre off the boat in the middle of the Atlantic was justice—you shut down an operation that was abusing and killing girls, and, in the process, may have brought down Cockwomble—the president of the United States. You say, 'We accomplished what we set out to do,' I find that hilarious."

"I guess we did do a little more than I'd hoped." Alexander smiled, but it faded quickly. "I'm sure we shut down the killings at the hotel—if not the hotel itself. We got Sunday, McIntyre, Olga, and maybe the president. We got one secretary to resign. On paper, that sounds good, but a lot of people who were directly involved are going to walk."

Jana rubbed Alexander's thigh. "They may walk, but I think the truth will come out eventually, and everyone involved will pay. They may not go to prison, but their lives will be turned upside down. You said it a few days ago, once the dominoes start to fall..."

"You're right. I hope we or any of the others aren't one of the dominoes."

"Could that happen?"

"Anything is possible. Two men are dead. Jerry took a shot at the president...more or less. We impersonated federal officers, planted evidence, and that's just off the top of my head. The good news is, Willie and his friends are really good at what they do. I think we're fine."

"So, the moral of the story is, don't fire CIA-trained assassins." Jana glanced through the glass door at the television. "There's breaking news on the TV. It may be about Bat's press release. Do you want to go in and watch it?"

Alexander took a sip of his scotch. "Honestly, no. I'd rather sit here with you and not think about it."

"I couldn't agree more." After a few minutes, Jana said, "We both had long naps today. Why don't we take our drinks into the bedroom?"

THIRTY-SEVEN

By morning, a video of Fort Lauderdale police detective Rick Amos holding a specimen jar containing a portion of the president's penis had gone viral. DNA analysis would still be needed to confirm the item in the jar once belonged to the president—a fact he was calling fake news from his hospital bed.

All the major news outlets except one read Bat's release verbatim, and their reporters were following up on the details. The one network that didn't air the release was still claiming the president had been hospitalized by an assassin's bullet. What little credibility that network had was quickly fading.

Meme creators, political cartoonists, and satirists were having a field day. Nicknames were sprouting like weeds in the spring. One reporter wondered aloud whether the president would order flags flown at half-staff.

In their suite inside the now-quiet War Room, Morgan awoke early and turned on the television. With the sound muted, she flipped through the channels, looking at the headlines. A bit later, Jessica began to stir. She struggled to sit up in bed.

"Do you need some help?"

"I got," Jessica said when she was upright.

"How are you feeling?"

"Better. My ribs hurt when I move, but my head's clear. What the fuck did you give me?"

"Just a little something to make you more comfortable."

"It worked. I feel like I've been floating on a cloud. I don't even know what day it is."

Morgan caught Jessica up on everything she'd missed or couldn't remember from the past couple of days. Jessica still had questions. Once they were answered, Morgan unmuted the TV. After watching one channel for a few minutes, she switched to another channel. When it was obvious that there was nothing new, she turned the TV off.

"You're going to be in pain for a few more days. I'm reluctant to give you any more of my meds. You're going to have to rely on OTC painkillers. Is that okay?"

"You're doctor. If I don't move, I'm fine."

"I think we should check out and go back to my place until you feel better. Unfortunately, that means moving."

"I can handle it. It will be nice to be at your house."

"Let me check your wounds, and then we'll pack and leave."

Morgan got fresh surgical dressings from her bag, unbuttoned Jessica's shirt, moved it aside, and removed the old bandages. She hadn't stitched a living human in years, but did a masterful job on Jessica. The scars would be barely visible. In a few years, she would have to look closely to see the reminders of the day she could have died.

"Looks really good," Morgan said. "There's no sign of infection."

Morgan finished dressing Jessica's wounds. "Whenever you feel up to it, we'll go home."

Jessica buttoned her shirt and took a long, slow breath. "I feel pretty good. Let's go...home."

*****

On Monday morning, Jerry and Sam checked out of the Grand Paradise Hotel. They stayed one night with Willie and Guerline before heading back to DC. They didn't watch the news and spoke only briefly about the events of the past few weeks. Instead, they discussed the future. Willie suggested that Jerry and Sam move to Florida. Maybe they could start a private investigation or security service. Jerry and Sam agreed to think it over.

The following morning, Willie was the only one able to fight back tears as Jerry and Sam drove away. Inside the car, they sat quietly, taking one last look at South Florida.

It had been an exciting few weeks, and now it was over. What started out as a theory—could the CIA kill a sitting president and pin it on a patsy—turned into a resounding yes. Jerry could have fired a second round and killed the president. That wasn't the plan. The only thing they didn't do, or attempt to do, was have a Jack Ruby silence Olga Sokolov. There was no point. She said she was a patsy, but all the evidence pointed to her.

"Orlando's about three hours north. Do you want to go to Disney World?" Sam asked.

"I'm ready to get home to my bed."

"Me too. Another time?"

"Sure. There is one thing I desperately want."

"What's that?"

"Where's the nearest Buc-ee's?"

Acknowledgments

First and foremost, I have to thank my awesome daughter, Robin, for an amazing job of proofreading. She has become so much more than a proofreader, offering suggestions to improve the style, flow, and sentence structure of my manuscript. Her input throughout the whole process was invaluable.

Once again, a big thank you to my "deer" friend Debbie, who not only encourages my writing but also finds some of those pesky typos that even Robin misses.

A special thank you to Sam (NOT the Sam in this novel) for her invaluable input and suggestions.

I'd be remiss not to thank my friend Bob for his technical support and for listening to me talk endlessly about my books.

Last but not least, I'd like to thank everyone who bought a copy of this book. Your support means the world to me.